The archer c[illegible]d, but appeared unbroken. Minobu could vaguely see a moving shape within. The warrior lived! Carefully, he began to peel the shard of armor locking the access hatch in place.

Minobu had snatched this man from death, literally taking the MechWarrior's life into his own hands. If not for Minobu's actions, the warrior would be dead, his future blown to the winds with his atoms. From now on, the karma the man earned, good or bad, was also Minobu's karma. The man's words, his deeds, even his life were now Minobu's responsiblity. *Bushido* demanded it.

The hatch was cleared. It opened with a groan of protesting metal, and the MechWarrior's neurohelmet appeared. Moving slowly, he emerged, battered and with his left arm hanging limp at his side.

"Looks like I owe you one," the pilot said, using his good hand to force his neurohelmet free from his head. Finally, Minobu could see the other warrior's face. The man he had saved was Colonel Jaime Wolf.

BATTLETECH®

WOLVES
ON THE BORDER

Robert N. Charrette

A ROC BOOK

ROC
Published by the Penguin Group
Penguin Books USA Inc., 375 Hudson Street,
New York, New York 10014, U.S.A.
Penguin Books Ltd, 27 Wrights Lane,
London W8 5TZ, England
Penguin Books Australia Ltd, Ringwood,
Victoria, Australia
Penguin Books Canada Ltd, 10 Alcorn Avenue,
Toronto, Ontario, Canada M4V 3B2
Penguin Books (N.Z.) Ltd, 182-190 Wairau Road,
Auckland 10, New Zealand

Penguin Books Ltd, Registered Offices:
Harmondsworth, Middlesex, England

Published by Roc, an imprint of Dutton Signet, a division of
Penguin Books USA Inc. Previously appeared in a FASA edition.

First Roc Printing, May, 1996
10 9 8 7 6 5 4 3 2 1

Series Editor: Donna Ippolito
Cover: Peter Peebles

Printed in the United States of America

To my parents, without whom I would not be what I am, and to ERJ and RW, without whom this book would not be what it is.

Cast of Characters

Jaime Wolf
Founder and mysterious commander of Wolf's Dragoons mercenary unit

Minobu Tetsuhara
Samurai sworn to the service of House Kurita, original Combine liaison to Wolf's Dragoons, later founder of *Ryuken* regiments

Grieg Samsonov
Warlord of Galedon Military District of the Draconis Combine, answerable only to Takashi Kurita

Jerry Akuma
Aide to Warlord Grieg Samsonov; later Draconis liaison officer to Wolf's Dragoons

Natasha Kerensky
Feared commander of the Black Widows, one of the independent units of Wolf's Dragoons

Hanse Davion
Prince of the Federated Suns

Takashi Kurita
Coordinator of the Draconis Combine

Subhash Indrahar
Chief of the Internal Security Forces (ISF), the Kurita secret service

Quintus Allard
Chief of the Ministry of Intelligence Investigations and Operations (MIIO), the Davion secret service

Michael Hasek-Davion
Duke of the Federated Suns' Capellan March; brother-in-law and arch-rival to Hanse Davion

Michi Noketsuna
Aide-de-camp to Minobu Tetsuhara, original Combine liaison officer to Wolf's Dragoons

Hamilton Atwyl
Commander of Blue Flight, a unit of Wolf's Dragoons Orbital/AeroSpace Operations Group

Jason Carmody
Commander of Wolf's Dragoons Orbital/AeroSpace Operations Group

Dechan Fraser
MechWarrior promoted to command Fraser's Company of Wolf's Dragoons Alpha Regiment, Able Battalion

Kenneth Quo
Commander of Hephaestus Station, Wolf's Dragoons' orbital space station

Anton Shadd
Commander of Seventh Kommando, Wolf's Dragoons Special Services unit

Fadre Singh
Former Dragoon MechWarrior, later a defector to the Draconis Combine

Prologue

Franchelco Province, Dromini VI
Dieron Military District, Draconis Combine
14 September 3021

The sounds of battle had ceased—along with all communications with Tercian's Company. *Tai-i* Minobu Tetsuhara could still see smoke rising from beyond the ridge. That oily smudge meant burning vehicles, and burning vehicles meant trouble for the counterattack by the Dromini Ducal Armored Hussars.

Tetsuhara's Recon Company had been ordered to support Tercian's unit after reports had come in that BattleMechs belonging to the invading Steiner mercenaries were in the area. If the enemy were about to make a major thrust, the forces of the Draconis Combine were in trouble. It would take more than Minobu's twelve 'Mechs to blunt any serious push.

With the rocky outcropping blocking his sensors as well as his sight, the only way for Minobu to learn what had happened was to go and see. Ordering a 'Mech lance to maneuver wide on each flank to block either end of the valley, he led his Command Lance in a straight line over the ridge.

The lance's three 35-ton PNT-9R *Panther*s moved with a grace that belied their size. From a distance, a casual observer might mistake a *Panther* 'Mech for an armored man at a run, but any resemblance to Humans would be shattered as soon as it passed a tree or building. Like all 'Mechs, it stood as tall as a three-story house.

The fourth machine of the lance was an OTT-7J *Ostscout*. Though it too strode forward on two legs, no one was likely to mistake the 'Mech for a man at any distance. Its long legs connected to a squat, egg-shaped torso and twin antennae poked from behind the small dome of the cockpit. Its arms were sensor arrays, skinny, tapered housings that waved and circled as the 'Mech advanced, gathering data for the machine's specialized scouting computer.

As the ground began to rise toward the ridge, Minobu had to slow down over the rough terrain. Just short of the ridge crest, he stopped and signaled the rest of the lance to do the same. He crawled his machine toward the edge, being careful to keep the *Panther*'s right-arm particle projector cannon clear of debris. Selecting the visible light spectrum for the first feed, he raised the 'Mech's head to let the scanners fill his cockpit screen with data.

What he saw in the valley below was a scene of carnage, scattered over with the smoking hulks of the light hovercraft of Tercian's Company. Minobu counted all nine of the vehicles he knew the company was operating. Half a kilometer beyond the nearest wreck stood a single enemy BattleMech.

Minobu identified it as an *Archer*, a seventy-ton machine. The 'Mech's bold blue and gold paint scheme was marred by scorch marks, and large portions were too blackened to reveal any identifiable unit or rank markings. The *Archer*'s armor was torn and breached in places and one arm hung limply, half-ripped from the moorings beneath the massive missile launcher on the 'Mech's shoulder. The giant machine had certainly paid for its victory.

Tactical doctrine usually called for *Archer*s to serve as heavy fire-support vehicles, but this one seemed to have been operating alone. Minobu wondered it its pilot had been out hunting other 'Mechs and the glory of a combat duel.

The Hussars had caught the *Archer* here in the open plain of the valley, where they could operate to best advantage. They had no doubt expected an easy kill. The MechWarrior must have surprised them, proving too much for the tanks, even though he was badly outnumbered. Such a warrior would be a redoubtable opponent.

"Skirmish wedge," Minobu ordered as he took his *Panther* over the top and headed down into the valley at speed. Well-drilled MechWarriors, his men in their *Panther*s closed up the flanks and followed him. Safe in the slot of the wedge, the poorly armed *Ostscout* followed behind, watching out for danger to its advancing fellows. The 'Mech was too valuable to risk in actual combat.

Minobu was 200 meters ahead of his lancemates when he came onto the smoother floor of the valley. Though his target was well within the theoretical range of his Lord's Light PPC, he knew the targeting system's limitations too well. It was an irony of thirty-first century warfare that incredibly powerful weapons were used at ranges that warriors of a millennium ago would have considered ludicrously short. Targeting circuitry was among the technologies lost to almost three hundred years of warfare among the five Great Houses of the Successor States.

Ahead of him, Minobu could see the *Archer* stir. It began to turn toward him, then it slumped. Well within range for accurate fire, the Combine 'Mechs moved closer, but the *Archer* did not react.

"Gibbs, scan report," Minobu ordered over the taccomm. "Is it a trick?"

"I don't think so, *Tai-i,*" the *Ostscout* pilot replied. "I think he just shut down." Gibbs sounded surprised. Certainly, Minobu was. He called up an infrared scan on his screen. The enemy 'Mech glowed with waste heat.

Minobu slowed his own 'Mech and ordered the lance to halt.

"Damn your fool code to the Buddhist hells!" MechWarrior Jerry Akuma's voice snarled across the comm frequency. "He's easy meat, *Tai-i.*"

"Pass my position or fire, Akuma, and it will be you who is meat," Minobu snapped. He had half-expected such an outburst from his lance second, but was disappointed to get it.

Inside his cockpit, transmitter off, Akuma cursed. The icy calm of Minobu's voice made his threat all too real for the charging MechWarrior. The *Tai-i*'s sense of honor had been touched by this battered hulk and its pilot. Akuma withdrew his finger from the firing stud and brought his 'Mech to a halt. "That is a *teki, Tai-i.* An enemy to whom we must show no mercy. It's a heavy BattleMech, which, in its weakness, we can destroy for no cost."

"No cost? You dishonor your ancestors. That pilot is a warrior, but his 'Mech will not respond to his commands. *Bushido* demands that we allow him his weakness now so that he can fight and die as a warrior at a later time. We will leave this valley now."

"Leave?" Akuma's voice rose higher. "You're turning your back on an enemy. You are . . ."

"Are you questioning my command, MechWarrior Akuma?" Minobu cut in.

Akuma knew the others in the lance were listening carefully over taccomm. All knew that to defy a commander's orders meant death. The lickspittle milksops he had for lancemates would back Tetsuhara, even in the face of his own more practical advice. Seeing the hatch over Kemsai's missile launcher already open, Akuma decided that capitulation did not mean defeat.

"No, *Tai-i* Tetsuhara. I do not question your command. I die at your command." The formal phrases came out smoothly. Akuma switched off his transmitter. "Your authority, no. Your sanity, yes. Your precious *bushido* code was dead before man left old Terra. It has no place here. This is real life, and we are at war.

"I shall remember this. You have shamed me once too often."

Minobu watched Akuma's *Panther* for any further reactions. He had long known of the ignorant Akuma's low opinion of the code, and had expected complaints and derision once the battle was over. He had not expected Akuma to come so close to disobeying an order, even though that order had its basis in the code. Still, the MechWarrior had finally bowed to Minobu's authority. The crisis point was passed, and Akuma's blood would cool.

Turning his 'Mech back toward the *Archer,* Minobu keyed on his external speakers. The enemy 'Mech's pilot had popped his hatch and was standing on the seat, visible from the waist up. A bulky neurohelmet hid his features.

"Warrior," Minobu said. "I, Minobu Tetsuhara, *Tai-i* in command of Reconnaissance Company Gold of the Second

Sword of Light Regiment, samurai of House Kurita, and soldier of the Draconis Combine, honor your prowess and your courage. We shall not kill you now. Return to your forces, if you can. Die in battle as a true warrior."

With that, Minobu turned and led his lance from the valley.

THE BORDER
BETWEEN THE DRACONIS COMBINE AND THE FEDERATED SUNS

CIRCA 3028

BOOK I

Honor

1

Tetsuhara Family Estate, Awano
Benjamin Military District, Draconis Combine
9 March 3023

Light from Awano's sun sparkled off the metal, dazzling his vision. Minobu squinted, but the glare still brought tears to his eyes and blurred his sight. He could not allow this to distract him because precision was of utmost importance now. If he missed his mark, it would be disaster. He waited. His vision cleared only minimally, but he was calm. The time had come. Between the beats of his heart, his hand descended. It was steady.

"Brother!"

The unexpected shout from the glade near the house broke his concentration. Minobu bit his lip as the paintbrush slid over the surface of the vase, marring hours of patient work and spattering gold flecks on the dark skin of his hand. He had not achieved *muga* today. Again. Not since the disastrous fighting on Dromini VI had he been able to truly reach the state of "mind and deed as one."

Once House Steiner had sprung its trap and unleashed its Regulars to join the mercenary Wolf's Dragoons, they had devastated the Draconis Combine forces attempting the relief of Dromini. The Combine troops had held the planet, but at the cost of severe casualities among the Combine troops. A month after the debacle, Minobu had been relieved of his command and stripped of his BattleMech. Those orders had come without explanation and from the highest source, the Coordinator's office. They were signed by the Coordinator himself, Takashi Kurita, ruler of the Draconis Combine. A promotion had accompanied the new orders, but Minobu still felt shamed, haunted by the thought that he had betrayed the ideal, that he had not lived up to the code of *bushido*. It was this worry and concern that barred him from *muga*.

Before Dromini, so small a thing as a shout would never have affected his brush stroke. He put the vase down. It was ruined on the surface, yet it might still serve, as would he. Decoration aside, the vase was still what it was, sturdy and strong. As he must be.

"Brother!" Minobu was still tidying his work area when Fuhito, panting from his run through the thin air of the plateau, burst into the room. The grin that split his face told Minobu that this interruption was, at least, because of good news.

"Your haste is unseemly in a samurai, little brother. Sit down and compose yourself." Fuhito did as he was bid, taking several moments to control his breathing and assume a calm demeanor. Minobu sat motionless, his face betraying none of his desire to hear whatever news had sent his brother rushing across the estate toward him. In control of himself at last, Fuhito bowed to Minobu.

"Elder brother, I have received a letter from the Bureau of Administration. In two weeks, I am to leave to begin my service as a MechWarrior." Fuhito's grin broke loose from his control, his joy too great to be contained. He searched his brother's face for approval, but his smile faltered when that approval was not immediately apparent. "I'm a fool, elder brother. Forgive me. In my pleasure at having a chance to prove myself, I've touched your own pain. You should be the one to receive the call to service."

Looking down, Minobu's gaze fell on the ruined vase. He was distressed that his control was so poor that even his unsubtle little brother could see his inner turmoil. The long months of isolation here on Awano were taking a toll that increased daily. He seemed unable to regain the calm that he had always known as a MechWarrior. He willed the muscles of his face to relax. "My personal feelings are of no matter, though I am pleased you have this chance to prosper, my brother. You shall bring honor to our family. *Katana Kat* is your 'Mech now."

Fuhito rose abruptly. "No. I won't go. It should be you piloting the *Panther.* I shall insist on it." He headed for the doorway, but jerked to a halt when Minobu called after him.

"Now you *are* being a fool. The 'Mech has been registered in your name for over a year. You have shown no reluctance to pilot it during your training sessions with me, and your progress has been duly recorded. Refusal at this point would only embarrass the family."

"But I thought you would be getting the 'Mech back eventually. This whole thing is unfair. You are a great warrior, maybe even the best in the family since old Jackson Hayes forsook his African heritage and took the name Tetsuhara. I shouldn't have gotten *Katana Kat* while you could still pilot it. You should be in the cockpit. You're not old, or crippled, or . . . or . . ."

"Dead? No, I am not dead. Nor am I any longer the master of the *Kat.*" Minobu rose and walked toward his brother. He put an arm around the younger man's shoulder and led him across the room. At the far end, they paused while Minobu slid open the panel that opened onto the veranda. Minobu looked out over the trees that separated his house from the main part of the estate. Beyond those trees were the family mansion, the retainers' barracks, and the training grounds. The Tetsuhara *Panther* stood on the practice field, its head visible above the tops of the trees.

"There is your duty," Minobu announced, pointing at the 'Mech. "You are the approved pilot of that BattleMech. It is to be your sword for battle, a samurai's soul. Do not darken its bright shine by foolish actions or ignoble deeds. Its sheen will reflect your honor as your honor will reflect that of our family. You now have a chance to wipe away any tarnish that my disgrace has placed on that honor. Sufficient restitution has been made. Your orders are proof of that, little brother. The Tetsuhara clan once again has the opportunity to bring honor to House Kurita." Minobu paused and stepped away from his brother. "Where are you to go?"

Minobu had hoped his speech would help Fuhito grasp the

realities of the situation. Fuhito's steady voice encouraged that hope, but the flat tone revealed his discouragement. "Benjamin District. The Seventeenth Regulars."

"Not a Sword of Light Regiment, then."

"I was not able to attend the Sun Zhang Academy like yourself, brother. I had no patron. They have little love for country-educated warriors in the Swords."

"Sadly, it is as you say. A man's honor and devotion should count for more than his school. It was too much to expect that you would be called to my former position. Still, Warlord Yorioshi is a loyal man and well-versed in the code. The Seventeenth is his own regiment, and he is District Warlord. It is a good appointment. You can prosper there. Show yourself a loyal soldier and a valiant warrior, and you will yet make it to the Swords."

Minobu watched his brother, who stood half-leaning against a post. Fuhito's head hung down, and he kicked at nonexistent pebbles on the oiled wood. Though in his twenties, he often acted as though he were still a headstrong child. Minobu felt that their father had shown weakness in allowing their mother to pamper and spoil Fuhito, her youngest son. It had left Fuhito with a fierce strength that could blaze up and often carry him through, but the fires had no reservoir of fuel, no constant source of strength. His skills and control were good enough that he would survive as a MechWarrior if he enjoyed the luck any soldier needed to last on the battlefield. Fuhito would never rise to command until he could find the inner strength, the calm that permitted action without thought or regret, decision without remorse. Before he could achieve that calm, he would have to accept his place in the universe.

"I have orders as well. I am to leave for an assignment in a week."

Fuhito's head came up, eyes bright. "A command? A new 'Mech? One of the *Grand Dragons,* I'll bet."

"Something other than that. I am to work with the Professional Soldiery Liaison."

"Mercenaries!" Fuhito sputtered angrily. "They have set you to babysitting honorless curs. This is an insult."

"It is not an insult. It is the order of Lord Kurita. He knows what is best for his realm," Minobu said, his tone matter-of-fact. "We are samurai and must obey our lord's orders. It is our duty. You must remember that duty always comes before our own desires."

"Just as it was the lord's will that you be relieved of your command." Fuhito stepped from the veranda into the garden. He reached down, picked up a stone, and threw it at the distant trees. "That your 'Mech be taken from you." Another stone followed the first. "That you be confined to Awano for over a year." A third stone. Fuhito turned to receive Minobu's answer.

"Yes."

"Then you agree with his treatment of you."

"I did not say that I agree." Minobu willed his voice calm. How could one agree with what one did not understand? "I accept it. I follow orders because I am samurai."

"But . . ."

"There are no 'buts' for a samurai. You will do well to remember this. You are now a Tetsuhara samurai, the pilot of the family's BattleMech. Look to your honor. It is more precious than anything else you possess."

"What about your honor?" Fuhito protested, rubbing the back of his neck. "You have been here in disgrace for over a year. Then you get an assignment to work with hired soldiers, credit-hungry dogs with no concept of honor and no belief in the triumph of the Dragon. You are shamed."

"I am ordered. I will do my duty."

Minobu walked down the length of the veranda. With his back still to his brother, he said, "At least these mercenaries have warriors among them."

Minobu turned around to find Fuhito watching him, puzzlement on his face.

"Karma can be strange, don't you think? I am to work with the unit that was my last opponent in battle." When he saw that Fuhito did not understand the reference, he added, "Now that Lord Kurita has taken their contract, I am to be Chief Liaison to Wolf's Dragoons."

"The Dragoons! They're the best fighters in the Inner Sphere," Fuhito exclaimed. "If the reports from the other states are to be believed," he added hastily. "And they're big, too. Some say they have more 'Mechs than all the Sword of Light Regiments combined. But you are only a

Sho-sa. Wait . . ." He cocked his head and looked suspiciously at his brother.

"I will wear the bars of a *Chu-sa,*" Minobu stated in confirmation.

Fuhito laughed. "You have been setting me up. This is wonderful news. A promotion and a position involving such a large force. In spite of all your moping, you have been restored to favor. The lord has remembered your loyalty and set you on the path. A command of real warriors is sure to follow."

"Perhaps you are right, little brother."

"Have you told Father?" Fuhito's voice was suddenly restrained.

"No."

"Surely he will relent and see you now."

"I don't think so."

"Then you won't even try?"

"No. You are not to speak of it, either," Minobu warned.

"You are stubborn."

"So is he."

An awkward silence fell between the brothers. "I must go now," Fuhito said finally. "There's much to be done before leaving. Perhaps we can have a final lesson in the *Katana Kat* in, say, three days?"

"That would be fine."

Minobu watched him go. As the younger man passed out of sight beyond the carefully tended cryptomeria trees, Minobu turned and entered the house. He crossed the room to a tall chest. From the top drawer, he took a case and a ComStar communique envelope. The envelope contained his orders in the form of a *shuga-to-hama,* a letter of joyous celebration, duly stamped and sealed by the Bureau of Substitution. He did not need to reread the words to remember that the date for his departure was in two days. Minobu knew that Fuhito would wait for their last lesson together to try again to convince him to speak to Father. Since that lesson was not to be, Minobu would be gone before their father even learned of this assignment, which would offend the old man's sense of propriety and confirm his low opinion of his eldest son's worth.

Minobu moved to his work area and knelt by his pots.

Laying the orders on the floor, he opened the small box that had accompanied them. On the velveteen lining lay twin rank insignia, the double bars of a *Chu-sa.* He pulled one from its backing, and it came out with no resistance. Using a work knife, he chipped the thin green metal plating that covered it. The bars were of cheap materials and had nothing to hold them in place, which told him that the promotion was only for show and not intended to be permanent. The new assignment was certainly a calculated maneuver on someone's part. How had he so offended House Kurita that his punishment should go on and on and his requests to atone be refused?

Minobu replaced the bars in the box. He got up and returned to the chest. Opening a panel, he activated the compad hidden within and entered a requisition for a senior Draconis Combine Mustered Soldiery officer's uniform and rank insignia, both to be paid for at his own expense. He had no doubt that the request would be honored; the DCMS lacked for little in material things. Minobu walked to the outer doorway. Before he closed the sliding panel to the veranda, he looked out. The flowers in bloom held out the promise of the coming heat of summer, and the late afternoon sunlight colored the clear skies. On the horizon, however, beyond the head of the *Panther*, Minobu could see the racing dark clouds of a gathering storm.

2

Bantan Airspace, Quentin IV
Draconis March, Federated Suns
13 June 3023

The primal violence of the planetary storm was a threat even to so tough a craft as Lieutenant Hamilton Atwyl's *Lucifer.* The AeroSpace Fighter bucked and pitched as it plowed through the turbulence of howling winds. The storm was bad enough without having to worry about the enemy DropShip out there, somewhere. That huge spacecraft would be less disturbed by the winds and pressure shifts that buffeted his own sixty-five-ton LCF-R15.

The Davion DropShip that he was chasing had broken away from the fight in the orbital space above Quentin IV. Atwyl's Blue Flight had been detailed to hunt it down. Even damaged, a *Union* Class DropShip was still a threat.

Days ago, the JumpShips of Wolf's Dragoons had flickered into existence at the system's nadir jump point. They had come for their first mission in the employ of the Draconis Combine, a raid on the Davion planet of Quentin IV. Officially, they had been in House Kurita's employ for three months, time spent crossing the volume of space from the realm of their former employer, House Steiner, to their new employer's border with the Federated Suns of House Davion.

When the Dragoon JumpShips had unleashed their cargo

of DropShips for the in-system trip to Quentin, the Davion ship had abandoned its own course toward the jump point and had fled from them. Flight Colonel Jason Carmody had suggested that it could be carrying cargo that might prove troublesome. It had also been close enough to get good data on the strength of the forces the Dragoons had brought to the Quentin system, something Colonel Wolf did not want revealed so soon. Carmody had advocated the immediate destruction of the Davion ship, and Colonel Wolf had agreed. Carmody's AeroSpace forces had mounted a pursuit, but the DropShip's Captain had been skillful enough to elude their fighters in deep space. Reaching Quentin IV, the DropShip had joined the hastily organized defense that the Federated Suns had mustered to oppose the sudden Dragoon raid.

When a DropShip had pulled away from the battle and headed planetside, the main battle computer aboard Wolf's *Overlord* Class DropShip, the *Chieftain,* had identified it as the one that had run from the raiders earlier. The orbital fight was still undecided, and all Carmody could spare was the hastily organized Blue Flight. Lieutenant Atwyl's aerolance of two *Lucifer*s and two aerolances of SPR-H5 *Sparrowhawks* had orders to chase it down.

Against an intact *Union* Class DropShip, they would not have had a chance, but Colonel Carmody had informed him that the six AeroSpace Fighters would be sufficient for a ship estimated to be seriously damaged. Carmody had not counted on the severe storm that caused the flight to lose track of its quarry.

With the way the *Lucifer* was being tossed about now, Atwyl was glad he was not in a *Sparrowhawk.* The thought of that tiny, thirty-ton ship that was little more than a cockpit strapped to an engine reminded him to check the formation. This was his first mission as a flight commander, and he was still getting used to having to worry about more than just himself and his wingman.

Atwyl's radar screen was fuzzed with junk readings, but showed several intermittent blips that should be the rest of his flight. His visual scan of the airspace outside his cockpit only picked out AeroPilot Gianni Bredel in the other *Lucifer,* glued to his left wing tip as usual. Raising power to punch through the interference, he called over the channel reserved for Blue Flight, "Let's close it up a little, children. There's a big, bad DropShip out there. Crippled or not, it can swat a *Sparrowhawk* out of the sky. I don't want anyone finding it by himself."

He received acknowledgement from Gordon, Hall, and Reischaur, but not from Morris. Shifting more power to the comm circuit, he tried again. "T.J., you out there, girl?"

"Sure am, boss man. What you want?" The words were distorted and barely audible, but T.J.'s jaunty tone came through. Hamilton was surprised at the relief he felt. AeroPilot T.J. Morris had just graduated from the Dragoon AeroSpace pilot program and was on her first mission. Her high scores and outstanding simulator performances did not keep him from worrying about her, however. Enthusiasm and training often counted for little in the field, especially with conditions as bad as they were now.

"Close up with Reischaur and the rest of the flight. Can't have you taking down that DropShip all by yourself, hot-shot."

"Roger, boss man."

Atwyl looked for the closing fighters. Off to the right, he could see the shapes of Beta Lance's craft break through the clouds. The bright yellow paint jobs of both fighters made them easily visible against the storm clouds. The dark, anodized metal sheaths of the Martell lasers that jutted forward on either side of the fuselage gave a *Sparrowhawk* the profile of a winged bullet. It took a lightning flash to reveal the dark wolf's-head against a red circle that decorated the tall, vertical stabilizer rising behind the cockpit of each ship.

Unable to see the fighters of Gamma Lance, Atwyl switched his communicator over to the band he shared with his wingman.

"Yo, Gianni. I don't have a visual on our little Gamma birdies in this soup. My scanners show them off to the left, I think. Can't be sure what's a real echo and what's a ghost. This storm has really screwed things up. Hope it's as bad for the groundpounders holding this rock."

"I'll give it a look-see, Ham." The speaker crackled and popped in accompaniment to his wingman's voice, which was calm and steady as ever. It took more than a bumpy ride in a wild storm and playing hide and seek with a hostile DropShip to fluster Aerospace Pilot Gianni Bredel.

"Not too far, Gianni. Don't want to lose you in this murk, too." Atwyl watched as the other ship vectored thrust and shot away from his side. In the patched and cross-wired technology of the Successor States, things had a too-common tendency to break down. Even in the long-ago era of the Star League, *Lucifer*s had been notorious for the fragility of their communication and sensor systems. Fearing that the recent communication problems might be due to more than the storm's interference, Atwyl didn't want his wingman out of sight.

"You and me both, boss man," said Bredel, but the rest of his words were drowned in a burst of static. Atwyl fretted while the other *Lucifer* moved out 200 meters, then pulled up even with him. As it did so, Atwyl's visual angle changed, making it seem as though he were being paced by a flying skeleton. The other *Lucifer*'s wings, both the canards under the cockpit and the main vee, had disappeared against the midnight blue of the ship's color scheme. The dark fighter's shape blended with the stormy sky, leaving only the white bars and shapes of highlighted panels and structural elements.

"Got 'em, Ham." Bredel's call snapped Atwyl from his musings. "Safe and sound."

"Roger, Gianni." Switching over to the flight frequency, he said, "All right, children. Let's keep it this way if we can." Resolving to hold his own attention on the job at hand, Atwyl returned to watching his sensor sweeps.

Minutes crawled by while the tempest tossed the flight's fighters about. Twice, Atwyl had to call for the young pilots to quit grousing about the rough ride and keep the comm frequency clear. During a brief lull in the storm, AeroPilot Friedrich Reischaur was the first to pick up the DropShip's readings. "Big mark on MAD sensor, Lieutenant," he reported.

"I've got it, too, Friedrich," Atwyl said. The *Lucifier*'s bigger computer had been even quicker at registering the target, but he revealed little of his excitement in finding the quarry. "Reading matches the Davion DropShip, and comp places it on the surface just shy of the Batan spaceport. If that's our baby, she'll be an easy target as long as we keep clear of the port's guns."

Atwyl punched in some numbers and waited for the fighter's battle computer to confirm his estimated flight plan. When it did, he laid out his plan to the flight. "We're going to go down on the deck and come in low. That should put us under the spaceport defenses. Comp says there's a forest that will screen us most of the way to the DropShip. Beta and Gamma, when we're down, stretch out your lead on us. I want you in fast with your eyes open for hostiles. Recon only on the first run. Bredel and I will come in hard and rip up the sucker after you give us the all-clear. After we've softened it up, it's an open turkey shoot. Questions?" Morris's channel lit up.

"What's a turkey, boss man?"

Atwyl laughed. Intentionally or not, T.J. had broken the tension that had been rising in him since he'd first caught the readings on the DropShip. He hoped her words had loosened up the others, too. "Never mind, T.J. What it means is that after Bredel and I hit the ship on our first pass, you guys can make your own attack runs."

"Roger, boss man. You crack the shell, and we take the turkey." That got laughter from Bredel and Hall. Atwyl quieted them down.

"Let's all go down together. Make it a six-eight degree glide slope down to three-zero meters off the deck. Then open throttles and go in. Got it?" Five voices chorused acknowledgement, while Atwyl keyed the final figures into his battle computer. It set up a countdown timer in the left corner of his head-up display.

"O.K. Recorders on. Three. Two. One. Punch it!"

Acceleration pushed Atwyl back into his flight couch. A small whine came from behind him as the pressure equalizer cut in. The system was supposed to infate bladders in his flight suit to prevent blood from pooling in his limbs under the weight of the tremendous gee forces of dives and high-speed maneuvers. If he lost power in the system, he could black out and lose control. Though the equalizer was noisy, it did seem to be working.

A sudden drumming announced the end of the clouds as waves of rain hit the hurtling ship. The water sheeted over the canopy, leaving everything gray and dim beyond it. Ahead of him, Atwyl could see the flames of the *Sparrowhawk*'s afterburners as the fighters leveled out and accelerated. Easing back on the control stick, he came out of the dive smoothly. Checking on Bredel, he saw his wingman following cleanly behind. Ahead, the lights of the smaller fighters' engines winked out as they reached attack speed. He vectored all thrust aft to bring his own ship up to speed.

The Dragoon fighters broke through the front of the thunderstorms. Under the clearer sky, the open, rolling hills of the countryside were visible around them. The roads Atwyl could see were deserted. In places, he spotted the rubble of towns and industrial complexes, highwater marks of the Succession Wars battles that had swept over this planet time and again. Right on schedule, the forest loomed ahead, in trees rising to almost a hundred meters high. The fighters roared up and over the forest.

When they reached the edge of the woods nearest Batan, a path of newly broken trees appeared. It was as though a giant, flaming hand had swept across them, splintering and burning them despite their sodden condition. As the last trees fell away, the cause became apparent.

Half-sunk in the fields outside the city was the immense sphere of the Davion DropShip. The pilot must had been making for the spaceport when disaster struck. The ship had gone down, skimming the trees and plowing into the open fields west of the city. Seven kilometers short of its goal, the DropShip had foundered.

A huge hole gaped on the upper surface, the edges blackened and warped outward. Debris was strewn in a trail from the forest's edge to the crash site. High on the elevated side, one of the great unloading doors was open to the sky, its protective armor crumpled and torn. Across one edge, limp as an unconscious man, was the shape of a BattleMech. The giant machine seemed small against the bulk of the transport spacecraft. Even as Atwyl registered the carnage, the *Sparrowhawks* were zooming over the wreckage, two on either side of the ship.

Just then, a startling twin flash of laser pulses split the sky, followed by the stuttering light of tracer fire from autocannons. The lead fighter of the left-hand pair crossed the streaks of light and disintegrated in a ball of fire. No sound reached Atwyl over the roar of his own engines. Reischaur was gone.

The author of the *Sparrowhawk*'s destruction emerged from the shadow of the downed DropShip. It was a *Rifleman* BattleMech. The wing antenna of the Garret D2-j targeting system was rotating as the machine's torso swiveled to bring the paired autocannon that made up each of its arms to bear on a new target.

Atwyl felt paralyzed, stunned by the sudden loss of his pilot. His hands were rigid on the *Lucifer*'s controls, but the other members of Blue Flight went into action. Beta Lance split and began jinking to throw off the enemy machine's tracking. Morris threw her *Sparrowhawk* into a steep climb, thereby avoiding the lethal streams of coherent light and armor-piercing shells that filled the air where her fighter would have been. Even Bredel was reacting. He launched a flight of missiles that impacted far short of the DropShip. The *Lucifer*s were still too far away to do any damage, but Bredel's attack had roused Atwyl from his shock at the loss of Reischaur. He took command again.

"Overthrust, Gi! We've got to get in there." Atwyl's voice was shrill with emotion. He had lost one man. He didn't want to lose any more.

"Roger." As always in battle, Bredel's voice was emotionless. "I'll take the 'Mech."

"No! He's mine. Strafe the DropShip." Atwyl wanted the killer for himself. He knew that wasn't a professional reaction, but he didn't care. Arming his missiles, he threw his craft into an evasive roll. Ground and sky flashed alternately across his cockpit. Once, he glimpsed Bredel's *Lucifer* in the midst of a similar maneuver.

Before they could close to firing range, Atwyl caught a flash of sunlight on metal high above the fields. A check of his IFF scanners revealed it to be Morris's SPR-H5 diving down on the crash site.

"No, T.J.! Abort!" Atwyl's fear for the young pilot came through in his strained voice. The small fighter was too light to go against a BattleMech that excelled at antiaircraft work.

No reply came from the AeroSpace Fighter weaving a crazy corkscrew path as it dove. All four of its lasers were blazing. Some of the beams caught the *Rifleman* and sent chunks of blistered armor spraying from its torso. The 'Mech's own fire cast a deadly net around the fighter, but the small ship darted like the winged predator of its name. A burst of fire from the *Sparrowhawk* caught one of the twin guns on the 'Mech's right arm, shearing it clean away. Then the fighter cut sideways and roared over the field, miraculously untouched by the *Rifleman*'s weapon fire. Now shielded from the 'Mech by the bulk of the DropShip, T.J. sped her craft toward the onrushing *Lucifer*s. Atwyl shook his head in amazement at this virtuoso display.

"Not to worry, boss man." T.J.'s voice was clear, though the words were slightly spaced as she caught her breath. "Those tin men are too slow to catch this—"

T.J.'s comment was cut off as missiles arcing up from a concealed position struck her fighter. One hit her port wing. Its explosive warhead and the speed at which she was traveling were enough to rip the wing away from the body of the craft. As the *Sparrowhawk* began to roll, the turbulence tore more pieces from the stricken craft. Trailing flames, it dropped lower. Morris's screams lasted until the fighter plowed into the ground and exploded.

With those screams echoing in his ears, Atwyl hit the firing stud. All of his forward-mounted lasers raked the ground at the point where he had seen the killer missiles rise. Clouds of steam rose as kilojoules of energy flash-heated the ground, then flame erupted as the launcher's ammunition exploded. The infantry team who had fired the SRMs ceased to exist. A savage smile split Atwyl's face. It vanished just as suddenly when his *Lucifer* rocked under autocannon fire from the *Rifleman,* which had now cleared the side of the DropShip.

A swift shift of thrust vectors let him sideslip the fighter away from the 'Mech's searing energy beams and pounding shells. Banking the *Lucifer* around, he came in from the other side of the DropShip.

The *Rifleman* was waiting for him, its remaining three guns brought to bear on the Dragoon fighter. Atwyl, lost in his fury, bore straight in. His craft's armor was vaporized by the hellish energy of the 'Mech's lasers and the pounding of its autocannon shells. He didn't care. Flight after flight of missiles roared out from the Holly LRM launcher beneath his cockpit. His aim was poor, and most of the shots went wild, streaking past the BattleMech or striking the ground beside it. Some burrowed into the heavy plating of the crashed DropShip to send scraps pattering harmlessly against the 'Mech and the scorched dirt around it. Some few others found their target, repaying the BattleMech some of the punishment it was dishing out.

Atwyl's lips were skinned back, baring his clenched teeth. Sweat rolled down his face, puddling under his eyes and blurring his vision.

The shutdown alarm shrilled, warning of heat burden above acceptable limits. His hand stabbed out to hit the override, silencing it. Another stab launched the last of the Holly's ammo.

The *Rifleman* loomed larger and larger. Atwyl cursed the heat, then loosed all of his lasers. Red fire lanced out.

As fissures opened in the 'Mech's armor, a small explosion came from within the machine, followed by a string of larger ones. The BattleMech rocked and toppled backward as its torso ripped open. The *Lucifer* screamed through the fireball where the *Rifleman* had stood.

Now Atwyl had to pay the cost. The heat burden had risen too high for the fighter's cooling unit to handle. The automatic cutoff had shut down the fighter's reactor. The ship was going down, and him with it. To correct a flaw in the LCF-R15's design, the engineers had created a new one. The fighter had no emergency ejection system.

Fighting the sluggish controls, Atwyl thought that it was lousy to die now after he had wasted the 'Mech. Struggling with controls, he thought that the *Lucifer*'s nose did finally come up, a little. *Enough*?

No.

Maybe.

He was glad he was in a ship that had at least minimal atmospheric streamlining. Some AeroSpace Fighters relied almost exclusively on their engines for lift. Lift that the *Lucifer* would need. To avoid crashing. . .

Crashing. . .

3

DropShip* Starblade, *Approaching Quentin IV
Draconis March, Federated Suns
13 June 3023

Nine days ago, the Kurita DropShip *Starblade* had uncoupled from its interstellar transport to begin its flight from the jump point into the system. Behind it, the JumpShip had settled in to await its return, unfurling the kilometer-wide jumpsail to collect the solar energy needed to recharge the hyperdrives.

Now, hours from reaching his destination, Minobu Tetsuhara contemplated the main viewscreen on the bridge of the *Starblade*. The magnified image showed the fourth planet in the Quentin system. The terminator bisected the principal continent of Aja, and in the darkened portion of the sphere, twinkling lights outlined the land mass and its smaller companion, Aja Minor. Lights marked the major population centers as well. Even in the midst of a major raid, there was no blackout for cities that did not fear attack. Their lights shone forth, callous as the stars in the greater darkness of space.

He shifted his gaze from the planet and sought out the glimmer of Nirasaki. Mere days ago, the JumpShip *Okomaru* had transferred from there to the Quentin system, crossing the gulf instantaneously by virtue of its Kearny-Fuchida hyperdrive. It would be years before the light Nirasaki emitted that day would reach Quentin. By then, Minobu would be elsewhere, his current business long concluded. Yet light from Nirasaki was here today, light from years gone by. The past mingling with the present.

Today, he mused, the past was meeting the present in more substantial ways. Today, forces of the Draconis Combine were assaulting the Quentin system. Once again, the Federated Suns and the Combine struggled for possession of these inhospitable worlds, just as those two states had for almost their entire history. The lure of Quentin was not that of friendly worlds, ripe for colonization, but a glitter that evoked the greed of the House Leaders. The third planet's mineral resources and the fourth's factories and research facilities were great prizes.

In the days when the Star League had ruled the Inner Sphere and its thousands of Human-settled stars, the battles for Quentin had been political. The League had tottered after Stefan Amaris had attempted to usurp the power of the First Lord of the League, and fallen apart when General Alexandr Kerensky abruptly vanished from the Inner Sphere in 2784, taking with him the bulk of the Star League military. When Lord Minoru Kurita claimed that he was rightful heir to the throne of the First Lord, the other Council Lords opposed him. The First Succession War had begun.

Five states had solidified out of the chaos within the Inner Sphere; for good or ill, each was strongly wedded to a ruling house. Foremost among those quarreling realms were the Draconis Combine and the Federated Suns. The Combine was ruled by the Kurita clan and the code of *bushido*. The office of Coordinator of the Draconis Combine was currently filled by the strong-willed, forceful Takashi Kurita. Under him, the Dragon was strong.

The Federated Suns was headed by its ruling family's scion, the shrewd Prince Hanse Davion. Minobu had often heard it said that Lord Kurita considered Davion one of the few foes worthy of the Combine.

Minobu was no master of a star-spanning kingdom. He was only a MechWarrior—and a Dispossessed one at that. It was true that each of those redoubtable House rulers had served as a Mechwarrior in his younger days, but neither one any longer fought in the battles of the Succession Wars. Lord Kurita and Prince Davion directed great states. They gave the orders while he, a simple soldier, obeyed them. His orders had brought him here to the Quentin system where, under the light of the present sun and the past stars, he would meet his future.

Wolf's Dragoons.

So far, his own route of travel along the lanes of commerce had prevented him from joining the mercenaries to whom he had been assigned. Having their own transport gave the Dragoons tremendous strategic flexibility, and they had traveled rapidly across the Combine, then moved into action.

Minobu had finally been able to intersect their course. Soon he would have his first actual meeting with Wolf's Dragoons, or at least, with those present for the attack on Quentin. He would meet the people behind the communiques and situation reports.

One mercenary regiment and several auxiliary units had rushed on, joining a raid in the Hoff system. A second regiment was on recovery furlough and serving as escort for the Dragoon support services and noncombatants as they moved toward their assigned home base on An Ting. That left three full BattleMech regiments involved in this action, an unusually large force. Likely, it was simply a matter of timing. The Dragoons were to be stationed in the Galedon District, along the Draconis border with the Federated Suns. As they moved through the Benjamin District, the opportunity for the Quentin raid arose. The Dragoons simply used the whole available force, for it would mean a quicker resolution of combat and a faster arrival at their garrison stations.

In the three months since he had received his assignment, all of Minobu's contact with Wolf's Dragoons had been secondhand, through reports and ComStar-mediated communiques. Soon he would be dealing face-to-face with the enigmatic mercenaries from beyond the Inner Sphere. Indeed, he still did not know what the Dragoon commander looked like. For some unknown reason, there were no solidographs or datapics included in the briefing materials, and Minobu realized he could not even be certain of Wolf's gender.

The name was no help, either. Minobu had met or served with at least seven persons named Jaime, and only five had been male. While all Combine materials used the masculine pronoun when referring to Wolf, that was not proof of gender. Combine forces had suffered serious defeats when the Dragoons had been employed by the Lyran Commonwealth, the other Successor State bordering the Combine. Many Kurita officers could never accept the idea that a female could function successfully as a military commander. If the Dragoons' leader were a female, Combine officers might have concealed and denied that fact out of shame at being defeated by a woman.

Minobu had studied all the available history of Wolf's Dragoons. Of their origin, there was nothing. They had simply appeared in Davion space in 3005 and signed on as mercenaries. Details of their later history were just as meager, except for a long list of victories and a much shorter one of defeats. For almost twenty years, they had fought for each of the contending Houses in turn, but always seemed to avoid conflict with their most recent employer. Minobu knew that the contact with House Kurita specifically precluded the use of the Dragoons against House Steiner, and he suspected that their previous contracts had included similar clauses.

The Kuritan Internal Security Force had provided organization charts, but the ISF's data were incomplete. To Minobu's mind, the most glaring gap was the lack of personal dossiers on most of the Dragoon officers.

Sho-i Rudorff, the ship's Second Officer, cleared his throat and interrupted Minobu's musings. "*Sho-sa* Terasu and *Sho-sa* Hawken are on their way to the bridge," Rudorff announced, his face showing concern for Minobu's position. The two Sword of Light officers had made it clear that they did not approve of Minobu's presence on the Bridge. Rudorff's warning was one more of the small kindnesses he had shown Minobu throughout the trip. Minobu acknowledged the man's unnecessary sympathy with a nod.

Because of the obvious rancor of the Sworders aboard ship, Minobu had tried simply to avoid them. With practiced ease, he scrambled up the worn steel of the ladder that connected the bridge with the ship's first deck. He had not quite made it to the cross corridor into which he intended to duck, when the two Sword of Light officers exited the lift. Honor prevented Minobu from showing an attempt to avoid them, so he continued on.

As their paths brought the three men nearer, Minobu stepped to one side of the companionway to allow the Sworders room to pass. Technically, he outranked them, but they held combat assignments and he had only a staff officer's position. Moreover, each of them was a commander in an elite Sword of Light Company and an active MechWarrior, while he was Dispossessed. The net effect put the Sworders in a superior social position, and they took full advantage of it.

Minobu sensed that they disdained him because of some secret self-importance that made their harassment seem justified. Ever since his transfer to the *Starblade* from a commercial DropShip docked at Nirasaki's zenith station, their petty indignities and deprecating comments had been ceaseless. Minobu ignored them whenever possible, though he knew they took it as a sign of weakness.

Today there would be no avoidance.

Sho-sa Brett Hawken of the First Sword of Light Regiment stopped as he drew abreast of Minobu. His long-distant ancestry on the Terran continent of Africa was as evident as Minobu's own, but he had made it abundantly clear in previous encounters that he would accept no hint of association with Minobu, however minor.

"It looks like our deskjock has been wandering around where he isn't needed," the man drawled.

"Or wanted," *Sho-sa* Gensei Terasu of the Seventh Sword of Light added venomously.

The two officers rarely agreed on anything except their dislike of Minobu.

"We are almost in range of the planetary defense, Tetsuhara," Terasu continued. "Shouldn't you be in your crash couch? I've been given to understand that it's much safer there."

"I believe you are correct," Minobu said, his deliberate ambiguity lost on the hardheaded Sworder.

"Then you had best get along," Hawken said, stepping so close to Minobu that the scabbard of the black Sworder's *katana* almost struck him in the crotch.

Terasu barked a laugh as Minobu twisted to avoid the contact, then stomped on down the corridor after his companion.

Minobu watched their backs, shaking his head. The code of *bushido* embraced a diversity of adherents. Some might even consider those two to be exemplary samurai. *De wa,* he thought. A man had to mind his own honor.

4

Batan Territory, Quentin IV
Draconis March, Federated Suns
13 June 3023

Hamilton Atwyl never remembered hitting the ground.

When he opened his eyes, the Dragoon Lieutenant was lying on his back, looking up at the sky. A cool breeze blew over his face. The rich smell of loam and humus almost covered the harsher stink of burning oil, plastic, and blood.

"Gianni, he's awake!"

Atwyl winced at the shout. The tensed muscles sent pain shooting through his head, closing down his vision to a pinpoint. The vibration of footfalls approaching at a run sent another wave of pain through his head. This one rippled through his back as well. The pleasant warmth of the sun disappeared as the remaining pilots of Blue Flight crowded around him.

Something pricked his arm, then Gianni Bredel's voice cut through the haze. "You O.K.? We thought you'd taken up farming when your *Lucifer* plowed in."

"So did I." Atwyl's voice scratched out of a throat raw from breathing the superheated air in his *Lucifer*'s cockpit. "Guess Colonel Carmody will have my rank disk for that stunt."

"Damn fool stunt," Bredel chided, "but impressive, Ham. Your cockpit recorder must've been working overtime on the last pass at the 'Mech. Too bad your heroism will go unrewarded."

Atwyl didn't understand what his wingman was talking about. Damn, but his brain was foggy. Bredel caught his confusion.

"The black box is dead," he explained, caressing the holstered laser pistol at his side. "There's no record of your suicide charge, and"—he winked at Gordon and Hall—"we'll never tell."

The other pilots nodded, grins brightening their faces.

Now Atwyl understood. His flight members had pulled the black box and destroyed it. With the box gone, so was the record of his lapse in command judgement. Carmody would never know. Blue Flight was rewarding the protective loyalty Atwyl had shown for those under his command. To them, such loyalty was much more important than some brass-trimmed Colonel's idea of professional detachment. Atwyl didn't even feel the pain his answering smile cost him.

The beeping of the communicator in Bredel's fighter interrupted them. Bredel heaved up and ran to answer it. Hall and Gordon were discussing something, but Atwyl couldn't focus on their words. Their voices faded from his awareness. His brain felt sodden. Finally, he decided that they must have given him a painkiller.

When Bredel returned from his *Lucifer,* he was carrying a rucksack. He stopped and spoke quietly with Hall and Gordon before bending next to Atwyl. "That was the man upstairs. He says it's time for Phase Two. And since we are so nicely situated here, he wants Blue Flight as part of the air cover for the Pathfinders."

Atwyl tried to get up, but Bredel was ready for that and held him down. "Blue Flight don't mean you this time, boss man. Your ship's a mess, and so are you. You're sitting out this part of the party."

Ignoring his protests, the pilots lifted Atwyl and got him onto a makeshift stretcher. They carried him up a slope and into the shade of the nearby forest. As careful as they were, the unavoidable jolting sent pain through the drug's shield of isolation. Bredel took care to prop him up while the others cut saplings and brush to build a blind. Hall spread a thermal blanket over the framework before covering it with brush. When satisfied that Atwyl was as well-concealed as possible, Bredel handed him a Binox image intensifier.

"Now, your majesty, you have a front row seat for the festivities. And your own private sound system." He patted the comm unit lying next to Atwyl. The wingman's smile dropped a little. "Stay put, Ham. We'll be back for you as soon as we can." Then he was up and calling for Hall and Gordon to get to their fighters. Feeling a detachment that he knew was chemically induced, Atwyl watched them trot down the slope to the waiting fighters.

A roaring in his ears brought him back from the dreamy fog into which he had begun to slip. He looked out to where the fighters of Blue Flight had been. They were gone. The noise, however, was still there. When shaking his head didn't stop the sound, he looked up for its source. Two Aero-Space Fighters with Dragoon markings shot out over his head. They screamed toward Batan and the spaceport at its edge. Behind them came a bulky *Leopard CV* DropShip, whose insignia showed it to be Colonel Carmody's flagship. Around the ship swarmed a dozen or more fighters, and he thought he saw the remnants of Blue Flight among them. As he watched, the small craft spread out in front of the big DropShip. Like the first pair of fighters, this flight dropped to the deck as they blasted toward the spaceport. Like Blue Flight before them, they were trying to come in under the port's defenses.

To Atwyl's blurred vision, the attempt at tactical surprise seemed to be working. Port defenses were slow and uncoordinated in response to the closing enemy. The Dragoon aerospace forces opened up on the spaceport as soon as they had range. The usual assortment of missiles and rainbow of energy weapon beams bombarded the defenses of the port. Despite the seeming chaos, Atwyl thought he could see the raiders concentrating on gun emplacements and avoiding the landing surfaces and port facilities. He fumbled for the image intensifier.

Just as he reached it, a wedge of three spacecraft cleared the trees. They followed in the path of the earlier ships. At first, Atwyl feared that they were Davion forces intent on smashing the Dragoons, but the grinning wolf's-head that adorned each tail fin told him otherwise.

The *Leopard* Class DropShip in the first flight could carry AeroSpace Fighters. Its complement of six were, no doubt, part of the swarm that accompanied it. The new arrivals were also *Leopard* Class, but were the more common design for carrying BattleMechs. Each ship could carry a full lance of four giant battle machines, as well as two AeroSpace Fighters. Atwyl guessed that the fighters from these ships were operating in the advance wave.

When the second flight was halfway between the forest and the port, another four DropShips rocketed down the path. These, too, carried the Dragoon wolf's-head, but they were a different type. They were *Fury* Class troop ships, each able to carry a company of troops and eight support vehicles.

Atwyl switched the comm unit to scan so that it would pick up the Dragoon battle frequencies. Then he focused the Binox on the port in time to catch the finish of the first flight's run. Several of the Dragoon craft were engaged with some atmospheric fighters that the Davion command had managed to get into the air. Atwyl wondered whether they were brave or stupid for pitting mere atmospheric fighters against the Dragoon aerospace craft. The transatmospheric ships were so superior that the outcome of the fight was a foregone conclusion.

The 'Mech carriers reached the landing field. Atwyl could see their landing gear still was retracted even though they were barely ten meters above the ferrocrete. When he noticed that the 'Mech egress doors were retracted, too, and that the ships were not slowing, he knew what was coming. In his ten years of service in Wolf's Dragoons, he had heard often enough about this maneuver, but he had never seen it. It took well-trained warriors and reliable equipment to pull it off. Dragoon MechJocks called it downloading. Lesser men called it crazy.

The *Leopard*s opened fire to suppress any hostiles who had survived the sweep of the fighter cover. The right wing ship dropped back to clear a fire lane for the starboard weapons of its partner as well as for its own port weapons. The Pathfinders' BattleMechs appeared at the edges of the bays.

The winds of the DropShips' passage buffeted the mighty machines. Atwyl heard the jump command come over his comm unit. In unison, the 'Mechs hurled themselves clear of the ships, some firing jets from back units, others using the jets set into their legs. In either case, the terrible momentum was slowed.

Sparks flew as the 'Mechs skidded to shaky stops on the landing field. One, a *Stinger,* crumpled to the ground as its left leg buckled on contact with the ferrocrete. The remaining BattleMechs began to spread out at top speed. Some opened up with their own weapons as they targeted on emplacements that the aerospace forces had missed. Behind them the *Furies* roared closer.

Again Atwyl's comm unit barked with a command. The BattleMechs on the landing field threw themselves prone and ceased their fire. Like the *Leopard*s before them, the *Furies* came in as a staggered vee with clear firelanes. Coherent light, charged particles, and missiles rained on the defenses.

A Davion BattleMech lance appeared near the control tower, but the lead *Fury* cut down the first two 'Mechs with its particle beams and missiles. The third 'Mech, an ENF-4R *Enforcer,* went to ground while the fourth disappeared back behind the tower. The prone 'Mech opened fire, bringing its autocannon to bear on one of the Dragoon 'Mechs. Shell craters pocked the ferrocrete and ripped into the target 'Mech's armor. The Dragoon MechJock held his fire. The Davion pilot probably never had time to wonder why as beams from the passing DropShips converged on the *Enforcer*'s position. As the only fusion-powered combat machine firing weapons on the tarmac, the *Enforcer* was an easy lock-on for the DropShips' targeting systems. Limbs flew as its ammo storage blew. The *Enforcer*'s Federated autocannon fired the last shells in its chambered cassette round as the arm assembly spun through the air.

While the guns of the DropShips were wasting the Davion BattleMech, a third order came through on the Dragoon battle frequency. Trooper after trooper leaped from the speeding *Furies,* each wearing an individual jump pack. Like the 'Mechs before them, the Jump Troops used the exhaust as a brake so they would hit the tarmac at something approaching a reasonable speed.

Having laid their troops, the DropShips leaped for the sky to rejoin the rest of the aerospace forces. They would be harassing the Federated Suns troops trying to flee the port, discouraging the arrival of any reinforcements. Atwyl knew that part of the mission well. He had flown on it many times.

The comm unit at his side came to life. Now that the time for split-second commands had passed, the channels were clear for normal battle traffic. The Dragoon 'Mechs were up and attacking again. The infantry, highly mobile with their jump packs, moved swiftly to hold what the 'Mechs had won.

Surprise and the lightning assault made the rest easy. In short order, the Dragoons were in control of the port. From his vantage point, Atwyl observed the Davion troops retreating in good order out of Batan. As they headed south and away from him, the battle calls and commands on the Dragoon frequency changed. Victory yells and postbattle chatter filled the channels as the *Furies* returned to unload the infantry's vehicles.

Atwyl relaxed as he listened to the excited talk. The tension of watching the battle had drained his strength. He was drifting off to sleep when the babble cut out suddenly, overridden by the command call buzz.

In the comm silence, Colonel Carmody's voice was clear. "Landing zone secure, Colonel Wolf. You may begin landings, as scheduled."

5

Batan Spaceport, Quentin IV
Draconis March, Federated Suns
14 June 3023

The gee forces made breathing hard, but they were not enough to explain the difficulty Minobu was having. He had made combat drops in the insubstantial ablative shell that protected a BattleMech as it fell through the atmosphere. He had ridden down through the firestorms of enemy defenses while locked in the cockpit of a 'Mech that was, in turn, locked in the belly of a DropShip. Those were harrowing times. Why a problem now?

He closed his eyes, blotting out the small stateroom. Was it because this was the first time he had landed on an enemy-held planet without being in the cockpit of a 'Mech? Was it the lack of a 'Mech's protective armor? Was it fear of death? No. Death held no fear for a true samurai. The old, old proverb of his spiritual ancestors said it best, "Death is a feather; duty is a mountain."

It was the duty, then, that raised his pulse and made his breathing shallow. Or rather the fear of it. The message with his assignment had been clear. He was walking a narrow line, facing concerns that were new to him. He feared failure and the shame it would bring. He had always been calm before battle.

Minobu forced his head around and opened his eyes to

look across the compartment. *Sho-sa* Gensei Terasu lay stiff on the lower bunk across the stateroom the Kurita officers shared. He was pale, with sweat beaded on his forehead, and his muscles were taut with more than just the strain of acceleration. Fear etched the face that a short time ago had been set with disdain for Minobu, the Dispossessed MechWarrior.

Minobu found it ironic that Terasu feared a descent outside his control. MechWarriors, accustomed to the feeling of vast power that came with piloting a 'Mech, often showed quirks and superstitions when traveling in machines piloted by other men.

Minobu turned away. To see a warrior in such fear only added to the shame of that warrior. Such enslavement to fear was pitiful, even in so crass and overbearing a man as Terasu. The man's combat record was superb, indicating that he had courage. Minobu wondered if Terasu's courage in battle was really fear of shame, which could overmaster him as thoroughly as fear of death did now. That would fit with his bullying attitude, too.

Between the rattling and creaking of the DropShip plowing through the turbulent upper air over the Ajan continent, Minobu caught a softer sound. It was a voice, soft and monotone, reciting a Buddhist chant. If it had been coming from anywhere other than the acceleration bunk immediately below him, he would never have heard it. Minobu had not expected *Sho-sa* Brett Hawken to have any religious inclinations at all, unless one counted his fervent devotion to House Kurita. Did Hawken feel the same fear that gripped Terasu? Did he intone the prayer from a true religious impulse or was the chant merely a focus to calm his mind? Did it matter?

As Minobu listened, the *Starblade*'s rattling lessened, but the roar of the drives continued. The ship had slowed its velocity. From his estimate of the time elapsed since they had started the descent from orbit, he calculated that they were beginning the final approach to Batan spaceport. The Dragoon AeroSpace Command had been as good as their word. The *Starblade* had come through unmolested by the Davion defenders.

The thunder of the DropShip's engines subsided. As the relative quiet of the hundred-year-old DropShip's normal creakings and hissings returned, *Sho-i* Rudorff appeared at the hatch to the stateroom. He apologized for the failure of the old ship's intercom, and assured them that it was safe to unstrap. Minobu released the restraints that had held him in place during the descent. As he started to swing his legs out from the confining couch, Terasu's head appeared. His face was flushed with returning blood. "Stay up there till the combat soldiers are clear, Tetsuhara."

He put a particular, haughty emphasis on the word "combat." Hawken, also up now, grinned maliciously at the comment, teeth shining in his black face. Minobu waited patiently while they slung their gear. The Sworders took their time, but Minobu recognized that there was more behind their actions than a simple desire to keep him waiting in the cramped bunk. A hasty appearance on the landing field would not suit a Sworder's dignity, especially on a field captured and held by mere mercenaries.

Terasu and Hawken finally finished. Terasu exited first, taking no notice as the Second flattened against the hull to give him room. As Hawken started through the hatchway, he said, "Make yourself useful, Tetsuhara. Tell the men to deploy the 'Mech lance into a guard patrol." Over his shoulder, Terasu yelled back, "Make sure *my* men are out first." Hawken frowned and hustled after the other Sworder. Their voices, raised in argument over precedence, echoed through the corridor.

Minobu found Rudorff had come to help him change from the drab gray shipboard fatigues into his uniform. "I don't know how you do it, sir. Those two are barbarians. Always ordering everyone around. Such arrogance! As if they were the Coordinator himself. But you are never perturbed. Like a zen master. Why do you let them speak to you so?"

"It is in their nature." As Minobu shrugged to settle the black tunic over his shoulders, the high collar folded and caught on the side of his neck. He straightened it before allowing Rudorff to fasten it. "Just as it seems to be your nature to speak so freely."

At that, the man fumbled a fastening. "I am a loyal son of the Dragon, lord," he stammered. "I meant no offense, lord."

"I take none. Here. Hold this box." From the box, Minobu removed his dress swords and placed them in his belt; first the short one, then the longer. Stowing the box again, he shooed the Second out of the compartment and headed for the ramp. "Have *Sho-sa* Hawken's order conveyed to the lance at your first convenience."

Rudorff bowed. "As you command, lord."

The walk through the corridor to the ramp was short, but Minobu was perspiring by the time he reached the exit. Even in the short time the *Starblade* had been open to the atmosphere, the arid planet had conquered the old DropShip's air-cooling capability. Minobu's sweat evaporated in the first, unfiltered blast of the hot, dry air of Quentin IV, and he could almost feel the water being drawn from his skin.

As uncomfortable as it was, the climate over most of the planet was far friendlier than that of its sister world, Quentin III. Even in the inhabited zones of that planet's great mesas, a man had to wear a full environment suit whenever he left the safety of a ship or building. Hoping he would not be outside long enough to dehydrate, Minobu looked out across the field.

Nearer to the control tower, an *Overlord* Class DropShip stood on the landing apron, its huge, egg-shaped bulk dwarfing the BattleMechs walking sentry-go. The presence of the sentry 'Mechs and the bustling activity around the ship suggested that the *Overlord* was Wolf's command ship. The Sworders had obviously reached the same conclusion because they had already started toward it. Minobu was about to follow them when he noticed a line of communication cables running from the ship to the tower building. With a small smile on his lips, he walked down the ramp and headed for the port building.

As he approached the entrance, the Dragoon guards drew to attention and saluted him in Kurita fashion, fists across their chests. Their posture seemed respectful. Most of the mercenaries Minobu had met in the past had been remarkably lax about military etiquette. Some had not even known how to perform a proper salute. Minobu found himself wondering if the Dragoons' visored helmets hid derisive smiles. It might be their idea of a joke to pretend to be respectful. It did not matter. They were only door guards and their thoughts were of no relevance. Minobu ignored them as he passed from the blazing sun into the shadows of the building.

Just beyond the archway waited a young Lieutenant in the camouflage field uniform of the Dragoons. He noted that her pale hair was cropped close after the fashion of most MechWarriors. Cool air from the blower units rushed past Minobu, to be lost in the sweltering heat outside as she stepped up, saluted, and said, "Colonel Wolf will be pleased to meet you, *Chu-sa* Tetsuhara."

He returned her salute without reply.

"If you will follow me, sir," she said, turning. "I'm sure the other officers will be along in their own time." She led him through the debris of yesterday's fighting, chattering at him over her shoulder. He had only enough time for single-word answers to her questions concerning his flight down from orbit and no time at all when she wanted his opinion of the local weather conditions. Before long, Minobu's attention drifted from this one-way conversation. His body followed hers through the corridors, but his mind wandered through other passages. Lost in thoughts of duty and what it meant to him and to his future, he was startled when she excused herself and left him standing before an archway.

Beyond it was a large open area that had recently been a passenger concourse. Its function had now changed. Scattered about were several tables and piles of electronic hardware. Techs, in an activity common to their kind throughout the Inner Sphere, bustled about, checking cables and exposed banks of circuitry. A heavy cable snaked through the arch to a large table where sat an inactive holoprojector and other machinery. Around the table stood and sat several soldiers in Dragoon uniforms. The late morning sunlight glittered off rank insignia. Five of those present wore the triple stars that marked them as Dragoon Colonels.

Understanding dawned on Minobu. He had spent over twenty years threading his way through the mazes of protocol and the labyrinths of status that underlay the Draconis Combine. This was an old game. One that was older than the Successor States, older than the Star League, older even than man's first departure from the cradle of Terra. That homeless mercenaries would set up such a test was unexpected and hinted at an unsuspected sense of propriety and proportion.

Now he knew the reason that no solidographs or datapics were included in the briefing materials. Only one of the five Colonels could be Jaime Wolf. Minobu must identify Wolf correctly or suffer a loss of face that would hamper all further dealings with these people. He would have to observe closely and rely on that. He calmed his mind and looked about him.

Nearest to him was a tall, angular woman whose dark blonde hair was pulled back tightly at the nape. She paced while speaking to an aide, and the spring in her step suggested that it was chained energy rather than anxiety that drove her. Her movements were fluid.

In her pacing, she went past the second Colonel. Because the man was seated at the table studying reports, his height was indeterminable. His uniform hung loose on a spare frame. Whenever the blonde passed, brown eyes in a face as dark as Minobu's own flicked up in distraction. The man's movements were as sharp-edged as his eyes.

The next was a short man with gray-streaked hair, erect carriage, and steady, economical movements. His uniform was tailored perfectly to the well-muscled body of an athlete. Though he was giving most of his attention to the fourth Colonel, he seemed to miss little of what the others were doing. His calm was a pool.

His partner in conversation was of a height with him. Her body was strong, hardened by use yet softened with feminine curves. Her dark hair showed no signs of age. Minobu took her to be quite young until he caught the wrinkles about her eyes that could only have been acquired from years of squinting into harsh suns. A brittle shell surrounded her, protecting a yielding yet strong center.

The last Colonel was seated, relaxing. He was a big man, massive through the chest and shoulders. He would stand tall, probably taller than Minobu's own two-meter height. No aides approached him while he sat back and listened to the others. Occasionally, he offered a comment. His strength lay dormant.

After only a few minutes, the pacing Colonel stopped, dismissed her aide, and gave Minobu an appraising glance before turning her attention to the table. She said something to the big Colonel who answered her. She laughed.

Minobu knew the time had come. He was expected to make his selection. To delay would be a loss of face, even if he selected correctly. He walked forward.

Drawing nearer, he pierced the curtain of white noise that had muffled the voices around the table and prevented him from hearing their conversation. At his approach, the talk stopped. He passed the pacer and moved around to the far side of the table, stopping behind the short man. "Colonel Wolf?" he said, making the polite interrogative into a statement. "I am to be your Liaison Officer."

The man turned to face Minobu. His cool gray eyes scanned up the front of Minobu's tunic, stopping momentarily at the Bushido Blade on the left breast pocket. He stared briefly into Minobu's eyes, breaking contact before the stare became impolite. "More than just a lucky guess, I think. What gave me away?"

"It was obvious." Minobu's voice was calm, almost casual. "Yours is the only *ki* in the room strong enough for the command you hold."

"*Ki,* is it?" Wolf, one eyebrow arched, glanced around at the other officers. "I think we are gong to have an interesting relationship, Colonel—or should I say *Chu-sa*—Tetsuhara.

"Let me introduce my officers. Footloose down there is Kathleen Dumont, Delta Regiment. This is Jason Carmody, AeroSpace Operations Group." With a thumb over his shoulder, he indicated the other female Colonel. "Wilhelmina Korsht, Gamma Regiment. The lazy bear in the chair is Andrei Shostokovitch, Beta Regiment. The young sprat is Kelly Yukinov." Wolf indicated a Major standing near Carmody. "He's the one who really runs Alpha Regiment.

"I'm afraid you'll have to wait to meet the rest of the command staff. Transport timing didn't work out."

"Colonel." The speaker was Major Yukinov. When he had his commander's attention, the Major inclined his head toward the archway. Through it, they could see the two Sworder officers approaching, led by the same blonde Lieutenant who had met Minobu. Her face was set and she was not speaking. No doubt Terasu or Hawken had commanded her to silence, for neither man thought much of a woman's conversational abilities. Without hesitation, the Sworders walked through the arch. Behind them, the Lieutenant shrugged and turned away.

"Which one is Wolf?" Terasu only looked at Minobu long enough to direct the question to him. Then, like Hawken, he scanned the assembled mercenary officers. Their disdain was evident in the way they held their bodies.

"I'm Wolf." The Colonel spoke before Minobu could.

"You will brief us on the current situation," Hawken commanded.

Wolf made a small bow of acknowledgement and began a rundown of the Dragoon dispositions. If he was annoyed by the peremptory manner of the Sworders, he showed no sign.

The bow was a surprise, though. It showed that the mercenary commander had made at least a cursory study of the forms of courtesy prevailing in the Combine military. Minobu wondered if Wolf was aware that no commanding *Tai-sa,* or Colonel, of the DCMS would ever make a bow-to-superior to a *Sho-sa,* or Major, as he had done. Perhaps he thought it appropriate from a mercenary to the soldiers of his paymaster. The Sworders certainly accepted it as their due. From what Minobu had seen today, Wolf might be merely playing to their arrogance the way one humors a small child. Minobu decided that this mercenary Colonel was a man who would bear watching.

Wolf apologized that the holoprojector was not yet operative and proceeded to sketch the situation in words. His briefing was succinct and clear, interrupted occasionally by comments or queries from the Sworders. They seemed more interested in Davion activity in the immediate area of the port and the aerospace above. Though their questions were pertinent, Minobu could tell from the structure of the mercenary's presentation that he would eventually have answered all their questions in the course of his outline. Once satisfied that matters were proceeding according to schedule, the Sworders announced that they would personally inspect the security measures taken to secure the port.

The briefing reminded Minobu that there were still military concerns in his world that would constantly affect him and those around him. The Sworders' obsession with safety matters seemed uncharacteristic. He had assumed that the presence of the officers and the companies they commanded in this operation was simply a chance to blood some of the newer members of the regiment or for the veterans to sharpen the edge. It was also an opportunity to test coordination, tactics, and, perhaps, loyalty in a relatively controlled combat situation. The First and Seventh Sword of Light Regiments certainly saw little action in their position as honor guards at the capital on Luthien. The planet had seen no military action in Minobu's lifetime. It was secure and safe, as the capital of the Combine should be.

"The city administrator is at the gate, Colonel." The soft voice broke into Minobu's thoughts. He looked around. The speaker was a slim Captain who had been standing by the table all along. A flat, metallic box fitted to the curve of the young officer's shoulder. A cord led from it to a receiver in his right ear, and another connected to the comp pad he held in his right hand. The boom-mounted microphone partially obscured his mouth. It was obviously a communications device, but Minobu had never seen its like before.

"Thank you, William. Pass him in and have Alpha's mobile HQ brought up." The Captain was murmuring into his microphone before Wolf had turned to face Major Yukinov. "Time for you to go, Kelly. Reports at regular intervals."

Yukinov snapped a quick salute, and along with several junior officers, headed for the exit. Each started to fasten on humidifier masks as he went. Minobu marveled that these mercenaries, so informal among themselves, could so quickly respond to orders, as was proper. At least, there were some soldierly virtues among these Dragoons. Wolf's voice caught his attention.

"Kathy, flick that thing on."

The blond officer, nearest to the holoprojector, did as he said, and a relief map of the Ajan continent appeared, floating in the air above the table. The terrain was depicted in a muted gray, allowing the bright reds and blues of unit dispositions to stand out.

"Let's get this show over with," Wolf said impatiently, "so we can get ready for our guest."

Around the table, the Colonels began adjusting their reports, conferring with their comp units, and dispatching aides. The jumble of action reflected Minobu's reactions to

Wolf's last comment. Puzzled, he asked, "What is this show, Colonel Wolf?"

Wolf left off studying the holomap. "Our visit from the Baron of Batan. He's here to meet the rampaging mercenaries, and we don't want to disappoint him."

"*So ka.* Then the guest you wish to prepare for is someone other than the Davion administrator?"

"Of course," Wolf said. His brow furrowed slightly for a brief moment. "Didn't they tell you? Your Coordinator wants to be a soldier again."

Minobu thought he had misunderstood Wolf's word. Perhaps the mercenary had confused the ranks within the Combine. He could not mean Lord Kurita.

"Takashi Kurita himself is coming to visit," Wolf said.

Suddenly, the Sworders' preoccupation with security became clear. In their pettiness, they had kept the information from him. Now that Minobu knew that the Coordinator of the Draconis Combine was coming to Quentin, he could only wonder way.

6

Batan Spaceport, Quentin IV
Draconis March, Federated Suns
14 June 3023

The road from Batan to the spaceport ran parallel to the landing field for a kilometer. The car traveling that road was a sober gray. From its right fender flew a flag showing the colors of the Federated Suns; from its left, the colors of the city of Batan. Looking out the car window, Baron Augustus Davis, administrative chief of that city, could see the invader marshalling his forces.

In the sky, a DropShip was on final approach vector to join others already perched on the landing field. Beyond the fence, its ragged gaps filled with strands of barbed wire, he could see vehicle parks, prefabricated barracks and, worst of all, row upon row of BattleMechs. Sensor towers stood guard in place of patrolling troopers.

The groundcar slowed as it approached the barricade that had been erected across where the road turned into the spaceport. Davis frowned when he saw the two banners on the flagpole at the guardhouse. One was the black wolf's-head of Wolf's Dragoons, which he recognized from holo reports of battles throughout the Inner Sphere. He knew the Dragoons were mercenaries, soldiers for hire, loyal only to the almighty C-bill. He had heard that those who served under the wolf's-head were better than most of that breed, but it hardly mattered, given the masters they now served. Above the wolf banner flapped their new master's flag, the hated Dragon of House Kurita.

The Dragon had brought war to the Quentin system for centuries, and with it, much suffering to both inhabited planets. The total annual output of the mines of Quentin III was less than a single month's quota in the days of the Star League. Quentin IV had fallen on even harder times. Its research facilities were gone, and the few industries struggled to stay alive. Now the Dragon was back, and Quentin IV would suffer again.

Davis's thoughts halted at the same time the car did. The driver opened his window, letting in a blast of hot, dry air, and he handed the guard a safe-conduct pass. The pass had been delivered to City Hall that morning, along with an invitation—or more accurately, an order—to attend the garrison commander.

Behind the opaque faceplate of his helmet, the trooper silently studied the papers for a while. Voice distorted from passing through the helmet's filters, he announced that they checked out. Turning from the car, the guard signaled his fellow soldiers to open the barrier. When the road was clear, he waved the groundcar through.

The car moved into the port, now an enemy camp where DropShips were disembarking men, equipment, and supplies. Mechanics and laborers wearing Dragoon uniforms were at work everywhere. Scattered among them were workers wearing heatsuits of local manufacture. Davis strained to recognize the turncoats whenever one was close enough, but his or her humidifier mask always defeated him.

Once, the car had to pull over to clear the way for a column of BattleMechs. The huge machines were mostly painted in brown, dull red, and gray to blend into the colors of the badlands that dominated the continent's interior. A few sported bright colors or fanciful designs as though the pilot were challenging his enemies to single out the BattleMech for battle. Seen from a distance, the machines had seemed only more impedimenta of war. As the 'Mechs lumbered past his car, Davis shuddered and sat back, his hatred vanishing under a wave of fear. He had known of their size, but the physical presence of the huge legs blurring past the window, each foot large enough to crush the groundcar, was unnerving. He took one of his shaking hands into the other. When that didn't stop the trembling, he held them between his knees. He was still holding them that way when the car began to move again.

When the groundcar reached the main building, he was met by an empty-headed blonde who chattered interminably while leading him through the carnage left by the attack on the port. If this trooper were any indication of the quality of the Kurita invaders, Davis thought that the Davions should have them running for the system's jump point in short order. Before he knew it, his guide was gone and he was looking into a room full of soldiers.

The first to catch his eye was a tall black man in the uniform of a Kurita senior officer. One of the triple-damned Internal Security Force troopers, no doubt. A dog set by the Draconians to watch their warhounds. Batan would be seeing more of his kind if the invaders were around for long.

The others all wore camouflage fatigues. One was, presumably, Wolf. Looking for a Colonel's rank insignia, Davis was dumbstruck to find five. *How was he supposed to tell which one was Wolf?* The mercs had probably arranged this to embarrass him, to put him off-balance. He'd show them. He examined the prospects carefully and found his man, a perfect picture of the barbarian at his ease, comfortable with the havoc he had caused. Davis approached, and with just the right amount of bored indifference in his voice, he said, "Colonel Wolf, I presume. I am Augustus Davis, Baron of Batan. I understand you wished to discuss something with me."

The man heaved himself up from the chair. The broad shoulders rose past Davis's eyes, leaving him staring at a chest full of campaign ribbons. "Davis? I don't remember asking for a Davis," he rumbled. Over the Baron's head, he said, "I'm going to take a nap. Wake me if anybody important shows up." The big man turned and left the room. Davis glared at his back, silently damning the Colonel's insufferable arrogance in calling him all the way out to the spaceport for a petty insult.

"Baron Davis?"

The noble swung about to find a short, gray-haired Colonel facing him with hand outstretched.

"I'm Jaime Wolf. I'm glad you could find the time to see me today. I'll try to make it brief."

Davis took the man's hand. The grip was strong. He knew he'd just made a fool of himself by introducing himself to the wrong man. Regaining the initiative would take some doing. Before he could say anything, Wolf spoke again.

"Don't be put off by Colonel Shostokovitch. His sense of humor is often difficult for those around him. Please take a seat and we'll get down to business."

"I . . . well. . . . yes, of course." The Baron had been thrown off-balance after all, leaving Wolf the initiative. Things were not proceeding as he had rehearsed. The man was not at all what Davis expected. Wolf seemed earnest, open. He had a cultured voice. Clearly, this was no common mercenary commander.

"I wish to apologize for the inconvenience of our presence here. I assure you that we are equally inconvenienced. Our arrival was unplanned. Your orbital defenses were a bit more determined than we expected." Wolf shrugged, a half-smile on his face. Davis was distracted by the shifting play of colors on the holomap where the disposition of Dragoon forces was displayed. This Wolf was not infallible, Davis gloated to himself. The merc no doubt thought the Baron would be too discomfited to notice the map, which might work to the advantage of the Davion forces.

"We have had to divert the bulk of our force here to assure safe landings," Wolf continued, seeming not to notice the Baron's interest in the holomap. "Batan is not our target, and I have no wish to bring the war here, Your Excellency. However, do not misunderstand me. Since we are here, I intend to hold the port as long as we are on planet. Its facilities are too convenient.

"Our troops will be moving out soon, leaving only garrison forces. The strain on your city should be small. Your cooperation can minimize that strain."

Ah, Davis told himself, *here come the invective and threats, followed by orders to supply the invaders with provisions and workers, all with no recompense.*

"If you will ensure that there will be no guerrilla activity or sabotage against my rear areas, I will declare the city a clear zone—no combat," Wolf said. "We will also need laborers, but there will be no slave gangs or forced labor. We will pay fair rates for fair work, 2 percent over current market rate for supplies . . . in C-bills." Wolf paused only briefly to let the Baron assimilate the offer. "Do you find these conditions unreasonable?"

"I think . . . well . . . no."

The merc Colonel had caught him off-guard again. The terms were generous and more than he could have imagined. The offer to declare the city clear and thus spare it the ravages of the invasion was too good to be true. There had to be catch. "Colonel, why are you offering this?"

"You are suspicious, and I can't blame you." Wolf gave him a conspiratorial look. "It's simple. We have no quarrel with your population. Our mission is an ordinary objective raid, but our forced landing here has complicated matters. Your cooperation will simplify things and make my job easier. For that, I'm willing to pay. Think of the people, Your Excellency.

"We are mercenaries. The defending BattleMech forces on Quentin are mercs, too—businessmen like us." Wolf gestured as though to suggest that Davis was also a businessman. "We are aware of the costs of doing business. There's an opportunity here for a clean military action. Certainly, this planet encourages it. City fighting can be very costly, and I want to avoid it if I can. Don't you?"

"Of course."

"Then we see eye to eye. I can count on your cooperation."

"Well . . . What you say does make sense," Davis stalled, stroking his chin. He asked about the administrative details, trying to keep Wolf talking while his own mind raced. It was a good deal. Batan would be spared war's ravages this time. It might even come out ahead because competition onworld, especially from Port Gailfry, where the mercs were heading, would be lessened. He could always report to the Duke that the mercenaries had held hostages and forced his cooperation. It wouldn't be too hard to cover up the profit he would make.

"Yes, Colonel, we have a deal."

* * *

When Wolf returned from escorting Davis to his car, Minobu noted that the mercenary seemed pleased with the results of the meeting. "All right, people, let's get back to work," he said, running a hand back through his hair. "William, clear that junk from the holo."

The air above the table shimmered as the image changed. Additional details of the terrain developed while colored images representing units flowed across the map. When they came to rest, the simulacrum was far different from what had shown during Baron Davis's visit. In particular, the blue, symbolizing Dragoon units, was more prevalent. New unit markers had appeared, most in and around Batan. None of the units previously shown, except for a few at the Batan spaceport, occupied the positions they had a few minutes before. Wolf had obviously intended the Baron to see the holomap and the false information it contained. Minobu wondered how much of Wolf's expressed intentions was accurate. The man was a clever strategist, operating on many levels at once.

The officers began to describe the operations of their commands, illustrating highlights of current deployment or planned movements by manipulating the holographic representation through their comp pads. Minobu learned the details of the Dragoon plans. No, he reminded himself, he was only learning what they wanted him to know of those plans.

Planned troop landings would be completed by 0600 standard hours tomorrow. Then, the bulk of Alpha and Delta Regiments, along with elements of Gamma, would begin their move south and west of Batan. They were ostensibly moving to join those components of Delta Regiment engaged around Port Gailfry, which was what the carefully controlled communications traffic would indicate. The move was intended to draw the Davion forces out to attack the tempting offered flank of the Dragoon thrust. That flank was actually to be a screen of units that would retreat under pressure, drawing the Federated troops further into Wolf's trap.

When the enemy was strung out enough, the Dragoons would strike, hitting the Davion flank and engaging them in a holding action. Meanwhile, the main force would attack the real target, the city of Fasolht and its BattleMech factories, whose defenses would now be weakened by the absence of units on their way to hit the supposedly vulnerable Dragoons. It was a complicated plan, one that Minobu would never have considered for Kurita House troops, let alone mercenaries. Wolf and his officers, however, did not seem to think the complications and contingencies unusual, and their tone was confident.

When Wolf announced his satisfaction with the results of the preliminary skirmishing and the preparations for further action, the discussion turned to the security of the Batan region. All was reported to be well. No enemy units had been sighted within one hundred kilometers of Batan for twenty hours. Wolf turned to Minobu. "Do our arrangements satisfy you, Colonel . . . er . . . *Chu-sa* Tetsuhara?"

"Assuming your reconnaissance reports are accurate, Colonel Wolf, I can find no fault. However, my colleagues may suggest some minor alteration in dispositions to demonstrate their tactical expertise."

"I understand," Wolf said, smiling. "Even so, I expect your Lord Kurita will have a safe landing."

"Yeah," Wilhelmina Korsht snorted. "Once he's down, he'll have his own bodyguards to look after him. If he gets into trouble then, he won't be able to blame us."

"Easy, Willie," Wolf chided. His next remark was addressed to all of his officers. "I think we're done for today, people. Dress uniform tomorrow in honor of Lord Kurita. He may only be a head of state, but he is our paymaster.

"Dismissed."

Shocked at the irreverence to Lord Kurita, Minobu watched the Dragoon officers disperse. They had handled the strategic and tactical discussion with impressive expertise and dispatch, yet their lack of respect was both distressing and confusing. Minobu knew that respect was integral to an appreciation of what was proper.

Then there was Wolf himself. He seemed to be a man of many faces, adapting to the circumstances. Minobu could not help but be intrigued.

He moved to where Wolf still stood at table. "Why do you play this game, Colonel? Hiding among your fellow officers?"

Wolf looked up at him, silent for a moment. "Tells me a little something about the people I'm dealing with."

"*So ka.*" Minobu nodded in understanding. "I, too, have learned something about the people I am dealing with."

"Did you now?" Wolf's look was sharp. He hefted his comp pad, then said, "You know, you're the first to get it right in quite a while . . . *Ki,* you said."

"Yes."

"I'll keep it in mind."

7

Batan Spaceport, Quentin IV
Draconis March, Federated Suns
17 June 3023

Minobu entered the command center in the company of Colonel Andrei Shostokovitch, the big Dragoon assigned to be Minobu's guide around their camp. The tour had started three days ago at the crash site of a Davion DropShip. The Dragoons were already refurbishing it as their own; their contract allowed them salvage rights to enemy equipment they destroyed. Since then, the two Colonels had been near-constant companions during Minobu's waking hours. "Liaison to the liaison," was how Shostokovitch put it.

The big man had answered Minobu's questions freely, breaking the veil of secrecy that seemed to surround Wolf's Dragoons. He was, however, uncommunicative about anything prior to the Dragoon service with House Davion.

Shostokovitch made sure that Minobu saw all the facilities the Dragoons had in service onplanet. The only place off limits seemed to be the upper decks of Wolf's command DropShip, the *Chieftain,* but Minobu did not find that unusual. Wolf was the lord of these men—and women, he reminded himself—and it was only proper for him to have private quarters. With a nudge and a wink, Shostokovitch had assured Minobu that Wolf kept a bevy of beautiful girls hidden there to while away the hours between battles. It was a joke, of course, something the big Colonel seemed to have in inexhaustible supply. Sometime during the second day, Minobu had capitulated to his companion's boisterous and good-humored insistence on being called by his nickname.

"Shos, will Colonel Wolf recall the commanders to meet Lord Kurita's DropShip?"

"Don't think so. It's starting to turn into real business out there, and Jaime won't let a little pomp get in the way of that."

The three-day delay in Lord Kurita's arrival had forced Wolf to allow his Regimental Commanders to disperse to their combat assignments. Now, it seemed, the pressure of combat command would keep them from reassembling to meet the Coordinator. Colonel Dumont had gone off to the northwest to supervise the harassment of Port Gailfry, while Colonel Korsht had joined Major Yukinov and the bulk of the Dragoon forces in the field. Shos and Flight Colonel Carmody remained at the port. Carmody, though he complained loudly about it each day, seemed content to control orbital operations from the ground. Shostokovitch, with no combat assignment, chaperoned Minobu and, in his own words, "hung around to intimidate the hostiles." Every time he said it, his booming laugh echoed across the landing field, but Minobu was not sure he understood the joke.

Wolf was still present. As the days passed and Lord Kurita's arrival continued to be delayed, he seemed to grow restless, stalking about the center, speaking rarely except to give an order or ask for information. Rather then being angry, as frustrated commanders so often were, he seemed distracted, removed. Each time a new report came in from the field, Wolf entered it into the holomap himself and projected endless variations of possible follow-up moves. He was trailed everywhere by his communications specialist, Captain William Cameron, who whispered in the Colonel's ear like a guardian spirit.

Minobu studied Cameron. The young Dragoon was at least thirty years younger than Wolf and overtopped the Colonel by a head. His slender frame was presided over by a plain, freckled face, which gave him a decidedly unprepossessing appearance. This, combined with his quiet manner, led to the man's being overlooked and ignored in the crowd of flashy officers surrounding Wolf. Unobtrusive he might be, but unimportant, no. Cameron's common appearance hid an uncommon talent.

William Cameron was Wolf's filter. Data relayed from the field and the main battle computer through the Tacticon B-2000 system aboard the Captain's CP10-Z *Cyclops* BattleMech were fed to the unit he carried on his shoulder. Thus, Cameron was able to monitor all Dragoon communications simultaneously, making sense of what would have been senseless babble to most other people. He was able to select and isolate important data, updating his commander's situation map and informing him of any vital communiques. Most important, his judgment of the value of information was reliable. Cameron's talent, allied with Dragoon technology, was a powerful combination that freed Wolf to exercise his considerable command powers—a freedom most leaders would have paid dearly to possess.

At an order from Wolf, Cameron started around the map table toward Carmody. He hadn't covered half the distance before he stopped suddenly and stood listening intently for a moment. When he spoke, Cameron's voice was low, with an uncharacteristic tinge of emotion. Eagerness perhaps? "A delta call, Colonel."

"Feed it here," the Colonel said.

Wolf's fingers flashed across his com pad. Unit readiness data twinkled into being above the holomap. Harsh red spots appeared about a third of the way from Batan to Fasolht. Lurid crimson light surrounded those spots, suffusing the terrain feature that stretched across every projected line of march Minobu had seen in the planning discussions. As Wolf became engrossed with the images developing on the display, Cameron returned to his side.

Unwilling to interrupt Wolf, Minobu turned to his companion. "Colonel Wolf seems disturbed, Shos. What is a delta call?"

"Means trouble," the big man said, the bantering tone completely gone from his voice. "Somebody has got himself into a situation."

"What kind of situation?"

"Ambush. Battle. Something big." Shostokovitch pointed at the image. "See. It's in Kelly's area, near a place the locals know as Fire Rift. Kelly's run into something, and as commander on the spot, he's determined that what's come up could affect the plan. So he's checking with the boss. Watch the map."

It was flickering again. The red-tinted portion of the map grew until it almost filled the image volume. Where unit representations had indicated battalions, the symbols for companies and lances appeared. Several of the strength rosters for the Dragoon units in the area registered casualties. A yellow flare, indicating ongoing conflict, limned several ridge lines. Behind those highlights, the ghostly red sparkling that marked suspected troop concentrations was prominent in the area Shostokovitch had indicated as Fire Rift. Somehow enemy troops had developed a position across the Dragoons' intended path.

"Jason, get me a terrain map . . ." Wolf's eyes flicked over to Minobu, then quickly away. Minobu gave no sign that he had seen. "Map data to augment the projection. I want good detail so we can all see the position. Then dump it, with any refinements, into Williams's Tacticon."

Minobu noticed a slight emphasis on the word *all,* an indication that the composition of the group around the table mattered to his order. Wolf had almost slipped and revealed something that he had been keeping secret, a hidden source of data that could supply *refinements.* There was no clue about what kind. Perhaps the ISF would know; they would certainly be interested.

From the moment Cameron had announced the delta call, activity around the map table had increased. More officers had shown up, their tousled hair, bleary eyes, and rumpled uniforms showing that some had been roused from sleep. Apparently, no one had seen fit to call in Hawken and Terasu from where they were readying their companies for Lord Kurita's arrival. Wolf looked up, rapidly taking in the officers gathered around the map table. "Kelly's got a hotspot. Several 'Mechs are down in an area called Fire Rift, some kind of geological anomaly."

Major Stanford Blake, Wolf's intelligence chief and the first off-duty officer to arrive, took up the situation briefing.

"The hostiles have been identified as belonging to an outfit called The Snake Stompers. William, bring up the merc file on them. These guys are long-term borderers with a big hate on for Kurita." A new data window opened in the holo image. "As you can see, preliminary recon and intelligence reports give a 90 percent probability that they have a battalion on Quentin III and another two here on Four. Prime base on planet is at Carson, with two companies detached to stiffen the garrison at Fasolht. The early reports indicate that it's only those two companies causing the ruckus. But that's enough to give us trouble."

"These are tough customers," Wolf summarized. "They're vets and they know the planet."

"Colonel, interception of Davion transmissions indicates that the opposition at Fire Rift is acting without specific orders," Cameron said. "It is an unauthorized advance."

"We may be able to take advantage of that." Wolf ran his fingers through his hair and pondered for a moment. "Right now, they're sitting where we want to go. If they can make a fuss about it or call in company, we will have to revise our estimates of the costs on this operation. With our visitors on the way, I don't want an embarrassment. I think I'm going to have a look for myself.

"William, scramble the lance.

"Jason, keep an eye on things, but I don't want any extra recon missions. Can't have your opposite numbers noticing our interest.

"Shos, you're back on the job. Hold the camp. You're on protocol duty if I don't get back in time to meet our guest." Each officer nodded acknowledgment of his orders.

Minobu watched Wolf's face as he gave out the orders and then headed for the landing field, where his BattleMech would be waiting. That face was free now of the nagging worries that had tightened his expression. The call to action seemed to have liberated the man's spirit. His energy was directed, focused. He was ready to act, decisive and in his element. Wolf pulled up short as he passed Minobu. "*Chu-sa,* you are here to observe how we operate. Want to come along with me?"

Minobu did not answer immediately. Surely, Wolf knew that he had no BattleMech. The mercenary was calling on Minobu to confess his dishonor. Very well. "I am Dispossessed, Colonel Wolf. I would be a liability."

"Nonsense," Wolf said, taking his arm. "We can fix you up. Come on."

The pressure on his arm and the attention of the room compelled Minobu to go along. The only alternative was to create a scene of indecorous refusal.

Once they hit the heat of the harsh Quentin sun, there was little time for thought as Wolf led him, Blake, and Cameron at a brisk walk. A faster speed would have been foolish because it would be asking for trouble to overheat the body *before* entering the cockpit of a BattleMech. Ahead of them the half-dozen BattleMechs of Wolf's Command Lance stood in the blazing sun.

Among the unfamiliar machines stood the *Cyclops* that would be Cameron's 'Mech. Minobu spotted a blue *Archer* with familiar gold trim. *So ka.* Had the pilot survived Dromini as well? There would be time enough to find out after the crisis. If it was the same pilot, that would be a warrior worth meeting.

Gathered in the shadow of the war machines was a small group of people. Three of them wore cooling vests, which marked them as MechWarriors. Like the officers who had just come from the command center, they did not wear humidifier masks. They were expecting to be out of the dry air soon and inside their 'Mechs, where the filtration systems would keep the air moist.

The faces of the MechWarriors were unfamiliar to Minobu. Any one of them could have been the warrior he had spared on Dromini VI, for they all had the look of veterans of the harsh battlefields of the Successor States.

The rest of the group, whose uniform markings showed them to be Techs, was equipped to work in the planet's brutal conditions. They were occupied with last-minute checks or in briefing the pilots on the status of their machines.

When Wolf's group arrived, a pair of Techs stepped up to help the Dragoon officers strip out of their uniforms. Once Wolf had on his vest and his helper was attaching the biofeedback sensors, he motioned for a woman wearing the insignia of a Senior Tech to join him. "Bynfield, I want you to find something for Colonel Tetsuhara."

"As you wish, Colonel." Even muffled by the mask, her voice conveyed the annoyance of a busy person being asked to take on a heavier workload. She turned to Minobu and said, "If you will follow me, sir."

Minobu did as he was bid, following the Tech to a hangar. As he entered, he looked back to see Wolf conferring with his lance members.

"What do you pilot, sir?"

Minobu noted that she used the present tense. There was no way that this Tech could know that he lacked a 'Mech, and so she assumed that it was simply unavailable. He need not make his disgrace obvious to one of her social standing; neither would he bother to lie. "My last BattleMech was a *Panther.*"

"*Panther.*" She consulted a desk comp. "Hmmm. Can't get you one of those just now. Got a VND-1R that we've just finished servicing in the vehicle park. How's that?"

Minobu had never handled a *Vindicator,* so he questioned Bynfield about its details as he studied the diagrams the Tech brought up on the console. A MechWarrior was supposed to be able to pilot any 'Mech. Theoretically, his training had prepared him for that, but as was so commonplace in the universe, the theory did not match reality.

Most BattleMechs had a similar humanoid shape. Regardless of shape, however, their controls had to be designed to interface with a Human pilot. That made them similar, but not identical. Even minor differences in the arrangement of the instruments could lead to a moment of hesitation that might cost a MechWarrior his life. Likewise, anticipation of a certain turning radius or rate of head dispersion that was not appropriate to the current machine could be lethal in the split-second world of combat. The problem was further complicated by the decline of technology in the Successor States. Modifications and jury-rigged systems were more common. Such modifications came in such a bewildering variety that no 'Mech academy curriculum could cover them all.

This *Vindicator*'s performance characteristics were similar to those of his old *Panther.* The 'Mech was jump-capable and had a comparable ground speed. Massing ten tons more, it also carried heavier armament and armor. The biggest difference was that the right arm mounted a Ceres Arms Smasher PPC instead of a battlefist. The weapon's sophisticated cooling jacket made it a less compact system than the Lord's Light PPC of the *Panther.*

The computer readout showed only one non-standard system—a Holly launcher replacing the Capellan-built Sian/Ceres Jaguar missile system. The Holly's discharge rate was slightly inferior to that listed for a factory-fresh Jaguar launcher, but its reputation among MechWarriors of the Inner Sphere was far superior. This unit's maintenance record was spotless, and the BattleMech's overall record was nearly as good.

"The *Vindicator* is adequate, Tech Bynfield."

Bynfield's voice was hard with sarcasm. "Glad you're pleased, *Colonel.* We try so hard to perform to adequate standards. If you could be troubled to step this way."

The Tech indicated a jitney that had arrived while Minobu was studying the computer files. On the passenger seat was a cooling vest, the feedback sensor cords coiled neatly on top. Minobu removed the garment and took a seat. He had barely settled in when Bynfield gunned the engine and directed the vehicle toward the back of the hangar. They roared through the open doors and headed for the vehicle park. As they approached, Minobu recognized the silhouette of the *Vindicator* from the plan views stored in the data file. A power lift scaffold nestled next to the 'Mech, and a pair of jitneys and a coolant truck were parked at its feet.

Bynfield brought the vehicle to an abrupt stop and jumped out. She headed for the 'Mech, her back stiff. Minobu climbed out and stood in the shade of the BattleMech to strip off his uniform and don the cooling vest. As he watched Bynfield supervise her crew's final preparations for powering up the 'Mech, her concern for perfection and technical expertise was evident. She moved and directed with the sureness of a master. Now he understood her attitude. He had treated her as a simple lackey, not as the artist she obviously believed herself. When she returned to announce the 'Mech was ready, Minobu bowed.

"I am grateful, Senior Master."

Bynfield stood for a moment, puzzlement written all over her face. Then she shook her head and started to reach for the pile that was his uniform and swords. "Your gear'll be at HQ, sir."

Minobu stepped in her way. "You may take the uniform when I am gone. The swords I must take with me." He lifted the *wakizashi.* Loosening the *sageyo* cord, he looped it over his shoulder, and retied it. He settled the sword where the blade would not get in his way when he clambered aboard the 'Mech. He did the same for the *katana,* his motions quick and practiced.

"Right. Well, the *Vindicator*'s all set, sir. The neurocircuits have been adjusted to an open setting, and so you shouldn't get any feedback. You can ride the lift up." She watched as he entered the cage. Minobu engage the drive and began to rise up the length of the 'Mech. "Crazy samurai," he heard her say to another crew member, though he knew Bynfield had not intended him to overhear. Then she picked up the uniform and walked away.

The lift jarred to a stop at cockpit level, where Minobu picked his way across the hot metal of the 'Mech's exterior. Before entering, he unslung his swords. Holding them both by the scabbard cords, he slid through the open hatch and into the pilot's seat. Swords safely stowed, he looked over the controls and checked the 'Mech's system monitors before reaching up to close and dog the hatch.

Sliding the neurohelmet free of its cradle, he settled it onto the padded shoulders of the vest and plugged the control leads into the console. He waited for the brief wave of dizziness that he knew would come. The neurohelmet was a sophisticated computer interface that fed data on the BattleMech's stance and position to the wearer. The 'Mech's control systems then utilized the feedback from the pilot's own sense of equilibrium to guide the gyros in controlling the motion of the machine. All this occurred below the level of the MechWarrior's consciousness, but the moment of connection was always palpable.

The vertigo came and passed quickly, only slightly more unpleasant than Minobu was used to because the frequencies were not adjusted specifically to him. A rush of adrenalin came with the sense of the machine's balance. He was in control of the BattleMech. The viewscreens, set to the visible spectrum, revealed the ground crew clearing away. As he moved the 'Mech out of the vehicle park, he lifted the PPC in salute.

Today, if only for a little while, Minobu Tetsuhara was a MechWarrior again.

8

Fire Rift, Quentin IV
Draconis March, Federated Suns
17 June 3023

The *Vindicator* moved through a hellish landscape. Minobu had seen no signs of animal life, and the only plants were scrubby bushes and rough grasses, all tinted with tawny chlorophyll analog that had evolved here. Everywhere he looked were columns of red rock, sculpted into fantastic spires reminiscent of the antique minarets and arches of Al Na'ir. Scattered among them were mesas of banded sediment aproned in talus piles and dusted with weathered gray pumice and ash. In several places, plumes of vapor rose from active volcanic vents. All of it was wrapped in the distortion of heat haze and a pall of smoke.

It was much hotter here than near the spaceport. There was direct solar heat from the blazing white sun, reflected heat from the dazzling ash, and activity heat from the 'Mech's movements. Heat was a MechWarrior's constant concern. If the internal heat of a BattleMech rose too high, its functional efficiency was impaired. Delicate systems could malfunction, and there was the danger of an ammunition explosion if the machine carried a missile rack or a ballistic weapon. And if the heat levels rose too high, automatic safety circuits could shut down the 'Mech's fusion power plant, leaving the MechWarrior helpless in the midst of a battle. He was only on the outskirts of Fire Rift now. Deeper into the region, it would be worse, for smoke plumes to the south showed that volcanic activity was greater there.

Minobu checked the *Vindicator*'s heat scale. It was still low, but that would change if he had to engage in combat. The Dragoon Techs had set speed governors and lengthened the recycle time for weapons on their 'Mechs to slow the crippling buildup of heat. He must not forget that if he was to use this 'Mech effectively. Status readouts indicated that the heat exchangers were operating at 52 percent of standard capacity. It would be far too easy to overheat this machine.

The *Vindicator* headed along the bearing Minobu had received from the command center when he left Batan, a course that was supposed to take him to the Alpha Regiment's field headquarters to link up with Wolf. The mercenary had not waited while Minobu was fitted out with the loaner 'Mech. He and his Command Lance had moved out, leaving their liaison to follow. Minobu wondered briefly if it might be another test, but decided that a more likely explanation was Wolf's desire to take charge quickly.

Communications had been fitful since he'd entered the Fire Rift area. When not screened completely by the masses of granitic extrusions in the surrounding landscape, they were broken up by static. Only when he crossed a hogback could Minobu pick up the Dragoon battle frequencies with reasonable clarity. The elevation also exposed the *Vindicator* to enemy observation, a risk not worth taking. Constant communications linkage was not critical at this time.

He had not been able to make contact with Alpha Command. Presumably, they remained at the location he had seen on the command map at the port. A check of the map display on his right showed that he was only forty-five or so kilometers from the site. Were the terrain clear, the 'Mech could get him there in two hours, even with its speed limited by a governor. That was a vain thought, however. The terrain was anything but clear, and getting worse. The trip would take considerably longer, but he could not predict how much.

Minobu maneuvered the *Vindicator* down a slope and onto an old lava flow. Because walking the 'Mech was easier on the relatively flat surface, he was able to increase his pace for awhile. When the flow began to lead away in another direction, he was forced to return to tramping over broken rock and scrabbling through the scree.

Distances were deceptive in these badlands. Erosion had sculpted many fantastic shapes, in many sizes, but size and shape had no connection, and the stone had no scale. Combined with the lack of ordinary measures, such as trees, vehicles, or people, it was almost impossible to gauge the distance to any of the natural features. What looked to be a tremendous tableland, kilometers away, could turn out to be a miniature mesa only meters off. It was all a giant illusion that would have intrigued and delighted his grandfather, a gardener in the ancient Japanese tradition of recreating the natural world in the microcosm of a garden.

Grandfather had often taken him into the family garden. In that quiet place, the old man had begun young Minobu's first training in the disciplines of *muga,* opening him to the paths of inner solitude that are the strength of a samurai. With Grandfather at his side, Minobu had walked those paths, inner and outer, among *bonsai* trees carefully cultured to make mounds into mountains.

Minobu's first sight of the wrecked BattleMech came as he passed through an arch of ruddy stone. Frozen in place against the background of spires and buttes, the 'Mech was gigantic, dwarfing the tablelands. Illusion and his memories had caught him. This was no refugee from a child's holo entertainment, no impossible machine standing hundreds of meters tall. It was an ordinary *Griffin,* destroyed in combat. The 'Mech was only fifty meters away, not the hundreds it had first appeared to be.

The left side of the machine's torso was armless and ripped open. Even a novice MechWarrior could have told that an ammunition explosion had destroyed this 'Mech. The battle damage was light, fingering heat as the killer. Probably an internal buildup followed by detonation of the warheads on its missiles. A similar fate could await his *Vindicator,* for it carried one hundred-twenty 87mm free-flight rockets, in racks of five. Any one set exploding in its rack would gut the BattleMech more surely than a hit from an enemy PPC. To ignore the high ambient heat level would be suicide.

The *Griffin* bore Dragoon markings, and so Minobu

scanned for the pilot. The IR was useless for finding a man's body heat among the furnace of rocks, however, and a visual check yielded no better results. The MechWarrior was gone or dead. Minobu entered the location on his map display for later salvage, and then moved on.

At one point, a geyser erupted nearby, spattering the *Vindicator* with drops of boiling water. Without conscious effort, Minobu sidestepped the 'Mech clear of most of the falling water. Once he and the 'Mech were safe, he realized that he had achieved *muga.* Action without thought. If only briefly, he had burst the barrier. Control of the 'Mech's movements became easier. Though the machine was sluggish because of the speed governor, he had carried out its movements as though they were his own. Suddenly, the way seemed shorter, and the landscape slid by.

An hour later, as he topped a rise, Minobu's receiver picked up a broadcast. He made a slight adjustment to the comm unit to bring the signal in clearer. Static still blurred many of the words, but he recognized the strained voice of Captain Cameron broadcasting a string of coordinates. Minobu waited until he finished, diverted power to his comm unit, then sent his own call. "Cameron, this is *Chu-sa* Tetsuhara. Do you copy?"

"Unity!" Static hiss distorted the words, but not beyond comprehension. "Colonel Tetsuhara, where are you? Wait. Keep transmitting so I can get a fix. We thought we'd lost you, too."

Too? Minobu wondered who else was missing. The sudden thought that it might be Lord Kurita terrified him. "What do you mean? Is the Coordinator safe?"

"Huh?" The question caught the Captain off-guard. His usual tranquility was shattered, lost in turmoil. "I think so. I mean, his ship hasn't landed yet. It's the Colonel, sir. We've lost contact with him."

"Calm yourself, Captain," Minobu said, taking his own advice now that he was assured of the Coordinator's safety. "Can you vector me to your location?"

"Yes, sir." The air went dead while Cameron consulted his computer. Minobu waited for him to transmit the heading. When the coordinates were broadcast, he changed his direction to match them. "Tell me what happened," he ordered.

"Command Lance moved out after you left to get your 'Mech. By the time we reached Alpha HQ, Major Yukinov had a confirmed count of over twenty 'Mechs, all flying Stomper colors, sniping from the Rift. He had three 'Mechs out of action and another four M.I.A. Alpha was having trouble pinning the Stompers down, and he wasn't getting anywhere.

"The Colonel was worried we'd have to shift too much firepower to deal with these guys and that it would tip our hand to Davion. Scans were garbage and communications intermittent. The Colonel wanted to know just what was happening, and so he headed out to see for himself. He left me and Major Blake here, and took the rest of Command Lance."

That meant Wolf had three other 'Mechs with him.

"About forty-five minutes ago, we got a burst transmission that they'd been caught in a Stomper ambush. Lieutenant Vordel's last report stated that the Colonel's antennae had been shot away just after he ordered the lance to scatter. Vordel lost sight of the Colonel in the badlands.

"We've called up Charleton's Company from reserve to keep those Stompers off our back while we look for the Colonel. Major Blake is up in his LAM."

That was interesting. Minobu hadn't known that the Command Lance included on of those rare Land-Air 'Mechs. Most Successor Houses had trouble keeping those multiform 'Mechs in fighting trim. That a mercenary force could maintain one said much about the Dragoons' technical staff and supply capabilities.

"Conditions are terrible. The long-range scanners aren't worth a ComStar repair prayer out there. With the Colonel's radio out, we've got to find him by visual."

"Then you will need all available pilots," Minobu stated. "How close am I to where the Colonel was last reported?"

There was a pause before Cameron's voice came back hesitantly. "Five klicks. North and east."

"Where are your other searchers?"

Cameron gave him the details of the assigned search sectors and the number of Dragoon 'Mechs in each. The number of hostiles was unknown.

"Very well. I will proceed into sector seven-delta-three-three because your coverage there is limited."

Changing his 'Mech's heading, Minobu ignored Cameron's protests that he come to the field HQ for his own safety. Minobu was Chief Liaison Officer to Wolf's Dragoons for the PSL. Knowing Wolf's whereabouts was his duty. If no one else had that information, he would have to get it himself. A samurai could not sit idle when his duty was clear.

Minobu felt a curious relief when growing interference swallowed up Cameron's voice. Was it simply the welcome lack of distraction? Was he glad to be free of reminders that his actions were more becoming to a simple soldier than to an officer, that he was neglecting his real duty in order to prove that he was still a MechWarrior? He concentrated on piloting, trying to ignore questions he did not want to answer.

The course changes forced upon him by the tortuous terrain brought him near the coordinates of the ambush. The comm frequencies were empty, save for the hiss and sputter of static. He decided to check the site. It was entirely possible that Wolf had returned to learn the fate of his lance. Lacking communications, the last place where they had all been together could be deemed a reasonable rally point.

The fight had been hard, and the land bore testimony to the fury unleashed there. Minobu studied the ground, envisioning what had happened. The Dragoons had been surprised by a sudden attack. Where it had come was marked by blackened craters and glazed patches of sand from near-misses. Not all the enemy's shots had been misses, however. Chips of armor and fused lumps of metal attested to that. A BattleMech arm lay half-buried in the dirt, severed raggedly by explosive force, but there were no other obvious casualties.

Minobu observed the ground where it was scarred by the rapid turns and accelerations the Dragoon machines had made to escape the fire zone. He could see that they had scattered in four different directions, probably hoping to lose their pursuers in the maze of the badlands.

He suddenly realized that he had no idea what type of BattleMech Wolf piloted. Three of the Dragoon 'Mechs involved in the fight had been heavy machines. He could tell their paths from the depth of their tracks. The fourth was considerably lighter, a *Wasp* or *Stinger.* It was the owner of the arm left on the field. That one was not likely to be Wolf's. A commander of his stature was too valuable to fight in so fragile a BattleMech. Of the others, any could be Wolf's machine.

Overlaying the tracks of the Command Lance 'Mechs were those laid down by many other machines as the Snake Stompers followed in pursuit of their prey. The signs indicated that these 'Mechs were lighter but more numerous.

A call on Dragoon frequencies produced no results, which did not surprise Minobu. Because any of the heavy 'Mech trails could be Wolf's, his decision was easy for a samurai. He followed the one indicating the passage of more enemy BattleMechs.

The trail soon became difficult to follow. The Dragoon was keeping to harder ground, no doubt believing that this would make his pursuers' job rougher. The enemy's scanners had to be crippled as those of the Dragoons, though that would also make it harder for anyone trying to aid the Dragoon warrior.

Signs of the Stomper 'Mechs vanished first. They were lighter than the machine they hunted. Then marks made by the Dragoon 'Mech became more scarce. Minobu had hunkered the *Vindicator* down in order to better use shadows in reading particular marks of passage when his exterior sound pickups brought him the sound of shifting gravel. As he was straightening his machine to a standing position, the new arrival announced his presence over his external speakers of his 'Mech.

"Move it easy and you don't get cratered, friend."

9

Fire Rift, Quentin IV
Draconis March, Federated Suns
17 June 3023

Keeping his 'Mech's movements slow, Minobu noticed that his rear scanners showed a BattleMech half-hidden in the shadow of a twisted spire of stone. No visible markings betrayed its allegiance, though its type—a fifty-five-ton *Shadow Hawk*—was clear. The newcomer's autocannon, locked into its firing position, pointed out over the left shoulder. The machine's right arm, bearing an externally mounted laser, was extended in Minobu's direction.

"At ease, MechWarrior," Minobu transmitted as he slowly pivoted his 'Mech. "I am *Chu-sa* Tetsuhara. We are on the same side."

Had the pilot been one of the hostile mercenaries, Minobu was sure the other warrior would have fired rather than spoken. Because they knew all their own BattleMechs by sight, an unfamiliar machine had to be an enemy and subject to immediate attack. The Dragoons, being from a far larger and better-supplied organization, were less likely to know all their own machines. That was definitely one of the Stompers' advantages in the maze of Fire Rift. Minobu pointed his PPC at the sky, but kept his finger near his jump jet ignition switch in case his reading of the situation was wrong.

"Tetsu—" boomed the voice from the *Shadow Hawk*'s speakers. "Whatchu doing out here?"

"If you care to switch to your radio instead of bellowing all over the Rift, I'd be glad to discuss it," Minobu answered over his own comm unit.

"Uh, right." The other pilot's voice was suspicious. A second or two later, the MechWarrior added, "Colonel."

"As to what I am doing, I am looking for Colonel Wolf."

"Ain't that a surprise." The suspicion was gone now. The Dragoons had enough confidence in their communications network that they believed it safe from interception. Only a Dragoon, or an ally, would know Wolf was missing. "I'm Sergeant Dechan Fraser. I thought I was the only one assigned to this sector, Colonel."

"I assigned myself. Colonel Wolf must be located soon."

"Don't that beat all?" As the *Shadow Hawk* moved forward to join him, its autocannon slid back into transport position. As the sunlight struck the dark blue 'Mech striding from the shadows, it revealed a stooping golden hawk on the machine's chest and a black wolf's head against a red disk on the left shoulder.

Fraser crouched his 'Mech and scanned the tracks Minobu had been studying. "Ain't been long. Sun hasn't dried the bottom yet." The *Shadow Hawk* straightened up, its left arm pointing. "Looks like he went that way. This Mech's got company. He's gonna need help, with them Stompers on his tail."

"We shall be that help."

"You know, Colonel, I like your attitude. Let's go."

Ten minutes later, their microphones picked up the distant sound of missile fire. They adjusted course and accelerated toward the noise, only slowing when Fraser reported sighting a BattleMech moving through the shade of a ridgeline. He and Minobu took their 'Mechs to cover to observe the situation.

What they saw were several Stomper machines ahead, stalking a target not yet in sight. Minobu counted four: a *Locust,* a *Stinger,* a *Javelin,* and a *Valkyrie*—all light 'Mechs with low-power weapons. The machines were moving cautiously, taking full advantage of cover. The pilots were probably worried about the firepower of their quarry. Except for the *Valkyrie,* none carried long-range weaponry. Any of the missing Dragoon BattleMechs could have outranged them.

Moving his machine forward, Minobu caught sight of the Stompers' target through a notch in a ridgeline. It was the blue and gold *Archer.*

The pilot had tried to cross what he must have thought was an old lava flow, but it was not old enough. The seventy-ton machine had crashed through the crust, falling in to its waist. Steam rose around it, and Minobu could see the glow of molten rock whenever the 'Mech's legs churned in its attempts to free itself.

He beamed a transmission at the struggling BattleMech to warn the pilot that help was on the way, but Minobu was not surprised that the *Archer* did not respond. The 'Mech's motions were slow and disjointed, as though the pilot were dazed or disoriented. The heat inside the cockpit would be debilitating, leaving the warrior helpless. If the warrior fired any weapons, he could cook himself.

"Your comrade is in serious trouble," Minobu transmitted to Fraser. "The Stompers haven't realized it yet, but he is helpless. He does not have much time."

"Then what are we waiting for, Colonel? Let's go get him." With that, the *Shadow Hawk* was up and moving, its autocannon laying down a barrage.

Minobu followed more cautiously. The Dragoon BattleMechs would normally have been more than a match for the Stompers ahead of them, but the light 'Mechs did not carry the heat burden of their heavier brethren. Their activity levels would be set higher, too. Here on Quentin, that might outweigh the armor and armament advantages of the medium 'Mechs.

The Stompers scrambled for cover at the sudden onslaught, but they fired as they moved. Keeping out of sight of the trapped *Archer,* they turned to deal with his friends first, the response of disciplined veterans. Even so, one Stomper did not make it to cover fast enough. Shells from Fraser's autocannon burst caught and staggered the *Locust.*

In a 'Mech battle, hesitation is death. Minobu loosed a blast from his PPC at the wobbling *Locust.* His body was bathed in sweat as the sudden heat of discharge threatened to overpower the *Vindicator*'s heat dispersal system. His target had more immediate problems. The hellish energy of the PPC vaporized armor and opened a path to the 'Mech's innards. It crashed to the ground in a shower of sparks and lay immobile.

First blood to the rescuers.

With the Stompers gone to ground, Fraser took his 'Mech to cover as well. With the surprise of the first rush gone, the MechWarriors began a deadly game of tag amid the badlands of Fire Rift. It was a game that the Snake Stompers had played before. They had the homefield advantage, and had used it to ambush the Dragoons' Command Lance. Now they were going to try to use it to destroy two more Dragoon 'Mechs.

As Minobu moved the *Vindicator* along a ravine floor, his microphones caught the roar of autocannon fire and the whoosh of missiles beyond the next hill. Before he could move up, a *Locust* flying the Stompers' banner from its whip aerial scurried around a bend behind him. The *Vindicator* was caught in the red glare of its laser. The pulses deeply scarred the 'Mech's rear armor, but Minobu's return blast sent the enemy pounding back for cover.

Their enemies were again four in number. At least four, Minobu reminded himself. Any number could be hidden among the twisting valleys. From the battle sounds he could hear, Fraser was engaging two of them.

The new *Locust* had disappeared out of sight behind a basaltic column. Minobu took the *Vindicator* over a small hillock to stalk it from the next gully over. As he crossed the ridge, he caught sight of the fourth Stomper 'Mech. The *Javelin* was climbing a talus slope, scrabbling for a position to fire on the trapped *Archer*.

The action at one with Minobu's thought, the *Vindicator*'s right arm lifted. A bolt of blue lightning arrowed toward the Stomper Mech to score on its leading leg. Armor vanished, and with it, some of the myomer pseudomuscles and carballoy structural members it had protected. Off-balance, the 'Mech toppled forward. Missiles arced skyward as it fell, a visual punctuation to the scream that echoed across the open comm frequencies. The *Javelin* hit the lava crust, broke through, and disappeared beneath the magma.

With the firing of the PPC, the *Vindicator*'s heat burden

soared. Minobu's heads-up display targeting crosshairs flickered and vanished under the heat surge, but he considered it a small price. The *Javelin* pilot had gone to his ancestors. Every MechWarrior dreaded death by fire, but Minobu thought it a suitable fate for a coward who would strike down a helpless opponent.

The destruction of the *Javelin* must have shaken the Stompers. One by one, they broke off stalking the Dragoon 'Mechs. Firing as they went, in retreat not rout, they began to move east. They had lost two, and the situation was now against them. Their BattleMechs were damaged, and the opposition outmassed them significantly. They retreated to fight again, but on a field of their own choosing.

Though Fraser's 'Mech had taken damage, he pursued the enemy, his autocannon roaring. In the confining terrain, the faster machines had been able to outmaneuver him, to strike and escape lightly. He charged on, seeking a kill.

Seeing the enemy in retreat before him, Minobu started to follow as well. A warrior did not let the enemy escape while he was capable of destroying them.

A warrior! The *Archer*!

Minobu pulled up.

A BattleMech's heat sinks could not long cope with the temperatures of magma. An *Archer* carried almost five hundred missiles at full load. Certainly, many of them would have been expended in combat. Just as certainly, the rising heat would make an ammunition explosion imminent. Even if only a few missiles were still on board, they would probably be enough to rip the 'Mech to shreds. He could not leave the *Archer*'s pilot to that fate. The Stompers could be fought and killed another day.

Minobu headed for the stranded *Archer,* which was still struggling feebly to pull itself from the pit. At each attempt, however, more crust crumbled around it. Minobu maneuvered carefully to avoid the same fate.

"Punch out, warrior!" he called over loudspeaker as well as comm unit.

The pilot did not eject. When Minobu reached the edge of the lava flow, he could see why. The *Archer* had taken missile hits on the upper torso near the shoulder-mounted missile launcher. Shreds of armor had peeled away and fouled the hatch. The 'Mech's weight was too great for the *Vindicator* to pull. The MechWarrior was sealed in a seventy-ton coffin.

Unacceptable. That was no death for a true warrior.

Minobu lowered his 'Mech down to the ground and carefully moved it out onto the crust. The skin of the magma dented beneath the *Vindicator*'s weight, but did not immediately crack. Minobu knew with every movement that the next one might be a sudden plunge through the crust into the molten rock below the surface. He edged forward ponderously until the *Archer*'s cockpit was within reach of the battlefist on the *Vindicator*'s left arm. Angling the right-arm PPC to distribute the 'Mech's weight, Minobu raised the upper torso of his 'Mech.

Ruby light lanced out from the 5cm Ceres Arms laser mounted alongside the *Vindicator*'s head. Centimeter by centimeter, the coherent light chewed through the heavier 'Mech's armor, outlining the cockpit area. Each centimeter was purchased with increased heat in Minobu's cockpit, edging his own 'Mech closer to shutdown. Following in the path of the laser was the battlefist, exerting incredible pressure and peeling back the weakened ceramet armor. It was slow work. Every moment brought the inevitable ammo explosion closer.

When there was enough space, Minobu closed the fist around the armored compartment that held the pilot. Rocking backward, he tried to pull the cockpit from the foundered 'Mech. The attempt threatened to topple the *Vindicator* over the *Archer* and into the magma. The 'Mech would not give up its warrior.

It took three more tries before the cockpit ripped free. Prize in hand, the *Vindicator* inched like a giant crab back away from the crack. As soon as he thought it was safe, Minobu brought his 'Mech to its feet and pounded for cover.

Before he could reach safety, the inevitable finally occurred, and the *Archer*'s missiles detonated. The pressure wave slapped the *Vindicator,* sending it flying like a rag doll. Minobu brought his 'Mech's left arm in across its chest and curled the machine around it.

The jar when the 'Mech hit the ground was phenomenal. A restraining strap split, and Minobu hurtled forward into the viewscreen. The neurohelmet kept his skull from splitting open, but the impact dazed him. The control jacks pulled free of their sockets, and the Mech sprawled as limply as its pilot.

Minobu fumbled the jacks back into place. The 'Mech lay on top of the *Archer*'s cockpit housing. He hoped that it was intact. To have crushed it after rescuing it from the explosion would be a cruel joke of fate. He rolled the *Vindicator* onto its side.

The *Archer* cockpit's metal shell was dented and distorted, but appeared unbroken. Minobu could vaguely see a moving shape within. The warrior lived! Carefully, he began to peel the shards of armor locking the access hatch in place.

Minobu had snatched this man from death, literally taking the MechWarrior's life into his own hands. If not for Minobu's actions, the warrior would be dead, his future blown to the winds with his atoms. From now on, the karma the man earned, good or bad, was also Minobu's karma. The man's words, his deeds, even his life was now Minobu's responsibility. *Bushido* demanded it.

The hatch was cleared. It opened with a groan of protesting metal, and the MechWarrior's neurohelmet appeared. Moving slowly, he emerged, battered and with his left arm hanging limp at his side.

"Looks like I owe you one," the pilot said, using his good hand to force his neurohelmet free from his head. Finally, Minobu could see the other warrior's face. The man he had saved was Colonel Jaime Wolf.

10

Alpha Regiment MHQ, Fire Rift, Quentin IV
Draconis March, Federated Suns
18 June 3023

"BattleMechs coming in from the east, Colonel." Cameron's voice was quiet, but it caught the attention of everyone in Alpha Regiment's mobile headquarters vehicle. "Not ours."

Wolf looked up from the holotank to check the chronometer on the forward bulkhead. "Timing's about right for our guests." His voice was harsh, still dry from his ordeal in the overheated BattleMech. Wolf sipped electrolyte fluid from the plastic bottle he held. "Put a recon lance out to intercept and confirm, William."

"On their way, Colonel. Intercept in ten minutes."

"Girard's Company on alert?"

"Yes, Colonel."

"Then until we get an ID on them, we wait," Wolf said, returning his attention to the holotank, which displayed the disposition of the combatants skirmishing throughout Fire Rift.

Observing the mercenary commander through the tank, Minobu thought Wolf looked haggard. He had refused the doctor's offer of a painkiller, citing a need to think clearly. When he moved, it was slowly and with great care to avoid jarring his left arm, held rigid in a preserving sleeve. The white sling was stark against the dark blue fatigues he wore. He was clearly exhausted.

Minobu knew that the human body was not meant to deal with the agonies Wolf had suffered yesterday, and the Colonel was no longer a young man. Minobu also knew that the body was resilient enough to heal swiftly from terrible injury if driven by a great will. He could only wonder if Wolf still possessed that will.

The mercenary Colonel watched the holomap as he had in the command center at Batan, though he played no variations with it. He dealt with the problems his officers brought to him, but initiated no discussions. His response to questions was slow, his speech slurred. There was no edge to the man. He seemed detached from his surroundings.

Was this the warrior who had brought troops from nowhere into the Inner Sphere, and then built a reputation as the elite mercenary unit of the Successor States? The tireless commander? The implacable foe? This was a man showing the effects of nearly twenty years of constant warfare. A shadow of the fox who had played dominance games with Minobu at their first meeting. Had the brush with death been a kind of tidewater for the man? Had Minobu saved Wolf's body only to lose the man's essence?

If the recent adventure were not a turning point for Wolf, it had certainly been one for Minobu. He felt renewed, in touch with his internal peace. Out in the badlands, he had known *muga* once more. Then, in the battle, there had been *mushin,* that peculiarly martial form of action-without-thought in which one was free from remorse. The action of the moment and its proper completion became the all of existence. A samurai's peace.

Cameron's voice caught his attention. The Captain was confirming that the approaching machines were the party expected from Batan. Wolf made no reply. The Colonel had fallen asleep where he sat.

Cameron did not repeat himself when he got no reaction from his superior. Instead, he positioned himself at Major Yukinov's shoulder. Business proceeded in the MHQ, Yukinov answering questions for Wolf and giving the orders that the Colonel would probably have given. No concern for overstepping command boundaries was shown. No one contradicted Yukinov or questioned his authority or seemed concerned that his orders might be countermanded, should Wolf awake. The Dragoons continued their operations free from the paralysis other units might have experienced without their commander at the helm. Minobu settled in to observe their performance.

"Kurita 'Mechs passing the pickets, Colonel," Cameron said, his hand on the sleeping man's shoulder. Wolf's eyes opened at once, then blinked at the light flooding in from the open hatchway.

"Time to go out and meet them." Wolf rose, wincing as his damaged arm bumped the edge of the holotank. The senior officers present left their posts to join him, and Minobu followed in their wake.

The air was chill with the cool of the night, too cold for the light coverall Minobu wore. When the party moved into the sunlight to face the northeastern end of the canyon, warmth flooded Minobu's body, and his shivering ceased.

In the distance, the morning light flashed on the Kurita 'Mechs as they filed through a gap in the walls of the canyon holding Alpha's field headquarters. The head of their column had already disappeared down into the shadows, where it would be negotiating the tortuous terrain between the entrance and the broad tableland where the MHQ was stationed. Two full companies passed while Minobu watched.

Beyond the cluster of reconnaissance vehicles that served the MHQ, activity continued undisturbed, as it had through the night. Alpha Regiment had set up its field repair and supply facilities in the same location. Some theorists have speculated that the double target of command and logistics headquarters was too great a temptation to place before an enemy, but the Dragoons seemed to feel secure. Even the damaged BattleMechs in for repair would be dangerous to an attacker. The functional vehicles of the Command Lance and the guard 'Mechs hidden in the surrounding terrain would make the cost of any attack very high. Certainly too high for the Snake Stompers, with what they could muster in the Rift.

Minobu watched the Dragoon Techs servicing the 'Mechs scattered around the canyon floor. Coolant trucks and ammunition lighters attended each in turn. The former tended a machine's heat exchanger system, flushing warmed coolant out and replacing it with a fresh, cold supply before the latter supplied the ammunition to bring each weapon's magazine to full capacity. Technicians swarmed over the 'Mechs, rigging replacement armor slabs, substituting new components for damaged ones, and improvising where they didn't have the parts. Though the Techs had labored through the night, they had proceeded at a leisurely pace, with light work loads for each shift. The fighting had been trivial so far, and there was no need for frenzied repairs to get machines back in the line.

One operation caught Minobu's attention. A *Wolverine* stood within a light alloy framework. Radiation sheeting hung from the scaffolding to keep the machine cut off from the rest of the field while a Tech worked on the fusion plant from the safety of a repair platform. That kind of work was usually done only in rear areas or after a deciding battle, which further underscored how confident the Dragoons were of the safety of their bivouac.

As the leading Kurita 'Mechs reached the field, Minobu's attention shifted immediately from the Dragoon repair operations. Anticipation rose in him at the realization that he would soon meet his master, Lord Takashi Kurita. He adjusted the angle of his swords in his belt, fretting about the suitability of the borrowed Dragoon coverall he wore. If only he had taken his own uniform with him in the *Vindicator*. Surely Lord Kurita would understand the pressures of necessity.

Unlike the forward elements that preceded a typical Kurita BattleMech company, this lance was not composed of light 'Mechs. Each machine massed at least fifty tons. Foremost was the tiger-striped *Marauder* that carried the white dragon-claw insignia of Brett Hawken. In a signal to the other machines, the 'Mech spread its forearms, broad and blocky because of the heavy cooling jackets encasing the paired weapons that ended each arm. They dispersed and took overwatch positions around the MHQ. Lowering itself down from its walking position, the *Marauder* settled back on it clawed legs like a scorpion waiting for its prey.

More 'Mechs came into view, among them a *BattleMaster*

with the serpentine dragon of House Kurita painted on its chest. Though most of the machines stopped a hundred meters away, the *BattleMaster* came on, followed by four others, all bearing the rank insignia of officers. They continued toward the group of Dragoon officers until their shadows covered the men on the ground and the vehicles behind them.

The *BattleMaster* loomed above the group, servomotors sighing as the giant machine came to rest. Soft hisses and crackling signaled the release of tension in motor components as the 'Mech settled into quiescence. As cooling vents popped open in the sides of the massive torso, the smell of hot lubricants drifted down to Minobu. The canopied cockpit opened, and the 'Mech's pilot emerged to begin the climb down his machine.

The man was well-built, with the hard muscles and belly of a *ki* adept. His motions were sure and steady, more like those of a man in his thirties than one who had seen over fifty summers. He wore a Kurita MechWarrior's standard combat gear, save that it carried no rank insignia and the belt buckle was made of ivory set in gold. Minobu knew him at once.

The man striding toward their waiting group was Lord Takashi Kurita, Coordinator of the Draconis Combine, Duke of Luthien, ultimate lord of all Kurita samurai.

Though Minobu had never met Lord Kurita, could any inhabitant of the Draconis Combine not know that face? It stared out at them from millions of patriotic posters and solidographs. The strong, square features were marred on the left cheek by small scars. Except for the pure white at his temples and a streak in Kurita's widow's peak, his close-cropped hair was raven black. Most striking were his eyes. Steely blue, they peered out from under slight epicanthric folds. These were the Eyes of the Dragon itself: cold, penetrating, keeping their secrets while peeling away the secrets of those on whom they gazed. At the moment, those eyes were taking in the members of Wolf's command staff.

Lord Kurita's gaze rested on Minobu. It took in the plain Dragoon coverall he wore and swept on to the swords at his belt before returning to his face. Minobu thought he saw recognition flash briefly before it became hidden behind the bland mask of a political man. Minobu realized how tense he had become by the relief he felt when, without a word, the Coordinator stepped forward, extending his hand to Jaime Wolf.

"Good day, Colonel Wolf. I am most pleased to meet you at last."

Wolf took the Coordinator's hand. Minobu could see the tendons in each man's hand stand out as he tested the other's grip. "You honor us with your presence, Lord Kurita."

"Not an unusual honor for you. You have served under all the Successor Lords, and now at last, me. I am looking forward to many visits with such a renowned commander. Perhaps, in one of them, you will tell me why you have resisted my offers for so long." The Coordinator's voice was mild, with no hint of accusation. "Your Dragoons have an unmatched reputation as warriors, and we know how to honor true warriors in the Combine. Perhaps now you have found a lasting home. Surely you will find our martial ways more to your liking than the effete mishandling you received under your Steiner contract."

"We look forward to a good working relationship, Coordinator."

"A diplomatic answer, Colonel." Takashi cocked his head at Wolf. "Perhaps not so diplomatic as your actions. You were not at Batan to meet me, and my officers were not pleased." A slight gesture indicated the officers who had come up from their 'Mechs. Among them was Gensai Terasu, scowling as usual. "They reported you had something that you considered more important than meeting the head of state."

"The military situation required my presence, Lord Kurita." Wolf's response was bold and honest, but he softened it in just the right way to soothe a Kurita lord. "I was sure you would understand that a warrior must do his duty."

Wolf had played it correctly. Takashi barked a short laugh. "I am glad to see that you put your duty before petty matters of protocol."

The expressions on the faces of the Sworder officers showed all too plainly that they did not agree.

"But I am remiss. It is clear that you still suffer from your recent misadventure. I will have my personal doctor attend you. He is the finest of the Brotherhood physicians."

"With all respect, Coordinator, my injuries are of no importance." Despite Wolf's words, Minobu could see that he had paled considerably during his talk with Lord Kurita. Wolf was toughing it out. Like a samurai, he betrayed no weakness and gave no admission that wounds mattered. The fire was still alive. Inside, where no one could see, Minobu smiled.

The Coordinator must also have noticed Wolf's pallor.

"At least, then, we can retire to the command vehicle, where we will all be more comfortable. We old soldiers know about wounds. Ah, for the days when wounds were my only concern." He walked beside Wolf to the MHQ. As they boarded, he said, "I am anxious to see your Dragoons in action."

The cooled air of the MHQ was an obvious relief to Wolf. Even so, he still looked shaky to Minobu. Wolf introduced his officers and deftly passed the work of the briefing to his intel officer, Major Blake, who outlined the situation for the new arrivals.

"As you can see, Coordinator, we have contained the salient at Fire Rift and are prepared to launch a thrust to blunt its threat. Our skirmishers have maneuvered the two companies of Snake Stompers that advanced without orders from Fasolht into position during the night. No reinforcements for them are expected. Indeed, intelligence intercepts of Federated transmissions indicate that they are refusing recall orders. The Davion forces are holding within their established defense perimeters at Carson and Fasolht."

Blake stopped to ostentatiously consult his watch. He smiled when he looked again at the gathered Kurita officers. "Five minutes ago, elements of Alpha Regiment began Operation Sleight. If you will direct your attention to the holotank, you will be able to follow the action."

In the tank, images of the battle unfolded, with Major Blake supplying commentary to supplement the chatter of the command channel piped into the MHQ.

The main force of Dragoons was moving west across the field. They had obviously been observed by the Snake Stompers, for several enemy machines moved to harass the column. As they approached, a detachment separated from the main body of the Dragoons. It was clear to those in the MHQ that this was no simple reaction to brush away a nuisance. The two companies of medium 'Mechs that moved out were under the direct command of Major Yukinov, but there was no way for the Davion mercenaries to know that.

The fighting quickly separated those first hostile 'Mechs from their fellows. The Dragoons intended to keep them that way. Through clever maneuvering and sharp rebuttals to countermovement, they succeeded. Unknown to those skirmishers, the rest of the Snake Stompers were being forced back, away from Fasolht and away from their comrades. They were being guided into a trap.

The bulk of the Stompers, fighting their usual hit-and-run battle, were forced slowly west, herded into a prepared position where the Dragoons turned the tables on them. The badlands that had sheltered the Stompers for days now provided cover for the Dragoon trap. Two companies of concealed heavy BattleMechs opened up on the Stomper force, taking down a quarter of their number in the first fusillade. Next, carefully sited demolitions and blocking units cut off the Stompers' retreat. Those canny veterans did not take long to realize their plight, and they began to surrender.

Smooth, efficient, and professional, the Dragoon operation had proceeded without a hitch. Cameron relayed the casualty reports; only two 'Mechs were totally out of action. Of the other fifteen that the Stompers had damaged or disabled, nine would be in the field by evening, with the rest functional again by late the following day. The Dragoon recovery and repair teams were as impressive as their soldiers.

"Cowards," Hawken said. "They surrender while they can still fight. They're worthless dogs."

"If they had been fighting Kurita soldiers, they wouldn't have surrendered, *Sho-sa*." Wolf's eyes were hard. "They would have died to the last man and taken many Draconians with them. Many would have died needlessly."

"Such a death is a warrior's death. A soldier can hope for no more." A smile crossed Hawken's face at the thought. "If they would fight to their last man, I would be proud to lead a charge against such determination. Proud to be the death of such dedicated foes. And they would be proud to die."

"There's no pride in useless death. What you describe is an unprofitable waste of men and material. Only an irresponsible commander would waste his resources so."

Hawken shrugged and turned his back on Wolf.

Minobu watched Lord Kurita, who had said nothing. Though feigning not hearing the exchange, he could not have missed it in the confines of the MHQ. Hawken had said no more than was expected of any Kurita soldier, but Wolf had spoken like an honorless merchant. He had also implied that a Combine officer was a fool. And yet, Lord Kurita said nothing. Was it possible that he agreed with Wolf?

Tiny in the holotank, a lone MechWarrior stubbornly resisted the inexorable advance of the Dragoons.

"What is next, Major Blake?" This came from a Kurita *Tai-i* whom Minobu did not recognize.

"Now we clean up the ambush site. We don't want the opposition to know just how much force we brought to bear. The Stomper skirmishers will be allowed to observe their opponents rejoining our column moving west. We plan to have them overhear quite a bit of radio traffic. They will not be allowed to observe where we hold up the column.

"This should go a long way to convincing them that we have passed on Fasolht and probably on Carson as well. The continued deception of our lead elements will add to the impression that our ground force is moving to the relief of Delta Regiment and the assault on Port Gailfry. We anticipate that the Davions will react by forming the mobile forces from Fasolht and Carson into a strike force. They'll try to hit us in our presumably unprotected flank before we can link with Delta and overwhelm the White Witches and the Port Gailfry Defense Team.

"We expect a right fine dust up when we hit them with the real bulk of Delta while they are chasing our screen. At that time, Alpha's planned assault against the industrial facilities at Fasolht will proceed."

"That is all excellent, Major." Lord Kurita's praise sounded sincere. He turned to Wolf. "I should like to see some of this action, Colonel Wolf. I will accompany you with Delta Regiment for the fight with the Davion 'Mechs. I wish a presence with the real assault as well. *Chu-sa*

Tetsuhara and *Sho-sa* Hawken and his unit will accompany Alpha Regiment."

"As you wish, Coordinator." Wolf was clearly not pleased, but then neither was Hawken. In fact, the only one in the room who seemed at ease with the announcement of the Coordinator's plans was Takashi Kurita himself.

11

Alpha Regiment MHQ, Fasolht, Quentin IV
Draconis March, Federated Suns
21 June 3023

Minobu was almost alone in the Alpha MHQ. Major Yukinov and his immediate subcommanders had left to oversee an assault on a Davion strong point at the Independence Weaponry manufacturing complex, leaving a skeleton staff to monitor operations. While Hawken dozed in the far corner, Minobu switched on the holotable. Accessing the Stratops file, he replayed, at compressed speed, the maneuvering since the action in Fire Rift four days ago.

Wolf's improvisation to the basic plan had worked perfectly. Davion intelligence missed the concentration of Dragoon forces, and so their forces were taken in by the deception. The Federated Suns commander stripped Fasolht and Carson of their mobile forces to catch a nonexistent Dragoon force in the flank. Once the Federated forces were committed, Wolf led the main BattleMech striking force of Delta Regiment into Davion's own flank. The 'Mech battles were brutal, especially when the fighting spilled over onto the Plains of Glass. More 'Mechs were lost there to heat problems than to enemy action.

At the same time, the Dragoon aerospace forces began to reassert themselves, scuttling any Davion hopes of shuttling troops by DropShip from the southern capital at Barnaby or from the lesser continent of Aja Minor. The defenders were tenacious. Even though Dragoons held the prime orbital lanes, Davion atmospheric fighters still contested Dragoon control of atmospheric space over the continent.

Once the bulk of the Davion forces was engaged, Major Yukinov led his team into the foothills of the Ridge Mountains to attack Fasolht. Progress was steady, and Dragoon gains came at little cost. Because the Davion commanders had been caught off guard, their opposition was spotty. As the Dragoons neared Fasolht, resistance stiffened, but not enough to worry Yukinov. The fighter pilots of the Fasolht Defense Team had proven too aggressive and competent for his tastes, however. He canceled the combat drop by Gamma Regiment, deeming the advantage of extra BattleMechs not worth the risk of losing the expensive machines. Instead, Yukinov pushed forward with the troops on hand. Perhaps Major Yukinov was regretting that decision, for the assault had bogged down yesterday.

The sudden commotion of Yukinov and his officers returning wrenched Minobu from his studies. The Major secreted himself in the secure comm booth while his subordinates busied themselves with their duties. One wiped Minobu's map clear to ready the holotank for new data. He made no apology.

Wakened by the disturbance, Hawken watched carefully. The rapid activity indicated that something was up, and Minobu recognized the smile twitching at the Sworder's mouth as a sign of anticipation. Hawken no doubt hoped that the Dragoons had found a way to embarrass themselves.

Yukinov left the booth and joined his staff at the holotable. "I've informed the Colonel. He can't break any of Delta free and wants Gamma down on the double."

"Unity! There goes the capture bonus, split all ways to Sunday." That from Major Patrick Chan, a strong note of protest in his voice. "Kelly, we'll take that dump in a few more days. Why can't Gamma just go on cooling their butts in orbit and leave the loot for us?"

"That's what we all hoped for, Pat, but things have gotten a little sticky. The Davion intel has finally twigged to what they're facing. A 'Mech force of the White Witches has punched through Dumont's screen around Port Gailfry and is headed to reinforce the Federated troops on the Plains of Glass. It could shape up into an expensive slugfest. The Colonel wants us to finish up business here before that happens."

With a smug expression, Hawken rose and sauntered over to the table. "You paid soldiers have no heart for battle," he said.

As the Sworder had so obviously planned, all eyes turned to him. Minobu watched Yukinov's face darken with anger as he spoke. He had risen easily to Hawken's bait. "I suppose you could do better?" he snapped.

"Of course." Hawken shrugged.

A Captain whispered in Yukinov's ear. He nodded. "What if I give you a chance to eat your words?"

The Kuritan smiled in reply. It was a shark's grin, reinforced by his cold, hard eyes.

"That's the bottleneck," Yukinov said, pointing into the holotank. "The Independence Weaponry complex. Think you can take it by tonight?"

Hawken looked over the holomap. "Those are your best estimates of the enemy strength?" When Yukinov nodded, Hawken barked a short laugh. "We will dine in their commissary."

The Sworder started for the door of the MHQ, then stopped to face Minobu before he had taken three steps. "Tetsuhara, I don't suppose you'd want to come along and see some combat."

"My orders do not include participation in assaults."

"Thought so." Hawken turned and headed for the door again. He didn't bother to check the reaction to his parting shot. "Well, we wouldn't want you damaging borrowed property anyway."

Minobu's cheeks burned.

Yukinov put a hand on his shoulder, no doubt intending a show of comradely concern. Minobu simply stared down at it. The Major quickly removed his hand.

"Uh, Colonel, I plan to watch this show from my 'Mech. I'd appreciate it if you would join me in yours."

Minobu stared at the man. He must be obtuse to have missed Hawken's reference to borrowed property. Something in Minobu's face made the Major flinch. Minobu Tetsuhara could not join him in *his* 'Mech. He owned no 'Mech.

"I will join you in the *Vindicator,*" Minobu said as he turned and headed for the door.

"Tol' ya, didn't I, Jenkins? Them wolf bastards was gonna come dis way. Dinna tell ya?"

"Yeah, yeah, you told me, Gramps." *Too many times, old man. Why did you have to be right?*

"They're too damn sneaky. Fought 'em up in Marik space back when they's working for ol' Max Liao. Their tricks are too fancy by half. Whupped my company damn good."

"You told me that story, too, Gramps." Jenkins was tired of the old man. He was tired of the losing fights against Wolf's Dragoons. He was just plain tired. He rolled over, hoping the old man would decide he was trying to catch some sleep while there was a lull. It didn't work. Gramps went right on. He told the whole story of his ill-starred merc company, right on through the slaughter of his family by the Kuritas on Bergman's Planet up to his joining the Snake Stompers for revenge.

The story was similar to Jenkins's. Hellfire, it almost was his own. Different details, different locations, but the same loss, the same need for revenge. Every MechWarrior in the Stompers hated the Snakes with good reason. All you had to do to join the Stompers was to swear "Death to Kurita!" That's what he wanted, to kill Snakes. Not mercs, least of all the thrice-damned Wolf's Dragoons. With them, it would be all blood and no payback. His ghosts would get no release. If only the raiders had been Kurita Regulars.

The Dragoons had brought blood with them, all right. They had suckered the Davion command right and proper. Now things were really in the pot. After the Fire Rift disaster, Stomper command had called for what was left of the detachment at Fasolht to join the rest of the battalion at Carson. They were to go with the mobile forces to hit the Dragoon flank. The lance had refused, the Lieutenant insisting that it was a diversion and that the real attack was coming down on Fasolht. Command wouldn't believe him, not even when Captain Edison, now commander of the mercs and the survivors of the Batan Defense Team who had fallen back on

Fasolht, had agreed with Stomper Lance Leader. Their arguments were for naught.

The Hard Riders, the other 'Mech unit defending the city, marched their machines out of Steel Valley, along with the armor and APCs of the Fasolht Defense Team. The Davion planetary ruler had horned in with threats to haul the mercs who refused to abandon the city before the ComStar Contract Review Board. Edison had told him to go to hell. Eloquent lady.

Events had proven the recalcitrant mercs right. The Dragoons had come to Fasolht. There would be no review board hearing. Vindication had only brought them hard knocks.

The Lieutenant was gone now, leaving Jenkins, Gramps, and some Techs the sole surviving Stompers in Fasolht. Jenkins rode the Lieutenant's *Phoenix Hawk* because his own *Stinger* was a smoking wreck three klicks north, at the edge of the valley. Edison's mercs had come straggling into Fasolht with only eight of her company's 'Mechs. Now he heard that only six were still running. The Batan expatriates were using light recon hovercraft in counter-assault duty. There was no hope of reinforcements before the Dragoon juggernaut rolled over them.

If they put up a good fight, they could expect honors of war. A far better fate than real Snakes would leave them. Small comfort. At least a regiment of Dragoons was breathing down their necks. It wouldn't be much longer now.

A sound came swelling from beyond the wall sheltering the Stomper bivouac. The pounding of BattleMechs moving at speed was unmistakable. Jenkins sneaked a glance over the wall while the ground crews scrambled for their weapons. Expecting to see the badlands' camouflage that the Dragoons used, his mind was slow to register what his eyes saw. The charging 'Mechs carried a scheme he knew too well.

"Lord in heaven," he groaned. "Sword of Light!"

His shout was enough to turn the disciplined turmoil of the camp into bedlam. One young Tech dropped what he was carrying and stood up, unmoving, eyes focused on some other place. Gramps howled and barged toward his 'Mech through the running figures. He squirreled up his *Commando* and into the cockpit. The 'Mech had been standing at idle, and he took off before the neurohelmet kicked in. Jenkins watched the machine sway and almost topple before the gyros came under guidance. Gramps was firing before he cleared the wall.

Seeing the old man light out galvanized Jenkins. He climbed up his machine. By the time he was settled into his own cockpit, ravening energy beams were cutting through the camp and rockets impacting on the surrounding buildings. On the other side of the wall, he saw Gramps reach the front rank of the Kurita 'Mechs. A shot from the *Commando*'s chest-mounted SRM launcher caught a *Jenner* with a full spread, staggering it. The old MechWarrior closed in for the kill, sending volley after missile volley into his foundering opponent. A Sworder *Panther* came down on him from nowhere and knocked the Stomper to the ground. Before he could rise, a second one loosed a PPC blast pointblank into the *Commando*'s cockpit.

Jenkins had no more time to worry about Gramps, for his own 'Mech was under attack. A crippling blast of charged particles wiped out half the actuators in the left leg. He staggered the *P-Hawk* to cover and tried to lay down suppression fire for the retreating ground troops of the Defense Team.

"Get out of here, you bastards," he urged them over his speakers. "Hell's own are here now."

Over by the main factory building he saw Edison's 'Mechs coming up. Her troopers were good, but clearly outclassed against the fanatics of the Sword of Light. Wild as the Kurita assault was, their gunnery was precise and their piloting superb. Before he could warn the mercenary 'Mechs off, one of them went down. Beyond Edison's machines, Jenkins caught sight of Dragoon BattleMechs moving to outflank the position. They would soon cut off the defenders completely.

"Edison, get out of here. They're cutting us off. Take to the hills."

"Hold on, Jenkins. We'll give you cover. We'll all get out together."

"Negative, lady. Leg's shot. Won't make it." He tried to keep his voice calm. "You'll only get caught, too. The Snakes don't take prisoners."

"But . . ."

"No buts. Get out and keep the fight going. The damned Snakes are here in person, lady. Send 'em back to the hell they crawled from." He breathed a sigh when he heard her give the order to withdraw.

A Kurita 'Mech passed his position. *Don't get too cocky, s.o.b.,* he said silently. *I'm not out of the fight yet.* The blast from his 8cm laser caught the enemy machine full in the back, its beam burning through the Kuritan's armor and flashheating a warhead to explosion. A chain of detonations ripped the 'Mech apart.

The heat overload alarm screamed for Jenkins's attention. Something from the explosion had shredded the cooling jacket on the laser and damaged the weapon. The laser wouldn't fire but continued a dangerous heat buildup. The *P-Hawk* was on its way to heat overload. He crouched the 'Mech and waited. One by one, he disabled the automatic overrides.

A Kurita *Crusader* approached. As the enemy passed, Jenkins pushed off from the wall. The *P-Hawk* stumbled toward the enemy. Lasers melted his 'Mech's armor, while missiles spalled and cracked it, but Jenkins didn't care. He got his 'Mech's one good arm around the enemy, hauling the two machines into close contact. Against the struggles of the *Crusader,* he brought the useless laser cannon around over the cockpit. On what he hoped was the Kurita battle frequency, he broadcast, "You're staying with me, you samurai Snake. We're going for a ride."

Then Jenkins shut down his heat exchangers, letting the heat destroy the magnetic containment on the *Phoenix Hawks*'s fusion reactor.

Minobu found Hawken leaning against the hulk of a burned-out Harasser hovertank while he bandaged his left hand. As Minobu approached, the man stood and called out, "A glorious fight, Tetsuhara. A fine victory."

Minobu searched the sweat-streaked face. He saw no concern for the carnage wreaked that day or for the lives spent to soothe the Sworder's ego and fulfill his desire to embarrass some mercenaries.

"You would not be able to hold it."

"Hold it? Against what?" Hawken asked, voice dripping

contempt. "We whipped the Davion dogs, and they ran with tails tucked. They will not return."

"And if they did?"

"We would whip them again, of course." Hawken was very confident of that. Minobu heard it in his voice and saw it in the way he stood.

"With what?" Minobu asked. "All your 'Mechs are damaged. A quarter destroyed beyond salvation and another quarter will be days in the repair bay. A third of your men are dead."

"There'll be more 'Mechs. There'll be more soldiers," Hawken said. "Any true Kuritan would gladly die for the chance to take part in such a glorious battle."

"Like yourself?" Minobu's tone was mild, simply inquisitive. He would not be baited as easily as the naive Major Yukinov. He ignored the implication that he might not be a true Kuritan.

"Yes," Hawken hissed, eyes full of hate. "Like myself."

The men stared at one another in silence for a few moments. When a medic came up to check Hawken's bandage, the Sworder kicked at the man. "Get away, fool," he shouted. "Go mother someone who needs it."

The man scrambled away from the Sworder, his expression confused and angry.

Hawken stalked away without another word to Minobu and joined a group of his soldiers in the shade of a demolished Davion *Scorpion*.

Minobu shook his head as the Sworder walked off.

"Colonel Tetsuhara," came a voice over the comm unit at his belt. "This is Yukinov. I've just received confirmation that we have secured the perimeter around Independence Weaponry's main factory. Thought you might like to see the loot before we pack it out."

"Thank you, Major. I'll be there shortly." Minobu headed for the main building.

Duty called.

12

Independence Weaponry Complex, Steel Valley,
Quentin IV
Draconis March, Federated Suns
21 June 3023

The vaults of Independence Weaponry were swarming with Dragoon Techs, most of whom were tagging crates and individual pieces of equipment to be moved by conscripted locals. Dragoon ground troopers watched the conscripts carefully as they loaded the loot into trucks or hoppers rigged for BattleMechs to carry. The work was proceeding briskly.

A few Techs manned the computer stations. Their job was more than mere identification of physical booty. They were trying to crack the security codes for access to encrypted computer data. Long ago, the industrial firms of the Inner Sphere had learned to keep their important data as nonportable as possible. Their factories were that much safer when an outsider who wanted the data knew that blowing his way in would cost him what he sought.

Senior Tech Bynfield was in charge of the scavenger teams. When Minobu and Yukinov entered, she called to the Major. Bynfield was excited and soon had Yukinov engrossed in what was on her console. Minobu paid them little attention, preferring to take his own survey of the operation.

Into the midst of this organized chaos walked *Sho-sa* Hawken. Like a lord moving among the serfs of his domain, he strolled to where Yukinov and Bynfield stood. Ignoring the Senior Tech, he announced to Yukinov, "This is all Combine property, Major."

"What?" Bynfield sputtered angrily. Her face reddened, drawing a satisfied smile from Hawken.

"At ease, Bynfield," Yukinov ordered. To Hawken, he said, "I think you may be a little confused, Major. Our contract specifies a split on all spoils and salvage, apportioned by risk and costs of operations borne."

"Your contract?" Hawken snorted. "A scrap of paper. You mercenaries are, I am sure, concerned with scraping up the debris that warriors leave behind, and so salvage is of great interest to you. Soldiers are concerned with military information and supplies." With a wave of his hand, he took in the building and the activity around them. "Such as this. It is all strictly military, and hence, property of the Draconis Combine."

"Military . . ."

"Bynfield!"

"You really should teach your underlings better manners, Major Yukinov."

"You slimy—"

"Bynfield!"

Bynfield heard the warning in Yukinov's raised voice. She blanked the computer screen and stamped off to another terminal.

Yukinov didn't bother to watch her go, but kept his eyes on Hawken. Controlling his temper, he said, "I think you'll find the contact specifies that . . ."

"You," Hawken interrupted, "will find that the Combine has classified all materials here as military supplies and information. Which makes all this the property of House Kurita."

"You won't get away with this. We'll take it before the ComStar Board if you insist."

Hawken merely laughed and walked away.

Yukinov looked around, located Minobu, and headed for him. The anger he had held in check while talking to the Sworder overflowed into his voice. "All right. You're supposed to be the Professional Soldiery Liaison. What's going on?"

"Calm yourself, Major," Minobu cautioned. "Your defense of your contract was adequate and accurate. However, Major Hawken is correct with regard to the disposition of properties here. That is, if they are declared as military priority."

While they spoke, some Sword of Light troopers came in and began to direct the changing of destination tags. Outside, a Kurita BattleMech arrived to guard the guardians of the conscript labor.

"What am I supposed to do now?" Yukinov demanded.

"For now, Major, I suggest you go along."

"All right. In the interest of amicable relations, I will. But I'm expecting a different tune when the Colonel gets here."

Go along they did, but with no joy. Minobu doubted that Hawken could see the difference, but he noticed a distinct drop in the efficiency of the Dragoons tagging and moving property. The air grew tense as the Sworders became more brusque with their orders. A fistfight between a Dragoon and a Sworder MechWarrior started, but was quickly broken up. Shortly after that, a second Kurita 'Mech joined the first outside the building.

So things stood when Lord Kurita and Jaime Wolf arrived, talking easily to one another as though they were fellow officers. Without a word, each took in the tension at the factory complex.

"What's the problem here?" Wolf inquired of Yukinov. The Major's explanation was brief and to the point, omitting nothing relevant.

"If it is military data, we are obliged to turn it over to the Combine," Wolf concluded. He turned to Takashi Kurita. "Is it so classified, Lord Kurita?"

The two men searched one another's eyes, cold blue meeting steel gray. Minobu could almost see their *ki* strengths thrust and parry in the space between them. This had become a test of wills and of loyalties. A long time later—a mere heartbeat—Takashi Kurita replied, "It is."

"So be it, Major Yukinov. See that House Kurita receives all the property due them."

"Well said, Colonel," remarked Lord Kurita with a smile.

"I am sure your underlings were merely being over-zealous. I myself often have to deal with such enthusiastic supporters." He placed his hand on Wolf's shoulder, turning him toward the door. As the Coordinator walked the mercenary Colonel from the vault, he lowered the pitch of his voice and spoke more loudly. Minobu had no doubt that Lord Kurita wished all present to hear his words.

"There is no problem, friend Colonel. I take no notice of anything out of the ordinary. It will be as though nothing had happened."

At the vault's great double doors, a courier met the pair of leaders. He handed a message to Lord Kurita, who read it quickly and stuffed the flimsy into a pocket in his uniform.

"I am afraid I must leave, Colonel. Duties of state call me back to Luthien." It was not long before the Coordinator had gathered together his officers and left to prepare for his journey. Work in the factory continued as before, while Bynfield approached the group of Dragoon officers.

"Malking samurai," she said, spitting onto the concrete.

"Military data, my left cheek. This stuff is pure Tech stuff. Unity! Half of it is just theoretical. At least they didn't get all of it."

Wolf rounded on her, his carriage stiff. "What do you mean?"

She held up a tape cartridge.

"This. It's good stuff, too. Axial flux patterns in fusion containment bottles, myomer stress reaction patterning." She went on, becoming more and more intricate in detail. Lost in her technical world, the Tech didn't notice that Wolf just stood there watching her, his face hard.

"Bynfield, you're confined to quarters until further notice."

"What!" She was shocked. It was clearly not what she had expected.

"You have jeopardized our position by disobeying orders. We agreed to pass that data over. All by yourself, you've broken our contract."

Bynfield's mouth worked, but no wound came out.

"Can't we just turn it over now?" somebody else asked.

Wolf turned on him. "You haven't been studying your briefings. We're stuck. If anybody finds out about that tape, we're in trouble. I lose face for not having control over my troops." His glance clearly indicated the "troops" in question. "Kurita loses face because he was generous in overlooking our little scene. Nobody wins.

"Kurita might decide we can't be trusted with anything. Then where are we? We sit out a five-year contract on garrison in the hinterlands. No combat bonuses. No loot shares. You all know that we can't afford that because the short contract with Steiner left us strapped.

"Besides, we have our reputation to consider. We're supposed to be the best, most reliable mercs in the Sphere. We break contract now and we start the slide down."

Into the silence that greeted Wolf's words, Minobu heard someone suggest, "We could pack up and head for home."

Wolf addressed his answer to all the Dragoons. "That's not an option right now."

The silence fell again. After a moment, Wolf turned to Bynfield. "Bury it deep, Talia. For five years, it doesn't exist."

Minobu could see her face reflect an inner struggle. An order to hide knowledge was obviously unpalatable to her. "Yes, Colonel," she said finally.

As the impromptu meeting broke up, Wolf noticed Minobu watching and his eyes widened briefly in surprise. In those eyes, Minobu could see that the mercenary Colonel had forgotten the Kuritan's presence, and that meant he had spoken freely. The mercenary's speech had not been a staged performance. Minobu made Wolf a slight bow, and Wolf nodded before heading out of the vault.

Minobu pondered the incident. Wolf's command of Combine custom was correct, and his solution was as elegant as one could hope from a man who was not samurai. No one would expect Wolf or his people to commit *seppuku* over this conflict. Yet Wolf showed a genuine concern for loss of face, especially before Lord Kurita. Was it possible that a mercenary could be a truly honorable man?

In the few days Minobu had spent with Wolf's Dragoons, he had learned that many things were not as he had believed them to be. His stay with the Dragoons was going to be interesting, he decided. Very interesting.

* * *

Lord Kurita still found time to make a proper exit from Quentin IV. He bid formal farewell to the officers of the Dragoons whom he had met during his stay. He even found a word of praise for the exemplary work Senior Tech Bynfield had done in organizing the stripping of the Independence Weaponry complex. Before he boarded his DropShip, he stopped to speak to Minobu.

"You look much better now that you are back in uniform, *Chu-sa* Tetsuhara."

Minobu bowed, unsure if he should respond.

"Wolf's Dragoons could be a lasting benefit for the Combine. I expect good service from them." Lord Kurita paused briefly, looking over the honor guard of Dragoon BattleMechs that had assembled for his departure. "Although a dutiful samurai should not expect it, a lord rewards good service."

"Hai, Tono," Minobu replied in response to the ancient proverb. He had heard that the Coordinator liked to couch his orders in such proverbs or in poems. He wondered if there were some special message in Lord Kurita's words or if his lord were merely stating a general principle.

Takashi Kurita turned then, indicating his intention to leave. Minobu bowed and immediately felt the heavy weight of the Coordinator's gaze on his back as he held the bow. All doubt about whether his lord had intended some special meaning vanished with Kurita's next words.

"Be a dutiful samurai, *Chu-sa* Tetsuhara."

"Hai, Tono."

Takashi Kurita boarded the DropShip that would take him to his JumpShip. Before long, he would be back home in his Imperial City on Luthien.

13

Hoshon Mansion, Cerant, An Ting
Galedon Military District, Draconis Combine
9 November 3024

The arrow thudded home two fingersbreadths from the previous shaft, completing the practice pattern on the fifth target. Minobu shifted his attention to the sixth target and selected another arrow. Fitting it to the string, he raised the bow above his head. He paused for an instant, then lowered the bow, bringing the arrow to full draw at the same time. He waited for the moment when archer, arrow, and target became one. He waited and . . .

"Husband!"

. . . the moment came—he released the arrow, letting it fly smoothly to its mark at the center of the target.

Now he could deal with Tomiko's interruption.

Minobu unstrung and racked the bow, then closed the cover to protect it and its fellows from An Ting's chill morning air. He turned to the house, shrugging his kimono on to his bare shoulders. In the doorway, his wife stood shivering in her robe.

When he stepped inside, she closed the panel behind him and reached to put her arms around his neck. "You are so cold, husband. Could you not practice your *kyudo* indoors?"

"If I did, I would have no need for you to warm me afterward," he said, gathering Tomiko in his arms. Minobu found her lips while his hand reached for the tie that secured her raven hair at the nape of her neck. As he pulled her down to their *futon,* her hair fell free, bringing a new night sky to shroud their privacy.

She pulled back from his embrace. "Your aide, Captain Noketsuna, called. There is someone to see you."

"Things are peaceful on the border." He slid his hand down her neck, past the edge of her robe, and caressed her breast. "Let them wait."

"He seemed concerned," she persisted, though her voice was husky with the thrill of pleasure.

"Pity the poor samurai whose wife is more devoted to his duty than to him."

She smiled teasingly as she poked him and slid free of his clasp. He returned her grin.

"If it is peaceful, there will be other times," she said.

"Other times, eh? All right, I will be off to my duty." A hint of mischief crept into his voice. "But I shall condone no complaints from my wife when I visit the pleasure quarter because she has no interest in me."

He dodged the pillow whose fine cedarcine wood would have raised a serious bruise. It tumbled past him to strike harmlessly on the floor. When she did not join in his laughter, he saw that her face was serious.

"It is something to do with those awful Dragoons, isn't it?" Her words were more a statement than a question. "They will be your misfortune."

"Most likely it is the Dragoons, but you should not speak of them so. Ever since I was assigned to them over a year and a half ago, they have been our *good* fortune. As their liaison, I have been assigned this fine home, where we live in comfort. Our son Ito has been accepted for the spring term at Sun Zhang Academy. Could you ask for a surer sign of favor? It will guarantee him a post as a MechWarrior."

She sighed, unconvinced. "Sometimes it seems like an illusion. I worry so. You spend so much time with those . . . mercenaries."

Tomiko uttered the word with such distaste. Minobu wondered if his own voice had revealed the same scorn when he had learned of this assignment. If so, the scorn was gone now. He had learned much in his posting to the Dragoons.

"I spend time with them because it is my duty."

"You needn't spend your free time with that Jaime Wolf."

"No, I need not." It was the old argument again. "That, at least, is by choice. Jaime is more than an ordinary mercenary soldier. He is many things, but foremost, he is a man of honor. Besides, does not the Coordinator encourage us to enlighten promising souls to the superiority of the Dragon? I am but doing my part."

She turned her back to him, signaling the end of the argument in a manner he knew too well.

He finished dressing without another word from her. When he was ready, Minobu looked again at his wife, who had not moved. He walked to the door, opened it, and stepped through to the corridor. "I will be in the office," he said, closing the panel.

The walk through the private quarters of Hoshon Mansion was short, but the dark wood accents and the finely made *shoji* panels created a sense of peace that settled his nerves. This house, with its simple, traditional furnishings, often had that effect on him.

Minobu entered his office by the inner door. In the outer room, he could hear the strident tones of Natasha Kerensky berating his aide. Poor Michi Noketsuna! The young *Tai-i* was too new at his job to have to deal with the fiery Captain Kerensky at this early an hour. Minobu sat at his desk and pressed the stud that would illuminate a telltale on Noketsuna's desk letting him know that Minobu was present.

Noketsuna must have been waiting for that signal. Almost immediately, he shifted his pleas for calmness on Captain Kerensky's part to specific requests that she sit down so that he could take care of some business in the inner office. She gave him no chance. "Oh no you don't, you little Japanese stonewall. I saw that light. I'm going in with you."

She was as good as her word.

Michi Noketsuna reached the desk first. Minobu's practiced eye saw that he was upset, but the young Captain managed to maintain his decorum. Not a strand of black hair was out of place. Michi's skin was darker than typical for most Kuritans of Japanese ancestry, and Minobu suspected that his coloring probably concealed any flush of embarrassment at the garb of their visitor.

As usual, Natasha Kerensky was dressed provocatively. Whether it was the silver cord with dangling onyx wolf's-head that tied back her dark red curls or the highly glossed boots of speckled *shant* leather, each garment she wore accentuated her renowned beauty. A custom-built Marakov slug-thrower was slung low on her hip, and the flash of light on the gun's ivory grips drew attention to the sway of her hips. The weapon added a menacing accent to her carefully cultivated image. She was well aware of her effect on men and had been known to take advantage of it.

Kerensky started to harangue Minobu as soon as Noketsuna began his explanation of the situation. Minobu could not follow either of them. "Please, Captain Kerensky, you will have my full attention just as soon as I can get the story of what has happened," he said, indicating the chair across from his own. She took it, but her foot tapped the floor in an angry rhythm. "Now, Captain Noketsuna, please start again."

He did. The story was simple and one that Minobu had heard before. Kerensky's Independent Company, the notorious "Black Widows," were once again in port on liberty, and once again, the Civilian Guidance Corps had detained members of the company on charges of drunk and disorderly, destruction of property, and sundry other incidents of mayhem. This time, at least, there were no charges of murder.

Minobu listened through his aide's reading of each circumstance, then he questioned him on specifics, asking Kerensky for clarification. Despite her terse and hostile responses, it soon became clear that the charges were all minor and Kerensky's protests merely perfunctory. She was displaying the fierce loyalty of a she-bear for her cubs. Indeed, Minobu had heard other Dragoons opine that those cubs, her troopers, would follow her through all the Buddhist hells. Such loyalty was enviable and the one who could inspire it was fortunate. Minobu found it pitiable that her social form was so unmannered and impolite.

As it was not the first time her troops had created a disturbance on An Ting, he decided that it was necessary to make a point. "Captain Kerensky, even though the revenues of An Ting are at the disposal of Wolf's Dragoons for the duration of the contract, the Dragoons are not the lords of the planet. The people of An Ting were here before the Dragoons came and will be here long after the Dragoons are gone. Neither you, your troops, nor any other Dragoons may make free with them. Upon release from Civilian Containment Quarters, your troopers are to be confined to the military reservation at Boupeig for the duration of their current stay on An Ting."

Kerensky started to protest again, but he cut her off. "Of course, the damages will be charged to the Dragoons. Colonel Wolf will receive a full report on the situation and your response, Captain."

Though obviously furious, Kerensky left without another word.

"She acts like a man," Noketsuna commented after she slammed the door to the outer office. Minobu almost chuckled at his inexperience.

"That should be no surprise. She has lived a man's life and has been a MechWarrior almost longer than you have been alive, my young friend."

"Impossible! She is barely older than I."

"Read her dossier. She was commanding a company before you entered the academy." Michi's eyes widened. "She is a remarkable woman, Michi-*san*. Just one of the remarkable things you will discover about Wolf's Dragoons. I have confidence that you will take it in stride. Otherwise, I would not have requested you for my aide. Now, before I swell your head further, what is the business of the day?"

Noketsuna directed his attention first to the military situation reports. Minobu felt pride when he saw that all the Dragoon units out on raids were reporting satisfactory progress. The elements of Epsilon Regiment engaged on Courasin signaled that operations were complete and that they were en route to their home base on Thestria. Davion activity in all sectors were minimal. In all, there were no surprises.

The next order of business was a review of the status of the Dragoon fighting units present onworld for furlough. Wolf had set up a regular schedule of relief rotations for the regiments. Each had a unit, sometimes as large as a battalion, on An Ting for rest and recreation at all times. It gave the troops a break from garrison duty or a vacation from the periodic raids along the border worlds.

It also meant that, in addition to the Dragoon dependents, An Ting had a considerable population of the fighting elements of the Dragoons at all times, almost as though it were a garrison station itself. Wolf had once told Minobu that this schedule was really Takashi Kurita's idea. The Colonel claimed that Lord Kurita had known Wolf would consider the planet assigned to the Dragoons for their dependents to be too close to the border and hence vulnerable to a deep-penetration raid. Wolf alleged that it was the Coordinator's way of getting a free garrison for a planet not listed in the service contract.

The rotation schedules were orderly. Branson's Company of Alpha Regiment was scheduled for return to Capra today to trade places with Specter's Battalion of Delta Regiment. Zeta Battalion was returning to An Ting for rest and refitting after the action on Bergman's Planet. Until the three companies from Gamma returned to the field, things would be a bit crowded at Boupeig. Minobu issued an order to open the southern barracks in preparation for Zeta's arrival.

The supply accounts were next. All was in order and by the book. Beta Regiment had filed a complaint, charging that the last shipment of cold-weather gear had been defective and inadequate to cope with the frigid temperatures of the Borealis continent's interior. Minobu initialed the note and issued a requisition for a replacement order to be sent through the Procurement Department. It was not like them to issue shoddy goods to a unit in the field. Gamma Regiment, Beta's companion on Misery, had no similar complaints. The only other item of note was a shipment of armaments from Ceres Metal that had arrived at An Ting's orbital station, pending transshipment to Delta Regiment on Capra. After reading the manifest and verifying its accuracy with Noketsuna, Minobu approved the transfer. There should be no problem in having the materiel reach the regiment before its next scheduled action.

The last item on the docket was a formal request from Training Command for clearance to commence practice maneuvers. They were intending a mock operation in orbit over the continent of Hotei in the northern hemisphere, and requested that the planetary defense network covering the zone be alerted to their presence. As ever, Colonel Wellman was cautious about the safety of his fledgling Dragoons. Minobu approved the request and forwarded it to the Kurita garrison commander for final approval.

As Minobu was putting the finishing touches on the note to the commander, Noketsuna returned carrying an envelope with ComStar seals appended. The somber look on the man's face showed his concern over the gravity of the missive. "This just arrived for you, sir. Eyes only."

The cover flimsy cited the point of origin as the DropShip *Chieftain*. Though the ship had been in orbit above An Ting for a week, Minobu had heard nothing from Wolf after the friendly announcement of his return. Minobu opened the envelope and read the contents at once. The dramatic delivery was merely Wolf's way of getting his attention.

Noketsuna was waiting, hoping that his superior would favor him with a confidence as to the contents. His patience was short. "Has Davion attacked? Are we to go into battle with the Dragoons?"

"It is only an invitation, Michi-*san*." Noketsuna wilted in disappointment. "It does, however, include you in its scope.

"Colonel Wolf is hosting a celebration of something he refers to as Resolution Day. It is to take place aboard the Dragoon orbital facility."

Noketsuna's disappointment vanished with the realization that he had just been invited onto previously forbidden ground. He beamed, obviously pleased by the honor.

Minobu, too, found it an honor. Once again, Jaime Wolf was holding out to him the hand of trust, a hand that Minobu had been proud to clasp in the past months. The invitation was a step further into Wolf's confidence and friendship. Minobu began to phrase his formal acceptance.

14

Hephaestus Station, An Ting Orbit
Galedon Military District, Draconis Combine
11 November 3024

Noketsuna opened the airlock door for Minobu and Tomiko, then stepped aside to allow them room in the cramped access passageway. Even so, the stiffened shoulders of Minobu's formal *kataginu* brushed him as the *Chu-sa* passed. Tomiko's formal kimono was no problem in that regard, but Noketsuna had to be careful not to step on her trailing hems.

In the softly lit corridor beyond, J. Elliot Jamison waited to greet them. The Colonel was as big and bulky as the assault BattleMechs he commanded in Zeta Battalion. A grin split his broad face, showing white teeth framed in the black of his beard and mustache.

"Good evening, *Chu-sa* Tetsuhara, Lady Tetsuhara," he said as they stepped through the hatchway. "Welcome aboard *Hephaestus Station.*"

"Thank you, Colonel Jamison," Minobu replied. "The station looked most impressive as we approached. I do not believe that I have seen its like before."

"Most likely, *Chu-sa.* Though most of it is Star League-design, we've added a few things of our own. *Hephaestus* is quite useful to us." Jamison led them along the corridor as he spoke. "This station has gained a bit of notoriety. You know that this is what the homebodies at Fasan Press call our factory. As if you could uproot a BattleMech factory and tow it around with you."

"Then you don't produce your own BattleMechs?" Noketsuna asked.

Jamison gave him a sharp look before answering. "This facility can handle final assembly and most repairs, but it is certainly not set up for heavy manufacturing or fusion power plant production. Your basic introduction to battle technology should have told you that those operations are best performed onworld."

"Please excuse my aide, Colonel," Minobu said. "He is young and curious. We are here on recreation, not business." Noketsuna took the oblique admonishment well.

"No excuses necessary," said Jamison with good grace.

Despite Minobu's words to Jamison and his rebuke to Noketsuna, he was just as curious to learn all he could about the Dragoons. His aide's question had gotten an interesting response. Though Jamison had described some of the station's capabilities, he had not actually denied that the Dragoons could produce their own BattleMechs. Even when revealing some things, the Dragoons kept other secrets. But secrets were business and this business upset Tomiko. He had felt her stiffen at Noketsuna's question. Best to turn the conversation back to the order of the day, the good-natured celebration that Jaime Wolf intended.

"I have to admit to some curiosity as well. Colonel Wolf's invitation referred to this celebration as Resolution Day. I do not recognize the reference. Perhaps you could enlighten me?"

"Indeed, I could. But because the Colonel mentioned it to you, I think he should be the one to explain it." Jamison's manner was by no means hostile, but he did seem to be hiding another secret. Where previously the man had evaded Noketsuna's question, now he seemed unsure what level of information should be available to the Kuritan visitors.

He seemed glad that they had just reached a final door, which hissed open to reveal a large chamber filled with civilians in brightly colored garb and Dragoons in their black dress uniforms. Most of the crowd was engaged in conversation or in making choices from the buffet, but several couples were swaying to a gentle dance tune on an elevated dance floor. The primary illumination came through transparent panels in the ceiling. The sunlight reflected by An Ting, visible in blue and white glory, was the source.

Jamison led his charges to the buffet and made sure they were well-supplied from the bounty on the tables. He even found enough delicacies to fill Tomiko's plate, despite her uncharacteristic fussiness over the selections of foods.

For Noketsuna, Jamison found more than foodstuffs. He provided an introduction to a young Dragoon lady, beautiful in a shimmering lavender gown. Had there been any lingering thoughts of business in the young *Tai-i*'s mind, they must have fled. Each youngster seemed to find the other fascinating. The constant motion of the crowd soon edged them into a corner, but they did not seem to notice or to mind.

Jamison's own companion appeared, and he introduced her as Jaella Domichardt. She wore a well-tailored high-collared Dragoon's dress uniform, with the twin stars of a Major on each sleeve. The conversation was light, but Tomiko's frosty manner seemed to annoy Domichardt. Before long, she was urging Jamison to dance, and he capitulated. Minobu and Tomiko were left to find their way through the throng.

Minobu greeted several Dragoons of his acquaintance, and they responded warmly. All the males were complimentary to Tomiko, who took in their flattery with an icy edge to her customary grace. Conversations were short-lived.

Among those they met was Dechan Fraser, the bold warrior Minobu had first encountered on Quentin. Fraser wore the silver disk of a Lieutenant now and shrugged off Minobu's congratulations as though they were no more deserved than his promotion. In another man, such a show of humility might have been false, but Minobu knew that Fraser's modesty was sincere. Not wishing to discomfit him further, he pretended to spot another friend and excused himself and Tomiko.

As they moved through the crowd, Minobu caught snatches of conversations—reminiscences, tales of past adventures and misadventures, both military and private. Everyone with whom they spoke was polite, and none refused to include the couple in their conversation. Some of the groups, especially those dominated by older Dragoons, seemed to falter when they noticed the Kuritan couple approaching, however. The talk always resumed quickly, but it was clear that the topic had changed.

At last, Minobu located Jaime Wolf near one of the huge silver punch bowls. The Colonel stood with a dark-haired woman whose pale blue gown fell in caressing folds over her shapely form. Even from a distance, Minobu could tell how relaxed the two were in one another's company. Seeing Minobu and Tomiko approach, Wolf broke into a pleased grin.

"Glad to see you could make it, Minobu-*san*." Wolf turned to Tomiko and bowed in greeting. "A pleasure to see you again, Lady Tomiko. You look lovely tonight."

"Your words are kind to an old woman, Lord Wolf."

"Nonsense. They would only be kind if untrue. As it is, they understate the truth."

"He is no flatterer, Lady Tetsuhara, as I well know." The eyes of Wolf's companion twinkled with amusement. "Allow me to introduce myself, since Jaime is so overcome as to lose his manners. I am Marisha Dandridge, sometime helpmate to this vagabond Colonel."

If Tomiko was offended by the forthright manner of the woman, she did not show it. She bowed.

"Our pleasure to meet you, lady," Minobu said. "Jaime has kept you as one of his Dragoon mysteries. Are you a military secret?"

Wolf hung his head in mock acceptance of the rebuke. "Simply an oversight and lack of proper opportunity, my friend. Marisha is even busier than I. She works on the civilian side of the Training Command. A finer children's counselor you won't find. She's not too bad with us grown-ups, either."

Dandridge nudged Wolf with her elbow before speaking to Tomiko. "Jaime tells me that your eldest son is to go to the Sun Zhang Academy."

"Yes, it is an honor for our family." Tomiko's reply was formal and brief. Even Dandridge's warm interest was not enough to thaw her reserve.

"Jaime said eldest son, Lady Tetsuhara. Do you have

other children as well?" Dandridge seemed determined to draw Tomiko out from her redoubt of detachment.

"Yes, a daughter and another son. They are somewhat younger." Again, she was brief and formal, but Minobu detected a crack in her reserve.

"Well, I know you would be interested in seeing the children's care and play facilities we have here." Without waiting for Tomiko to respond one way or the other, Dandridge took her arm and began to lead her away. Though Tomiko seemed reluctant to go along, she was even more unwilling to create a scene. She submitted to Dandridge's enthusiasm.

"What was that about, friend Jaime? I would not have expected your lady to be so . . . domestic."

"She might surprise you. But you're right, she usually isn't," Wolf said. "She's near as devious as I am, though. We thought this might be an opportunity to improve your lady's opinion of us, so Marisha's taking advantage of it. Besides, she knew I wanted to talk to you alone for awhile."

Minobu tilted his head in question. In reply, Wolf led him around the table to the wall and pressed a panel in the decorative design. A doorway opened, and the two men walked into a small office. Wolf directed Minobu to take a seat, pulled up a chair next to him, and sat down. Both men faced the room's window, through which they could see two of An Ting's lesser moons moving in stately procession across the stars.

As usual, Wolf came directly to the business at hand. "What can you tell me about Warlord Samsonov?" he asked. In the early days of their relationship, this abruptness had disconcerted Minobu because it was at odds with the typical Combine practice of approaching a subject obliquely. Draconians went through a series of irrelevant preliminaries intended to measure the mood and temper of the participants. Only close acquaintances and old cronies could dispense with these introductory formalities. Over the months of working with the Dragoons, Minobu had learned that they were all precipitous in this fashion, but he had finally gotten used to it.

"Why the sudden interest?" Minobu asked.

"That's one of the things I'd like to know," Wolf said. "We've been in his District for more than a year, but only now has the Warlord decided that it's time we have a talk. He's coming to An Ting for a meeting, and I thought you might be able to give me an idea of what to expect."

Wolf waited while Minobu marshaled his thoughts. Minobu had only met Warlord Samsonov twice, but he had no trouble conjuring an image of the tall, vigorous, gray-haired Warlord who was always so careful of his appearance. Wolf was not inquiring about appearances, of course, but wanted to know what manner of man was Samsonov.

"I have had a few dealings with him in regard to the operations of the Dragoons," Minobu began. "General Samsonov is an interesting man. In honor of our friendship and knowing that you will keep what I say in confidence, I will speak frankly.

"His appearance is distinguished, in all ways that of a proper general. He always speaks with respect for the Coordinator and presents himself as a loyal son of the Dragon. He has an admirable military record and has been awarded the Order of the Dragon in recognition of the territorial gains he has made for the Combine.

"Yet something in his manner seems out of place. I fear he may harbor personal ambitions beyond those proper for a samurai of House Kurita."

Wolf perked up at that. Minobu, noticing the interest, tried to explain.

"His treatment of his inferiors is less than respectful. One wonders if a man who does not treat his inferiors with respect can properly respect his superiors. A man who does not respect his superiors may seek to replace them.

"Of course, all men harbor ambition of some sort, and so it may be that the General is not so unusual after all. What is important is that a man does his duty, and in this, General Samsonov is hard to fault. He cares well for his office, and so Galedon District prospers. The units under his command are well-supplied and maintained, though I have heard it said that he uses unusual methods to achieve those ends. Such comments are surely only rumors, and who knows but that they may be due more to the envy of his rivals than to the facts.

"As you know, he holds the title of Warlord of Galedon. As a Warlord, he stands high in the power structure of the

Draconis Combine, with almost total command over the District. Warlord Samsonov is also an honored councilor to the Coordinator. He is overlord, in Lord Kurita's name, of more than sixty star systems and guardian of almost half our border with the Federated Suns.

"He is a most powerful man. As a friend, helpful. But as an enemy, most dangerous," Minobu concluded.

Wolf sat silently for a moment.

"I appreciate your honesty, Minobu. You've given me a bit to think about," he said, then slipped again into silence.

Minobu let him think for a while, using the opportunity to ponder for himself the reason for Samsonov's visit. Something was up. But what? Minobu did not have enough information to reason out an answer.

He looked at Wolf out of the corner of his eye. In the past months, they had grown to trust one another, each respecting the other's strengths. Minobu had given little thought to Jaime's private life. Certainly, Wolf never mentioned it. Tonight, Minobu had met someone who was obviously important in Wolf's life. Once again, the secretiveness of the Dragoons . . . Once again, Minobu was reminded of just how little he knew about this man he trusted so well.

"Marisha Dandridge seems a fine woman, friend Jaime," he commented into the silence.

Wolf seemed a little startled by the change of subject. His recovery, as always, was quick. "A man could not ask for better."

"Yet, in all these months you have spoken little of her. For that matter, you have not spoken of family at all."

"No, I haven't. We Dragoons try to keep family separate from business. But sometimes the business won't let us," Wolf said bitterly.

"Ah, the New Delos incident. That was an honorless deed. It was your brother that Anton Marik had killed, was it not?" Minobu knew his comment might open an old wound, but Wolf seemed to be signaling a willingness to talk.

"That's the public version." The bitterness had fled as quickly as it had come, to be replaced with regret in Wolf's soft voice. Several moments passed before he continued.

"Anton Marik tried to take control of the regiments. He tried to force us to his will by making hostages of our families on New Delos. We brave warriors wouldn't bend to his will," Wolf said, sarcasm lacing the words. "We stood up to him.

"It wasn't just my brother who died there. My wife and our two youngest children were with the civilians Marik slaughtered."

That was not what Minobu had expected. A brother lost in the tumble of political maneuvering was one thing. Joshua Wolf had been a soldier, and soldiers expected death in the political and military turmoil of the Successor States. Wanton murder of family members was something else. Even the Dragoons' storming of the New Delos Palace and killing Anton Marik might not be enough to lay innocent ghosts to rest. "My friend, I had not meant to stir such memories."

"It's all right." Wolf gave Minobu a faint smile of forgiveness. "That was ten years ago. I can talk about it now. Marisha has been a blessing in that regard. She has gotten me through the worst and taught me to face the future again. But, by all the gods of space," Wolf continued, voice turning to steel, "I won't let anything like it happen again."

Silence fell once more. Each man looked out on the stars, lost in his thoughts. To end the awkward pause, Minobu assayed, "You implied you had other children."

"That's right." Wolf's voice was far away, but the harshness was gone. "You never miss a trick, do you, Minobu?" Minobu inclined his head humbly. "I have a son. He's in Beta Regiment."

"Beta? There is no Wolf on the regiment's muster."

"That's right, too. He fights under another name. And no, not even you, my friend, will get that name out of me." Wolf chuckled, much to Minobu's relief. "There would be no fair treatment if he were known as mine."

"Shall he miss out on his heritage then?"

"No. He will come into it when he has learned to stand on his own feet. There are no free rides in the Dragoons. Nepotism only works when the favored can earn their own way. If he deserves my place, he'll have it.

"But right now, my place is host to this party. Let's go back and join it. Eat, drink, and be merry, eh?" Wolf laughed in an attempt at good cheer, but Minobu thought it forced. Not all the shadows had fled, despite Wolf's brave speech.

"Yesterday is done and tomorrow will bring its own problems," he said, clapping Minobu on the shoulder. "After all, how often are the stars so quiet?"

15

Cerant City, An Ting
Galedon Military District, Draconis Combine
12 November 3024

Galedon Warlord Grieg Samsonov arrived at An Ting orbital station at 1300 standard hours, precisely on schedule.

Two hours later, he disembarked from his DropShip *Winter Dragon* at Cerant spaceport, entourage in tow. Among them was a man Minobu recognized at once, though he had not seen him in years. It was Jerry Akuma, a tall Japanese wearing the smartly tailored uniform of a *Sho-sa,* or Major in the Eighth Sword of Light Regiment. A small pin bearing the Galedon seal marked him as an aide to the Warlord.

Wolf had not been able to assemble his usual battery of Colonels to meet Warlord Samsonov. Only Ellman of the Training Command and Jamison of Zeta Battalion were on hand. As the group of visiting officers neared, an aide stepped forward with a packet. Coming before the Dragoon Colonels, he extended the packet and asked for Colonel Jaime Wolf. "Credentials and protocols, sir," he said, handing the envelope to Wolf. The aide scurried back into the crowd around the Warlord, leaving the way clear for Samsonov himself to step up. Now that Wolf was identified, the Warlord paid no attention to anyone else in the Dragoon group.

"I am pleased to meet the illustrious Jaime Wolf," he rumbled, though his voice indicated something other than pleasure.

"The honor is mine, Warlord Samsonov," Wolf replied with a bow. Minobu knew that Wolf did not feel particularly honored, but the mercenary's voice betrayed nothing.

Samsonov's squinty eyes roamed Wolf's face as the mercenary spoke, taking his measure. His own face settled into an expression of disdain. The condescending tone that the Warlord took for the rest of the preliminaries told Minobu that he considered Wolf an inferior, a mere hireling soldier. Minobu wondered how long before the Warlord learned that he had made a mistake in underestimating the mercenary.

The reception group and the visitors organized themselves for the trip to Dragoon Administrative HQ, where facilities had been prepared for the meeting. Samsonov climbed into an opulent groundcar that pulled away almost at once, escorted by the lightly armored cars of Cerant's Civilian Guidance Corps. While Wolf and his officers boarded the second vehicle, the Warlord's aides scrambled for places in the remaining groundcars. Before Minobu could join Wolf, Akuma cut him off.

"You look well in your *Chu-sa*'s uniform, Tetsuhara," Akuma said with a cold smile. "Is it comfortable?"

"I am doing well enough, *Sho-sa*." Minobu had not seen Akuma since Dromini VI, where dealing with the man had become trying. Akuma had performed his duty and was always respectful when others were present, but in private or on the field, the story was different. Akuma had questioned Minobu's decisions, always pushing, always deriding and belittling the code of *bushido*. Now the two crossed paths again. As an aide to Samsonov, Akuma would be in a position to affect relations with Minobu's charges, the Dragoons. It would be best to humor him.

All but one car had pulled away. The two men turned and strolled down the colonnade toward it. The brisk breeze flapped their uniforms about them and occasionally pelted them with fugitive petals from the flowering trees that lined the boulevard. The Sworder was trying to be nonchalant, but his eyes were carefully measuring Minobu's reactions.

"You certainly seem to be on top of things, which should give you a clear view of all around you. Perhaps there are clouds that make your sight a bit unclear," Akuma suggested airily.

Minobu was puzzled by Akuma's approach, but refused to allow him the satisfaction of knowing it. He kept his face impassive and said nothing.

Akuma was undaunted. "You have been piloting a BattleMech in your forays with these hireling soldiers, haven't you?"

"Yes."

"Don't you find it even slightly interesting that your name is still listed on the rolls of the Dispossessed in the books of the DCMS?"

The reminder, coming from someone Minobu knew to be a poor pilot at best, stung. He found that he had to leash his temper. The man definitely knew how to needle him. "I am aware of that."

"Careful of that tone, Tetsuhara. One must be polite to a MechWarrior."

"It is as you say, MechWarrior." *Insufferable puppy. Puppies must be taught their place.* "Is it not also true that a junior officer is expected to show respect to a senior?"

"Indeed it is, *Chu-sa,*" Akuma replied, with suave urbanity. "Even when the bars have no stays."

Minobu looked up sharply. How could Akuma know of the rank insignia that had been sent along with his promotion? Had he a hand in Minobu's disgrace after Dromini? Was he ISF? Was that the reason for the constant baiting? Minobu had always assumed that it was personal, a difference in philosophy. Could it be something more?

To buy time to gather his composure, Minobu directed Akuma's attention to the practice field, where some Dragoon trainees were at work in a mock battle. Their simulator 'Mechs careened about the field firing low-power beams at sensor-studded armor. A computer recorded and evaluated hits, freezing portions of the machines when damage was estimated at sufficient severity.

"Did you know that the Dragoons train most of their MechWarriors themselves?" Minobu asked.

"*So ka.* Can they not find enough soldiers from the dregs of the other Houses?" Akuma countered.

"The Dragoons are good soldiers, not dregs. They are

competent and efficient warriors. They are, in fact, more knowledgeable concerning the honor of a warrior than you will ever be."

"Watch your temper, *Chu-sa,*" Akuma chided. "You will upset your precious *wa,* and then who knows what silly things your code of *bushido* will demand of you?"

And so it went. Akuma finding ways to needle Minobu, and Minobu attempting to demonstrate the quality of the mercenaries with whom he worked. They drifted further afield as Minobu showed more and more of the Dragoon facilities to the Sworder. Behind them, Noketsuna trailed along, a silent shadow. Forgotten, the last car had left for the city.

An hour passed before Minobu caught on to Akuma's ploy. He meant to keep Minobu from the meeting with Samsonov. For some reason, his new master did not wish the Liaison Officer to be present, as he should.

Claiming a need to check in with his office, Minobu excused himself to use a nearby communicator. Once out of sight, he exited by a back door and summoned one of the private taxis at the port, ordering the driver to head for the central plaza.

The fact that he'd left Noketsuna to occupy Akuma and field his protests did not worry Minobu. His aide was clever and did not have shared history with Akuma that the man could use for bedevilment. Besides, after Natasha Kerensky's invective, not even Akuma's would seem as blistering. Noketsuna might find Akuma to be a trial, but it was one the young Captain should be able to handle.

There were traffic delays, and by the time Minobu arrived at the meeting, it had been underway for some time. He slipped into a chair near the door, apparently unnoticed by the Warlord. One of Samsonov's aides was narrating a film of recent action on Courasin. His words built a picture that was unflattering to Epsilon Regiment, with hints of incompetence scattered throughout his commentary. If the meeting was a typical Samsonov production, things were being orchestrated to a climactic point, when the Warlord himself would step in to make his point.

Wolf sat woodenly throughout the spiel. The senior men were also remarkably quiet, but some of the junior officers shuffled papers and looked decidedly uncomfortable. Minobu could feel tension emanating from the Dragoon side of the table, but the Warlord and his people seemed oblivious to it. When the aide finally finished, Samsonov stood up, taking advantage of his height to tower over the seated Dragoons.

"As you have seen and heard, Colonel Wolf, your officers have continually balked at the proper chain of command. In some cases, they have gone so far as to arrogate command responsibility to themselves." The Warlord stalked about the room as he spoke, gesturing theatrically. "The worst offender has been this Korsht woman. How you could allow a woman so much responsibility beyond her place is baffling to me."

When he got no reaction from Wolf, the General seemed to take it as agreement. Minobu wondered how the man could be so blind, but Samsonov drove on to his point. "I am here to allow you to place your units directly under my command, effective immediately."

"Warlord Samsonov, that is in direct violation of the contract," interrupted Minobu.

Samsonov looked up, clearly displeased at the interruption. When he saw the source, the muscles on his face tightened, tugging his features into a vicious scowl. Minobu felt the sudden wave of hatred. Had the man been a *ki* master, the power of his emotion would have been dangerous.

"*Chu-sa* Tetsuhara is correct," said Wolf. His voice was quiet, but it snapped the Warlord's attention back to him.

Samsonov's face contorted. He was not used to being contradicted by those he considered his inferiors. He slammed the papers in his hand violently onto the table. "I wanted this meeting to be amicable. The evidence is clear. Your hostility and resistance are unimportant. The Coordinator will order this when I ask him."

"Then ask him," Wolf said.

It was a dare.

"If you don't wish to have a discussion," Wolf continued, "you won't mind if we send along a little evidence of our own."

"Send what you will," Samsonov replied to the challenge. Puffed with his own importance, he added, "I am a Warlord of the Draconis Combine and have the favor of Lord Kurita. You are a homeless hireling. My position is irrefutable."

Wolf stood. From across the table, he looked up into Samsonov's eyes. "I will retain command."

"You will not."

Wolf's gaze never wavered. "Don't bet your life on it," he said.

Interlude

Unity Palace, Imperial City, Luthien
Pesht Military District, Draconis Combine
16 December 3025

Takashi Kurita entered the maze of corridors that made up the lowest level of the Unity Palace. The proper turns engraved in his memory, he took each without hesitation. When the passage finally came to an end, it was crossed at a right angle by another corridor. Without stopping, Takashi proceeded directly ahead and passed through the far wall.

That wall was a hologram. Immediately behind the image was a flight of uneven steps, which Takashi took with an ease born of habit. Anyone not familiar with the way could easily be thrown off balance and fall to the bottom of the stairs, where two of the Coordinator's most loyal *Otomo* stood guard at the entrance to the Black Room.

Of all places within the borders of the Draconis Combine, there was none so secure as this room. Its existence within the palace was hardly a secret, for every Successor Lord had his or her own version of it. The exact location of Takashi Kurita's was known only to the top leaders of the Combine and to select members of the Household Guard.

Access to the Black Room was limited and strictly monitored. The level of the palace on which it was located was accessible only by elevator. Getting to the level required a special code.

The obvious purpose of the room was secrecy. To that end, its five walls, ceilings, and floor were shrouded with technological barriers and sheathed with materials to foil the prying eyes and ears of spying devices. To foil microwave transmission, specially formulated black paint—which gave the room its name—covered all the interior surfaces. Chief among the defenses was a magma-pulse magnetic field that activated when the door was sealed.

Takashi reached the bottom of the stairs, where Chamasa and Potemkin, two of his trusted Household Guards, flanked the doorway. The red light, which allowed them to maintain their night vision in case of power failure, did not leak through the hologram masking the stairway. The ruddy illumination glittered off the high points of their breastplates and helmets, lending them the air of guardian Myoo spirits.

"Seal the room, *Tai-i* Chamasa."

"*Hai,* Coordinator!"

Takashi did not wait for the acknowledgement or even hear it when it came. Obedience was expected. He strode through the open doorway into the small room. Behind him, the door slid shut.

Awaiting him in the room were the Director of the Internal Security Forces and the Warlords of the Draconis Combine's five Military Districts. The only senior council member missing was Takashi's cousin, Marcus Kurita, nominal Chief of Strategies. It was unlike Marcus to be absent, Takashi thought. Ever since the Coordinator had removed him as Warlord of the Rasalhague Military District six years ago, Marcus had been faithful in attendance, even though it must be clear to him that he was not really chief of anything. Takashi still listened to his valuable advice, but Marcus showed signs of bitterness over the loss of his power base. Those signs told Takashi that he had done well in relieving Marcus as Warlord. To gratify dangerous ambitions, the younger Kurita might have stooped to treason.

Takashi took his place at the head of the table, greeting each Warlord in order of seniority. He concluded by welcoming Hirushi Shotugama, recently appointed Warlord of the Benjamin Military District, to the council. There was no mention, however, of the cloud under which his predecessor Yorioshi had been removed. After acknowledging the presence of Subhash Indrahar, the ISF Director, Takashi settled back in his chair and called for situation reports from each Military District.

Each of the Warlords presented a favorable report. Each also was questioned and corrected by his fellows. Takashi watched the byplay carefully. He played a dangerous game in balancing the rivalries of his Warlords. Always, he had to watch for changes in the equilibrium, shifts in the undercurrents.

After the District reports came a general discussion of the strategic situation. The Generals argued noisily about one another's performance and the priorities of the Combine, which seemed most often to lie with the priorities of each Warlord's district. As usual, Takashi gave the Generals leeway, listening carefully to sort out the nuggets of real concern from the dross of self-interest. When he was certain that he could gain no further enlightenment from their bickering, he called a halt to the debate. "Thank you, Warlords. General orders will be issued after I have meditated on your advice."

Takashi then turned to Indrahar. "Director, I know that you have some matters to bring before the council. Please, proceed."

Indrahar rose from his seat to take the floor. After polishing the archaic spectacles he affected, he favored the assembly with a brief smile.

"The correlated data secured from the raids on Davion BattleMech facilities on Quentin and Hoff have proven beyond a doubt that a technology transfer is occurring between the Federated Suns of House Davion and the Lyran Commonwealth of the Steiners. Captured documents of recent date contain data from the Lyran facilities on Hesperus II, Coventry, and Alarion. These documents were found at both raid sites. One Steiner technical file even carries a citation by Doctor Robert Willis, a Davion scientist last reported to be working in the Federated Suns' top-secret BattleMech development program.

"A diplomatic pouch has been dispatched to Maximilian Liao by special courier, carrying documentation on the Davion-Steiner military trades. This information should motivate him to some action, for he has even more to lose from this coalition than do we.

"There are other signs, perhaps even more ominous, that Davion and Steiner are drawing closer together. Prince Davion has admitted Lyran officers to his highly touted New Avalon Institute of Science, which my investigators report is more a military academy than the research institute that Davion propaganda claims. Davion military advisors have also recently been observed on the Lyran front. ISF analysts believe that this explains recent improvements in the Lyrans' battlefield performance.

"All these signs point to a deeper and stronger bond between Houses Davion and Steiner than has yet come to light. It's possible that Prince Davion has secretly agreed to Archon Steiner's cease-fire proposal of 3020, though we have not seen any evidence of the assurances necessary to seal such an arrangement. To date, all of the benefits, beyond an improvement in trade allowances, seem to be to the Commonwealth. Surely, the Davion fox has a deeper plan."

Indrahar took his seat again, content to let his audience mull over his words. The Warlords were clearly upset by Indrahar's presentation.

Takashi was gratified to note their concern. An alliance between Steiner and Davion could be disastrous for the Draconis Combine. It would wed the strongest economy in the Inner Sphere to the military might of the Federated Suns. A potent combination, even without the wily Hanse Davion in command. After a suitable interval, Takashi quieted his councilors to allow Indrahar to proceed to his next point. The Director stood again.

"In the matter of the disastrous campaign on Galtor, media coverage has been satisfactorily contained. According to our popular media, we have achieved a victory—" Indrahar looked pointedly at General Samsonov—"despite the military situation."

Samsonov's eyes narrowed at the implied criticism. "We may have lost the Star League cache, but it was not due to any failure on my part. The Coordinator himself has taken that position."

What Samsonov referred to was the ceremony in which Takashi had publicly refused the Warlord the right to commit *seppuku* for his "failure to achieve the goals of the Combine." Takashi had cited the Combine's continuing need for the General's services. Samsonov's co-commander in the invasion, Warlord Yorioshi, had been broken in rank and banished to an obscure staff position deep within the Combine's interior. The Coordinator's absolution had persuaded Samsonov that he had been justified in goading his rival to rash action and that he was strong in Lord Kurita's favor.

Takashi found it amusing that Samsonov did not to look to the Coordinator for a confirmation of the position he espoused. The man was very sure of his lord's support. That was satisfactory. Samsonov would be even more unbalanced if it ever became necessary to withdraw that support.

"Yorioshi was the reason for the failure," Samsonov continued. "When he abandoned my troops on Galtor, the man showed himself as a traitor and an incompetent, totally unfit to command the Benjamin District." The Warlord neglected to mention that he had goaded Yorioshi into that action by continually undermining the man's leadership and endangering it through his own actions and non-actions.

The Warlord turned to Shotugama. In an effort to twist attention away from himself, he struck out at a colleague. "We must look to the future," he said. "All Galedon District units are back to at least 75 percent strength. Can Yorioshi's successor match that?"

Shotugama was slow to answer, allowing Vasily Cherenkoff, Warlord of Dieron, to jump in. "I fear our new comrade is made timid by the company he now keeps. Maybe he needs to consult one of his nuns?"

Takashi was surprised by Cherenkoff's reference to Shotugama's upbringing in a monastic environment. With his personal habits and ill-bred comments, the fat Cherenkoff was often offensive to those around him, but he rarely made any effort to do research for his half-veiled insults. This time, he—or more likely, some lackey—must have probed Shotugama's background. The open hostility in the Dieron Warlord's voice showed that he had developed a deep dislike for his new fellow. This would have to be taken into consideration, especially if the feeling was returned. Benjamin District lay between Cherenkoff's Dieron District and the rest of the Combine. Beyond Dieron lay Terra, and beyond the homeworld, the Combine's unsteady allies. An internal struggle could cut lines of communication. That would be calamitous.

"All necessary consultations have already been made, General Cherenkoff," Shotugama replied. "Though I have no reputation to match the bulk of yours, I do know my job." The small man's demeanor was quiet, but he showed spirit, matching Cherenkoff's attack without abrasiveness. He kept his hostility in check to his higher duty to the Combine. Shotugama was a good appointee, Takashi decided. The balance was maintained.

"By March, we will have made up equipment and pilot losses in units participating in the Galtor adventure," Shotugama continued. "Current strengths vary, but the average is approximately 68 percent of authorized strength. Most serious is the morale deficit. Former Warlord Yorioshi's disgrace has had a widespread effect in the District."

"The dog did not get what he deserved," Samsonov growled.

"Enough!" Takashi commanded. It would not do to have his actions as Coordinator brought into question, even here. "Our losses on Galtor have weakened our border with the Federated Suns. But House Davion has paid a price for their military success, and is now weakened as well. We will allow them no rest. Though we may not be able to mount any major effort without jeopardizing our security, we can keep the pressure on Davion.

"I therefore order the Fifth Sword of Light transferred to Dieron. They are to raid throughout the corridor that Davion maintains to Terra. If a weakness is found, exploit it.

"Our friends in the Capellan Confederation and the Free Worlds League will be encouraged to attempt similar probes. If we can cut off Davion and Steiner from one another, it will nullify the threat of any alliance between them."

"Can those states be reasonably expected to provide a serious threat to our immediate enemies?" Kester Hsiun Chi asked. The Warlord of the Pesht District always had an eye on events outside his District. Was the old man being wasted in the quiet of Pesht? Takashi wondered. Might he better serve in a more active District? Benjamin had just received a new Warlord, and matters in the other Districts were acceptable. This was not the time for a transfer.

Noticing that Takashi was lost in his thoughts, Indrahar answered for him. "The Free Worlds League is, as usual, busily concerned with internal bickering. The ISF believes that one or more of their factions might be persuaded that it would be worthwhile to make an attempt on our enemies. However, any Marik faction so persuaded is unlikely to strike across the Capellan Confederation at the Federated Suns. The Lyran Commonwealth is their only likely target, but we can expect little result from them. With luck, they can occupy some of the Commonwealth's attention. Archon Steiner may perceive a greater threat than the adherents of House Marik can provide.

"As for the Capellans, they will certainly occupy Davion's attention in some fashion because Maximilian Liao seems to have identified Hanse Davion as his principal enemy. Though some military action is possible, it is more likely that Liao will utilize intrigue to weaken our mutual foe."

"In the long run, the actions of other states will not matter," Takashi said. "If we must go to war, the Draconis Combine will do so. Turn your minds in that direction, my Warlords. Soon or late, it will come to war."

Takashi made to stand up, a sign that the session was over, but Samsonov spoke up. "*Tono,* there is another matter that I believe merits your attention—Wolf's Dragoons."

"Your attempt last year to have them placed under your command was uncalled for," Takashi said coldly. "I was satisfied with their performance and told you so. Do you wish to raise the issue of their tractability again?"

"Iie, Tono!" Samsonov responded, but the bitterness in his voice put the lie to his denial. "Their record of success argues against any complaints. I am more concerned about their loyalty."

He paused, sweeping the room with his gaze. He clearly wanted everyone's attention now. "Are you aware, *Tono*, that they have sent an officer to Galatea, the so-called Mercenary's Star?"

From the corner of his eye, Takashi caught a confirming nod from Indrahar. "This has been brought to my attention. Why does it distress you?"

"It is not personal distress. I worry for the sake of the Combine. The Dragoon contract still has more than two years to run. Yet their officer is entertaining recruiting agents from any and all comers. Is this not clear evidence that the Wolf's Dragoons mercenaries do not intend to renew their contract?"

"Perhaps they merely wish to raise the price of renewal. They are mercenaries, after all," Hsiun Chi commented.

"It is possible," Samsonov conceded. "But we must consider the alternative. If the Dragoons should leave the Combine's service, it would gravely weaken our forces on the Davion border. We must act to prevent them from defecting to our enemies."

Takashi knew Samsonov had more than the interests of the Combine at heart in this situation, but the Warlord raised a valid point. The loss of the Dragoons could be devastating, especially if the military situation deteriorated. House Kurita had no units that combined the fast-strike capability and the tactical adaptability of the Dragoons. *So ka.* It need not remain that way.

"While we have the Dragoons under contract to us, we shall take advantage of their presence and let them serve as teachers. We will create a new unit to work at their side. That unit will learn how to fight as do Wolf's Dragoons and so add Dragoon capabilities to the Arm of the Dragon. Their Liaison Officer shall command the new unit. As he already has some experience in observing Wolf's methods, he has a head start."

Samsonov flushed, infuriated. His ploy to wrest control of the Dragoons had been diverted. Takashi's sudden solution had cut off his chance to present the documents his aide Akuma had carefully prepared. The Coordinator's order that Tetsuhara command this new unit would give more power to the stiff-backed troublemaker whom Samsonov had looked forward to breaking in rank once a Liaison Officer was no longer needed. The Warlord quickly covered his rage under frowning brows and hardened expression.

Takashi offered him an opening to save face. "General Samsonov, I expect you can find a suitable officer to fill the liaison position."

The Galedon Warlord's face lightened.

Takashi did not know what devious plan had just entered Samsonov's mind, but it was clear that inspiration had struck.

"I have just the man for the job," Samsonov said.

"Even though I wish to see a Combine unit with the capabilities of Wolf's Dragoons, I do not want to lose the service of those mercenaries," Takashi announced. He hoped that his statement would keep Samsonov from any excesses. He turned to Indrahar.

"Director Indrahar, see what can be done to persuade the Dragoons to stay. Encourage them to see that their future lies with the Draconis Combine. If they cannot be persuaded, we should have some sort of insurance in case the Dragoons decide to enter an enemy's service." Takashi spoke as he rose from his seat. This time, no one offered an interruption.

Takashi watched as his councilors left the room. The Warlords' squabbling was a necessary evil. While they were busy watching each other, they were not planning revolution. He found it a necessary, but disheartening, strategy. If only he could trust them to have no ambitions for the Coordinator's seat. If they would unite together behind him, no power in the Inner Sphere could stand against the Dragon. An idle wish, he mused. An illusion. He must never forget that reality was the cruelest of masters, with a heart as bleak as the walls of the Black Room.

BOOK II

Loyalty

16

Hoshon Mansion, Cerant, An Ting
Galedon Military District, Draconis Combine
15 August 3026

Late afternoon sunlight threw long shadows across the courtyard of Hoshon Mansion. The outer wall's shadow ran down the edge of the archery range where Minobu and Jaime Wolf were shooting. The great tower set at the corner of the wall was built to resemble an ancient Japanese castle keep, and its shadow bisected the still sunlit ground. When the image flickered with movement, Minobu looked up from the veranda to see Tomiko and Marisha looking out over Cerant from the balcony of the second level. Minobu caught Wolf's attention and pointed out the women to him.

"I am glad you're finally back, and that you and Marisha could find the time to visit us here. It has been too many months. Tomiko has missed your lady. The plan you initiated two years ago on the *Hephaestus* has borne wonderful fruit. Tomiko and Marisha have become like sisters."

"It wasn't *my* plan," Wolf said, smiling. "But I, too, am glad they've become friends. Tomiko had always seemed so distant, and now she is even polite to me, a bloody-handed mercenary barbarian. She even tries to teach me civilized manners." Jaime paused, his eyes resting on the two women. "It's good for Marisha to have someone to talk to outside of the Dragoons."

"And you have no such needs to fulfill by coming here?"

"No need to fish for compliments," Jaime said with an easy grin. "It's not the same with us. We are brothers, no matter what, sharing the profession of arms as we do."

"I share my profession with many people, but I would call few brother. Even friends among those rare men of true honor are uncommon."

"Now you're trying to flatter me."

"Certainly not. You need nothing to inflate your ego."

"What!" Jaime raged, though his eyes showed the fury to be a sham.

"Calm yourself. A show of temper is uncivilized, but uncivilized you certainly are. That monstrosity of metal and plastic that you call a bow, for example. No *civilized* man would use such a thing."

Jaime was caught up in his friend's sportive mood. Years dropped away and cares were forgotten in favor of playful banter. "It's the product of the most advanced technology available to archers in the Inner Sphere. It's balanced, strong . . ."

"It is dead." Minobu dismissed the bow with a wave of his hand. "How do you feel the shot through all that lifeless hardware?"

"I don't have to feel it. The sighting equipment allows millimeter-precision in the aiming point. With this bow, an archer doesn't need any of your mystic nonsense about 'becoming one with the target.' And the pulley system will deliver more power than that bound bamboo longbow of yours."

"Power? There is no power in that device."

"Oh yeah? Watch this." Wolf adjusted his bow's tension settings, selected an arrow, and sighted carefully on the target before releasing. The arrow buzzed through the air to bury its head more than seven centimeters into the solid backing of the target post. It stood out from the center of the inner ring, blue feathers gleaming against the golden shaft. Wolf turned to Minobu and grinned, clearly proud of his shot.

"A fine shot," Minobu agreed.

Minobu selected one of his own arrows. He fitted it to the string, then stopped to concentrate for a moment. In that moment, he focused his *ki,* drew the bow and then loosed the arrow with a motion that was rapid but smooth. Stillness followed the brief flurry of motion; he held the release position until the arrow reached the target.

The arrowhead shattered Jaime's shaft and passed into the target's backing. Only the fletching remained visible in the target circle.

Jaime shook his head in disbelief. "Could you show me how to do that?"

"I have tried to show you the way, but you found the methods unacceptable."

"You mean that business about shooting at a target only thirty centimeters away. That's pointless."

"A man must walk before he can run."

Jaime shrugged. Ignoring Minobu's disappointed look, he sent another arrow at the target. "At least you've had more success in teaching me Japanese."

"You have the capability. It is simply a matter of focusing."

"So you have told me often enough. Jaime Wolf, secret master of *ki,*" he said in mock seriousness, then laughed. "Guess I'm just too old a dog. You'll have to be satisfied being *sensei* to Michi."

Minobu took the time to loose another shaft before speaking. "Michi is a good aide, always trying hard to please. He has the heart of a fine samurai and shows great promise as a MechWarrior, but his *ki* is as yet weak."

"He will come into his own. The new generation always does." Wolf selected an arrow for another shot. After he loosed, he said, "Kelly tells me that the Draconis Command has assigned you a BattleMech for a command vehicle."

With his friend, there was no need to hide behind the impassive face a samurai must present to the world. Minobu let his pleasure at no longer being Dispossessed show in his smile. "It is true. A DRG-1N."

"A *Dragon*? That's not your type of machine at all."

"The type seems very unimportant to me right now. I have a 'Mech again and I have been restored to honor under Lord Kurita. I cannot be ungrateful by disputing the model selected for me."

"Have you tried it out yet?" asked Jaime.

"Yes. It is very different from my old *Panther,* but then my position now is also different. I am adjusting."

"Having problems feeling the shots through all that 'dead hardware'?" Jaime asked, waving his pulley bow for emphasis.

"A BattleMech is different."

Minobu paused to consider. Jaime was a strategic and tactical genius, with the intuition and understanding of people required of a successful general. He was also a magnificent warrior, honed in the hard school of the Succession Wars for over twenty years. Despite all that, he was unable to grasp the core of the spirit of *bushido,* to appreciate the spiritual nature of the samurai's code.

"In the old days, a samurai's sword was his soul. It was a part of him, a channel through which his *ki* could flow. Today, we samurai of House Kurita carry the swords as symbols only. The BattleMech takes the place of the samurai's sword as the channel for a warrior's *ki.* A MechWarrior enters his 'Mech and almost literally becomes one with it. It is a symbiosis that an ancient samurai could never achieve with his sword.

"Not all warriors are samurai, to channel their *ki* through their 'Mechs. Of those who are samurai, not all have 'Mechs that would seem to be the best match for them. Most often these assignments are arranged by unenlightened bureaucrats.

"The type of machine does not really matter. What really matters is the warrior who pilots the BattleMech. The warrior's spirit is the real strength, not the technology."

Minobu looked into Jaime's eyes. He could read the lack of true comprehension, but a flare of appreciation showed. If Jaime could not understand, at least he respected the code and those who followed it. Jaime's own code might be different, but he still walked a path of honor and that was something Minobu respected. On that mutual respect, they had built their friendship. Devotion to honor had bound the two warriors, despite their different backgrounds and all that they could not know or understand about one another.

"As to a 'Mech matching its pilot," Minobu said, "look at yourself. An *Archer* would not seem the best choice of

BattleMech for the commander of the largest and most successful mercenary unit in the Inner Sphere."

"You might be right on that. Certainly, there have been times when I would have liked something tougher or faster. It's a matter of prestige. The Dragoons have a lot of *Archer*s, all of them our special model. It's almost a signature machine. Seeing me pilot one gives the troops an identification with their commander.

"That's something to keep in mind now that you are a commander."

"*So ka.* Now you become the *sensei.*"

"No," Jaime said, shaking his head. "No, I'm not a teacher. I'm a doer. There's too much action out there. Too much to be done. Maybe you'll get a little friendly advice from time to time, like just now, but I can't be your teacher." Something had entered Jaime's voice, a hint of yesterdays passed. "The battlefield is the real *sensei,* the only way to learn to command."

"If you truly believed that, your Dragoons would not maintain the Training Command with the regimental instruction programs."

"Not so. Some things can be learned in practice. *Must* be learned. Your own *kyudo* art demands constant practice. So do any warrior skills.

"Command is more than just another skill. You can't train a man to make command decisions in split seconds and live with the consequences. A man has to learn that for himself. If he takes too long to learn or he fails to see that he never will learn, good people die. And he still has to live with that." Wolf stopped and took a deep breath. He seemed to come back to himself and to the present. "Touché, Minobu. You got your lecture from *sensei* Wolf. But by the look in your eyes, I don't think I told you anything you didn't already know."

"A man needs to feel that he is not alone even when he knows it is so."

"Ah, the wisdom of the Dragon." The banter was back, covering exposed emotions. "My friend, we are getting entirely too serious for the day. Shall we return to more mundane matters again? Tell me how the organization of your unit is going. Logistics headaches are about the most mundane things I know of in this universe."

"That is very true, but in this case, you may not have found your cure. The Coordinator has named us *Ryuken*, the Dragon Sword, and it seems he wants his sword well-cared-for. Our equipment is of excellent quality and our supply levels are high. The principal headache I face is where to store everything until I have the personnel to use it."

"You're short on MechWarriors?"

"Not really. Some are having to travel long distances to join the unit. Others do not have the necessary experience as yet. It is but a temporary problem. You see, I have been allowed to request pilots from other units. There have been many volunteers as well.

"If the Ryuken is to fight like your Dragoons, I must have a certain breed of MechWarrior. I have been selective, and yet have found many fine candidates among the Combine's soldiery. However, once I select a pilot, especially one to serve as an officer, the ISF must approve of his or her loyalty to the Combine."

"You don't sound too pleased with that last condition."

"Let us just say that the ISF and I do not always agree on a MechWarrior's qualifications."

Wolf nodded in understanding. His brow wrinkled briefly as he registered a phrase Minobu had used. "You said 'his or her loyalty,' didn't you?"

"Yes. Does it surprise you that a samurai of House Kurita would consider seeking out women for positions in a fighting unit? Many women serve in the Combine's military. Though I do not expect them to excel at a man's work, I do expect all my MechWarriors to perform to their utmost. I expect them all to work together as a team in a balance of strengths and weaknesses, as your MechWarriors do. A commander cannot afford to ignore talent and competence, and so I have made my choices looking for those qualities.

"Besides, I have seen women working well in the Dragoons. Therefore, many of my choices have been women. So far, it is proving a boon. They are grateful for the recognition of their prowess. They work hard, often harder than the men, and perform well. An additional benefit is that the ISF has fewer objections to the women I choose for my MechWarriors than the men."

"A noble attitude."

Minobu could tell by Jaime's smirk that he was amused, but had no idea what the mercenary found funny. Confused but undaunted, Minobu continued to fill in his friend on the progess of the Ryuken.

"The training proceeds well with the soldiers on hand. First Battalion should be operational in another month, in time for the raid on Barlow's End."

Minobu and Jaime, bows forgotten in their hands, were just getting down to the fine details of the Ryuken's readiness when they were interrupted by the arrival of Tomiko and Marisha. "See? I told you they would be talking business," Wolf's lady announced.

"You sound like that's all we ever do, dear," Jaime responded.

"Sometimes it seems that way."

"Husband," Tomiko said, cutting off the good-natured argument before it could get rolling. "I have asked Marisha to join us for the evening meal."

Minobu turned to Wolf. "Which means, my friend, that I am to issue the same invitation to you."

"I would be delighted, but I have a previous engagement."

"Business," Marisha said in disgust.

"Afraid so," Jaime confirmed. "But there is no reason for you to pass up the Tetsuharas' hospitality. With luck, I won't be gone long and can rejoin you later."

Jaime started to excuse himself, but Minobu cut in and insisted on accompanying him on the short walk to the Dragoon administrative building. Jaime seemed uncommunicative, and lost in his thoughts during the walk, but Minobu found that acceptable. A stroll in the gathering twilight was pleasant. It was made more so by the comfortable, if silent, presence of a friend.

As they drew near their destination, Minobu saw a knot of Dragoon officers gathered outside. It included two Regimental Commanders, Baxter Arbuthnot and Wilhelmina Korsht, several Majors, and a few lesser officers. Among those gathered and doing most of the talking, was Natasha Kerensky. Even though she was technically outranked by half the officers there, her actual status was almost as high as that of the Regimental Commanders. She was commander of an independent company and had, more than once, refused promotion. All present seemed to be giving serious consideration to her words.

The group was agitated and disturbed. Though Minobu could sense no imminent violence, the local constabulary obviously did not share that sense of safety. Four members of the Civilian Guidance Corps had gathered at the far end of the block, and the quartet watched the Dragoons nervously. One of the men in the red-and-white striped uniforms was speaking into a comm unit.

As soon as one of the assembled officers pointed out Jaime's arrival, the whole company moved to meet him. The Dragoons were vociferous, and the cacophony of voices made it hard to determine just what the trouble was. Minobu could tell that Jaime was having trouble sorting it out as well.

"Please take the discussion inside," Minobu said, voice deepened to override the babble. "It is not seemly to air your grievances in public. You do nothing for the reputation of the Dragoons."

Wolf took advantage of the sudden silence. "*Tai-sa* Tetsuhara is right, people. Let's take it inside." He started for the entrance. "Coming, Minobu?"

"Wait a minute, Colonel!" Kerensky blurted, stopping Jaime's progress towards the door. Kerensky pointed at Minobu. "He's Kurita!"

A chorus of grumbling showed agreement with her statement and all it implied. Jaime silenced it with a monosyllable charged with the force of his will.

"So?"

"So, it's Kurita we've got complaints about. The Snakes are doing us dirty and he's one of them."

"Do you have a specific difficulty with *Tai-sa* Tetsuhara, Natasha?" Jaime's use of her name was intended to bring things to a personal level, a deliberate reminder that she was speaking of a man and not a faceless, nameless "Snake."

Kerensky faltered, but only for a moment. Though her voice betrayed a slight loss of conviction, her pose remained as arrogant as ever. "He's still a Kurita officer. How can we trust him not to go running to the ISF and report us as mutineers?"

"I trust him. That should be enough for all of you." Jaime's eyes swept the assembled company. "I'll want his opinion on the validity of your complaints after I get your story. It'll be easier if he hears it for himself."

"Perhaps it would be better that I not be there, Colonel Wolf," Minobu said in a placatory tone. "I am no longer your Liaison Officer."

"You were before and you know the new one. Your troops are going to be working alongside ours. You're still deeply involved in this, my friend."

In a dimly lit room in Government Center, a tall, thin man smiled as he reached across his marble-topped teak desk and switched off the monitor that relayed signals from the comm station below. The image dissolved before the sound faded, taking away the gesticulating figures before the contentious voices vanished as well.

"It seems matters are proceeding quite nicely," he said. His hands held a Dragoon undress cap, one finger tapping a rhythm against the black wolf's-head of the unit ID patch. He tossed the cap to the taller of the two other men in the room. The scarred blond man put up a hand and caught the hat. Without any apparent effort, he made it disappear from sight.

The thin man got up and walked to the window that surveyed Cerant. A satisfied laugh filled the room. That laugh had a nerve-grating quality to it, but the two men in black Kurita uniforms showed no reaction at all.

17

Hoshon Mansion, Cerant, An Ting
Galedon Military District, Draconis Combine
16 August 3026

"Michi," Minobu called over the intercom.

Noketsuna appeared immediately. "Yes, *sensei.*"

"I want to show you something in the garden."

"Is there a problem, *sensei*?"

"Perhaps." Neither spoke as they strode through the passages, soles slapping softly on the oiled wooden floors of Hoshon Mansion. It was not until they were walking among the carefully tended plants and away from the walls of the mansion that Minobu spoke again. "I want to discuss a matter that may have great bearing on the future of the Ryuken."

"Why do you speak to me, *sensei*? Surely your Executive Officer or some other member of the command staff would be of more help to you. Perhaps your friend Colonel Wolf?"

"I have already spoken somewhat to Jaime Wolf. You were with me when I was PSL officer, which gives you a perspective that my other officers lack. Besides, if I call the whole staff together, the ISF would know what was said before the minutes of the meeting came off the printer. It might be well to avoid that." Minobu watched Noketsuna react with a moment of dismay that was quickly replaced by trust in his superior.

"The ISF would need to be informed of treason, *sensei.* I am sure I will have no need to speak to them."

"You are honorable and trustworthy. Michi-*san*. And bright."

"Thank you, *sensei.*"

"But I think the time has come that you should stop addressing me as *sensei,* especially when we are alone. We are both soldiers and have weathered the storm of Combine and military bureaucracy together. Let us speak as friends."

"I am most honored by your trust, *sen . . .*" Noketsuna stuttered, at a loss for the correct form of address. The sudden offer of comradeship from an older man, and a military superior at that, clearly flustered him.

"Minobu will do in private," Minobu prompted.

"Minobu," Noketsuna repeated hesitantly. He drew himself up, almost defiantly. "I shall agree to your request, but you shall still be my *sensei.*"

Minobu shook his head resignedly, but proceeded to outline for Michi the problems the Dragoon officers had brought to Wolf's attention on the previous night. Noketsuna listened carefully. Minobu could see that he was reaching a conclusion even without all the details. Rather than continuing, Minobu asked, "Well, what do you think?"

"The Dragoons are justified in calling *Chu-sa* Akuma an obstructionist. He is using his position as PSL officer to make their lives difficult."

"A year ago, you would have said that mercenaries should expect no better treatment or that Akuma was justified in making their lives difficult. You have changed."

"I've been learning from you, *sensei.*" Michi's use of the honorific was unrepentant.

"Have you learned to predict what the Dragoons will do?"

"That was something I thought even the master could not yet do."

"Well spoken, imp. They are indeed hard to predict in many things. Jaime Wolf is a man as bound by his honor as we are by ours, and he will stand by his contract. Most of the others will follow his lead without question. The one I worry about is Natasha Kerensky. That one has a wild streak. She is impetuous and at the moment most unhappy with her employers. I fear she will do something . . . hasty . . . that will cause bigger problems."

"Surely she will not disobey Wolf's orders."

"Let us hope not. Things are confusing enough in this situation, even without such a volatile personality. For example, the supply shortages that the Dragoons are experiencing do not make sense, especially in light of our own abundance."

"Could *Chu-sa* Akuma be setting them up for the 'company store' approach? Setting them up to be plunged into debt to the Combine?"

"Perhaps. I cannot say for sure. He has offered no Combine alternatives, with the attendant higher prices, to replace the balky sources on which the Dragoons rely. If that is his plan, it will fail. The Dragoons are too resourceful."

"But you said that they were having trouble even with shipments from their long time suppliers like Ceres Metals."

"That is another curious fact. From hints that Jaime has let slip, I had the impression the Dragoons held stock in that company. Major Seward of the Contract Operations Group reported increased tariffs and communications problems. Why would that be? There are unknown factors operating here."

"If they are unknown, how can we deal with them?"

"As best we can, Michi-*san.* As best we can." Minobu stared at the wall that blocked the view of Cerant. "I begin to believe that many recent events are interrelated in some way I do not yet understand.

"This latest order, for example, requiring that each military cargo be inspected and verified by a PSL officer, who will then accompany that shipment. The Dragoon officers are upset about that. Spies, they say. Spies set to learn their secrets. I think they may be right."

"That would seem to be a reasonable assumption," Michi said.

"Are we not the same, my young friend? We have been set the task of learning the methods behind the success of Wolf's Dragoons and copying those methods to better serve the Combine. We are also to learn their weaknesses."

"Why does that make up spies? To copy their success is

wisdom. Is it not also wise to identify another's errors that you may avoid them yourself?"

"Yes, it is. Somehow I do not think that it is quite that simple and innocent. I fear that someone wants us to find those weaknesses so that a plan might be developed to exploit and to destroy the Dragoons, should it become necessary."

"If they are a threat to the Combine, should they not be destroyed?"

"It is always a Kurita samurai's duty to destroy threats to the Combine," Minobu said with conviction. He took a deep breath and closed his eyes. After a moment, he spoke again. "I think we can discern little more at this time. We have work to do and troops to train."

"At least that is something we can do with a full heart, Minobu-*sama.* It is a good work that is well underway."

Minobu nodded, eyes on the sky. "But, my young friend, I fear that Akuma's work has only just begun."

18

Greggville Province, New Mendham
Benjamin Military District, Draconis Combine
19 September 3026

"Your papers!"

John Norris grimaced at the Kurita officer. Papers! As if the camera and recording equipment weren't enough identification. The bloody Donegal Broadcasting Company logo was plastered on every piece of hardware they carried and prominently displayed on their white caps and armbands. Norris fumbled in his satchel for the papers.

If the Draconian was annoyed at the delay, it didn't show. He stood patiently, the bright sunlight turning the dark brown of his combat jacket and the tan of his fatigues to pastel shades. In the shadow of his helmet's wide dish, his face was impassive.

Norris finally fished out the documents and placed them in the man's outstretched hand. As though waiting for that cue, the holotech, Berger, plopped his own passes right on top.

The Kuritan studied them for several minutes before announcing that they were in order. As he handed them back, his harshness slipped away in favor of curiosity. "Why are you fellows here in Kempis, so far from the front?" he asked. "This sector is pretty quiet. Not much action for a news team."

"Just passing through," Norris lied. "We're on our way to Seldez to do a story on that guy from the Eleventh Benjamin. You know, the one who held the pass against the Davion thrust last week."

"Sergeant Yamato?"

"Yeah, that's the guy. He's quite a hero."

"He is," the *Tai-i* agreed. "It's good to see the outside media recognizing the true heroism of the soldiers of the Draconis Combine."

"Yeah, sure is. Long overdue, too, I say."

"Well, you gentlemen have a safe trip," the *Tai-i* said, nodding approval of the reporter's attitude.

"Geez, he bought that malarkey," the stocky holotech remarked, as the officer walked off to continue overseeing the refueling operation for the truck convoy his platoon was guarding.

"Keep it down, will ya? These Dracs can get touchy," Norris hissed.

"Aw, he can't hear me over them engines."

"Well, he might have friends who can. We don't want him back asking more questions."

Berger looked annoyed. No wonder the wags at the network called this guy Nervous Norris. The reporter was always worried about something. "We ain't spies. We're legit newsmen. He can't touch us."

"If he decides we're spies, he'll touch us all right," Norris retorted with an air of authority. "I once spent two weeks in a Davion cell waiting for the network to prove I was legit. The Dracs don't bother with cells. They *shoot* spies."

Berger didn't quite go pale, but he quit grousing. "Think that tip we got on a Davion push for this town is straight?"

"We'll know soon enough. If it is, we'll get an exclusive." Norris leaned down to whisper in Berger's ear as though to include him in a secret. "I know just where I'm gonna spend my bonus."

"I'll bet." Old Nervie would probably blow it on a racy novel, Berger thought.

Before Norris could enlighten Berger as to his plans, the Kurita sentry in the watchtower sang out, "Mechs coming in!"

Kurita troops scrambled to take defensive positions. Local

citizens scrambled for cover. A team of Draconians unloaded a tripod-mount laser from one of the trucks and headed for the edge of the village. The *Tai-i* lit out for the watchtower, making only a short detour to grab a pair of binoculars.

Norris turned, intending to tell Berger to find a good spot for filming the action. The holotech, meanwhile, was already on his way up an exterior staircase on a nearby building. A quick glance around told the reporter that he was the last person standing in the street. With a half-vocalized bleat, he scurried after Berger.

The vantage point the holotech had chosen offered a clear view of the nearby fields. Advancing from the west were the BattleMechs. Because of their solid black paint scheme, all four stood out starkly from the green of the crops they trampled. In the lead was a *Warhammer.* Close behind came a *Marauder,* and moving wide on either flank were a *Crusader* and a *Griffin.* Even the *Griffin,* the lightest of the four at fifty-five tons, would be more than a match for the Kurita soldiers.

Norris could feel the sweat roll down his back, and he knew it wasn't because of the hot sun. No man could look at those mountains of aligned-crystal steel and destructive weaponry without feeling a chill of fear down his spine. They were behemoths of a lost age, nightmares come to life to devour innocent men. A voice calling from the watchtower broke his reverie.

"Stand down," the *Tai-i* cried. "They're friendlies."

Around the village, the Kurita soldiers emerged from their hiding places. These troops were ill-equipped to take on BattleMechs, and so relief was evident even in the way they stood. The two troopers carrying SRM launchers began to fold away the sighting mechanisms. The laser team gave up assembling the cannon and began to break it down again.

"Stay put," Norris ordered Berger. "Davion's using mercs too. Maybe the Drac got his ID wrong."

Berger gave Norris a look that made no bones about what the reporter could do with his orders, but he did stay put. After all, there was no point in taking unnecessary—that is, uncompensated—risks.

The *Tai-i* did not seem to share that attitude. He had descended from the tower and was advancing across the field to meet the oncoming machines, his right arm raised in a friendly greeting.

In that pose, his torso suddenly exploded as laser fire from the *Warhammer* superheated the water in his body's cells. Then the other 'Mechs opened fire.

The blue lightning of particle beams scorched the village, blasting the startled soldiers. The explosive fury of missiles and autocannon shells mowed down groups of troopers. Laser sought out and struck down the stragglers. Large-caliber slugs made short work of those the lasers missed.

"Damn!" Norris screeched in a voice high with fear. Without taking his eyes from the carnage, he whispered, "Berger, you getting this?"

Berger didn't answer. He was too busy filming the onslaught of the 'Mechs. Sweat beaded his forehead and slimed the grip of the holocamera.

Below them in the village, terror reigned. The first 'Mech to reach the buildings was the *Griffin*. The laser cannon crew died then, as the BattleMech's foot crushed them and their weapon into an unidentifiable smear.

One Kurita trooper stood directly before the advancing *Warhammer*, an SRM launcher slanted over his shoulder at the rampaging 'Mech. When he fired, the soldier disappeared momentarily from Norris's view in the smoky backblast of the missile's exhaust. The rocket struck the BattleMech cleanly in the left leg, pitting the thick armor.

Leaning back slightly as though affronted that anyone dared fire upon it, the *Warhammer* halted its firing as its torso twisted to find the offender. By the time the Draconian's second rocket had impacted against the 'Mech's glacis, scarring the armor, the *Warhammer* had turned to face the lone man.

Whether rooted in fear or driven to insane defiance, the trooper stood his ground. In a gesture of utter futility, he dropped his empty launcher to the ground, drew his sidearm, and began firing at the *Warhammer*. No handgun could hope to penetrate the armor of a seventy-ton BattleMech. He was still firing when the *Warhammer*'s pilot opened up on him with the machine's antipersonnel guns. The man's body jerked and tumbled as the heavy-caliber slugs tore through it, but the *Warhammer*'s pilot continued to fire long after life had fled the body of the defiant soldier.

Back and forth through the village stalked the marauding 'Mechs, tearing into buildings where they suspected Kuritans might be hiding. If they found one, the trooper didn't last long. Though they showed no concern for civilian casualties caused by their hunt, the marauders did not go out of their way to chase down those villagers who fled from their path.

Before long, the four war machines turned their attention to the convoy trucks that had survived their onslaught. Using its hands, the *Griffin* began to load crates into containers attached to the backs of the other 'Mechs. Before loading the *Warhammer*'s pack, however, the *Griffin* removed a bulky object from the container and handed it to the *Crusader*, which headed with it to the outskirts of the village. The *Griffin* resumed its looting.

"Look what that *Crusader*'s doing," Norris said, poking Berger to get his attention. "What's he got there?"

Berger focused his camera on the machine Norris indicated and zoomed in. "Geez, it's a BattleMech arm."

"What?"

"Wait a minute. There's some kind of marking on the arm." Berger fiddled with the controls on his camera. "Yeah, that's it."

"Frackencrack! It's a Federated Suns crest! What the hell is going on here?"

A loud, mechanically augmented voice boomed behind them. "Nothing you ought to know about."

The newsmen froze. Slowly, they turned to face the *Marauder* towering above their perch. Neither had any wish to excite the pilot of the machine that had come up behind the building where they stood. Norris and Berger exchanged hopeless looks while the MechJock, forgetting he had his external speakers on, called to his leader. "Widow, got me a pair of rare birds over here."

The *Marauder* pilot ordered them to descend to the street while the black *Warhammer* approached.

The *Warhammer* stopped nearly on top of them. A hatch popped open at the back of the 'Mech's upper surface. Steel rang as a chain ladder was thrown clear of the interior, to come rattling down the machine's back and hang swaying.

A lithe figure crowned with dark red hair descended the ladder. The woman was clad in little more than a cooling vest. A tempting vision, until one noticed that from her belt hung a holster containing an ivory-handled gun of eccentric design but ominous lethality.

She stepped through her 'Mech's legs, and Norris blinked as a shaft of sunlight flashed on the black crystal spider hanging in the vee neck of her cooling jacket. Two triangular bits of ruby glistened in the insect's abdomen. Berger whistled softly, leaving Norris to wonder if he was more impressed by the obvious wealth the woman wore or by her body and the feline grace of her movements. Her eyes were hidden behind mirrored goggles.

"Well, well," she said in a husky contralto. "What has the Widow caught in her web today?"

"We are representatives of the Donegal—" Norris began.

"Can it, Skinny," she ordered. "I've got eyes."

She reached for Berger's camera. He resisted letting go until Norris took his arm. The reporter gestured with his chin at the *Marauder,* which had swung its carapace in their direction. The double barrels in each blocky forearm implied death and destruction as payment for resistance. Berger relinquished his grip on the camera.

The woman triggered the cartridge release and caught the boxy film magazine as it fell. She dropped the camera onto the pavement. She smiled at Berger's moan of pain and protest, and continued to smile as she tucked the film cartridge into her belt.

"You're gonna kill us now, aren't you?"

Norris thought that Berger's voice was steadier than it had any right to be.

The MechWarrior laughed. "I may be called the First Lady of Death, but I don't waste my time with pointless effort. I have your film. Without it, no one will believe you."

She turned her back on them, walked back to the ladder, and began to climb. The newsmen stood and watched. When she reached the hatch and had drawn up the ladder, she called down, "Killing you two would just waste my time."

The hatch slammed shut. Within two minutes, the four

black 'Mechs were headed back toward the horizon, laden with their loot.

"Malking sun!"

Norris ignored Berger's cussing. He concentrated on putting one foot in front of the other.

"Malking Widows!"

Norris trudged on, ignoring him.

"They didn't have to trash every piece of transport in the town, did they?"

Norris tried to pretend he hadn't heard, but the backhanded slap Berger gave his shoulder made that impossible.

"Sure they did," Norris said in a voice cracking from the dryness. "It makes it harder for the survivors to get the word out."

"Yeah, well, these two survivors are gonna get the word out. They're gonna pay for what they did back there. And they're gonna pay for my camera."

Norris had no answer for that. He, too, wanted to see the Widows pay. First, though, they had to reach a friendly haven. It would be a long walk. They had barely started up again, when Berger shouted and pointed at a hill fifty meters in front of them.

"Bloody hell! Tank up ahead!" The holotech headed for a copse of trees. "Grab some cover!"

Norris looked up. "Too late, Berger. They've spotted us." He didn't know if that was true or not, and he didn't care. He was too weary to run.

The vehicle Berger had spotted was a Striker wheeled tank. Its late-summer camouflage scheme revealed no affiliation as it crested the ridge ahead of them and moved down the slope. Then two more tanks appeared, and the three vehicles headed toward them at speed.

The leading vehicle slewed to port, its great wheels chewing up the soft earth, stopping a scant three meters from the drooping reporter. The commander's hatch opened, and a *Chu-i* hauled himself out of the tank. The man climbed down off his vehicle, getting dust on his neat uniform. He stopped to brush it off before approaching Norris. Even to the tired eyes of the reporter, the tall, lanky shape seemed unusual for a tanker. One should not question salvation, Norris told himself.

"I am very glad we found you gentlemen." The officer waved his hand, signaling Berger to join them. When the holotech came up, he and Norris exchanged puzzled looks. Neither had any idea why anyone, especially a Kurita officer, would be looking for them.

"My men and I have just come from Kempis," the officer explained.

"Then you know about the massacre," Norris stated.

"All too well. I want to take you two to Greggville. It's a free city. You'll be able to use the ComStar facility there to file your story and tell the Inner Sphere about this atrocity. The Draconis Combine will not tolerate such rebellion from its hired soldiers."

The trip to Greggville was uneventful. They did not see any BattleMechs on the way, for which Norris was very grateful. When they reached town, it seemed peaceful, with its people going about their business as though no battles were raging over the horizon. Nor was there much evidence of military presence in the town other than the three Kurita tanks. Indeed, the townspeople paid the armored vehicles scant notice.

The Draconians took Norris and Berger directly to the ComStar facility, halting the vehicles just outside the northeast gate. Like many ComStar compounds, this one had six gates, one for each of the great Houses and one to serve the general public. Each of the five House gates bore the symbol of a particular Successor Lord. This arrangement was supposed to be symbolic of ComStar's neutral position in regard to their centuries of warring. Because each state had its own gate, each Successor Lord—theoretically—had his own unrestricted access to ComStar, even on a planet ruled by a hostile state. The sixth gate was supposed to embody ComStar's mission to mankind as a whole and was open to any who wished to use the services of their interstellar communications network.

The northeast gate bore the black dragon of House Kurita. Their Kuritan military escort assured the newsmen of the immediate attention of a ComStar Acolyte, and dispatched them into the building to record and transmit their tale of treachery and atrocity. When the two newsmen came out an hour later, they found the *Chu-i* still waiting for them. He seemed concerned that they take away a good impression of Kurita soldiery. Norris, despite Berger's venomous looks, refused several offers of transportation.

"Thanks for your help, *Chu-i,*" the reporter said, starting off down the street. "When this story hits the network, those Widows will get what's coming to them. Their attempt to blame it on Davion by leaving that 'Mech arm won't help them at all. We saw the Widows do it. They'll pay."

"I certainly hope so, Mister Norris."

The man in the uniform of a *Chu-i* watched the newsmen walk down the street. When they had reached the far end, he turned to the squat, hard-faced man beside him. "I understand the traffic is heaviest near the business district. Arrange an accident."

"Hai, Chu-sa," the man replied and headed off.

At that slip of the tongue, the man in *Chu-i*'s garb scowled deeply. Obedience could be increased with training, he decided, as his underling walked away, but it seemed that brains disappeared in proportion. The sound of hard soles slapping on the paved walk interrupted his thoughts, and he turned to see a cowled and robed figure approaching from the main building. The officer bowed as the figure reached him.

"Good day to you, my son," the ComStar Adept said.

"A very good day, Adept Sharilar," the Kuritan replied. "I was told you would have something for me."

"I do, indeed."

He handed her a cartridge of holofilm. On its side was the logo of the Lyran Commonwealth's Donegal Broadcasting Company. Taped to the cartridge was a thick envelope. The Adept held the package briefly as if weighing it, then made it disappear into her robes.

"This will be held in trust until needed," the Adept said. "As agreed."

The Kuritan started to turn away, but seemed to remember something else he wanted to say. "The gentlemen I brought to your facility had a message for their network."

"They did, and it was recorded in complete fidelity. Alas," Sharilar said with mock seriousness, "an improper ritual was performed and some data transmissions were lost to the void. I fear that their story was among that lost data. Perhaps, at some future date, it may be recovered through the diligent prayers and hard work of my brothers and sisters."

The man in the *Chu-i*'s uniform nodded his understanding. The "recovery" would come when it was politically expedient. As he remounted his tank, he smiled in satisfaction.

From across the street, unseen in an alley, feral eyes watched the exchange.

When the Kuritans had gone and the Adept had vanished once more into the building, the unkempt man stumbled to his feet and sauntered to the public entrance of the ComStar compound. As he walked, he mumbled to himself.

"Widows! Heh, heh. Billy boy, you knows a way to make this 'un pay. The Hunter'll pay C-bills for a lead on the Widow."

When he reached the window, he told the Duty Acolyte, "Wanna sends a message to mah friend on Solaris."

The Kurita bills he produced to pay for the message's transmission were clean, a sharp contrast to everything else about the man.

19

Shaw District, Barlow's End
Draconis March, Federated Suns
29 September 3026

Chu-i Isabella Armstrong watched the screens of her BattleMech, which showed a large mass moving beyond the scattered redwoods on the forest's edge. That would be the Davion patrol 'Mech, right on schedule. She checked her visual to be sure the rest of her lance was well-concealed among small copses of lesser trees, presumably invisible to the approaching enemy. This raid on Barlow's End was the Ryuken's first combat mission, as well as her own first assignment as a lance commander. She didn't want anything to go wrong.

The Davion 'Mech, a sixty-five-ton *Thunderbolt,* appeared. Moving with little caution, it advanced through the thinning trees from the denser forest behind it. Suddenly, the *Thunderbolt* staggered and lurched back a step under the impact of at least twelve missiles. Such a response was more likely surprise on the pilot's part than because of damage to the 'Mech. Those few high-explosive warheads would make little impression on the sixty-five ton machine's armor. Smoke swirled around the *T-Bolt,* obscuring it from view.

"Hiyaah! First blood! I claim first blood," came the voice of Mech Warrior Hiraku Jacobs over the Ryuken taccomm.

Jacob's voice confirmed what Armstrong already knew

from observing the missile strike. Besides her own *Catapult,* Jacobs' *Whitworth* was the only 'Mech in the lance that was capable of launching such a missile spread. The impulsive hotblood had broken ambush by firing prematurely on the enemy. Even now, his 'Mech was bulling through the small trees that had provided a screen from the advancing Davion *T-Bolt.* He was moving in for a better shot.

"You are on report, hothead," Armstrong noted, though no one could hear her in the cockpit of her *Catapult.*

Armstrong's own position let her see a hundred meters past the *T-Bolt* and down the trail it had been following. In the shadows cast by the giant trees, she could see the blocky shapes of more 'Mechs moving. Damnation! There was only supposed to be a single machine on the patrol circuit. She keyed her command frequency. "We've got extra guests for our party, lance. Fast strike, in and out. Let's use what little surprise Jacobs left us."

Acknowledgements from MechWarriors Frost and Toragama came in as she fired her jump jets. The sixty-five-ton 'Mech leaped clear of the trees to land with flexed legs on the top of a nearby rise. Even before the *Catapult* had straightened, Armstrong loosed a flight of 75mm rockets from the paired launchers mounted on the back of the 'Mech's carapace. She didn't bother to aim. The approaching enemy was still bunched on the trail, and what didn't hit the first machine had a good chance of impacting on one behind it. In any case, the sudden fusillade might intimidate and confuse the enemy.

At that moment, Frost moved his *Panther* up on Armstrong's left, loosing particle beams into the milling BattleMechs just inside the trees. Meanwhile, the other *Panther,* piloted by Toragama, came up beside Jacobs. Together they searched for a target. Between their angle and the smoke from Jacobs' first attack, they were screened from the rest of the Davion lance. When the two 'Mechs began to fire on the *Thunderbolt*'s last known location, the object of their attentions suddenly appeared. Bursting from the smoke, the *Thunderbolt* crashed forward, its enormous right-arm laser blazing red light at the *Whitworth.*

"Watch out!" Toragama called, alerting Jacobs to the danger.

Jacobs managed to dodge that first shot, but the enemy pilot was more than his match. The second laser shot came much closer, and Jacobs' evasive shift took him straight into the flight path of missiles from the *T-Bolt*'s Delta Dart launcher. Craters appeared in the *Whitworth*'s upper torso and shoulder armor. Even after the cloud raised by the warhead explosions dissipated, smoke rose from the jagged gaps that the missiles had torn through the 'Mech's armor. Jacobs may have scored the first hit, but the *T-Bolt* pilot scored the first significant damage. The *Whitworth*'s left arm hung limp.

Armstrong had little time to consider her mate's plight. The Davion pilots had rallied with their leader's charge, and a *Valkyrie* was barreling through the thinning redwoods now, launching missiles as it came. The enemy MechWarrior snap-fired a laser blast at Armstrong's *Catapult*, momentarily blanking her screens as the flash compensator reacted to the coherent light playing over the 'Mech. She had no worries about damage, though. At over three hundred meters, it was too hard to lock on long enough to burn through even the lightest BattleMech armor. The Davion pilot had to be a novice. Armstrong was withholding her own laser fire for more effective ranges.

She targeted on the *Valkyrie*, a light 'Mech. If she could take it down early, the odds would be much better. She sent a double flight of missiles at the *Valkyrie*. The rocket exhausts flared past her viewpoint, powering their destructive loads toward the Davion machine.

Frost must have matched her reasoning, for he was concentrating his own fire on the same 'Mech. Blue-white lightning from his PPC crackled the air. The bolt seared away paint from the *Valk*, revealing metal, which slagged under the intense heat.

The center of so much unwanted attention, the *Valkyrie* pilot panicked and fired his jump jets before he had completely cleared the treeline. The 'Mech plowed into the foliage of a solitary giant. Branches cracked and tore clear as the 'Mech rose, but they stripped off most of the *Valk*'s antenna assembly. The thirty-ton machine arced away from the fight toward a hilly patch to the northeast. From its erratic flight path, either the 'Mech or its pilot had taken damage from the Draconian attacks.

Armstrong did not have time to see if the enemy warrior had landed safely before turning her attention to the other two Davion 'Mechs emerging from the woods.

The *Valkyrie* remained a potential threat, but was out of the fight for now. The new 'Mechs were a bigger and more current danger. First in line was a fifty-five-ton *Shadow Hawk,* followed closely by a sixty-ton *Ostsol*. Together they outmassed all three of Armstrong's lance-mates. In BattleMech combat, greater mass generally meant greater fighting capability.

"Lance, we've got trouble with a capital T," Armstrong radioed. What was supposed to have been a one-sided ambush was about to become a skirmish—with her force at a definite disadvantage.

"Withdraw," she shouted over the command channel. "Fire by extraction!"

Armstrong backed her *Catapult* down the reverse slope. Just before her 'Mech's bullet-shaped body dropped below the crest, she fired another double flight of rockets.

Scanners showed Frost withdrawing according to orders. His *Panther* was firing as it moved from cover to cover, working its way to Armstrong's position. The hill blocked Armstrong's view of Toragama and Jacobs, but the taccomm suddenly crackled to life.

"Jacobs is down! He hasn't ejected. I think he's hurt!"

"Keep it calm, Toragama." That was bad. With one 'Mech down, she didn't need to lose another pilot to panic. "What happened?"

"The *T-Bolt* raked him with missiles and he went down. His 'Mech's not moving. I think he's hurt."

"Confirmed, *Chu-i,*" Frost broke in. "Got a LOS on them. The *Whitworth* is down, with Toragama covering against the *T-Bolt*'s advance. The other Feds are headed that way. ETA of first hostile is two minutes."

Thank the Dragon for Frost's cool head. Armstrong knew they had to get out of here, but if Jacobs was still alive, she couldn't abandon him. With him still in his 'Mech, they would have to drag them both. Her own *Cat* had no arms, and a single *Panther* was too light for the job. It would take both *Panthers* to drag the forty-ton *Whitworth* clear of the field. With the Davion 'Mechs on top of them, that would be impossible. Something had to be done.

"Frost, listen up. You and Toragama are going to have to drag Jacobs' butt out of there. I'll give you cover and try to pull the Feds away. Meet you at the rally point."

"Hai, Chu-i!"

"Get moving!" Frost's 'Mech was in motion even before the order reached him, his machine racing along out of sight of the enemy.

Armstrong's machine rose on a column of superheated steam. It cleared the ridge, coming down in the open, eighty meters from the leading Davion 'Mech. As the *Cat* landed, Armstrong jolted violently, having misjudged the slope of her landing site. The shock skewed her aim, and the spread of laser fire she sent at the *T-Bolt* did little more than catch the pilot's attention. The ponderous 'Mech turned in her direction, and its partners changed vector to angle in on her as well. To distract the Feds while her lance members worked to make good their escape, Armstrong began the deadly dance of dodge and fire.

"Strike Command, this is Pouncer One," she broadcast desperately when the hostiles gave her a second's breather. "We've got trouble. Come in, Strike Command."

It took two more tries before she got an answer. By then, she had taken multiple missile and autocannon hits that had pocked and shattered armor plates, but failed to penetrate and rupture the more delicate structures beneath. Far worse was the shot the *Cat* had taken from one of the *Ostsol*'s 8cm lasers. The heavy beam had breached the 'Mech's leg armor and damaged an actuator. She was finding it hard to dodge with a limp.

"Strike Command to Pouncer One, what's your situation?" The comm officer's voice was calm and detached. He could afford to be, sitting safe in the MHQ.

"Mech down. Two on recovery assistance. Three heavy hostiles in pursuit."

"Understood, Pouncer." There was a pause. Armstrong prayed that it was to order a couple of 'Mech lances to their relief. Relief that she prayed, even more fervently, would arrive in time. A new speaker replaced the comm officer.

Armstrong recognized *Tai-sa* Tetsuhara's voice. "Negative on available ground forces, Pouncer."

Armstrong's throat dried. This was it then. If the Iron Man was on the line, it was to tell her that it was stand-and-die time, time for dignity and honor. Damn! She wanted to cry, but that wasn't dignified.

Sacrifice for one's comrades was noble in theory. In the hot cockpit of a BattleMech, facing death in the shape of three enemy BattleMechs, theory wasn't so attractive. Survival—now that was attractive! Far more than some abstract like the unit's honor.

"Pouncer," the *Tai-sa* called.

Frackencrack! she thought. *Here comes the death order.*

"We have diverted an aerospace lance to your coordinates. ETA is six minutes. Can you hold?"

What? For a few seconds, the unexpected words made no sense to Armstrong. While she was thus distracted, the *Shadow Hawk* rounded a copse of trees and caught the *Catapult* with a pair of missiles. Armstrong reacted on the reflex and drove her 'Mech in a skittering run for the cover of a granite boulder.

"Pouncer, can you hold for six minutes?"

"Do I have a choice?"

"Time is unconquerable, *Chu-i*. Do your best. I expect no less from my samurai."

"Hai, Tai-sa!" He had called her a samurai. In ten years of service with the Combine, no officer had ever accorded her the honor. The Iron Man was doing his best for her. She could do no less in return.

Those six minutes were the longest days Armstrong ever lived as the battle became a lethal game of hide and seek. As the *Cat*'s heat burden built up, more failure lights flared red in every encounter with the Davion enemy. Her missile stock shrank, and she had no idea how many more brushes she could survive. The next might be the last.

"Pouncer One, Pouncer One, you still out here?"

Armstrong shed tears of relief with no thought of her dignity when that voice came over the taccomm. "Barely. Thank the Dragon you made it."

"Say rather, Blue Flight of Wolf's Dragoons, ma'am." A burst of static blurred the link briefly. "We've got four

'Mechs on our screens. Can you give us a beacon for our run? Wouldn't want to lose you by accident."

"Roger on the beacon," she said, setting up a repeating pulse on her taccomm to identify her 'Mech to the friendly fighters.

Two *Lucifers* sporting black wolf's-heads came screaming down out of the sky to rain explosive destruction on the Davion 'Mechs. The Federated MechJocks were not tyros, but could do little against the swift-moving fighters. None of their machines was configured for ground-to-air work, and so the enemy 'Mechs headed for cover.

Armstrong didn't wait around. As soon as she saw the first rockets thud home, she throttled up and ran from the field at full speed. She wanted to put as much distance as possible between her *Catapult* and the Davion 'Mechs that had mauled it.

The Dragoon fighters made another pass, but it had less effect since the Feds had gone to ground. The Dragoon Lance Commander radioed his concern to Armstrong, "Gotta go, ma'am. We've got other calls to make. Hope you got enough of a lead 'cause I don't think we took any of the Fed 'Mechs down for the count."

"It will be enough," Armstrong said determinedly. "Warrior, to whom do I owe my life?"

"The name's Atwyl, ma'am. But you don't owe me anything. It's all part of the service. Good luck!"

The fighters disappeared into the distant haze, heading for the Shaw River Valley.

It took an hour for Armstrong to reach the rally point, but she was sure that she had eluded any Davion pursuers. The rest of her lance was waiting for her. The *Whitworth* was lying on the ground with its cockpit hatch open. Frost and Toragama stood beside the supine machine. Even before she cracked her own hatch, she knew what the word would be.

"Jacobs bought it, *Chu-i,*" Frost said after she had dismounted.

Armstrong shrugged off her cooling jacket and sat down on a convenient boulder. The cool forest air was balm for her body, if not her mind. "Well, he asked for it, and he got it."

"That's pretty callous, *Chu-i,*" Toragama blurted belligerently. "Hiraku Jacobs died in battle as a warrior. He should be honored for that."

"He should be tried for disobeying orders! When he broke ambush, he nearly set us all up to be killed."

"His was an honorable act. First blood for a warrior," Toragama protested.

"Honor, my ass. His honor lay in following orders, in serving his lord. Jacobs was reckless and heedless of his duty. His death has cost House Kurita a warrior and almost three more. It cost two 'Mechs heavily damaged, and it could have cost a whole lance totally lost.

"If Jacobs had used his head, he would be alive now. Davion warriors would be licking their wounds and burying their dead.

"We are Ryuken. We are responsible to react to the situation, not to follow orders blindly or to perform pointless acts of personal bravery. We must always keep our mission in mind. You got that, Toragama? *Wakarimasu-ka?*"

The chastened soldier nodded. *"Wakarimasu, Chu-i."*

20

Alpha Regiment MHQ, Ryuken Field Camp,
Barlow's End
Draconis March, Federated Suns
30 September 3026

The orderly threaded his way through the crowded mobile headquarters vehicle. Impartially bumping into Dragoon and Kurita officers alike, he apologized as he went. Reaching Minobu, the man held out a packet. "From Colonel Wolf, sir."

Minobu took the envelope, whose markings indicated that the message had not come over the military net. Minobu raised a questioning eyebrow to Major Kelly Yukinov, who shook his head to signify that he had no inkling of the message's contents. Minobu opened the envelope and unfolded the flimsy inside. A smile grew as he read the message.

"It is the Colonel's good wishes for the success of our first joint mission."

"We've got some work ahead of us," Yukinov said, "if we are to fulfill those wishes."

"Surely you exaggerate, Major."

Heads turned toward Jerry Akuma when he spoke.

Minobu could tell that the PSL officer relished the effect he'd made by finally breaking silence. Though the tall Japanese's presence had shadowed the proceedings in the command vehicle, he had said little, seeming to choose his moments with a timing that Minobu envied.

"The great Wolf's Dragoons are not noted for defeatism," Akuma said.

"Not defeatism, *Chu-sa* Akuma," Yukinov said. "Realism. This operation is not on schedule.

"You were here yesterday during the incident with Armstrong's failed ambush. The reports from both Ryuken and Dragoon Recon Lances are just as ominous. There's a heavier Davion military presence here than Kurita intel predicted."

"Perhaps," Akuma drawled. "The recon reports are just the over-reaction of half-trained troops and mercenaries eager to pad the enemy's numbers to increase combat bonuses." If Akuma was disappointed that neither Minobu or Yukinov rose to the bait, he hid it well. "If the reconnaissance reports are true, it only means that Davion's lackeys have good reason to protect what we seek. The prize must be more valuable than the ISF believes."

"It also means we'll have to 'work' harder to get it," Yukinov countered.

"The amount of 'work' is, of course, your concern. Your Colonel Wolf accepted this mission, and now you are obligated to produce results."

"You'll get them."

Akuma smiled. "I know I will." Standing unobtrusively behind him were his two aides. One was a blond man as tall as Akuma, but considerably more massive. The other was a squat and compact Japanese. They accompanied the *Chu-sa* everywhere, presenting ever-grim and impassive faces to the world.

The PSL officer held out a hand, and the shorter aide handed him a sheet of paper. Holding up the paper, Akuma said, "Already I have results. This is a message from our informant at the Achernar Proving Grounds in Landova. The agent's report indicates that the Davion commander plans to move Professor McGuffin's prototype to a more secure location four days from now."

The Ryuken and Dragoon staff officers exchanged worried looks at that information. It upset the raiding team's timetable. Akuma, satisfied with the turmoil he had created, stepped back, taking himself out of the circle around the holotank and the discussion that was starting there.

"Are they on to us?" asked Major Patrick Chan, his expression troubled. Chan's battalion made up most of the force from Alpha Regiment that was present for the raid.

"Well, Pat, we have to assume, at the very least, that they know what we're after," Colonel Jamison said. His own expression showed that he didn't much like the idea of the enemy knowing his objective either.

"Maybe we can use that to our advantage," Minobu offered.

Yukinov perked up. "How do you mean?"

Minobu wondered if Yukinov knew what he had in mind and was just giving him the opportunity to put the plan on the table. "If we put in the expected assault on the facility, they won't be expecting an attempt on the transfer convoy."

"That sounds good." This was from Captain Kristen Stane, commander of an augmented company of light BattleMechs notable for its air elements and fast-strike capability. Stane always favored plans involving sudden and unexpected attacks. She claimed that the speed and uncertainty agreed with her. With typical Dragoon thoroughness, she added, "If there's a good ambush site."

"There may be one," Minobu said, punching a code into his console. The holotank responded by zooming in on the Landova sector. A principal highway headed south from the city, then turned west and crossed the Shaw River Valley over a flood-control dam. After passing over the dam, the highway paralleled the west-northwest trend of the river until the dense woods of the Renbourn Forestry Reserve forced it to veer away. "Look here," he said, keying a zoom to focus on the area on the south side of the Shaw River.

"I see it," Chan and Stane said in unison. They looked at one another, both caught off guard by the other's remark. Each was known in the Dragoons as a master of the BattleMech ambush. Each also respected the other's expertise. Stane deferred to rank, and Chan said, "There, where the road passes through the edge of Renbourn Forestry Reserve. It looks like a perfect location."

Now Stane spoke up. "Exactly. That's why the ambush

should be sited here, in Millon's Woods. Before the road gets to the obvious site."

"No good. We wouldn't have a line of retreat if it drops in the pot," Yukinov objected. As officer in charge of Dragoon forces onworld, he must remain concerned with the preservation of those forces.

"There is a line of retreat," Minobu said. "If the attacking force is carefully selected."

"Huh?" The Dragoons looked puzzled. Minobu had leaped ahead of them. Minobu's own staff were even more confused, being already ill-at-ease with the interplay of a Dragoon-style planning session. They were unaccustomed to the speed at which options were accepted or discarded. Only Michi Noketsuna wasn't lost. He had seen where Minobu was looking while the Dragoons talked, and his face showed it with a half-smile.

"The Shaw River is a seasonal phenomenon," Minobu continued. "At this time of year, the valley is completely dry and its floor well-compacted. It would make an almost perfect road for a light 'Mech force."

"Still no good," Chan objected. "The banks are veritable cliffs. Fifty meters, if they're one."

"Ah," Minobu said. "That is why the attacking force must all be jump-capable . . ."

". . . So they can hit the convoy, smash through them, and jump down into the valley," Yukinov said, finishing the thought. While Chan was objecting, he had figured out what Minobu was leading up to. "I like it."

Minobu bowed his head in acknowledgement. "If our onworld reconnaissance is accurate, no more than half of the Davion 'Mechs in the vicinity are jump-capable. The proportion of these that accompany the convoy is likely to be somewhat less."

"How do you figure that, *Tai-sa*?" asked *Sho-sa* Charles Earnst. Of all of Minobu's staff, he was the most outspoken. One or two of the other Ryuken officers also signaled curiosity by nodding agreement with Earnst's request for enlightenment.

"If McGuffin's prototype is indeed valuable to House Davion," Minobu said, "they'll want a strong force to defend it, in case the convoy runs into trouble. A strong force means heavy BattleMechs, and most heavy 'Mechs are tied to the ground. Due to his requirements to defend other possible targets, the Davion commander will also wish to keep sufficient mobile elements to respond to our maneuvers. Mobile elements mean light BattleMechs, preferably jump-capable.

"That means something less than half the escort force will be available to pursue our raiders through the valley. Now, see the alternate channels that the river has carved over the eons. The Federated Suns commander will not know which channel we plan to use for our escape route, and he'll be forced to split his forces to cover all the possibilities. Some of his 'Mechs will end up in channels diverging from our route, effectively removing them from the battle. Others will reach dead-ends and the same result."

"There's still a hole in this plan," Chan put in, probably upset that his choice for an ambush site had been rejected. "The other convoy 'Mechs will be able to follow along the bank. They could provide direction to the pursuit as well as harassing fire, and their height advantage would be devastating."

"It might, if they were allowed to take advantage of it." Minobu had everyone's attention again. "But the Davion 'Mechs on the south bank will be occupied. After our main force makes the expected attack on Landova, we'll leave a skeleton force there to demonstrate our nonexistent intent to invest the proving grounds. Another contingent will form a cordon around the city, while the main force moves to engage the Davion 'Mechs with fire from the north bank of the Shaw. As soon as the ambush force is clear, the covering forces will disengage. The forces in Landova will also pull out and head for the DropShips. There should be no more than the usual problems in getting offplanet with our prize."

"Sounds workable," Yukinov said. "Who gets what assignment?"

"The hit-and-run nature of the ambush force would be best left to the Dragoons, I think," Minobu suggested.

"Got that right!"

"Thank you, Captain Stane." The admonishment in Yukinov's voice had no visible effect on the ebullient woman. "I agree. That leaves the Ryuken and our heavier machines for the Landova operation."

"Yes. But I think the lighter elements of the Ryuken can provide distraction for the Davion forces by moving—"

"Wait a minute. Wait a minute," Chan interrupted. "Look at the dam here. It's got access paths down into the river bed. The Feds could pull their heavies back to it and move them down there to chase our raiders. If their lights maintain contact and slow our troops, we could have real trouble."

"Respectfully, Major Chan," Michi Noketsuna said, heels clicking as he performed a sharp bow. "If they do, they shall have the same trouble you feared they would provide our raiders."

"Humph!" Chan looked sour. He did not like having his own objection brought back to shoot down his argument, especially by a whippersnapper Kurita officer, no matter how respectful. A glance at the holotank brought another idea. "What if they didn't go down but came back across? Whether they went after our covering force on the north bank or headed for Landova, they'd be in trouble."

"I think you are right, Major," Minobu conceded. "The dam will have to be destroyed after the convoy crosses it."

"Kristen, your airpower going to be up to the job?" Yukinov asked.

"Too busy with the Davion flyboys."

"Looks like we'll have to do it from the ground. What about those diversionary forces of yours, *Tai-sa* Tetsuhara?"

"They are the choice of necessity. Once we've encircled the Achernar facility, they would be available to make the strike." Minobu considered the distances involved. "They should arrive at the dam just after the convoy reaches the ambush site. That timing may be later than Major Chan would wish, but they should still be able to destroy passage down or over the dam well before the Davion commanders consider any options along those lines."

When the discussion moved to specific problems, such as timetables, jump-off points, zones of responsibility, and designating resupply points, Akuma lost interest. He found such trivia boring. He had listened intently to the earlier discussion, however, and agreed that the plan was well-formulated. It was a good scheme, with an excellent chance of success, and would suit his own plans very well. In the buzz of discussion that filled the MHQ, no one could hear him when he turned to his aides and said quietly, "Tonight."

21

Ryuken-Dragoon Field Camp, Barlow's End
Draconis March, Federated Suns
1 October 3026

MechWarrior Malcolm Spence dropped two sugars into his coffee and looked up at the clock on the wall of the monitor hut. Unity! It was only 0130. There were still four and half hours till his relief arrived. It was going to be a long night. The Feds didn't know where the raider camp was, so they weren't likely to be making any attacks. But Stone Face Chan didn't care. "Full standard surveillance," he had ordered, and Spence had ended up with the dead-man's shift. What had he done to piss off old Stone Face? Oh well, nothing for it but to muddle through. He would just have to stay awake, but that's what coffee was for. If only it wasn't so quiet.

When a knock sounded at the door, he nearly spilled the hot liquid into his lap. Before Spence could say anything, the door opened to reveal a tall, muscular Ryuken MechWarrior. The outside moonlight turned his close-cropped blond hair to a silver skullcap, and the scar down his right cheek might have made him sinister if not for the man's easy grin and manner. "Hey, didn't mean to startle you."

"That's O.K.," Spence said, mopping up the mess. "What's up?"

"Nothing. Couldn't sleep. Nerves, I guess. Figured whoever had monitor duty might be wanting to talk awhile to kill some time. I've had the watch myself and know how boring it can be."

"Too straight," the Dragoon agreed.

"Name's Kahn," the visitor said, holding out a hand adorned with a heavy gold ring that glinted in the light. Spence shook the man's hand, impressed at the strength of his grip.

"First or last?"

"Your choice," the Kuritan answered, pulling up a chair.

They fell into the easy talk of fellow MechWarriors. Kahn was sympathetic to Spence's problems with a glitch in the jump jets on his *Shadow Hawk*, for it turned out that he had had the same problem with his own 'Mech two years ago. He and his Tech had never been able to trace it down. It had taken a complete replacement of the jet systems to clear up the problem.

Spence was caught by surprise when Kahn opened his eyes wide and leaned forward. "What's that?"

"Where?"

"Monitor four. There behind the 'Mech." The Kuritan got up and leaned over Spence's chair, left hand pointing at the screen. Kahn's right hand rested on Spence's back and swiveled the Dragoon toward the bank of monitors. Kahn's ring was cold where it touched the skin on the back of Spence's neck.

Spence squinted at the screen, but he saw nothing out of the ordinary. "I don't see anything."

"Thought I saw something move. Must have been my imagination." Kahn rubbed his eyes with his left hand and went back to his seat. "I'm not used to the distortions on these nightscope video cams. It's not the same as the light amplification circuits on my 'Mech. Must take some getting used to."

"Yeah, some."

"You been working them long?"

"Longer than I like." Any time was too long. Unity! He was tired, ready for sleep.

"Still got a haul on your shift?"

"Huh?" It was an effort to concentrate on what Kahn was saying. "Yeah, long haul."

"Your relief will probably be late, won't he?" Kahn's voice was insistent, assured, and convincing.

"La . . . late . . ."

"But it won't matter, will it?"

"Na . . . no . . ."

"The night is quiet. Nothing to be seen on the monitors. All is boringly normal."

Kahn's voice was utterly convincing.

Spence made no response.

Kahn gave a satisfied grunt and rose from his seat. He moved to the monitor console and brought an image from the bivouac area to the main screen. After adjusting the image quality, Kahn took a slim black case out of his tunic pocket. He placed the object onto the screen's casing and touched a button recessed into the upper edge. A set of small green letters and numbers began to glow at one corner of the case. They repeated the time and location codes from the video screen. Smaller letters on the case spelled out the word "recording."

Within a minute, a figure in dark fatigues appeared on the screen. A patch on his shoulder caught a stray flash of light to reveal an open-jawed wolfs-head against a circular field.

The stocky shape walked casually past the tent bearing the personal insignia of Minobu Tetsuhara and disappeared briefly into the shadows. The man appeared again beside the tent and stepped up to the hovercar parked there. He lifted the hood and bent into the darkness beneath it. He did something and then shut the hood, looking around as though to see whether he had been observed. After a moment, the man vanished into the dark.

Kahn adjusted the controls on the console. The image he settled on showed a section of the perimeter fence. The green symbols on the box changed to match the new codes on the screen.

This time, it was nearly fourteen minutes before anything moved on the screen. The same man Kahn had just observed entered from the left, moving at a trot to the coiled wire fence. With a lithe spring, the man was over the wire, and landed in a crouch on the other side. He disappeared into the murk beyond the range of the camera.

Eight minutes later, he was back. He reentered the camp by cutting his way through the fence. Once inside, he spent a while burying small objects around the area. Still working at his task, the man moved out of the camera's field of view.

After Kahn could no longer see the man, he shut down his black case and put it back in his pocket. He took a small cylinder from another pocket and placed its end against Spence's jugular, creating a soft hiss from the cylinder. Kahn checked Spence's pulse and nodded in satisfaction as the counteragent for the drug he had administered earlier brought the Dragoon's pulse back up. The cylinder went back into Kahn's pocket. Before returning to his seat, Kahn replaced Spence's coffee with a fresh, full cup.

Kahn began to talk in a monotone. He spoke of boring things, creating clear, detailed word pictures of dull video monitors and duty shifts punctuated by cups of coffee.

"Must have faded out for a second," Spence said eventually. His words were slightly slurred, but Kahn didn't seem to notice. He must be half-asleep himself, Spence decided. "What were you saying?"

"Wasn't important. I'm pretty beat myself. Think I'll turn in."

"Lucky you. I can't leave till my relief signs on."

"You'll be O.K.? Won't drift off again?"

"Naw. I just got this cup of coffee. It'll keep me going for a bit." He took a sip. "Yuck! Must need this coffee. I was so drowsy that I forgot the sugar."

Kahn smiled and shut the door behind himself.

Two hours later, the first explosion ripped the night.

Minobu was off his cot and dressing before the blare of the warning klaxon sounded. The blast of the first explosion had awakened him. Tunic halfway on and belt still in hand, he shouldered aside the flap of his tent and stepped into the cold, predawn air. The sounds of explosions and gunfire were coming from the southwest perimeter. The sentry 'Mech in that quadrant was flashing its searchlight around, groping to reveal the intruders. Soldiers were running in that direction. Most were half-dressed like Minobu, but all carried weapons. Among them was Kelly Yukinov. Minobu moved to intercept him.

"What is happening?"

"Not sure yet," Yukinov said. "Looks like a commando raid on the southwest fence. Didn't think the Feds knew where we were."

"Mechs?"

"Not that I know of. I'm on my way to check it out."

"My skimmer will get us there faster."

"Right."

Michi, still rumpled from sleep but buckling on his sidearm nonetheless, stumbled from his own tent just in time to see the two officers leap aboard the hovercar. The engine roared to life, drowning out his shouted questions. Then the craft rose on its air cushion and roared away into the night, leaving Michi behind. Both disappointed and annoyed, he stood watching it go when the hovercar suddenly jerked to port and spun out. One skirt caught a boulder and the vehicle flipped high into the air. Silhouetted against the flare of a perimeter explosion, Michi saw a body tossed doll-like from the skimmer before the machine crashed heavily to the ground, where it lay in a broken, tangled mass.

Michi ran toward the wreck, stopping where he had seen the body land. Despite his prayers to Buddha, the body proved to be that of Kelly Yukinov. One leg was twisted back along itself, but the Dragoon's moan of pain showed he was alive.

"MedTech!" Michi shouted into the chaos of the night.

Michi looked about for his *sensei,* praying that Minobu had also been thrown free. The passing searchlight threw the scene into harsh relief. Stark whites and inky blacks chased each other across the wreck, making a grotesque picture. The hand that protruded limply from the crumpled skimmer made it all too real.

Michi left the Dragoon Major to fare for himself and dashed to the wreckage. Minobu was pinned within, and there was blood everywhere. With trembling fingers, Michi felt for a pulse. When he found none, tears flooded his eyes, but Michi did not let go of the *sensei*'s hand.

22

South of the Shaw River, Barlow's End
Draconis March, Federated Suns
3 October 3026

Dragoon Lieutenant Dechan Fraser looked up at the sky and tried to decide if it was going to rain, but a careful scrutiny of the clouds left him no more enlightened than before. He walked back under the thermotec canopies that screened the waiting 'Mechs from aerial and orbital IR scanners. The shrouding diffused their heat signatures while complex camouflage patterns printed on the fabric masked the machines from optical observation.

The Lieutenant ambled over to a group of MechWarriors. Except for his own lancemates, he had never worked with any of them before. They were here in Millon's Woods on detached duty, a special "light company" assembled for the ambush from different lancers of Alpha Regiment elements present on Barlow's End. Like soldiers everywhere, the troops were grousing and trading scuttlebutt to kill time and to relieve the palpable tension that always preceded battle.

As Dechan approached, he recognized the pretty blonde MechJock who was speaking as Jenette Rand from Laskowski's Company. He'd hoped to get to know her better, but she didn't seem to have noticed him among all the other MechWarriors. "Anybody know what happened to that

Draco Colonel?" she was saying. "The one the Ryuken Jocks call the Iron Man?"

"Heard the Fed commandoes did for him in that raid two days ago," said Sergeant Kerri Tennler. The stocky redhead was the pilot of a *Grasshopper,* which at seventy tons was the heaviest 'Mech in the ambush team. Though Dechan hadn't met her, either, he'd heard about Tennler's reputation as a tough customer. When Corporal Thom Dominguez brayed out a laugh at her comment, Dechan thought he might get to see that rep in action.

"Where *do* you get your info, Tennler?" Dominguez managed when he caught his breath. Every 'Mech battalion had its scrounger and Dominguez was it for Chan's Battalion. Unlike most scroungers, he was as good at gathering information as he was at acquiring spare parts looking for a new home. He had little patience, however, with those who merely dabbled at what he considered an art. "It wasn't any Feds. The Draco was in the same skimmer crash as the Old Man. Don't know yet if he's a farmer, but the MedTechs who rushed him off to the Draco D-Ship had real long faces."

"Too bad if he invested," Dechan mused. Noticing the many sour looks around him, he added, "He helped me save the Colonel back on Quentin. He's all right . . . for a Snake."

"Hey, Dominguez. Since you've got the poop, what's the word on the Old Man?" Rand asked.

"Gonna be laid up for a while." Dominguez was preening in the spotlight. "I saw him that night. Leg looked like it had an extra joint. Very messy."

"He gonna lose it?" The new voice was Private Erik Johansson. Like Dominguez, he was a member of Fraser's Lance. Unlike the scrounger, Johansson was a novice, fresh out of Alpha's Training Company. Despite the mildness of Dominguez's description, the kid looked a little green around the gills.

Dominguez shrugged. "If he does, Wolf will see to it that he gets the best, a full replacement with myomer artificials. Nothing's too good for the Colonel's fair-haired boy."

"Why shouldn't he get good stuff?" Tennler bristled. "He may be a little old, but he's a good CO. Takes righteous care of us."

The snide reference to an officer she respected riled Tennler more than Dominguez's earlier slight of her own abilities. She started to get up, ready to make the scrounger eat his words. At the same moment, Private Donal Cameron also rose from his seat next to her, as if by coincidence coming between Tennler and Dominguez. Dechan knew better, however. Cameron was his lance's peacemaker and had plenty of experience in heading trouble away from the scrounger.

"Yeah, Yukinov's a good man," Cameron said to placate Tennler, but hoped to quickly change the subject. "Now we got Jamison upstairs. Hope he remembers we don't all ride Assault 'Mechs."

"Nothing to worry about," Dominguez assured him, oblivious to the near start of mayhem. "Old Jamison has been herding 'Mechs for longer than most of us have been around. Zeta Battalion may be full of Assault 'Mechs, but I'm sure he knows a light from a heavy. Why, I haven't heard of him sending a *Locust* up against an *Atlas* in two or three weeks."

Laughter rippled through the group, defusing any remaining tension. The idea of a twenty-tonner duking it out with a massive, hundred-ton *Atlas* was funny. *That is, if you weren't the Jock piloting that Locust,* Dechan thought.

"At least, he ain't like that prissy Satoh. Don't know how the Ryuken Jocks can stand him," Rand remarked when things calmed again. For some reason, she seemed fascinated by the Draco command. Dechan decided that might be a way to catch her attention.

"Could be worse. I'd thought that Akuma creep would take over," Dechan offered. That got nods of agreement, including one from Rand.

"Naw, he left," Dominguez said, taking center stage again. "Think he went out on the same D-Ship with Iron Man."

"No lie? Thought he'd want to be around to take whatever it is we're after." Rand mimed, clutching something valuable to her heart. Her act got more laughs.

"Damp it!" Tennler cut in, voice low. "Here comes Stone Face!"

Major Chan was indeed headed in their direction, accompanied by Captain Amy Laskowski of the hastily assembled Light Company. Behind them, Dechan could see the other company commanders heading off to their own units.

"All right, troops. Our spotter has called in," Chan announced. "Our pigeons are on the way and will be here soon. I know most of you have new lancemates for this operation. Keep it in mind! Don't rely on a buddy who isn't there. I don't want any losses because somebody is running on reflexes instead of brains. Got it?"

Among the chorus of "Yessirs," Dechan also heard a dutiful "Yes, Daddy." He couldn't tell who the wise guy was, but Chan hadn't heard it. Laskowski might have, though. There was the ghost of a smile on her face as she returned Chan's salute. The Major sprinted off toward his *Crusader-L.*

"Saddle up!" the Captain ordered, and the MechWarriors scattered to their machines. Johansson ran alongside Dechan, grinning from ear to ear in anticipation. "This'll be easy."

"Don't get too cocky," Dechan cautioned him. "We still got to get through the Fed heavies."

"We'll do it. All the Feds here are low-class mercs. The White Witches are the best they got on this rock, and I hear they didn't do so well against Delta on Quentin. Delta, for Unity's sake! Now they're facing Alpha. We're the best."

While Johansson clambered into his *Javelin,* Dechan started up the chain ladder hanging from the cockpit of his own *Shadow Hawk.* Once seated, he slipped on the neurohelmet and buckled up as the 'Mech's systems came to full power. As Lance Commander, he checked with the others and received ready signals from all three. Dechan then linked into the taccomm circuit to report his unit ready.

When all lances signaled readiness, Chan fed the video from the scout position to all commanders. The Federated Suns convoy looked tiny on Dechan's cockpit screen. The dozen BattleMechs pacing the trucks and hovertanks in the column could have been armored men running alongside toy cars. Dechan knew better.

Moving along the highway at about 40 KPH, the Davion column passed the hidden position of Fraser's Lance. The BattleMech lance providing advance guard had already passed out of sight, headed down the road away from the ambush site. Still to be seen was the rear guard that the scout had reported, another 'Mech lance.

"Hit 'em!" Chan barked over the taccomm when the Fed column was in position.

Chan's Command Lance cut loose with a barrage of long-range missiles to open the attack. The rockets fell among the lead elements of the column. Their main target, the convoy command vehicle, disappeared under a cloud of black smoke.

From where Dechan stood concealed in Millon's Woods, he could see the confusion wrought by the sudden assault. The loss of the command vehicle and the sudden appearance of more than a dozen enemy BattleMechs had thrown the Davion convoy into chaos. The cargo trucks jerked to a halt while fighting vehicles and 'Mechs started to spread out in uncoordinated formations. Dechan could pick up their chatter on the comm. Though the words were hidden in electronic codes, the patterns plainly indicated their confusion.

Chan's team took advantage of the Feds' disarray to close the distance between the forces. The Dragoons moved forward at full-tilt to cut off the head of the column. While the Major's lance deployed to meet the expected return of the advance guard, the rest of the team, Uchimaya's Company, moved to attack the column.

At last, the Davion defenders began to react. Saracen and Scimitar hovertanks fanned out from the road, their blowers finding the rolling terrain almost as congenial as the paved highway. The flanking 'Mechs began to form a line between the Dragoons and the Fed trucks, whose cargo the Dragoons sought.

Before those trucks could organize an escape from the battlefield, the rest of the Dragoons broke cover. Fraser's Lance was running right flank guard to the main strike force of Stane's Company and the Light Company. Half a klick away to the south, Captain Waller led the jump-capable 'Mechs of Yukinov's Battalion to oppose the Feds' rear guard.

Stane's Company had little trouble swarming past the few 'Mechs and tanks that had fallen back to intercept them. Dechan spotted one Davion BattleMech and three or four tanks smoking on the field, all bearing the naked, white-haired sorceress insignia of the White Witches. The survivors recoiled on their own forces, which were themselves being pressed by Uchimaya's Company.

"Easy as falling down, boss," said Johansson, commenting on the lack of opposition Fraser's Lance met in their dash to the highway.

Dechan ignored him as he ignored the futile small-arms fire from the troops with the trucks. He was too busy relaying Laskowski's orders to direct the fire of his lance in support of Stane's Company. Fraser's Lance and the rest of Light Company provided cover while Stane's 'Mechs ripped open the trucks. They were looking for crates marked with the black bird symbol, which the Kurita spy had said would signal the components of the loot they sought.

"Company coming," Dechan warned the Captain as he spotted a lance of Witches preparing to mount a spoiling attack.

While Stane's troops continued loading up, the Light Company sent the Davion mercs reeling back with a storm of missiles and energy beams. Then Stane called the order to scoot over the taccomm. In seconds, the Dragoon 'Mechs had deserted the highway.

As his lance headed away from the road, Dechan looked back to confirm that the rest of the Dragoon raiding force had cleared the Davion battleline. As near as he could tell, everything was aces. Stane's Company and the rest of Light Company were covering ground in good order, with Stane herself carrying the biggest of the crates marked with black bird symbols. Waller was headed up the highway; apparently, they had never had to engage the Davion rear guard. In the northeast, Chan's team was conducting a fighting retreat toward the Shaw.

"Caught 'em with their pants down," Johansson crowed, referring to several of the Davion heavies that had positioned themselves across the Dragoons' presumed path of retreat. They were caught out of range when the fast-moving raiders continued across the highway instead of retreating back to the woods.

"Wishful thinking, kid," Dominguez said, deliberately misconstruing Johansson's reference. "Those Witches aren't interested in green meat. They only take veterans."

The Davion machines had yet to mount any serious pursuit by the time Fraser's Lance reached the edge of the Shaw. Dechan cut off the banter between his lancemates as he thundered toward the rim.

"O.K., guys! Let's go!" Dechan triggered a burst from his *Hawk*'s jets and launched his machine out over the void. Johansson's *Javelin* rocketed past him, the lighter 'Mech almost twice as fast in the air as the *Hawk*. The rest of the lance followed.

When the *Javelin* neared the ground, it became trapped in a glittering web of energy beams. Armor melted and flowed as unimaginable energies struck. The staccato roar of a heavy autocannon beat a macabre tune to which the light 'Mech jerked in rhythm. Even a novice knew when a BattleMech had taken all it could. Johansson punched out.

It might have been an accident, or it might have been malevolent intent—the ejector seat's path intersected with a charged particle beam. Structural metal and fragile flesh vaporized under the blue lightning, and the seat's fuel flashed to explosion in the sudden heat.

"Erik!" Dechan shouted uselessly.

To avoid the same fate, Dechan continued his jump, making random movements all the while in an attempt to break targeting locks. Smoking from hits by hostile energy beams, the *Shadow Hawk* struck ground with a violent jolt. The 'Mech's autocannon almost snagged the machine to a halt before it tore loose from its housing and let the *Hawk* continue on. Dechan headed for cover before he dared check the source of the lethal assault on Johansson.

In the meantime, the hostiles had begun to direct their fire on the new targets drifting down into the valley. Dechan watched far too many take serious damage from the fusillade. With the enemy's attention diverted, he risked popping his 'Mech up for a look at the unknown assailants.

At least a full company of BattleMechs was advancing down the riverbed toward his position. They were not Witches—that was clear from their markings. Each 'Mech prominently displayed a yellow disk with a black figure. Dechan focused his optics on the leading *Centurion* and brought up the magnification.

The yellow disk carried the black silhouette of a prancing

stallion, which Dechan instantly recognized as the unit badge of the Eridani Light Horse. The Horsemen were the only serious contenders to the Dragoons' title as the most elite mercs in the Sphere. They were tough and tricky.

Dechan knew that if things were bad before, they were now about to get very messy.

23

Ryuken Field Camp, Barlow's End
Draconis March, Federated Suns
3 October 3026

The Ryuken command hut was hot and the air stale, for it did not enjoy the air conditioning that Alpha Regiment's fusion-powered mobile headquarters vehicle boasted. The hut also lacked the MHQ's computer and holographic display facilities.

Nonetheless, for the two days of skirmishing leading up to the diversionary attack on the Achernar facility and the ambush of the Davion transport column, *Tai-sa* Elijah Satoh had been directing the Ryuken from the prefabricated structure. Upon taking command, Satoh had refused to enter the Dragoon MHQ and had ordered the hut erected as a sign that he, in Lord Kurita's name, was in charge.

Michi Noketsuna stood next to the commtech monitoring the radio band linking the commanders to the ambush team. Prior to the attack, radio traffic had been kept to an absolute minimum to avoid detection. Dragoon Major Chan had broadcast the attack command to headquarters as well as to his troops, signaling that the ambush had begun. Since then, traffic had been erratic and not very informative. But that was understandable because it required so much attention to coordinate the raid. He checked the time. Soon, Chan should be transmitting confirmation that the raiders had achieved their objective and were heading for the Shaw River valley.

Michi looked across the hut at *Tai-sa* Satoh. The man's uniform was pristine, his motions fastidious, and his disdain for the junior officers readily apparent. He was not a man to inspire warriors. Not like Minobu-*sensei,* Buddha care for him!

Days had passed since Michi had watched the MedTechs pry Minobu's battered body from the wreckage of the skimmer and load him onto a hovercraft bound for one of the DropShips' medical facilities. Minobu had been alive then, but the chief medic had seemed dubious about his continued survival. There had been no word on Minobu's condition since. Akuma, who had gone along on the hovercraft, had refused all of Michi's calls. Instead, he had sent Satoh and left the planet on the DropShip that carried Minobu away.

Tai-sa Satoh arrived the morning after the accident. His observer's commission from Warlord Samsonov contained a clause allowing him to step in as commander of the Ryuken in the absence of a senior officer in the chain of command, which he had done. He also carried Akuma's proxy as Liaison Officer. In an address to the Ryuken officers, Satoh spoke of the good fortune for House Kurita that he, an experienced officer of command rank, was on hand to step into the gap when an accident had claimed the Ryuken commander.

"Claimed Minobu," the man had said. As though Minobu were already dead! Michi found Satoh's presumption infuriating. Minobu-*sensei* would not die. He was too great a warrior to die in an accident.

Regardless of his concerns, Michi was chained to the present. His loyalty to House Kurita bound him to serve under Satoh, much as he wanted to follow Minobu, to stay by his side.

A loud voice near the center of the hut caught Michi's attention. It was Dragoon Colonel Jamison approaching Satoh about his worries. "Look, the ambush has come off. It's time to give our people some cover."

"*Your* people, Colonel," Satoh corrected punctiliously. "The Achernar Proving Grounds are not yet invested. Until then, your 'Mechs are to continue to participate in this portion of the operation. It is all in the master plan."

"At least send your light 'Mechs down to cut the highway across the dam."

"Not possible at this time, Colonel. They will go when the Achernar facility is isolated. The timing of all phases is specified in the plan."

"Plan! Plan!" Jamison shouted. He set his jaw and breathed noisily through distended nostrils. "The plan doesn't call for unnecessary deaths. If you stick to that piece of paper, you'll be killing people."

"There are always deaths in battle, Colonel. Once we've encircled the Achernar facility, we will proceed to the next phase of the plan."

"Then you'd better do your part. Zeta has already taken its objectives, according to the *plan*. It's your troops that haven't come through."

"I am aware of that, Colonel." A hint of annoyance crept into Satoh's voice and one corner of his mouth dipped into a petulant frown. "The Ryuken has run into unexpected resistance. A Davion mercenary unit, previously unanticipated, has appeared in the city. There will be a slight delay in completing the encirclement."

That was too much for Jamison. He threw down his stylus and turned his back on Satoh. The Kuritan shrugged off the Dragoon's gesture and went back to reviewing reports from the Ryuken officers and comparing them to the maps spread on the center table.

Michi took advantage of Satoh's preoccupation to catch Jamison's eye. When he had the Dragoon's attention, he pointed to the commstation, then to his own ear, and finally at Jamison. The Colonel nodded and moved to the commdeck the Dragoons had set up to relay data from Alpha Regiment's MHQ. Jamison picked up a headset to listen, but kept his eyes on Satoh.

Once he was assured that the Dragoon was being brought up to date, Michi gave Satoh the word that the ambushers had themselves been ambushed by the Eridani Light Horse. The *Tai-sa*'s face was impassive as Michi relayed the request for support from the beleaguered Dragoons. When Michi finished his report, Satoh acknowledged the news with a curt nod. Dismissing *Tai-i* Noketsuna with a wave of his hand, he returned to study the maps.

Jamison tossed down the headset and stormed up to Satoh. "Wasn't word from the Shaw enough to get you moving? My people tell me that it's the Eridani Light Horse that's been holding up things in Landova as well."

"Yes, Colonel," Satoh said in a bored voice. "I believe that was the identification from the field."

"And do you know their strength?"

"Not exactly, Colonel." Satoh paused to collect a flimsy and peer at it carefully. "Battlefield intelligence reports in excess of two companies in the city."

"Two companies! Unity, man! That means there's more than a battalion of Horsemen out there! This changes everything. Give up on this sham attack in Landova and pull out! We've got to regroup our forces until we know what we're facing."

"No." Satoh's visage was grim and unmoved, a rock to Jamison's storm waves.

"I'm not going to wait until they hand us our heads," Jamison warned.

"Colonel, I would think very carefully before taking action in defiance of the plan approved by your PSL officer, the Coordinator's representative. Consider your contract."

Jamison pulled himself to full height, towering over the man he faced. In a hard-edged voice, he said, "The contract requires us to fulfill our part in any approved plan. Zeta Battalion has fulfilled its objectives in that approved plan. To. The. Letter."

Jamison turned on his heel and signaled the other Dragoon officers in the hut. They dropped what they were doing and followed him out. The last to go pulled the commdeck behind him, not bothering to close the door.

Satoh stood stiffly, arms at his side, watching them go. When a Kurita guard closed the door, Satoh turned to Michi.

"*Tai-i* Noketsuna, record that the Wolf's Dragoons commander-on-planet has abandoned his post. This hour. This date."

"*Hai, Tai-sa,*" Michi acknowledged.

Duty compelled Michi to do as he was ordered, and Minobu had taught him that duty was all to a samurai.

Jamison's evaluation of the situation made sense. Satoh's rigid adherence to the plan went against the principles that Minobu held for the Ryuken. Things would have been different if he had been here. But Minobu was not here. Satoh was. Michi's stomach churned as he did what he was told.

24

Shaw River Valley, Barlow's End
Draconis March, Federated Suns
3 October 3026

"Dom, watch the left!" Dechan Fraser called, while himself firing on a *Commando* that had broken cover to close for a missile volley. His *Shadow Hawk*'s Martell laser grazed the Eridani 'Mech. Though Dechan could see no real damage, the enemy Jock scurried his machine back for cover.

Heeding Fraser's call, Dominguez pounded 90mm shells and laser fire into a pair of hostiles trying to advance in the shadow of the embankment.

The retreat up the river valley had been underway for the better part of an hour. The Light Company and Captain Stane's people had been leapfrogging each other, by turn firing then running. Having found some cover, Light Company was providing covering fire for Stane's unit.

Early on, Captain Laskowski's 'Mech had gone down when its leg collapsed. With the Eridani 'Mechs pressing forward, Dechan had been forced to abandon the Captain or lose the company. If the Captain survived, she could surely be ransomed from the Horsemen. In the meantime, Dechan was in charge of the company.

"Yo, Fraser!" Sergeant Tennler called over the taccomm. "Where's the help?"

"How the hell should I know? Ask Major Chan. He's in charge of this operation."

"Tried to, sweetheart. Comm channel's full of static."

"Great." Dechan hoped that didn't mean that Chan and the rest of the Dragoons had gotten caught. He tried to tell himself that it was just the Unity-forsaken rocks eating the comm frequencies.

The Horsemen were pressing hard and not giving him much time to worry about the others. Dechan recognized the pattern. The Eridani 'Mechs stepped up the pressure just before they got support from the high ground along the banks of the dry river bed, which meant that the White Witches, trailing along the south bank, had caught up again. He looked up. Sure enough, the pale blue *Zeus* that had been spearheading the Witches all along appeared on the lip of the embankment.

"Cover, troops. Hostiles at two o'clock high!"

The *Zeus* and its companions concentrated on the easy prey of Stane's Company as the Dragoon 'Mechs hurried to reach the meager cover that the Light Company held. Fire poured down on the fleeing machines. Like its namesake, the *Zeus* hurled down thunder and lightning.

A full spread of missiles caught Stane's *Phoenix Hawk,* sending it crashing to the ground. The 'Mech hit hard and lay still. Stane's troops reacted instantly, closing in to cover their leader. Forgotten now were the crates they had been sent to acquire. Hurrying toward their fallen Captain, a *Griffin* and a *Wolverine* grabbed the *P-Hawk* and dragged it away while the rest of the company returned fire.

"Give 'em cover," Dechan called.

The Light Company responded with a blistering sheet of fire that drove the Horsemen back. All the 'Mechs on the embankment, except the *Zeus,* pulled back as well. The battered machines of Stane's Company made it to Fraser's position. Once its prey had gone to ground, even the *Zeus* pulled back rather than be the sole target for vengeful Dragoons.

Silence descended over the valley, giving both sides a respite and a chance to vent the crippling heat buildups incurred in the last furious exchange.

Dechan used the time to count up the surviving Dragoons.

The Light Company still had eight functional 'Mechs, while Captain Stane's company had nine, including the Captain's own. A check by one of Stane's troopers told Dechan that the Captain's 'Mech might still be capable of fighting, but she was out of it for the duration. That left sixteen battle-capable 'Mechs. No, seventeen. At some point, one of Captain Waller's men had become separated from his own company and had joined the group. Every machine had been mauled.

Dechan, who had dreamed of commanding a company, was now senior officer for two companies. Instead of a dream come true, however, this was a nightmare.

The BattleMechs of a unit could fight for some time before their numbers were appreciably reduced. Eventually, the cumulative damage would begin to tell. Machines would fall and men would die. The term Combat Loss Grouping came unbidden to Dechan's mind. He had learned the formulae used to calculate CLG in the academy. Those harsh mathematics stated that, given an even volume of fire, BattleMechs of the same weight class were likely to reach dysfunction at, for combat purposes, the same time. An unpleasant thought, but one he could not avoid, faced with the battered remnants of his two companies. They were not far from devastating losses among their lightest members.

The ammunition situation was even worse. Dechan knew his own SRM ammo bay had run dry, and a quick check with the others revealed that all were low on expendable ammunition. Some had only one or two rounds, which would soon reduce them to energy weapons. All in all, the balance sheet had too many zeroes on the bottom lines. If the battle went on much longer, they would be into red ink.

To make matters worse, the unit was out of contact with Major Chan's team and Captain Waller's Company. They were on their own.

"So, where's the help, Fraser? We're being slaughtered!" Tennler again.

"Unity! How should I know?" Dechan shouted into the taccomm. "Maybe they got caught by the Horsemen, too."

As soon as he had spoken, Dechan bit his lip. He was losing his cool. The other Jocks looked to him as the only officer left. Shouting wouldn't solve anything and could only make morale worse. When he felt calm enough, he said, "I think we're going to have to get out of this on our own."

"What about the loot?" asked a voice Dechan didn't recognize. It had come over Stane's Company's frequency.

"We could make another grab for it," Corporal Rand suggested halfheartedly.

"We could get our asses shot off, too," Tennler objected. "Why don't we just jet out of here and head for the D-Ships? The Feds will let us go if we leave them their toys."

"I don't think so," Dechan said. "Once we're back on the plains, we'll be an easy target for the Witches. Our CLG is too high, we'll be leaving bodies behind before we can clear their range. Besides, the Horsemen have enough jumpers to keep the pursuit hot."

"Why should they bother?" Tennler countered.

Corporal Dominguez cut in to answer her. "We're Dragoons. Right now we're easy meat. The Witches remember Quentin. They could use the rep of having swatted us. The Horsemen don't need the rep, but they're more trouble. They got pride. They got memories of Hoff, too. None of our friends out there are going to want to see us leave this party before they've had their fun."

"And since our real friends haven't shown up," Dechan interjected, "we're left with the emergency escape plan. We have to keep falling back along the riverbed. The river banks get lower to the west and the land rougher. When we get there, we can use the terrain as cover for our retreat without worrying about anybody targeting on our naked backsides."

There was some grumbling, but no one offered a better idea. Dechan had started to sort the survivors into short lances when missiles impacted near them. Two caught his *Hawk* and another one hit Donal Cameron's *Javelin.* Most shattered only the rocks above the 'Mechs, sending fragments clattering down on them.

Dechan looked up to see the *Zeus,* its arm swinging to track the target for its next volley. Other 'Mechs joined it in firing down on the startled Dragoons. The Witches had worked their way around behind the Dragoon position. From the height of the embankment, the Fed mercs had a clear field of fire down to the crouching 'Mechs.

Dragoons started down the riverbed, looking for better cover. Dechan stood his ground and tried for a target lock-on. He wanted to pump a few LRMs into their nemesis. Before his target reticule flashed green, the enemy 'Mech staggered back from the brink, its armor dissolving under heavy laser and PPC fire. The Witches pulled back.

Dechan didn't understand what was happening until a massive *BattleMaster* loomed up on the opposite bank. The 'Mech's glittering reflective coating dazzled his eyes, but not before he had seen the grinning wolf's-head.

"You guys need a hand?"

The *BattleMaster* continued to fire on the retreating Witches while its pilot spoke to Dechan. Then an *Awesome* appeared on the *Master*'s left and a *Stalker* rumbled up on the right. Zeta Battalion had arrived.

"What took you guys so long? We thought we were orphans."

"A little trouble with a hardheaded Snake." The frivolous words were delivered in a grim tone. "Hold it. Colonel Jamison wants to talk to you."

There was a delay while the pilot set up the relay.

"Who's commanding?" Jamison's gruff voice barked.

"Guess it's me, Colonel. Lieutenant Fraser, sir. I've got Light and Stane's Companies here, sir."

"What happened to Major Chan and the others?"

"They took off through other channels to try and draw off most of the Horsemen. We lost contact with them an hour ago. Captain Laskowski went down and is presumed captured. Captain Stane's with us, but she's unconscious."

"Unity!" Jamison was quiet for a moment. "Where's the prototype?"

"Down here on the riverbed, out in the open where it was dropped when Stane got hit." Dechan hesitated, then resolved to give the Colonel the full situation. "Nobody wants to go get it. It's a killing zone out there, and we're on the edge of a CLG. Even with cover from Zeta, we'd lose at least half our people in the attempt."

Dechan was cut out of the circuit while Jamison checked in with his subcommanders.

"I've got contact established with Chan and Uchimaya," Jamison announced as he cut Dechan back in. "They're thirty-five klicks down river, but Waller's unit is still unaccounted for. The situation stinks.

"Fraser, its time to cut our losses. Get ready to move out." The link stayed open while Jamison spoke to his Captain in the *BattleMaster*. "Lucas, blast that damnable piece of junk to atoms. If we can't get the prototype out, we won't leave it with the Feds. Then give cover for Dechan's troops to get out of there.

"We're going home. Let's hope we find Waller's people on the way."

"What about the Ryuken?" Dechan asked.

"They left you folks to the Feds, so we'll just return the favor."

25

Ryuken Field HQ, Barlow's End
Draconis March, Federated Suns
4 October 3026

"Kantel's Recon Lance reports that the Dragoon ambush force has joined Zeta Battalion and is continuing to move north toward the landing zone," Michi reported. *Tai-sa* Satoh only nodded.

Michi stood staring as the unresponsive *Tai-sa* remained slumped in his chair. Could he not understand what that meant? Most of the fighting force that had landed on Barlow's End was now retreating from battle. The Ryuken was in danger of being surrounded, especially if Federated forces broke off pursuit of the Dragoons and turned toward Landova. Davion troops were forcing the Ryuken out of the city. Before long, their advance forces would reach the command camp's perimeter.

Something exploded outside the command hut, followed by more detonations. Time had run out. The Davion forces had arrived. The guard 'Mechs fired in response to the assault.

Satoh started at the first noise, but then slumped into listlessness again. His lack of reaction set off a wave of alarm through the Kuritan Techs and troops manning the command post. With the sounds of battle growing ever nearer, a panic began.

Michi waited for Satoh to give orders for the defense of the camp, but others did not. *Tai-i* Wakabe, commander of the Headquarters Lance, ran to direct his MechWarriors; the rest scrambled in all directions. Some took it on themselves to grab weapons and join the support troops firing on the enemy. Others simply dispersed in terror, a few to temporary salvation and ultimate capture in the wilderness, while most merely ran into the arms of death. In moments, the hut was deserted except for Satoh, Michi, and a single commtech.

"The Davion forces are surrounding us," Michi said to his unresponsive superior. "We must pull back to the DropShips, *Tai-sa*."

Satoh slowly turned his head to look at Michi for a long moment, his eyes dull and face slack. Then he said, "It wasn't supposed to be like this. I was promised."

The *Tai-sa*'s comment seemed disconnected from the drastic situation at hand. Michi ground his teeth in anger at this poor excuse for a commander.

"Brace up, *Tai-sa,*" he exhorted. "We are not beaten yet. You must take command of your troops."

Michi caught the commtech looking nervously from him to the *Tai-sa*. The man had something to say, but he didn't know to whom to say it.

"Speak up, man," Michi snapped. "What is it?"

"A call from the commander of the Eridani Light Horse, sir. He wants us to lay down our arms and surrender."

"No surrender," Satoh mumbled.

Michi looked at him in disgust. A surrender refusal should be made with force, to impress with determination.

"The *Tai-sa* is right," Michi told the commtech. "We will not surrender. Tell the Eridani commander that we refuse his request."

"I can't, sir. All frequencies are being jammed."

"Then he really does not want us to surrender."

Michi glanced at Satoh to see how he took that news. The man was listlessly pawing through the maps, seemingly oblivious to what would be a death sentence for the Kurita forces on Barlow's End. If the Davions could not accept a surrender, no one could fault them for killing all the Kuritans they found. They would claim that any attempts to give up were mere tricks to get closer before attacking.

The end was in sight.

Michi turned to the commtech, "You can no longer serve here. Find a rifle and join the brave soldiers defending the camp."

"We must hold here," Satoh mumbled softly. "We must complete the plan . . . the plan . . . the plan will succeed."

The commtech had not moved, despite Michi's order. His face was a study in fear, his eyes begging salvation from the young officer.

"You have an order, soldier," Michi said harshly. "Now move!"

The man almost ran into the door in his haste to leave. Michi watched Satoh as the *Tai-sa* shuffled through his maps—maps that were hours out of date. Satoh was lost in his own mind. Unnerved by the disaster unfolding around him, he began to give orders to subordinates who had been reported killed or captured in the fighting with the Davion forces.

Satoh's failure of will and his retreat from reality betrayed the men under his command, his last order condemning each of them to a useless death. Minobu's carefully nurtured troops would be wasted, thrown away uselessly.

This could not be considered good service to Lord Kurita, Michi decided. His face hardened into a grim mask as he saw what needed to be done.

Against the roar of the battle outside, the sound of a single pistol shot was lost.

26

Office of the Commander, Galeden City, Galedon V
Galedon Military District, Draconis Combine
2 November 3026

"Warlord, the ComStar Precentor of Galedon requests an audience."

The aide stood at rigid attention, his right fist over his heart in the formal Kurita military salute. Speaking to Jerry Akuma, Samsonov ignored the aide. "That is an interesting reversal. I usually have to visit with a battalion at my back to get a moment of the Precentor's precious time. What do you make of it?"

"Perhaps the venerable Precentor Phud is motivated by something more impressive than three dozen BattleMechs."

Samsonov coughed a rough laugh. "There is little more persuasive than that, unless it is more 'Mechs."

"Even ComStar Planetary Coordinators are men, Warlord," Akuma said, face lit with a knowing smile. "Most men find self-interest to be a powerful motivator. Perhaps our Precentor desires a favor."

"You may be right. If he wanted to make trouble, he would have barged past anybody in his way, wailing about the sanctity of his office. He must want something." Samsonov thrust out his lower jaw and stroked it with his hand. "Whatever it is, it'll cost him. Let him start with a wait."

Samsonov's eyes speared the aide. "Bring the Precentor here in an hour."

"*Hai,* Warlord."

Exactly an hour later, the Precentor was ushered into the Warlord's office, but the man who walked through the door that Akuma held open was not Jhi To Phud.

The formal robes of office swayed around a man taller and thinner than the fat old bureaucrat they had dealt with in the past. Light gleamed from the expensive fabrics and ornaments the man wore, as well as from his bald head. The passage of many years was evident on his face, but the new Precentor's firm step gave no sign that advanced age had brought him infirmity. His motions were those of one assured of his own dignity and power. He approached the Warlord's heavy teak desk, bowed, and said, "The blessings of the Sainted Blake be upon you, my son."

Samsonov gave the man a cold stare. The unannounced change in Precentors was clearly an attempt to discomfit him. Two could play that game, he decided. Rather than reply to his visitor, the Warlord indicated a chair with a wave of his hand. The Precentor showed no outrage at this latest petty insult. He sat where indicated and said no more.

Silence stretched, each man waiting for the other to buckle under the tension. Curiosity piqued and temper rising, it was Samsonov who broke the silence. Smiling coldly, he said, "To what do I owe the honor of your visit, Precentor?"

"The honor is mine, Warlord. I regret to inform you that Precentor Phud has been called to other duties." The Precentor paused for a moment, a look of formal sadness on his face. "He had reported to the First Circuit that his relationship with you was smooth and beneficial to all concerned. That is a pattern I believe to be worth preserving.

"I am Alexandre Kalafon, his replacement. I have come to establish my credentials. All the proper documents are contained in the weekly message pouch that my secretary is holding in the outer office."

"Surely you have another reason for your visit?"

The Precentor smiled blandly at what they both knew was a statement of the obvious.

"Is this man to be present?" Kalafon said. His eyes never

left Samsonov and he made no motion, but there was no doubt he was referring to Akuma, who still lounged near the door.

"Certainly. He has earned my trust many times over in loyal and discreet service."

"As you wish, Warlord. I am sure you are a good judge of your men. One who enjoys your trust would never need to fear the punishments House Kurita reserves for those who betray its secrets." On that ominous note, the Precentor began to speak of the rigors of his journey to Galedon and his pleasure at the mild weather that met his arrival.

Samsonov knew that the man was filling the air with nonsense in the approved Kurita fashion of chitchat before business. Samsonov also knew that the first to get to business lost face, according to Kurita custom. It was another of the nuisances he faced every day. Unlike many in the Combine's power structure, he did not feel himself bound by formal ritual and notions of honor. Such things were only of use to him when they could advance his cause or trip up a rival. The Precentor was not of House Kurita and he *was* annoying. The sooner the man was gone the better.

"You must be a very busy man, Precentor," Samsonov interrupted. "As am I. Let us dispense with the formalities and speak as old friends do, without preamble and going directly to the business at hand." The Warlord leaned forward and said earnestly, "What do you want?"

"It shall be as you wish, Warlord," Kalafon agreed.

Samsonov could detect no sign that the Precentor was disturbed by the Warlord's breach of etiquette. Perhaps this was a man with whom one could do business.

"I fear that you misunderstand the purpose of my visit," Kalafon continued placidly. "I want nothing from you. Rather, I have something to offer to you." He paused and smiled benignly. "I have by chance come into possession of information that may be of value to certain of your current undertakings."

Samsonov's suspicions were immediately roused. What did this old man know about his "undertakings?" The Warlord's eyes narrowed. "What kind of information?"

"Let me tell you about a soldier. A MechWarrior by the name of Fadre Singh."

"I'm not in the habit of buying soldiers, Precentor," Samsonov snapped. "I thought you had information."

"MechWarrior Singh is a most interesting fellow, Warlord. Do you know his recent history?"

"No," Samsonov grunted in irritation. The Precentor was not responding to intimidation and seemed determined to run the conversation his own way. So much for him being a likely business partner. The sooner the old man finished with his prepared babble, the sooner he would leave. "I am sure you can tell me all about it."

"To some degree I can," Kalafon replied, his tone still placid. "Singh's most recent success was with Wolf's Dragoons. He produced a brilliant performance in the Hoff raid of 3023—one worthy of a Kurita samurai. I am told that he led a charge from which his superior quailed and thus turned the tide of the battle. The raid on Hoff ended well for the Combine, did it not?"

Samsonov was silent. He let Kalafon take the silence as assent and confirmation of his sources.

The Precentor continued, "Alas, the unfortunate Singh was ill-treated. The embarrassment he had created for his commander seemed to weigh more heavily than his military success. The jealous officer had poor Singh disgraced and dismissed from the unit.

"His next assignment was a lonely outpost on Misery. It is a bleak world, cold and unforgiving over most of the continents, but hot and vile in the active volcanic zones. It was a virtual exile, totally unsuited to a hero.

"On Misery, he met a fellow MechWarrior. A mercenary, I think. She was sympathetic and greatly soothed his mind. It was from this wandering samaritan that I learned of the unfortunate Singh's plight."

Kalafon stopped, waiting.

Samsonov took time to consider just how a disaffected Dragoon could be useful. This was bait, he decided. Still, a smart fish can steal the bait and leave the hook untouched. "So, this Singh is unhappy with the Dragoons," he said.

"That is what I have been given to understand," Kalafon replied noncommittally.

"Why should I be interested?"

"Ah, of course. You do not buy soldiers. Forgive my failing memory. There was something else.

"Once of a long, dark night on Misery, MechWarrior Singh had a lengthy talk with his friend. In the course of it, he mentioned something to this lady, something he called the Hegira Plan. He claimed that this plan involved a full-scale exodus of Wolf's Dragoons from Kurita space. Would that be of any interest to you, Warlord?"

"That is a foolish question and you are not a fool, Precentor. What's the price?"

"Do not speak of price, Warlord." Kalafon spread his hands in a gesture of openness. A smile emphasized the wrinkles in his face. "I cannot sell you anything. I merely offer a gift out of good will."

"Good will is maintained through further good will, isn't it?" Samsonov said, staring into Kalafon's dark eyes, which shone with cool and calculating intelligence. *There is a dangerous man behind this well-mannered facade,* Samsonov told himself. Caution and circumspection would be required.

"I am pleased to see that you are as wise as I have been told, Warlord."

"Wisdom is slow in coming sometimes," Samsonov said, joining the game of politeness and euphemism. "You must let me meditate on this MechWarrior's sad story. Perhaps I can find a way to ease his burden."

"The Blessed Blake looks kindly on generosity." Kalafon rose. "I shall leave you now, Warlord. There is much to be put in order at our compound. You may, of course, reach me there. The blessings of Blake, my son."

With that formality, the Precentor moved toward the door, which Akuma opened for him. The ComStar official strode past Akuma, ignoring the Sworder's open stare.

"A most interesting man, Warlord," Akuma offered. "He shall be much more entertaining than Phud."

"More dangerous, too."

"That's what will make it interesting."

Samsonov searched his aide's face and found nothing but confidence. "You'll stick your hand into the fire too long someday, Akuma."

Akuma's eyes glittered. "I assure you that I am always careful when I play with fire."

Akuma's words set Samsonov to considering what he knew really of his aide. The man had first come to his attention after he'd requested a transfer into the Eighth Sword of Light Regiment. There had been a rumor of reprisals being planned against the young officer because of his small part in the disgrace of a commanding officer. Normally, that would mark him as a dangerous subordinate, but the ISF had assured Samsonov of Akuma's devotion to the Combine. They attributed the problem to Akuma's rejection of the hard-line code of *bushido*. Now, that was an attitude Samsonov understood. He considered that outmoded code and its devotees to be so many nuisances. They got in the way of business. If Akuma shared that attitude, a man who understood business could be useful.

Besides, Akuma had disgraced one of Warlord Yorioshi's officers, and the disgrace of the subordinate had reflected on the superior. Samsonov had decided to reward Akuma for his inadvertent aid. He had approved the transfer to the Eighth Sword of Light.

Once on Galedon, the Sworder had shown traits that reminded Samsonov of himself in younger days. Akuma was efficient, smart, and ambitious, and his only scruple was a sense of debt. He repaid those who touched his life, for good or ill. Such a man is a boon to one who has earned his gratitude, and so the Warlord arranged for Akuma to be grateful to him.

That done, the Warlord promoted Akuma and made him an aide. A fortunate decision, for Akuma served well as an advisor and agent. He was loyal and productive.

Yet, the glitter in Akuma's eyes worried the Warlord. A strong hatred fueled that fire, and it hinted at fanaticism. Samsonov believed that a fanatic was a dangerous man. In his obsession, a fanatic might forget the importance of anything else. Perhaps it was time to abandon this pawn. It would all depend on how well Akuma still responded to the demands on him. If he had stopped thinking clearly, he would be a liability. "What do think about this Hegira Plan?" Samsonov asked. "Is is real? Can we use it?"

"Let us leave aside the question of the reliability of the Precentor's source," Akuma began, almost pedantically. "If it is an escape plan, we would do well to learn its details.

Were the Dragoons to learn of our arrangements, they might decide to leave. Knowing where they would go could be invaluable."

"And if they don't go, worthless."

"Of course," Akuma agreed. "Did not the Coordinator ask for 'insurance' against just such an eventuality?"

"He did." Caught up in his concerns over the mercenaries, it did not occur to Samsonov to wonder how Akuma knew what the Coordinator wanted. "How do relations with your charges progress?"

"As per your orders, Warlord. I am pursuing all avenues of legal harassment open to me. The Dragoon position steadily weakens. Battle losses rise and certain members of their forces have been left behind on enemy planets, missing in action. Regrettably, timetables have often forced the abandonment of those unfortunates on enemy planets before a proper search could be performed. It is most unpopular with the Dragoons. I have regularly expressed my condolences, but in each action, I have been forced to point out that the orders to depart were completely legal, by contract. Thus, the Dragoons were required to obey, by contract. Some of these unlucky warriors have been subsequently recovered by the Dragoons, but such rescues are expensive.

"They are less and less able to afford the expense because they are having monetary concerns. Though their pay is supplied strictly according to contract, revenues from An Ting are, regrettably, down. There seems to be little interest in the Combine marketplace for products from that planet. Then, too, there is the high cost of supplies. It is most distressing, but unavoidable because of the economic pressures our enemies place on the Combine. I have offered the Dragoons military sources, but they seem to prefer other suppliers. They may soon find that certain vital supplies have become totally unavailable from conventional sources beyond our borders. I will have warned them. Other plans, too, are coming along as well."

"Such as?" Samsonov prompted.

"Such as getting their staunchest defender removed from the field."

Akuma could mean only one man. Since joining the Warlord's staff, the Sworder had shown an unreasonable, but not unreasoning, hatred for Tetsuhara. Had the cold calculator succumbed to a hot-blooded impulse? "Have you assassinated Tetsuhara?"

"Assassinated Tetsuhara?" Akuma repeated indignantly. "I am no crude killer."

No, Samsonov thought, *not crude.*

"I was about to inform you before the Precentor arrived," Akuma said, his calm restored. "One of your most loyal officers, Elijah Satoh, now commands the Ryuken. It seems *Tai-sa* Tetsuhara was involved in a skimmer accident."

"Killed?"

"Badly injured only . . . unfortunately. The Brotherhood physician aboard the Dropship was very loyal to his professional code of ethics," Akuma said. One corner of his mouth twitched, as though in irritation at some annoying memory. "The physician was very skilled, and Tetsuhara has survived. He may be able to return to duty after his convalescence.

"The Barlow's End operation was not compromised, however. Satoh was left with an excellent plan, which he should be able to execute and so return with glory. Even a healthy Tetsuhara will be hard pressed to oust a hero," Akuma concluded.

"Let us hope you are right. Satoh is unimaginative but devoted. Through him, I can control the Ryuken. They will be a lever in the days to come. The Dragon's Sword might even provide me with a counter to the Dragon's Shadows, should that become necessary."

Akuma sat back in satisfaction, watching the Warlord take in the success and consider the possibilities. Samsonov was a rising star that could be directed to carry a clever man quite high. Better than anyone. Akuma knew himself to be a clever man.

After a tactful interval, he reminded the Warlord of the waiting message pouch, which should contain dispatches on the outcome of the Barlow's End raid.

"The timing would be right," Samsonov agreed, opening a panel on his desk to access the computer console within. As the screen rose from its recess, the Warlord keyed in his request for the appropriate message texts. "They are here," he said.

Amber light flickered over the Warlord's face as words scrolled over the screen. Akuma watched as the muscles of Samsonov's jaw twitched, his eyes going wide, his face reddening. Something had gone wrong.

"Betrayed!" The storm broke. "The spineless mercenaries ran from battle!"

Samsonov started to rant about the Dragoons, but Akuma didn't listen. He swiveled the screen to face himself and read the text. A retreat by the mercenaries was the last thing he had anticipated. Frackencrack! It was hard to think about what all this meant with the fat old fool raving. The man really had little self-control, Akuma thought, much like himself a few years ago. At least Samsonov wasn't pointing the finger at Akuma's actions. He would have to calm the Warlord before they could deal with this disaster.

An hour later, Samsonov sat with hands clasped before him on the desk. His rage had subsided for the moment, but it still burned below the surface. "Wolf's Dragoons have embarrassed and insulted me too many times," he said. "I will see them destroyed."

Akuma drew back from the Warlord's coldly spoken resolution. He too wanted the Dragoons destroyed, but to him, it was not personal. Their destruction was a way to hurt Tetsuhara. Such a destruction was a thing to be carefully planned. It was a step-by-step process. A thousand little details orchestrated until there was no escape. Small bits might go awry, but the gathering momentum had to be nursed until nothing could stop it. Rash actions taken in a fit of anger were more likely to go wrong and upset the plan. Such actions could be as dangerous to the destroyer as to his target. If Samsonov did something foolish, the two of them could get "invited onward." Akuma had no intention of slitting his own belly. He sought to caution Samsonov. "Is that wise without the Coordinator's leave?"

"No," the Warlord said. "No, it isn't."

A rare smile of pleasure creased Samsonov's face. Akuma hoped that it signified the dawn of a brilliant plan and not simply the anticipation of bloodletting. "We'll just have to be subtle about it." He laughed harshly. "Call the Precentor back."

Though Akuma feared that he had lost control of the Warlord, he had no choice but continue to do his bidding.

27

Royal Court, Avalon City, New Avalon
Crucis March, Federated Suns
15 November 3026

Quintus Allard passed the guards at the entrance to the private wing of the palace, giving them no more than a friendly greeting. The old man and the worn, slightly oversized business suit he habitually wore were well-known to the Royal Guard, who served Prince Hanse in his palace in Avalon City. The guards sent word ahead to the Prince that his Minister of Intelligence, Information, and Operations had arrived.

As the heavy door to the private audience chamber slid open, Hanse Davion looked up at his visitor with a smile of welcome. "Special delivery, Quintus? Not bad news, I hope."

"I am not sure whether it is news at all, my Prince." Allard drew a green and gold holodisk from his pocket and held it up.

Hanse was puzzled. If Quintus Allard wasn't sure, circumstances must be confusing, indeed.

"It's not that the circumstances are confusing," Allard continued, as though reading the Prince's mind. "What confuses me is the motivation that urges your beloved brother-in-law to send this message. I am wondering what he hopes to gain."

"Well, you've got me wondering as well. Let's see this message."

Allard nodded and placed the disk in a slot on the viewer. The lights dimmed as the viewscreen came to life. The first image was that of Michael Hasek-Davion's personal heraldry, a golden lion against a green field. The artwork then dissolved into an image of Michael seated at his desk. The holotech had carefully composed the shot to place the lion's eyes where Michael's own green ones would appear. The conceit identifying Michael with the noble beast was marred by the restlessness in the real eyes. The voice that came from the speaker was a better match. It was a politician's voice, deep and sonorous.

"Salutations, brother. I hope that these greetings from Marie and myself find you well. I know what a tiresome job it is to rule the Federated Suns, and so I will take little of your time."

Hanse and Allard exchanged glances at that. Both knew how quickly Michael would grab that "tiresome job" if he could. In the holofilm, the Duke of New Syrtis twitched his long braid of black hair off the shoulder of his spotless uniform. "I have recently come into a bit of information that might interest you," he said.

Michael flicked his hand at someone out of the recorder's view. The holo image changed, flattening to an ordinary black and white video. The scene thus revealed was a darkened room, lit fitfully by a flickering blue glow-globe on the center of a table. A small, rumpled man sat at that table, the light throwing strange shadows across his sharp features. The man's shifty gaze ran about the room before focusing on something or someone not in the picture.

The sparse furnishings and grubby walls were little help in identifying its location. Alcohol advertisements proclaimed it as belonging to a drinking establishment, and so it was probably the back room of a seedy bar that could have been almost anywhere in the Inner Sphere.

Michael's voice explained. "My agent intercepted this on Le Blanc. It was addressed to a certain Sten Weller, a notorious freelance hunter. I believe it was data intended to accompany an invitation to partake in some work."

The Duke stopped talking just as the man on the screen

began to speak. "I told you in the 'gram. Wuz her, all right. Couldna been anybody else. They wuz even black 'Mechs.

"Wents out to Kempis town myself, I did. After things was quiet. Talked to a guy'd seen her. Nailed her phiz and red hair. Even told me 'bout that fancy iron she carries. Gots the word on her *Hammer* from another rube.

"They wuz real professional-like. I seen the Fed 'Mech arm they left ta throw the trail. They wuz in and out real quick. Gots what they wanted and cleaned them Snakes out real good. Real pros. It all ties up. Had to be them.

"Done good work for ya. I did."

Another man came partially into view. The cyan light from the glow-globe reflected off a cuirass and vambraces heavy with compartments and protuberances. Though the man's head was in shadow, stray gleams revealed that he wore a helmet as well. The reedy snitch flinched as the armored man moved forward, hand outstretched. That hand opened to drop a wallet onto the table. The rat-faced man snatched it up as though afraid it would disappear. Then it did, into his shabby clothes.

"Lordy, man. It's good work. Like a real detective, I wuz."

"It had better be good cop, my well-paid friend." The armored man's voice was electronically modulated, indicating either that his helmet was sealed from the environment or that he had an expensive voice distorter to conceal his voice as the helmet concealed his face. "If it's a set-up, Billy, ain't no place you can hide from me."

"It's good cop. Honest. On my life." The man was plainly frightened of his associate.

"That's right." The cold voice made it a promise.

The scene dissolved, bringing Michael's face back to the screen.

"If you haven't already guessed, brother, the subject of that conversation is the notorious Black Widow, Natasha Kerensky. It seems that she and her ragtag collection of misfits and malcontents have been committing atrocities against House Kurita on the planet of New Mendham.

"As the little man said, they are real professionals. Professional killers, not soldiers.

"I know of your fascination with Wolf's Dragoons, and I

thought this might open your eyes to see past their glamour. They are little more than bandits, rogues from the Periphery. It's true that they are well-equipped in these days of hand-me-down 'Mechs and half-functional factories. No doubt they have plundered some forgotten waystation left over from General Kerensky's exodus.

"Well-equipped or not, they are mercenary scum hiding behind the carefully constructed lie of being professional soldiers. They are professional *looters,* working their way through the Sphere, and they should be crushed rather than courted.

"As you know, I have only the best interests of the Federated Suns and our own glorious House at heart. I thought that you should see this before your agents on Galatea conclude a deal that could affect our prestige.

"I said I would take little of your time, and so I will sign off, leaving you to consider this revealing information." Michael's face changed from earnest seriousness to his bland, everyday smile. "Farewell until we meet again, brother."

The holo faded and Allard brought the room lights back to their normal level.

Hanse was frowning. "Atrocities. That's not like the Natasha Kerensky I knew twenty years ago."

That Kerensky was twenty years younger and had not lost a lover to a Successor Lord's betrayal, Allard thought. *She could have changed.*

"I'll grant that she's bold and outspoken, but she's a showdown type. She's not a backstabber." In spite of his defense of Kerensky's character, Hanse found it necessary to ask, "Is the story true?"

"That's what confuses me," Allard confessed. "A Kurita supply convoy was looted and destroyed in Kempis on the date in question. Many civilian casualties occurred as well. There is no doubt that the atrocity occurred.

"The question of the identity of the perpetrators is open. The mercenary expeditionary force we dispatched to New Mendham reported no contact with the Black Widows, and my subordinates cannot reliably determine the location of the Widows during that time period. It is possible that Kerensky's company was on New Mendham and behaved as the witnesses report."

"Why is Michael sending us this tape now?"

"If the allegation is true, he is acting as any loyal Davion concerned for our honor."

"Michael, loyal?" Hanse laughed.

"As much as he wants what he thinks is due him, even Michael would not see the Federated Suns destroyed by her enemies," Allard reminded the Prince. "Whether the story is true or false, he may simply be a message boy, passing on things that the friends of his Liao friends wish us to hear."

"An intriguing possibility," Hanse said, his expression becoming thoughtful. "Despite my 'well-known fascination,' I have lost track of what Wolf and his people are up to these days. Weren't they in on that business on Barlow's End?"

"They were, my Prince. Battle intelligence reports that the raiding force was composed of the bulk of Alpha Regiment and Zeta Battalion, along with a substantial Kurita component."

"House troops? Was that some kind of response to Operation Galahad?"

"Reports indicate that the Kurita raid on Barlow's End was planned before we staged our war games."

"Still, they caught the Eridani Light Horse in transfer." Hanse tapped a stylus against his chin, considering the possibilities. "How much can they have learned?"

"Little, I think. The battle went badly for them. The Dragoons abandoned the Kurita House troops shortly after the Light Horse became involved. Presumably, they deemed it impossible to achieve the goals of their mission. That left the Kurita unit unsupported. After another day of fighting, the Kuritans pulled out, too.

"We took losses ourselves, mostly minor, though the only existing prototype of Professor McGuffin's jump stabilizer was destroyed. The professor is, of course, furious. I am sure Doctor Banzai will be distressed as well. He put so much work into the design.

"There was an unusual item in the after action report from the Light Horse, though. The Kuritans did retreat, but those House troops seem to have been fanatics. We found the Kurita Commander dead in the command camp with a sword in his hand. He had been shot in the back of the head. It was some kind of ritual killing, perhaps a variant form of *seppuku*."

Hanse shook his head, unable to understand a code that required a life for a simple military reversal. Enough lives were spent on the battlefield. "So you think that the Kuritans will be too busy piecing their units back together and placing the blame to understand the significance of the nature of our defenders?"

"I do," Allard replied. "Galahad's cover is most likely still safe from them. I think, however, that the Dragoon intelligence network may be a step ahead of the ISF."

"What do you mean?" Hanse asked suspiciously. "What have they been up to?"

"As you know, we have had agents recruiting mercenaries all over the Sphere, particularly on Galatea. The Dragoons also have an officer on that world who stays in touch with the market for mercenaries. Though still cool to our offers to jump contract, she has taken some interest in our hirings.

"Then there are the visits the Dragoon JumpShips have been making to some of our systems. Too many of those sites are our transfer lay-overs."

"Not fighting. Just checking up on us," Hanse observed, and Allard nodded agreement. "I don't think that is authorized surveillance. The Wolf is double-checking ISF intel. He's watching his rear."

A sly smile began to grow on Prince Davion's face. "Perhaps things are not so cozy between the Dragoons and my old friend Takashi. How long does their contract run?"

"Almost another year and a half," Allard answered promptly.

Hanse looked disappointed at that. It was a long time.

"What's going on inside the Dragoons?" the Prince asked. "Didn't we get an agent in there?"

"We tried, but the Dragoons rarely recruit from outside their own organization. They are almost a closed shop. The recent plan to infiltrate them has met no real success. Our agent posed as a potential recruit. We assumed that a MechWarrior with a new machine like the *Hatchetman* would interest the Dragoons because they always seemed so interested in new and unusual technology during their contracts with us and with House Steiner. We thought their commanders would be tempted enough by the chance to get their hands on a *Hatchetman* that they'd accept our agent."

Hanse snorted mildly and shook his head. "Sometimes I think that Wolf is more a fox than I am. They found a way to get our 'Mech without taking our agent, didn't they?"

"They did," Allard confirmed. "They offered our agent a trade, one of their special-model *Archer*s for his 'Mech. They also offered a slot in Carter's Chevaliers, a subcontracting mercenary unit. They said the position was 'for a trial period.' In order to preserve cover, our agent had no choice but to accept."

"Fortunes of war," Hanse said resignedly. Not every gambit could succeed. At least, this one wasn't a total failure. It might still bear fruit in the future. Until then, they must try something else. "With things getting a little tense on the other side of the border, maybe we can stir up the pot. Do we have any combat footage of the Dragoons pulling out on Barlow's End?"

It was Allard's turn to look puzzled. "Some."

"Have it edited to emphasize the timing of the Dragoon departure and to de-emphasize the strength of our forces. Then let a Kurita agent acquire the film. Maybe Takashi will help us out by turning on the Dragoons. They may not come to us, but at least they won't be working for him."

Allard accepted the order in silence. He started for the door, but before he reached it, Hanse called his name. The minister turned and made a fumbling catch of the small object the Prince tossed to him. It was the holodisk he had brought.

"While you're sending out packages, see if you can find an anonymous way to get that to Jaime Wolf. The Wolf is an honorable man. If there is some plot to discredit his people, he won't like it. He might even break his contract off short."

Hanse smiled at his own cleverness. No one had ever denied that he deserved his nickname of "the Fox."

28

Hoshon Mansion, Cerant, An Ting
Galedon Military District, Draconis Combine
24 November 3026

Morning sunlight slanted in from the garden, throwing rippling shadows over the wooden floor. The open panels allowed the cool air to move through the room in a gentle breeze, but Minobu did not feel the chill. He was absorbed in his painting, completing a delicate chrysanthemum on the black vase he held in his left hand. The sable sheen of the ceramic shape reflected the light in subtle and harmonious ways.

Minobu held up the vase and turned it in the light. Satisfied with his work, he placed it on the drying stand and cleaned his brush. He had just turned to face the inner door when the panel slid open to reveal Jaime Wolf standing there. Though the lintel was low, the mercenary did not need to duck as he crossed the threshold.

"Finally found time to visit the invalid?" Minobu said as the Dragoon came forward.

"Things have been a little hectic since Barlow's End," Jaime replied evenly, though the harsh note in his friend's voice surprised him.

"I expect they were." Minobu's days had not been busy, but they had been full of pain as his battered body gradually healed. The convalescence had been long and slow, empty of the support of friends. He had seen little even of Tomiko, for she had fled the room at first sight of his prosthetic arm and leg.

"Marisha is with Tomiko," Jaime offered.

"My wife will enjoy the company." *Perhaps now things will change,* Minobu thought. *Marisha may be able to help Tomiko accept the new reality of her husband.*

Jaime's visit might be a sign of the end of his estrangement as well. In the seven weeks since his accident, Minobu had felt deserted. Even Michi's return a week ago had brought no relief. The young *Tai-i* was distant and reserved, all business. Much about him seemed changed. It was as though he, rather than Minobu, had been injured on Barlow's End.

No, thought Minobu, caught in self pity. *Not Barlow's End—Minobu's end.*

"I was remiss in not thanking you for the report you sent concerning the action on Barlow's End," he said woodenly. "It was most enlightening."

"Don't pull this inscrutable samurai crap with me," Jaime said, annoyance flaring. "We've been friends for too long."

Now Minobu was taken aback. Lost in his own problems, he had failed to notice that Wolf was troubled, too. "When first we met, I knew you were perceptive, my friend. I did not know your perceptions would make you a pain in the butt."

A faint smile touched Minobu's face but it vanished with his attempt to stand. He swayed from the pain that shot through his leg. Shifting his weight onto his cane, he steadied himself. The knife-sharp pain subsided to an ache under the driving force of his will. "I have enough pains right now."

Annoyance struggled with sympathy on Wolf's face.

"I apologize for my lack of courtesy. Come, have some tea," Minobu said, gesturing with his free hand.

Minobu and Jaime moved out into the garden. Walking along the gravel paths, they passed miniature castles and carefully tended dwarf trees. As they reached the top of the bridge over the stream, Minobu halted.

"You have done what you could," he said, picking up the earlier thread of the conversation. "If I am disappointed with the Ryuken's performance on Barlow's End, I should not take it out on you."

"It was a bad break to have the Horsemen show up there. You couldn't have anticipated it. Problems like that can make even experienced units look bad." Wolf's comment told Minobu that Jaime also had concerns over the outcome of the ill-fated raid.

"Kelly says your people were doing just fine until Satoh got hold of them."

Satoh! Minobu frowned at the mention of that name. Samsonov's pawn had been incompetent and unthinking—a dangerous fool! Minobu mastered his passion and relaxed the muscles of his face. There were more suitable topics for polite conversation. He would not speak of that man and what he had allowed to happen on Barlow's End, not even to Jaime.

"How is Major Yukinov?"

"I got him the best available. He's been back to duty for a week, limping a little though. The myomer implant didn't set quite right."

Jaime's voice faltered as he realized that he had touched on a subject that was difficult for Minobu to face.

During the weeks in which he'd waited for his own surgery, Minobu had not seen Wolf. Kurita Brotherhood physicians had attended him and replaced the mangled arm and leg with artificial limbs. They assured him that he would be able to do everything almost as well as before the accident. The prostheses Minobu had received could not compare to the myomer substitution technology that Wolf had arranged for Yukinov, however. Minobu was grateful that he could still pilot a 'Mech, even if it was at reduced efficiency, but he couldn't help but feel some envy. Still, his *ki* would help to overcome any remaining disability.

Jaime tried to revive the conversation by turning to business. "Kelly's busy whipping Alpha back into shape. Already I'm hearing gripes that they had it easy with J.E. in charge. Kelly runs a much tighter operation and doesn't allow the latitude Jamison gives Zeta's hellions. Alpha will be back in action soon."

"Your losses were serious?"

"Serious enough," Jaime said. Just as in the old days on

Quentin, he offered no details, keeping his secrets. "We'll recover, though. We have our ways."

"Ah, yes. Your mysterious source of supplies and troops that lies out in the Periphery. The greatest of the Dragoon secrets."

Wolf stopped and stared up at his taller companion. "Look here, Minobu. What are you playing at with all this baiting?"

"Am I baiting you?"

"Unity! There you go again. I'm not one of your zen students to be answered with a question." Jaime shifted to his drill-field voice. "What's the game?"

"If it is a game, it is not frivolous," Minobu answered gravely. "There is tension, distance, between us today. I know my own concerns, but not yours. I do know you well enough to see that you're avoiding something unpleasant. Speak frankly."

Minobu and Jaime locked eyes for a moment. Without signaling any surrender, Jaime said, "Let's cut the games, then."

Minobu nodded.

"I came to talk to you about what's happening with the regiments," Jaime began. "This Akuma bastard is still making trouble every time I turn around. It just keeps getting worse. I've got officers calling for his head. We're headed for a flash point.

"I smell Samsonov's hand in it. He's certainly letting Akuma jerk us around. We've also heard that he's been dropping hints all over the Combine that the Dragoons are out of control. That we are too strong. That we are a threat to Combine security. *You* know better than that!

"I think they're going to try to break up the regiments again." Wolf's shoulders slumped. Having finally spoken of his problem, his energy seemed to ebb.

"Which you will never allow." Minobu put his hand to his head. It ached again as much as in the first week after the accident, but it could not be from his injuries. Those headaches had stopped a month ago. "Why have you come to me?"

"The Dragoons are threatened," Jaime answered softly.

"And you will do anything, even use up your friends, to protect them."

"Yes." There was no contrition in Wolf's voice.

Minobu spent a long time gazing out across the pond. Jaime stood silent at his side. Wolf's admission brought a new light into their relationship. Each knew that Minobu's response would affect their friendship irrevocably.

"What would you have me do?" Minobu asked.

"You understand our situation and you know that the Dragoons are giving the Combine good, honest service. Talk them out of it. Tell them the truth and uncover Samsonov's lies. You were appointed by the Coordinator himself. You've got weight. I'm asking you to use it."

"If I try to do as you ask, I can make no promises about results. And there are things I need to know." When Wolf frowned, he added, "I am not asking for your secrets. I need to know what you will accept. What is the limit?"

"Bottom line?"

"Yes."

Wolf wet his lips and drew a breath. "The bottom line is that each regiment must stay together. I won't have even one of them broken up, and I won't let the independent units be isolated from the rest. As long as we have An Ting, I'll keep up the rotations to the planet because I won't leave our civilians defenseless."

"I would not think of asking that." Neither man felt it appropriate to mention that others might request that very thing. Minobu looked out over the garden, weighing Jaime's words. "Your position is not unreasonable. Perhaps the Coordinator will listen."

"But you expect Samsonov will be hard to argue down."

"Yes. He is a Warlord. The failure on Barlow's End has given him reason to flex his muscle. The action of your troops there will be hard to deny."

"We won't deny it," Jaime said matter-of-factly. "We did what we had to do. I'll give you all the data I can—tapes, transcripts, sworn statements. Anyone with half a brain will see that we only did what had to be done.

"The Dragoon combat record is good, better even than most Sword of Light Regiments. We are valuable to the Combine. Takashi Kurita will surely see that my troops are worth more to him than satisfying some megalomaniac's ego."

Minobu studied Jaime's earnest, imploring expression. The Colonel was calling on Minobu's loyalty to a friend and comrade in adversity. That would be enough for many men, but Minobu was also bound by other chains. Because he had saved Jaime Wolf's life, he was responsible for Jaime's actions. Under all laws, Jaime, as a commander, was responsible for his troops. That meant Minobu was also responsible for their actions. If the Dragoons acted against the Combine, Minobu would be responsible. He could not allow the Dragoons to be forced into unjustified acts of rebellion.

"Very well, friend Jaime. I will try."

29

Hoshon Mansion, Cerant, An Ting
Galedon Military District, Draconis Combine
1 December 3026

Michi opened the door to Minobu's study, expecting to see his mentor at work, but the room was vacant. In one corner lay the shards of several shattered vases, their delicate shapes destroyed forever. Curious, he stepped into the room. Near the workstation, he found traces of blood.

Fearing the worst, Michi threw back the panels to the outside and burst onto the veranda of Hoshon Mansion. The garden was empty and quiet as well, its harmony undisturbed in the twilight.

If something had happened to Minobu, surely he would feel a disturbance here, Michi thought. He tried to focus his inner senses as Minobu had taught him. Yes, something had distorted the flow of energy over the ancient building. It was high, above the level of the walls.

Michi looked up at the corner tower. Minobu was standing on the third level, lit in the glory of the setting sun. His kimono flapped about him in the breeze, its motion contrasting with his stillness as its pale color contrasted with his black skin.

Michi's breath huffed out in relief. Minobu was safe.

He ran to the tower and mounted the inner stairway, his holstered laser pistol slapping against his leg as he climbed.

On the third level, a brazier was lit; smoke curled from charred pieces of paper to crawl along the ceiling, seeking escape. Michi ignored it and stepped out onto the balcony. He caught his breath before speaking. "I found blood in your study. Have you injured yourself?"

Minobu did not look at Michi. He continued to stare out over Cerant as he held up his right hand. A stark white cloth was wrapped around the palm. "It is nothing important."

Perhaps the cut was not important. Michi could tell that something else was. "You are disturbed. I felt it."

"Yes."

Michi waited for more, but Minobu did not seem inclined to offer it.

"What disturbs you, *sensei*?" he prompted. "Perhaps I can help?"

"What disturbs me is the news that the Ryuken is to expand," Minobu said, finally turning toward his aide. "Each of its companies is to form the cadre of a new unit. These units are each authorized to expand to regimental strength. It seems that the experiment is a success, despite the experience on Barlow's End."

"That is good news," Michi asserted. He did not understand. The success of Minobu's training program and the acceptance of the Ryuken concept should have brought him joy, not this dark mood. The folly of Satoh was being ignored and the genius of Minobu-*sensei* exalted. Why was he upset? Something was not right.

"Why, then, are you disturbed?"

Minobu continued to speak in a monotone, as though he had not been interrupted. "Assignments are to An Ting, Capra, Misery, Thestria, Delacruz, and Marlowe's Rift. Does that suggest anything to you?"

Michi thought about it. He knew of no connection among those six systems, except their proximity to the Federated Suns and their location within the Galedon Military District. That was too obvious and simple. Minobu had been receiving messengers from the Dragoons all week. Perhaps that was the connection. "The first four are all planets where the Dragoons are present. I do not see a connection between them and the other two systems."

"All are now garrison systems for Wolf's Dragoons. Alpha has been assigned to Delacruz, while Beta is to go to Marlowe's Rift. Increased Davion activity has been 'discovered' near those systems."

Now the assignments made sense to Michi. Each unit of the Ryuken was to share a garrison with a unit of the Dragoons. That was good. The Ryuken would complement the Dragoons, learn from them.

The riddle of Minobu's melancholy remained unsolved, though Michi was beginning to suspect the answer. Six regiments would be a formidable force under the command of a general. Loss of command must be the reason for Minobu's depression over this news. Michi forced himself to ask, "Are you to command the Ryuken?"

"There is to be no general for the Ryuken regiments. Each is directly answerable to Galedon. If our resident Warlord cannot control the Dragoons, he will control the Ryuken."

"Then you are to be retired." Michi tried to put the sympathy he felt into his voice.

Minobu did not notice. His voice was as distant and cool as it had been, neither accepting nor rejecting what was offered. "No. I am to command Ryuken-*ni* on Misery."

Second regiment? Why not first? The Ryuken was Minobu's creation, and he deserved the pride of place. "What of Ryuken-*ichi*?"

"Ryuken-*ichi* is based on An Ting under the command of *Chu-sa* Jerry Akuma, Professional Soldiery Liaison to Wolf's Dragoons."

Michi was shocked, both by the appointment and by Minobu's passive acceptance of it. "That is an insult. You cannot accept it."

"There are many things I cannot do. At this time, foremost among them is refusing to accept this. Warlord Samsonov has informed me that it is Lord Kurita's wish."

"At least Akuma has not been promoted to stand over you," Michi declared defiantly. "You don't have to follow his orders."

Minobu turned to look up at the stars beginning to appear in the sky. His voice was as distant as their cold presence. "My young friend, you still have much to learn."

30

Dragoon HQ, Farsund, Misery
Galedon Military District, Draconis Combine
8 April 3027

"At ease," Wolf said. "Congratulations on your promotion, Captain Fraser."

"Thank you, Colonel," the young MechWarrior replied, relaxing his stiff-backed stance. He wondered what was up. The Colonel didn't call in shiny new Captains just to pat them on the back. Was it possible that Dechan had finally risen high enough to be let in on some of the unit's secrets? Seven years now he had fought with the Dragoons and he still didn't know where, other than their DropShips, they called home.

"I expect you're wondering why you're here." Wolf said, ignoring the start his words gave Dechan. "I am putting together a special team for a fast strike. The team will include lances from all the regiments, people who are not used to working together. That's something you had some experience with last year on Barlow's End. Your group performed well there and again here on Misery.

"I'd like you and your lance on the team. But it's all volunteer . . ."

An all-volunteer mission was unusual. The grouping of units from all the regiments was even more so. "I don't understand, Colonel. What's the deal?"

"About the mission or the team?"

"Both, sir."

"The deal with the team is simple. I want somebody from each of the regiments on this operation as a statement to our employers.

"The mission is a raid. One of our system recon ships intercepted a Davion communique. The Feds have uncovered part of a previously unknown supply cache that we have had occasion to use. If we get in there fast, it's ours. If we don't, intel predicts that the gear will go to re-equipping the same Seventh Crucis units that we just invested so much in cutting down here on Misery.

"You want another shot at the Lancers?"

The Crucis Lancers were the raiders who had just hit Misery. They were also Davion House troops, a rare quantity here on the border. In the past year, most of the opposition had been merc units instead of the Fed regulars that were the Dragoons' rightful targets. Dragoon intel briefings had mentioned House troops moving along the border, striking, and then winding up in another location instead of heading home. The pattern was an oddity, but nobody, not even information-scrounging Dominguez, had any idea what was behind it.

It meant that the Dragoons rarely got a chance to fight Davion Regulars. But here was an opportunity to follow up on some of those Regulars to make the damage the Dragoons laid on them really stick this time. That is was going to be the Seventh Crucis who got the short end was just icing on the cake. "All right, Colonel. We're in."

"Good. Have your Techs set up the 'Mechs for Udibi. They can access the operation file from the *Chieftain*." Wolf handed Dechan a computer-access code disk. "It's going to be a bit of a jump for your people from the snow here to the dunes there. Udibi is quite a ways into Davion space, so make sure your D-Ship is stocked for a long run. You've got a week to get things done."

Wolf paused and threw Dechan a stern look. "This is important, son," he said. "No passes for those who are going. No letters back to dependents on An Ting, either. This has to be kept quiet."

Wolf's insistence on such extraordinary security made Dechan curious. "Sir, this isn't a breach of contract, is it?"

"No, son. It's letter-by-letter legal. We need some supplies, and we're making the arrangements to get them for ourselves, per contract. Our employers aren't going to care for us taking an excursion across the border, though. They might not understand the situation quite right, so we just won't tell them about it."

Dechan didn't like the sound of that. The scuttlebutt must have been right about the cash flow. "Is the supply situation that bad?"

"It's not good, son. I don't want it to get worse. Our friends in the Kuritan PSL office have been pushing us harder and harder since they changed the garrison stations last December. It wouldn't be good business to push back, so let's just say that this time we're doing a little sidestep."

31

Gakken County, Benet III
Draconis March, Federated Suns
19 May 3027

"Recon, this is Command," Natasha Kerensky repeated. "Clavell, can you hear me?"

Boshemoi! How could he? She could hardly hear herself over the clatter of small arms rattling off the sloping hood over the *Warhammer*'s cockpit.

The Fed infantry that her lance was wading through was the weakest enemy force they had faced since grounding a week ago. Without anything heavier than rifles to use on the 'Mech in their midst, the Feds were wasting time and ammo. The best they could hope for was a series of lucky hits to scrag the BattleMechs' sensor probes. The chance of such a hit was very, very slim. They had guts, she had to give them that. No one would get *her* to stand up to a BattleMech with nothing more than a rifle.

The Widow 'Mechs moved single-file through the pass, ignoring the harmless groundpounders. Why waste precious ammo?

Colin MacLaren suddenly seemed to get another idea. His *Marauder* lunged out of the line toward a concentration of the Davion infantry. Like a beast of prey, the alien shape of the BattleMech stalked forward. With blistering laserfire emanating from its blocky forearms, it sought among the entrenchments for its victims.

The Feds held their ground until MacLaren opened up with the 120mm autocannon. Its snout ranged back and forth above the 'Mech's carapace, spitting explosive death at the infantry. The destruction so wrought was enough for the Feds. They broke.

MacLaren declined to pursue. They were just groundpounders after all. The *Marauder* returned to its place in the formation.

"Lose your temper, old man?" Kerensky asked, smiling in the privacy of her cockpit.

"I heard the Captain trying to reach Recon Lance, and I thought she might appreciate some quiet." As always, Sergeant MacLaren addressed his superior in the third person.

"You are very considerate. Thank you." She took advantage of the lack of distractions to try again while her lancemates took up defensive positions. The newest attempt brought no better results. For some reason, the Recon Lance was out of touch. She tried the rest of her company. "Command to Fire, report."

"Command, this is Fire. Trouble on homeplate."

That meant something had happened at the DropShip. This whole mission was one problem after another. "Where are you, Ikeda?"

"In the hills above homeplate. Had some guests nosing around earlier. We sent them away, but I expect they'll be back with friends soon."

"What about the ship?" If the Feds had determined the DropShip's location, they would make it a target in an attempt to isolate the Widows.

"Don't think they marked it, but they must be wondering what a lance is doing out here in the boonies."

"Excuse me," MacLaren's gruff voice cut into the taccomm, "but I thought the Captain might like to know that we have Davion 'Mechs moving up the valley."

"Thanks, Colin," Kerensky replied. "Hold tight, Ikeda. I've got to check on this."

Kerensky brought her *Warhammer* up to where Hayes's *Griffin* crouched by a boulder some forgotten glacier had discarded. From there, she could see MacLaren's *Marauder* and Sheridan's *Crusader* further down the ravine. Beyond them, a lance of Davion BattleMechs advanced up the valley.

The Fed machines were in open order and moving slowly. Apparently, they had neither scanned the Widows nor been informed of their presence by the retreating infantry. Lambs to the slaughter.

"Hold fire till I give the word, people," Kerensky called over the taccomm. "Let them get close, then concentrate fire on the leader. We don't want a real fight just now. If we can spook them by taking out their pointman, they should pull back and leave us alone for a while."

As the Davion BattleMechs continued their advance, Kerensky waited for the leading *Enforcer* to close to thirty meters from Sheridan's position. When it did, she sidestepped her *Hammer* clear of cover and triggered both her 'Mech's Donal PPCs. The beams ripped into the target's torso as she shouted the command to fire over the taccomm.

Her lance responded with a rainbow of energy beams. Before the Feds could react, the *Enforcer* was a smoking hulk, its pilot riding his ejection seat to safety.

The Widows turned their attention to the rest of the enemy lance. Facing opponents of unknown numbers and already down to three-quarters strength, the Feds decided to withdraw. Their weapons spoke often in their retreat, but they caused no real damage to the Widow 'Mechs. The Dragoons scored better, but didn't bring any more of the Davion machines down.

"Good show," Kerensky congratulated her lance. "Hayes, scoot down and look for a way off this mountain that won't take us through the Feds. Colin, Sheridan, keep your eyes open. I'm going to get Ikeda back on the comm."

Kerensky had to move her 'Mech further back up the pass before she could get clear reception from the Fire Lance. "Any sign of our Draco helpers, Ikeda?"

"Negative, Widow."

Never trust a Snake, she reminded herself. Without the Kurita unit that was supposed to land on Benet to support them, the Dragoons had insufficient force to punch through the Davion forces. As yet, her company had not run into any insurmountable problems. Unless Recon Lance's silence meant otherwise, they were still in reasonable shape. Things were getting hotter all the time, though, and they had not come near to completing their objectives. If the rest of the Dragoons weren't doing any better, they could be looking at big trouble. "What about Epsilon?"

"They're stuck in heavy traffic up on the escarpment. Colonel Arbuthnot is expressing interest in packing his suitcase."

Kerensky gave vent to a string of Russian curses. Ikeda, used to Kerensky's vocal tantrums, waited patiently for her to finish and resume normal conversation. "We're coming in, Ikeda. If you hear from Recon, call them home."

She hoped the raid on Udibi was doing better. With the growing supply problem, the Dragoons needed whatever they could grab there. She had wanted to go, but the Colonel thought it better if her high-profile company stayed where the Kuritans could see it, a distraction of sorts. So the Widows had been stuck with this hopeless jaunt on Benet, which, it was beginning to look, the Snakes didn't want any Dragoons to survive. That didn't mean she was going to let this operation turn into a suicide run.

"All right, lance," Kerensky called over the lance circuits. "Time for all us little spiders to head for the web."

The Command Lance began the trip down the mountain. Hayes reported that Davion forces had all the easy routes blocked, but that he had found a trail near a firewatch station, which led around to the east face and then switchbacked down. Wanting to avoid entanglements with the Federated Suns troops, Kerensky decided to use the path.

By the time they reached it, a small Davion contingent had occupied the station. In a short, sharp firefight, the Widow's knocked out a *Valkyrie* and a VTOL 'Mech-hunter and drove off the rest of the Feds. Hayes's *Griffin* took a hit in its already-balky jump jets, forcing him to shut them down till they could be repaired. The rest of the Widows took only minor damage, and moved on.

Twice they spotted VTOLs searching for them. The first must have lacked IR gear, for the heated BattleMechs would have stood out even through the cover they grabbed at the forested edge of the trail. That Fed passed them by. The second was better-equipped, or else the pilot was more observant. His attention was his death warrant, however. A spread of missiles from Sheridan's *Crusader* turned the Davion scout into a fireball.

Cursing Sheridan's impetuosity, Kerensky urged her lance forward. She knew the crash would bring Federated Suns troops as surely as a radio report from an observer. With luck, they would be able to cover enough ground to force the Feds to run a wider search pattern and spread their forces out to cover all possible routes that the black 'Mechs might have taken. That would give the Widows a much better chance to slip away.

The path they followed narrowed steadily until it was barely wide enough for a single 'Mech to pass. Kerensky sent Hayes on ahead. His *Griffin* was the lightest and most maneuverable of the machines in the lance, and so he could best react if they ran into trouble. Despite his protests, Kerensky sent MacLaren next. The Sergeant wanted to stay near Kerensky to protect her. She convinced him that if Hayes ran into trouble, the awesome firepower of the *Marauder* might be enough to blast through and keep the Widows, and thereby Kerensky, from being bottlenecked. Sheridan went next because Kerensky reserved rear guard for herself. If the Feds caught up to them on the narrow track, she wasn't going to have one of her people sacrificing himself or herself to allow the Widow to escape.

For twenty nerve-wracking minutes, the Widows picked their way down the mountainside. At almost every step, the ponderous fighting machines sent showers of pebbles and loose gravel plummeting over the edge to rattle away down the steep slope. MacLaren had the most trouble. The non-humanoid shape of his *Marauder* made some of the required balancing acts doubly dangerous. Whenever she checked in with MacLaren, Kerensky could hear his 'Mech's gyros whining in the background.

Davion pursuit failed to materialize. Kerensky was just beginning to think they were going to make a clean getaway when a deep boom came through her external mikes. A growing rumble accompanied the pressure wave that buffeted the *Warhammer,* nearly toppling the 'Mech. Struggling to keep the *Hammer* upright Kerensky backed up the machine. When one foot caught the edge of the pathway, seventy tons of BattleMech was too much for the weathered granite. It crumbled.

Kerensky shifted the machine's balance to the right. Though she risked a fall on the path, that was preferable to pitching down the side of the mountain. Her maneuver succeeded, but was ultimately futile.

The rumble had continued throughout her gyrations. Its source hurtled down upon the *Warhammer* as hundreds of tons of rock came free in an avalanche. The 'Mech was swept from the track.

Lynn Sheridan let out a scream of impotent rage. While she sat helpless in her *Crusader,* Natasha Kerensky's black *Warhammer* vanished in a billowing cloud of gray rock dust.

Sheridan's cry halted the rest of the Command Lance. Heedless of the danger, MacLaren whirled his 'Mech in an about-face and stormed back up the trail. He reached Sheridan's position to find the *Crusader* bent over the edge, directing its sensors downward. The path beyond it was choked with debris.

"I can't read her 'Mech, Sarge," Sheridan reported.

"Keep scanning," MacLaren ordered. He began to call for the Captain over and over on the taccomm, but there was no response.

32

Gakken County, Benet III
Draconis March, Federated Suns
19 May 3027

Long after the roar of the rockfall had turned to silence, Colin MacLaren was calling. Hayes and Sheridan tried to convince him that the Widow was gone, lost to a freak of nature. Believing that Natasha Kerensky could not be taken from him this way, he refused to stop calling for his Captain. His lancemates began to discuss how they might force him to head for the DropShip.

When a faint crackling became audible on the lance circuit, all three Widows stopped what they were doing and boosted power in the comm circuits. A faint voice came through.

"Calm down, old man. You haven't lost me yet."

Sheridan and Hayes whooped for joy. For all his earlier concern, MacLaren stayed calm, but he couldn't keep the emotion from his voice. "Is the Captain all right?"

"I'm alive, which is more than I have any right to be. *Black Lady* has seen better days. Lost my aerial in the slide. Took me a while to rig the spare. Sorry about worrying all of you."

"The Captain needn't apologize," MacLaren returned. "If the Captain will give us her coordinates, we'll be down to join her."

"I wish it were that easy, Colin. I'm in some kind of chasm. The walls are too steep to climb, and trying to come down would be suicide without jump jets. The talus slope from the rockfall is very unstable and would probably slide again if a 'Mech were to try to walk on it.

"See if you can link with the *Web* to use the ship's comp to give us a tacmap. This thing must come out somewhere."

MacLaren did as he was ordered. When the *Widow*'s *Web* computer fed him the map for the area, he located the chasm and saw that it finally leveled out twenty klicks to the northeast. He relayed the information to Kerensky.

"That's it, then," she said. "We'll rendezvous at grid seventy-two, reference three-seventeen. Get a move on. You've been exposed up there too long."

"But the Captain will be alone."

"No 'buts,' Colin. We haven't any choice. You can't slide down after me. Get going."

"Yes, Captain."

Kerensky could picture the *Marauder* moving like a sulky child denied its wish, and the thought lightened her mood considerably. Her people would give their lives for her, but it was no less than she would do for them. The Black Widow Company was the best, though once they had been the dregs of Wolf's Dragoons. She had turned that band of gamblers, criminals, and discipline problems into damn good soldiers, and then into the most formidable company in the most formidable mercenary unit in the Inner Sphere. It was an achievement that even one of her ancestry could view with pride.

Now she must deal with the present, however. She faced a twenty-kilometer march in a battered 'Mech. Her cockpit was already hot because several heat sinks had been damaged in the fall. The dysfunction lights indicating the failures in the heat exchangers were almost lost in the crowd of yellow and red lights on her systems board. One of the Donal PPCs was completely out, but all other weapons registered as functional. Assuming that the telltales were themselves reliable, Natasha reminded herself. She hoped she wouldn't have to fight.

The chasm was floored with blocks of granite and mounds of glacial till, much of it taller than her 'Mech and probably weighing five or more times as much. The massive rocks blocked most of her sensors and all of her comm frequencies. Visual range was reduced to handfuls of meters. Yes, she definitely hoped she wouldn't have to fight.

Before she had gone half a klick, the first blip showed on her Mass Anomaly Detector. Opting for avoidance, she altered her course. Twice more, she evaded what read as 'Mech-size masses moving among the rocks. When the fourth appeared directly in her only available path, Kerensky advanced cautiously. When she reached a visual observation point, however, there was nothing to be seen.

She ran a check on her MAD sensor systems, which came up green. Either the check system was faulty or she was chasing ghosts. Investigating three more blips gave the same results. It had to be the sensor system. There were no such things as ghosts, she told herself. Here amid the gloom and giant stone reminders of an ancient time, her rationality seemed subordinate to those old Human fears of the dark and the unknown. The *Warhammer* moved on, its cautious motions reflecting its pilot's growing nervousness.

"Bang! You're dead," came a distorted voice over the taccomm.

Kerensky whirled the *Warhammer* around, searching for the mark that had appeared on her MAD sensor. A voice meant a foe she could face, not some nameless shadow. She found the target, snugged into a cleft in the rockface, the collapsed folds of a camouflage screen draped over its clawed feet. It was a bright green *Marauder* with silver credit symbols glittering on its carapace.

The protective hatches on the *Warhammer*'s SRM launcher opened and her functional PPC came up as Natasha recognized the 'Mech. It was the Bounty Hunter. She didn't know his name, and she didn't want to.

The dorsal hatch of his BattleMech was open, and the pilot stood there, arms spread wide. Kerensky stopped herself from triggering any weapons, unable to burn down someone who had put himself at her mercy. Even this scum. It appeared that the Bounty Hunter wanted to talk. Maybe he would give her a reason to change her mind.

"Don't shoot, Widow Lady. At least, not till you check your rear."

Three more 'Mechs had moved out of concealment, an *Orion,* a *Quickdraw,* and a *Shadow Hawk.* That was a hundred and ninety tons of trouble added to the seventy-five in front of her. Even if her *Hammer* hadn't been battered by the last week's fighting and her recent slide down the mountain, Kerensky knew she probably wouldn't have been able to get away from this ambush.

"Can't you at least say hello, Natasha? I know we didn't part on the best of terms back on Le Blanc, but it cost me quite a bit for your comm frequency."

Kerensky disdained to reply. The last time she had met with this man-with-no-name, they had fought. Michael Hasek-Davion had informed the Dragoons that he was holding a family of renegade Techs, and Wolf had sent her to make sure the Techs were not runaways from the regiments. When Kerensky arrived on Le Blanc, the Duke offered her employment and a share in the services of Techs. She still wondered why he thought that would tempt her. When he refused to let her see the Techs and her Widows moved to take them away, the Duke sprang the Hunter and his dogs on the Dragoons. The Hunter had bagged two more Dragoons that day. The Widows had grabbed the Techs and gotten away, but so had the Hunter.

Her *Warhammer* stood motionless now. The Hunter and his bullyboys had the drop on her, and so she'd let him make the next move. If it was hostile, he would be cinders before the *Black Lady* went down.

"Come on, Widow Lady. Anything in the past between us was just business. You burned old Michael H-D when you scampered with his Techs. Let's call it even between us on that one."

"We'll never be even, scum. You've cost me too much!"

"Ah, those dulcet tones. Never say never, my dear Widow," he chided, relieved that he had gotten her talking. It would be downhill from here. First, she needed to be reminded of exactly where she stood because it would make the negotiations easier. "If I'd wanted your butt today, you'd be hanging on the wall. But, I'm in a good mood," he said expansively. "I've got a deal for you."

"Shove it up your exhaust ports." How could he expect her to trust him? She had "dealt" with him before.

"Now, is that any way to talk to someone who's trying to do you a favor?"

"The only favor you can do me is to drop dead."

"You're trying my patience," he said, the harshness in his voice due to more than the electronic distortion. "Let me make it clear. I've got a contract on you and you're under the guns of my boys. You don't walk out of here unless I go with you. Which is exactly what I want to do."

"Never."

"Now what did I tell you about that word? Listen, we've both got problems. Your pet Snakes ain't showed. They've left you Wolves on the rack to dry. You're stuck on this rock until you take the tracking station at Beaux Pawl, unless you want to lose half your DropShips on the way to orbit. You ain't taking that station till you get through twice your number in defenders.

"As for me, my boys and I have offended our friends somehow, and they've decided they don't like us anymore. We been double-crossed and our ride out of here has been chased off. So we're stuck, too.

"We've got a lot to offer each other. You've got Jump-Ships insystem. I've got a friend in Beaux Pawl who's very good with explosives. Not only that, I'll cancel the contract I have on you. All it takes is a ride out of this system on your JumpShip. A DropShip hitchhiker is a small price to pay to keep that silky skin intact."

"I don't travel with cold-blooded killers."

"That's not what some people are saying."

"What do you mean?"

"I had a call from a friend of mine. He placed you on New Mendham eight months ago. Same time that a bunch of black 'Mechs trashed a town held by Kurita. Very messy. Those Jocks tried to blame it on Davion as well."

"My company was elsewhere."

"*I* believe you, sweetheart. You wouldn't lie to me. But you can't prove it, can you?

Kerensky thought hard. No, she couldn't prove it without compromising Dragoon security. That would mean big trouble with Wolf, something she was unwilling to risk. The Hunter took her silence as his answer.

"Thought so. My friend says there're pictures to back up

the story." Inside his helmet, the Bounty Hunter smiled at Kerensky's curse. "You know, Widow Lady, I think you and your buddies are being set up. Somebody's got a real mad on for you. You're not the only Wolvie brass I was offered a pass at."

"Who would do such a thing?" she asked, letting her indignation leak into her voice. The Hunter might want to gloat and thereby let something slip.

"That ain't for me to say," he replied. *Sorry, Natasha,* he said silently. *I'm not that easy to catch.* Aloud, he continued. "Client privilege, you know. I'll tell you that my employer wore a badly disguised Waco Ranger's get-up, because that doesn't really tell you anything. Everybody in the business knows about old Whacko's Death Oath. It's an obvious cover for anyone who wants to target Wolvies.

"Of course, once we're out of this system, I might recall some significant details. I might also name a few names and dates that might be worthy of further pursuit."

"Do so now!" Kerensky ordered, abandoning both subtlety and any hope of worming information out of the Hunter.

"Uh-uh, Widow Lady. Not while we're in this system." *Not,* he said to himself, *ever, but if I tell you that, I'm stuck here.*

Kerensky fumed. The Hunter was too slick for her to catch him out while she was still shaken from her slide down the mountain. She was too rattled to play at word games. Her earlier outburst revealed her strong desire to get the cowards who stooped to setting bounty hunters after her and ruined her negotiating position.

"Very well," she said. "I accept your offer. We get you out of the system and you give me the names. I want the villain behind this!"

"I'm sure you do, little lady." Kerensky realized that he had been speaking over a circuit open to his men when he said, "Let's go boys. We've got our ticket off this rock."

33

Davion HQ, Kitchuken Barrens, Udibi
Draconis March, Federated Suns
22 June 3027

As Captain Frank Woomack gazed out over the barren landscape, motion off to the left caught his eye. He watched as one of the local *gyru* lizards slithered from its sunny perch into the shadow of a rock outcropping as a hovercraft bearing the sun-and-sword roared by. The vehicle's engines were audible even through the plastiglass. The machine cut across Woomack's line-of-sight and accelerated toward the perimeter of the complex. A second, then a third, followed the first.

"The Feds are stirring out there," the Dragoon announced to his companions.

"Think the Colonel has sent somebody after us, Captain?" Corporal Kathy Keegan's voice was full of hope. The internment at the Davion base had hit her the hardest of the three. Even though their captors had allowed them a fairly free run, she chafed at the confinement within the climate-controlled buildings of the Federated Suns outpost.

"If he has, Kathy, we'll be heading for orbit before nightfall," said Steve Geiger confidently. The loss of his *Stinger* and his own wounds had done little to damp the private's ebullient spirits.

"Don't get her hopes up, Geiger," Woomack warned. "We don't know what's going on. It could just be maneuvers."

"But, Captain, we've been held here for over a month. If the Feds were going to ransom us, we would be gone by now. They must have refused," Geiger concluded. "The Colonel won't leave us here to rot."

"You're right on that, Steve. The Dragoons don't abandon anybody," Woomack said, directing his reply to Keegan. "The Feds must be dragging the negotiations out for some political reason. If so, we sit and wait. It could be worse. They're treating us more like guests than prisoners."

"I guess you're right, Captain," Keegan conceded, hugging herself. "It's so hard sometimes. The walls. Not being able to go outside. It's really starting to get to me."

Keegan had started to shiver as she spoke. Woomack moved to her and put an arm around her shoulders. "You've got to keep it together, Kathy. We'll be out of here soon." Keegan stifled a sob. Woomack bit his lip. Sending people into battle had always come easy for him. Morale problems always disappeared in battle. Here, there was no battle for distraction. Feeling out of his element, he tried again. "Would it help if I could get them to authorize a trip outside?"

"It might," Keegan answered in a small voice.

"Then that's what I'll do." Woomack gave her a pat on the back and turned to Geiger. "Kid, see if you can get ahold of one of those Feddie officers."

"No problem, boss," Geiger said, tilting his head at the door.

Woomack turned his head to see a Federated Suns Leftenant standing in the open doorway, arms folded across his chest.

"Captain Woomack," the Davion officer said. "Major Whitfield wants to see you again."

"Does he? Well, I don't think I want to see him." If the Feds were going to baby them, maybe he should act like a sulky kid to see how far he could push them.

"I don't believe you have that option, Dragoon."

"You gonna carry me, Feddie?"

"Not personally. I can, however, have it arranged," the Leftenant said with calm assurance. His voice left no doubt of the firmness of his intention to enforce the invitation.

"Tell you what, Feddie. You take my people for a walk outside and I'll go along peaceably."

The Leftenant laughed at that. "Your peacefulness is unimportant, Woomack. If your people want to take a walk, they'll have the company of some of my troopers. It's no big deal. After all, where are they going to go?"

Woomack cast a glance at Keegan. Already her eyes were lit with anticipation of getting out into the open. Woomack may not have impressed the Feddie, but he had gotten what he wanted.

"All right, Feddie. Let's go see your Major." Woomack pushed past the Leftenant and started down the corridor. The Davion Leftenant just shook his head and followed after.

Woomack did not wait for his escort. He knew the route. He ought to. The Major had been calling these talk sessions three times a week since the Seventh Crucis had pulled out three weeks ago. Two or three hours of boredom each time. Things had been more interesting when McKinnon's Raiders were in charge of the prisoners. It had been fun to bait Kate Nomura. She was gorgeous when she was mad.

The Dragoon waited once he reached the Major's office, but not for long. The Leftenant was only a few steps behind him. When the officer caught up, he keyed open the door. Woomack strode through.

Major Whitfield was seated at his desk. At his left, as usual, was his secretary, manning the recorder. A white-haired stranger was seated at the other side of the desk. The business suit he wore was a rare sight at this military installation. Woomack figured he was probably some kind of psych specialist here to analyze whatever the Dragoon said.

Whitfield indicated the empty seat to Woomack, and the Dragoon took it. Once his visitor was settled, Whitfield said, "Captain Woomack, I would like you to relate your part in the recent raid by Wolf's Dragoons against the Federated Suns planet Udibi."

"Again?"

"Again, Captain."

Woomack shrugged. He told the tale of the Dragoon raid and their successful escape with most of the material uncovered in the supply cache. This time, he made an effort to emphasize the Dragoon accomplishments and their strict adherence to the Ares Conventions of War. Woomack didn't know who the old guy was, but it wouldn't hurt to play to Dragoon strengths and might even improve the Dragoon reputation if the old geezer had any influence. Woomack finished his recitation with a politely phrased request for the formal ransom that was customary for captured mercenaries.

"I assure you, Captain Woomack, that you will be returned to your unit as soon as possible." Whitfield was as earnest and sincere as he had been every other time he'd made the same assurances.

"I heard that one, Feddie," Woomack came back. "I heard it from Ryder when he took my parole. I heard it from McKinnon before he left. I've heard it from you for three weeks. From where I sit, it seems to be a lot of hot air."

"No need to get testy, Captain," the white-haired man said. "I am the reason for the delay."

Woomack gave the man a calculating look. The geezer didn't look like much. "So who are you, old man?"

"My name is Allard. I am a minister in the government of Prince Hanse Davion." Allard gave the Dragoon a pleasant smile. "I am here to finalize the arrangements for your return to the Dragoons."

"Not more bureaucratic nonsense."

"Bureaucratic, perhaps," Allard said with a chuckle. "But I certainly hope you do not find it nonsense. You and your companions, as well as what remains of your 'Mechs, will be conveyed to a rendezvous on Le Blanc. There will be no ransom."

Woomack closed his mouth. "What do you mean no ransom?"

"You only have to perform a single task."

"So that's it," Woomack snapped. "I'll have you know Dragoon soldiers are no traitors."

"No one mentioned treason, Captain. We merely wish you to perform the services of a courier. Prince Davion has a rather lucrative offer he wishes to convey to Colonel Wolf."

34

Dragoon Administrative HQ, Cerant, An Ting
Galedon Military District, Draconis Combine
29 June 3027

Warming sunlight drenched the central plaza of Cerant. The tall shape of Government House, seat of Kurita planetary authority, glowered at the former office complex that was now the Wolf's Dragoons' Administrative Headquarters. Unaware of, or at least unconcerned with, the tensions between the two parties, the civilians of An Ting went about their daily affairs. Food vendors and trinket hucksters vied for the attention of the noonday crowds. Here and there could be seen the bright red and white stripes of Civilian Guidance Corps men intimidating criminals and disruptive influences with their mere presence. Everywhere people bustled about, concerned for their own interests. A knot of Kurita soldiers moved through the throng, headed for the Dragoon building.

At their head was Minobu Tetsuhara, deputized by the absent PSL officer. Following him was his aide Michi and *Sho-sa* Charles Earnst, his second-in-command of Ryuken-*ni*. With them was *Tai-i* Dela Saraguchi and a detachment of six of her security troopers. The group's grim faces cleared their path without the need to speak a word.

They climbed the long stairs at the front of the office building and passed into the shadows of the portico. As they crossed the line of supporting pillars, Minobu looked up at the fierce faces of the guardian Myoo into whose shapes the columns had been carved. The resolution there was unmistakable. *Grant, oh great spirits, that my own resolve be as strong,* he asked of them.

A quartet of Dragoon sentries stood by the door, their faces showing only puzzlement and concern. The Kuritans swept past them without acknowledging the ragged salutes.

The warm air of the lobby was an abrupt change from the temperatures outside. As he walked up to the desk, Minobu noted the modifications that had been wrought in the building since the Dragoons had occupied it. Gone were the inspirational posters showing Lord Kurita urging the government workers to productivity for the Combine. Gone, too, were the works of art set there to inspire the spirits of those same workers. The Dragoons had stripped the place for utilitarian efficiency. If they could have removed the Myoo without damaging the building, they probably would have.

"Where is Colonel Wolf?" Minobu asked the Lieutenant seated at the reception desk.

"The Colonel is in the middle of a session in the conference room, *Tas-sa* Tetsuhara." The man was good at his job and showed no surprise at the armed security troopers. Maintaining his pleasant tone, the Lieutenant went on, "If you and your party will take seats in the waiting area, I'm sure he will see you as soon as he is finished."

"Secure the desk," Minobu ordered without looking at his men. "Noketsuna, take over the commnet."

Before the Dragoon Lieutenant could protest, two of the troopers had him by the arms. The stunners in the hands of the rest of the Kurita soldiers stifled the captive's attempt to protest. Outnumbered and with no desire to experience the unpleasant effects of those weapons, he let himself be marched to the waiting area. As his captors led him from the desk, the Lieutenant could see the lone figure of Minobu striding down the interior corridor. It had all happened so quickly and quietly that the guards outside were undisturbed.

Minobu had no trouble finding the conference room. He had often been there in happier times. His PSL-validated keycard overrode the lock and the door hissed open. When Minobu entered the room, heads turned in his direction, and all discussion ceased.

He surveyed the faces. Some showed minor annoyance at an interruption. Others looked confused or surprised. A few revealed naked hatred. Minobu presumed it was not directed at him personally. His *ki* senses agreed that the ill-will was directed at his uniform. The Dragoons had been given reason to hate the symbols of House Kurita.

Seated at the far end of the table was Jaime Wolf. His face showed nothing of his thoughts, and Minobu could not sense the mercenary's emotions. Jaime was an enigma.

Natasha Kerensky broke the tableau. "You didn't get an invitation. What do you want here, Snake?" she hissed. Hers had been one of the openly hostile faces.

Minobu ignored her and addressed Jaime Wolf. "I have just received a communique from Warlord Samsonov. It is a matter that bears immediate discussion."

"We are in the middle of a strategy session," Wolf stated.

"It is your strategies that are at issue here."

"Very well. Take a seat." As Minobu moved to do so, grumbling rose around the table. "Damp it, people," Wolf ordered. "We're going to hear him out."

As Minobu approached the table, Colonel Shostokovitch rose and gestured for Minobu to take his seat. The big bear of a man then moved down the length of the table to stand beside Wolf. He seemed content to observe the proceedings, standing with arms crossed across his chest.

Minobu settled himself in the vacated chair, and placed a message flimsy on the table. He made no move to open it or to pass it to the Dragoons on either side of him. "The Warlord has sent me an account of last month's action on Udibi."

Minobu waited for a reaction or an explanation from Wolf, but none came. Silence stretched uncomfortably. He tried again. "The Warlord states that Wolf's Dragoons have made an unauthorized incursion into enemy space. In response, he has filed a formal protest of insubordination with the Coordinator's office."

"Not treason?" Colonel Korsht asked.

"No. Treason is impossible from mercenaries," Minobu pointed out.

"But that's what he means, isn't it?" Korsht continued.

"I am not privy to the Warlord's thoughts, Colonel. It is

possible. In any case, the charge is serious." Minobu's eyes passed across the faces of the other officers. "The Warlord has prepared a number of other charges as well, not the least of which is breach of contract."

That excited a babble of protest, as Minobu had known it would. Just as Akuma must have known it would, too. Minobu wondered if the former Sworder had deliberately chosen him as a messenger in a move to focus Dragoon hostility against Minobu rather than himself. There was nothing Minobu could do about it. The Warlord had ordered him to take the place of the PSL officer on this mission, and he could not refuse.

"The Dragoons have taken no actions that violate the strict wording of our contract with the Draconis Combine," Wolf said.

Minobu had hoped that his friend would deny the charge and offer proof to back up that denial. Instead, Wolf's words left Minobu with no doubt that the Dragoons had conducted the raid on Udibi, just as Samsonov reported. The carefully chosen wording meant that Wolf was relying on legalistic interpretations. A merchant's trick, not a samurai's solution. "Then you do not deny that the Dragoons have conducted a raid on the Federated Suns planet of Udibi."

"As commander of the Dragoons, I will neither confirm nor deny anything until I see the specifications of the charges."

"Very well, Colonel Wolf."

Minobu thought he caught a flash of distress in Wolf's eyes at the formal address, but he could not be sure. Wolf sat today as master of his troops, not as Minobu's friend. There had been a bond between them, but it was strained and perhaps broken now. For the sake of what once was, Minobu felt compelled to speak.

"The wording in Warlord Samsonov's account of the Udibi action shows that he is furious. He is a man who does not take kindly to being embarrassed. As far as he is concerned, your success speaks against you in this. It has also been related to me, in private, that he has sworn the destruction of the Dragoons if they break faith with House Kurita. Regardless of your fidelity to the Combine, he seems to feel that your actions have touched his honor. A shamed man may take drastic steps. Even when such steps may not be in his own best interest, shame may drive him on."

Wolf sat quietly for a moment after Minobu finished. He interlaced his fingers and ran them back and forth across each other. Still looking at his hands, Wolf asked, "Are you saying that he will try to destroy us anyway?"

"I am not sure what he will do." Minobu took a deep breath. "He has warned me that he will have the head of any Kuritan who aids Wolf's Dragoons against the Combine . . . or against him."

"We don't need any help against that toad-licking slime snake," Kerensky boasted. "The Dragoons can kick his butt to Aldebaran and back. If he tries anything, that's just what we'll do."

Dragoons around the table chorused agreement. Out of the midst of the insults and complaints about ungrateful employers, Kerensky's voice rose again. "Let's cut them off now, Colonel. Unity knows they've asked for it."

"There is much to what Captain Kerensky says," Korsht seconded. "Perhaps it would be best to break contract now and forfeit the bond." Many other officers nodded or voiced their agreement.

"And where will we go?" Wolf asked. "Nobody wants a merc unit that runs away when things are tough."

"They'll understand," Major Patrick Chan protested. "Nobody will fault us for leaving Kurita."

"You're wrong, Pat. The Successor Lords watch our every move," Wolf reminded him. "If we break faith with one of them, each one will assume we'd to the same to him or her if we get unhappy. What seems like a good reason to us doesn't look the same from the other side of the paychest.

"Even if we have a good business reason to break contract, we still have our own honor to worry about. We gave our word. If we break it, what are we worth? We'll be the cheap sellswords they claim we are. Can any of you say you want that?"

The only reply was silence.

"We'll keep our contract, to the letter," Wolf continued. "If the Combine steps over the line, then we can act in all honor. Until then, we work for House Kurita."

The acknowledgements were soft, but they came forth,

Minobu noticed that some of the Dragoons, including Kerensky and Korsht, said nothing. At least they did not disagree. Despite their outspoken opinions, Minobu did not think they would disobey Wolf.

"Your devotion to honor is most ennobling, Colonel Wolf," Minobu complimented him. "It will stand you in good stead."

Wolf looked up sharply. "There's something else, isn't there, *Tai-sa* Tetsuhara?"

Whether or not Wolf had felt anything earlier, Minobu experienced the sting of the formal address. He inclined his head, took a deep breath, and released it. He pushed the message flimsy forward on the table before raising his gaze toward Wolf.

"Lord Takashi Kurita summons you to Luthien to account for your actions."

Interlude

Unity Palace, Imperial City, Luthien
Pesht Military District, Draconis Combine
28 August 3027

The small Dragoon contingent arrived at Unity Palace. There were only six of them, all that the travel passes accompanying the summons would allow. Jaime Wolf had wanted to go alone, believing that the fewer who went, the fewer might be made hostage. Major Stanford Blake had made the case that, as intel chief, he would be needed to present the Dragoon position. Major Olga Kormenski had included herself, claiming that her job as Wolf's Security Chief required her presence. The three others in the group wore the uniforms of Dragoon officers, but looked as though they'd be more at home in muddied combat armor. It was Kormenski who had insisted that they come. If she couldn't take BattleMechs to protect Wolf, she settled on the next best thing: troopers from Seventh Kommando, the highly secret Dragoon Special Forces Team.

A squad of *Otomo*, the Coordinator's fiercely loyal bodyguards, met them at the palace gates to serve as escort. The *Tai-i* of the Guard wore a black leather holster and the traditional two swords, each bearing the insignia of the Sun Zhang Military Academy. The white tunic of his dress uniform contrasted sharply with the red and blue uniforms and polished ceramet defenses of his squad. Those guardsmen wore the ceremonial armor of the palace, and each carried a heavy-barreled stunner at port arms. The weapons looked almost delicate against their bulky chest plates and gauntlets.

The *Tai-i* greeted the Dragoons with a stiff, formal bow before leading them in silence through the gardens surrounding the carved splendor of Unity Palace. The group passed wondrous topiary creations and splendid examples of horticultural art as they moved through gardens unrivaled in the Inner Sphere.

Once they entered the Palace, with its predominantly teak architecture and woodwork, they found that the interplay of light and shadow among the carved decorations created an impression that was both strong and airy. The *Otomo* led them through hall after hall until they came to a small *shoji*-paneled room.

"Colonel Wolf, your party will await you here." The *Tai-i* indicated a row of straight-backed chairs, distinctly out of place against the pervasive Japanese decor. "Only you shall enter the audience chamber."

"Major Blake is to present relevant data," Wolf objected.

"All data may be entered here." The man clapped his hands, and one of the guards rolled back a gorgeous gold foil screen to reveal a glittering chrome and plastic computer console. The *Tai-i* bowed, again stiff and formal, and left them alone.

"This doesn't look good, Colonel," Kormenski said.

"It's even worse than I thought," Wolf said gloomily. "They're not going to listen."

Blake looked up from the computer console. "You don't know that for sure, Colonel."

Wolf stopped massaging the bridge of his nose and rounded on Blake.

"Don't I? You're supposed to be an intelligence officer, Stan. Look around you. Look at how they're treating us. What other conclusion can there be?"

"Being a stubborn old man won't help," Kormenski chided, and Blake nodded agreement.

Wolf scowled at his staff officers. "I may be stubborn and I may be old, but I'm not fool enough to waste my strength. Not even a young man can single-handedly reverse entropy."

Having served under Wolf for years, Blake and Kormenski knew when to back off because the Colonel was simply not receptive to their arguments. After exchanging helpless glances, Blake returned his attention to the console while Kormenski pretended interest in one of the five Fudo statues adorning the room. Wolf stood in silence, his back to them both.

Half an hour later, the *Otomo Tai-i* and two guards returned to escort Wolf through the great arch into the lesser audience chamber. Before them were two massive teak doors carved with scenes from the history of the Kurita clan, with a guard to either side. The *Tai-i* stopped halfway across the room and indicated a row of chairs. "Please be seated, Colonel Wolf. Warlord Samsonov will join you shortly."

Sure enough, Samsonov came boiling through the archway before long. The Warlord drew a sharp breath when he spied Wolf already seated and waiting. Without a word, Samsonov stalked up to the great wooden doors to the inner chamber. Behind him the dapper Akuma trailed, ice to the Warlord's fire. The Sworder nodded a polite acknowledgement to Wolf as he passed. Wolf stood and joined them.

As the massive doors opened silently, they revealed the inner audience chamber. Though the architecture was simple, clean, and functional, it was opulent in its own way. The finest woods gleamed in oiled perfection, accented subtly by the gold fittings where beams joined. In the few niches were pedestals displaying exquisite masterworks of carved ivory. Standing at the far end of the chamber was a stocky figure in a black kimono of glistening *daigumo*-spider silk.

The man kept his back to them for a few moments after their footsteps began to echo in the room. Then Takashi Kurita turned to face his visitors, inclining his head in greeting to each of the officers in turn.

"Warlord Samsonov, welcome again to Luthien.

"*Chu-sa* Akuma, you are welcome also.

"I am pleased to see you, Colonel Wolf. It has been a long time since Quentin, and we had no time to chat after I presented you with the Bushido Blade on Benjamin in '26." Takashi made no reference to the summons that had left Wolf little choice but to come to Luthien.

"You have gone to a lot of expense for a little chat, Coordinator," Wolf said.

"As Coordinator, I can often judge such whims." There was a hint of regret in Takashi's voice. "I wish that were the case this time. Warlord Samsonov has had some harsh things to say about your Dragoons, Colonel Wolf. I thought you might want the opportunity to face your accuser and reply to his charges."

"There is nothing he can say that will stand against the facts," Samsonov shouted. Takashi and Wolf turned to look at him, surprised at his sudden, vehement entrance into the conversation.

"Be very sure of your facts, Warlord," Wolf warned.

Samsonov looked ready to say something more, but held his peace as Takashi cleared his throat.

"Facts are, gentlemen. They exist as separate entities. It is the interpretation of facts that concerns us here. I have studied your situation summaries, and now I will listen to your presentations." Takashi seated himself on the low dais and waved his arm to indicate that the officers were free to use the mats at the edge of the dais. Wolf and Akuma knelt. Samsonov remained standing. "Warlord, state your case," Takashi said.

"Wolf's Dragoons are a danger to the Draconis Combine and the security of House Kurita," Samsonov began in his typical bombastic fashion. "Their officers are cowards—afraid of the inevitable losses of battle. They hoard their troops, to the detriment of the military operations to which they are assigned. And this practice ultimately harms the Combine. We cannot allow such insubordinate incompetents to maintain powerful positions in the military structure. Uncontrolled, the Dragoons threaten to cripple our border defenses against the imperialistic House of Davion."

When Takashi did not contradict Samsonov, the Warlord flashed a savage grin of victory at Wolf and launched into a detailed assault on the history of the Dragoons' service to the Combine. Whenever he faltered for a name, date, or statistic, Akuma supplied it in a cool, detached voice.

The verbal attacks continued for an hour. When Samsonov seemed satisfied that he had finally driven home his point, he raised his haughty face to the Coordinator.

"Surely, the Coordinator can see that the Dragoons, by their very nature, endanger the Draconis Combine. That threat must be eliminated. Their leaders, criminals all, must be eliminated."

Takashi had remained perfectly still throughout the tirade. He noticed that Wolf had done the same, almost as though the mercenary were deaf to Samsonov's words. "You have spoken strongly for your case, Warlord."

The look that Samsonov gave Takashi seemed to say he didn't believe that the Coordinator really appreciated the danger he outlined. With slow, awkward movements, the Warlord knelt on his mat.

Takashi turned his gaze to Akuma. "*Chu-sa* Akuma, what have you to say?"

Akuma bowed smartly and then rose to his feet. "I have no emotional case to plead, Coordinator. There is little I can add to what the Warlord has already said. As Professional Soldiery Liaison, I have worked in the best interests of the Draconis Combine, always trying to shepherd the Dragoons into better cooperation with the plans of House Kurita. It has not been an easy task. The Dragoons are headstrong.

"My written evaluation covers this delicate matter adequately, Coordinator. I believe there is nothing I can add to it. If, in your wisdom, you have discerned any areas that I have not explicated completely, I will try to the best of my ability to rectify that failure."

"Thank you, *Chu-sa*. I have no questions for you at this time. Leave us now and attend to your other duties."

Akuma acknowledged his orders with a deep bow and retired toward the back of the room. The carved doors opened at his approach, and the Sworder strode through them without a backward glance. When the massive teak panels had closed behind him, Takashi turned his head toward Wolf.

"Now, Colonel Wolf. You have heard the case against you and the Dragoons. What have you to say?"

Wolf remained where he was. He did not bow. When he spoke, it was in a quiet voice. "The Dragoons are what they are, Coordinator." Despite the softness of his tone, the words were clear and distinct and would have carried through a larger room than the audience chamber. "Their leadership is inseparable from their nature. They will accept no other leaders than their own. You cannot remove the father and expect a family to accept a new man as head of that family."

"An interesting rebuttal, Colonel Wolf." Takashi sat silent for a moment. From the corner of his eye, he could see Samsonov frowning, his jaw working with barely suppressed rage. The Warlord was expressing more than enough emotion. It made a displeasing comparison to the cool and detached Wolf. "You have not denied any of the charges."

"An account of our actions since undertaking contract with the Draconis Combine is contained in the data file that Major Blake fed into your computer system. I stand by it. Beyond that, there is little point in my saying anything, Coordinator. We are prejudged."

"Not so. I have made no decision."

"Why not?" roared Samsonov, leaping to his feet. "The situation is intolerable. You have heard the evidence. You have seen this craven worm fail to deny anything his rogues have done. I demand that Wolf's Dragoons be immediately placed under my direct orders. I demand that Korsht and Dumont be relieved of their regimental commands. I demand that the criminals, especially the foul Kerensky and the butcher Arbuthnot, who instigated the bloody suppression of the unruly populace on Kawabe, be immediately tried and sentenced to death for their atrocities."

The Warlord punctuated each demand by shaking his fist at Wolf.

"You demand nothing of the Coordinator, Warlord." Takashi's voice was harsh as he glared at Samsonov. "The Dragoons will remain under the independent command of Colonel Wolf."

Samsonov's gesticulations stopped, but his expression grew wilder as Takashi spoke. His color went from red to purple and his breathing became stentorious. "I respectfully remind the Coordinator of his duty to the Combine," Samsonov said in a strangled voice.

"I remind *you*, *Tai-sho*, of your duty to *me*."

Insulted by the use of his lesser title and shamed by the Coordinator's tone of voice, Samsonov snapped his mouth shut. His silence lasted but a moment.

"I see. I shall return to my district and my duty, then."

The Warlord gave a stiff, formal bow and turned on his heel. Before the guards closed the doors to the audience chamber, Takashi and Wolf could hear the bellowing insults

Samsonov heaped on the aides who came to attend him. A heavy thud and a metallic clatter were the last sounds heard as the heavy teak panels swung shut, cutting off the tumult in the lesser chamber.

As he rose from his seat, the Coordinator spoke as though nothing extraordinary had happened. "I believe I need some fresh air, Colonel Wolf. Please join me on the balcony. The view of the city is superb."

Wolf followed Takashi through the open doorway, where the breeze was cold enough to cut through their clothes. Takashi swept out one arm, encompassing the view, which was breathtaking. Luthien's Imperial City was one of the most beautiful cities in the Inner Sphere.

"This is the heart of the Dragon's realm. From here, I rule more than four hundred stars. It is not an easy task. There are always hard questions to be answered and difficult decisions to be made. Constant demands on my time leave little space for release, for finding the small pleasures of life.

"When we met in Quentin, I sensed a kindred soul. A man who could see beyond the petty tasks of these latter days. A man of vision. Where is that man?"

"If by that you mean me, I am here at the order of my employer. Now, as then, I simply command the Dragoons."

"There is nothing simple about it. The Dragoons are a formidable force. You are a formidable officer. I would like to retain the services of Wolf's Dragoons."

"It hasn't been indicated."

Takashi detected bitterness in Wolf's words. "Things can be better. Improved resources. More suitable liaisons. Richer assignments."

"I'll take your offer under advisement."

"Don't think too long, my friend. Some people believe a long delay is the same as a refusal."

"Does that mean you, Coordinator?"

"I did not say that, Colonel. Your anger is misplaced."

Takashi turned to look out over the city. The glitter of lights soothed him a little, took the edge off his own irritation at the mercenary's stubborn wordplay.

"We are men of the same stamp. We share a view above the heads of the mob. We should be friends, Jaime Wolf."

"Your words speak of friendship, yet you allow what has

happened. Does not your philosophy teach that a man be judged by his actions as well as his words?"

"Yes."

"So does mine."

Takashi was stung by the rebuke.

"Think well on what has happened here today, Jaime Wolf. You are in dangerous space. There are hostile, misguided souls who might seek to wipe out what they consider a blot on the Combine's honor. In the worst event, such . . . persons . . . might claim to act on my behalf while taking violent action against your Dragoons."

Wolf said nothing and showed no reaction that Takashi could detect, but the Coordinator did not bother to probe Wolf's *ki* aura. He had learned from their bouts on Quentin that the mercenary could defy his probes. He let the silence continue for a full minute.

"Enjoy a week here at the capital while you think about my offer. I will be available, should you wish to speak to me."

"I'll keep it in mind."

Wolf turned and walked across the chamber to the doors, which did not open immediately. The mercenary stood stiffly until the panels had opened wide enough for a man to pass, then slipped through and was gone.

Takashi waited on the balcony until he saw Wolf and his party exit the lower level of the palace. He studied the small group as they walked swiftly through the gardens. *No need to hurry, Colonel Wolf,* Takashi admonished silently.

It was clear to Takashi that Wolf had been holding his thoughts under tight rein. All through the meeting, the mercenary had seemed elsewhere. Takashi knew that Wolf was wondering how much was show, how much was sincere, how much could be trusted. He had not taken the Coordinator's offer seriously. Takashi did not believe that Wolf would return to the palace.

The return trip to An Ting would take the Dragoons longer than the one that brought them to Luthien. There would be no Command Circuit JumpShips waiting to ferry their DropShip quickly from one jump point to the next, where another JumpShip would be waiting. This time, they would have to wait while their JumpShip recharged its drives at each stop along the way.

Takashi stepped back into the room long enough to look up at the ceiling and say, “Send the holofilm of the meeting to Director Indrahar.” Then he returned to his contemplation of Imperial City. This time, its glitter did not offer even the slight comfort of a few minutes before.

The Coordinator’s job was a hard one. Always he was faced with the age-old conflict: *ninjo* or *giri*. It was ever a choice between his feelings for others, which was the way his heart would lead him, and the inexorable call of obligation. As Coordinator of the Draconis Combine, Takashi knew which way he must choose. Indeed, when all was said and done, he had no choice.

Giri. Duty always ruled the ruler. Hard decisions had to be made and personal feelings or desires always subordinated to the iron law of duty. He could allow nothing to endanger his realm if it were in his power to avert that danger. Fellowship had no place in a Coordinator’s world, and people were only pawns in the game he played with history, pieces to be moved to improve the position of his ruling House.

It was a lonely game.

BOOK III

Duty

35

Ryuken-ni Command Center, Outside Boras, Misery
Galedon Military District, Draconis Combine
22 December 3027

Cold air blasted Michi Noketsuna's face as he stepped from the doorway of the mobile headquarters. He moved immediately to pull down his goggles and pull up the breath mask that would warm and humidify the chill, dry air of Misery. With hands made clumsy by overside thermal gloves, he fumbled the protective devices into place. Not a moment too soon, for the icy wind hit him with streamers of smoke and condensate steam from the engine stack as he stepped down from the vehicle. Even the heavy coldsuit could not keep Michi from shivering. Peering through the blowing snow, he could see no sign of the incoming Command Lance.

Michi leaned into the wind and headed for the vehicle shed. Though the walk to the lee of the shed was short, the frigid blast made it seem like kilometers before he finally reached the building and ducked through the open door.

Six months ago, he had been on An Ting during the cold season, but Cerant was nothing compared to this world, locked in an ice age. Why, he wondered, could not the Ryuken headquarters have been set up far to the south, in Laerdal, near the magma mines. It was true that the air there had an unpleasant, sulfurous tang, but at least it was warm.

From the shelter of the shed, Michi looked back across the

field. Through the swirl of the wind-driven snow, he could see Ryuken-*ni*'s old but recently refurbished mobile headquarters vehicle. The MHQ's internal combustion engine was new, but it would always be a poor substitute for the original fusion engine, removed long ago to use in some BattleMech. The vehicle's electronic facilities were far from the standard enjoyed by the Dragoons, but it belonged to the Ryuken. That made it superior. The MHQ bore the unit's proud symbol of a dragon coiling around a *katana*. It also carried the image Minobu had decreed for the regiment, a fierce feline head wearing an ancient Japanese *kabuto* helmet. Those two symbols made Michi proud, prouder than the serpentine dragon of the Combine did of late.

At the heavy sound of clumping feet, Michi gazed beyond the field, knowing it had to be the tread of BattleMechs. Sure enough, three dark shapes loomed in the swirling snow, coming in from the plateau beyond the MHQ.

Masked in part by the headquarters vehicle, the first machine was visible only from the waist up, and for a moment the swirl of white made it look like a snow dragon scenting for prey. The illusion was shattered as the silhouette moved completely into sight. Its blocky legs were where the snow dragon's neck should have been, the dream beast's snout resolved into the forward-jutting torso of a BattleMech, and its great ruff was transformed into the machine's humped shoulders. It was *Tai-sa* Tetsuhara's *Dragon*.

Michi had not been the first to imagine the dragon pattern in the DRG-1N BattleMech. The elongated configuration of its main armament, a Telos DecaCluster missile launcher, dominated the central torso. The low dome of the cockpit contributed to the saurian imagery. Many *Dragon* 'Mechs were painted with white-fanged dragon mouths to accentuate the resemblance.

The sixty-ton BattleMech trudged through the open arch of the vehicle shed and clomped onto the striped zone next to Michi's *Ostroc*. A second machine followed soon after. Ice crystals sparkled from the cylindrical body and projecting horns. Tong's *JaegerMech* paced into place behind the newly arrived *Dragon* and shuddered to a halt. Icicles, black with frozen lubricating fluid, clattered to the concrete from the paired weapons of the 'Mech's right arm.

Last in was Willoughby's 'Mech. The *Panther* seemed slight next to the two heavies that had preceded it. Willoughby noticed Michi huddled by the doors and raised his 'Mech's right arm in salute. The *Panther* slipped into its designated berth and became motionless as Willoughby started the shutdown procedure.

With the Command Lance safely inside, the great bay doors began to rumble shut. Michi strolled across the floor to the *Dragon*. Five meters above his head, Minobu was starting down the chain ladder hanging from the bottom of the 'Mech's snout. Bulky in his coldsuit, Minobu descended from his 'Mech in movements made doubly awkward by the icy climbing surfaces.

When he reached the last rung of the ladder, he dropped the final meter to the floor and landed smoothly, with flexed knees. No one would have guessed that only one of those legs was real. Before greeting Michi, the *Tai-sa* spoke with the Techs who had come up to service the BattleMechs. Satisfied that his chief Tech understood the problems that had cropped up during the recent outing, Minobu turned to his aide.

"What urgent news brings you out into the cold, Michi-*san*?"

"I wished to speak to you."

Minobu nodded his understanding that this was to be a private talk and waved at the approaching Tong and Willoughby. "Go on in to the ready room and get something hot," he called. "We will join you in a few minutes. I will want your preliminary evaluations of the exercise then."

The MechWarriors sketched salutes and veered off. Michi watched them until they disappeared through the door, then turned back to find Minobu gazing at him expectantly from behind the tinted perspex of his goggles. The noise of the Techs' work would prevent their conversation from being overheard.

"Is it wise for you to leave now?" Michi asked, his tone leaving no doubt about what he thought was the wise course.

"Now. Later. There is little difference."

"Now is not a good time. There's been another fight in Bharryspost. Three Ryuken and two of Major Jarrett's Battalion. Nothing serious this time, at least not physically. But this will not be the last incident."

"If there is to be an explosion, there will be one. *Shigata ga nai.*"

Michi ground his teeth together. Minobu had used the phrase to dismiss Michi's concerns with frustrating regularity. Ever since the accident, the *Tai-sa* seemed resigned to whatever happened around him. Michi would not let it drop this time. "If you go now, you will be responsible for the trouble."

"Nonsense. You are here to keep things steady. You have grown into your own responsibilities over these last months and can easily keep Major Jarrett clear of the pitfalls of rash action. Besides, Colonel Arbuthnot will be traveling to An Ting as well. His officers will do nothing drastic while he is gone."

"Then you still intend to go to An Ting?"

"Of course. I must see my family," Minobu said matter-of-factly.

Michi was not fooled. Minobu had not had much to do with his family since his recovery. "That is not your real motive. You could delegate someone to that task."

"And what is my real motive? Have you determined that, as well as what I should and should not do?" Minobu spoke without heat.

"You are going to talk to Colonel Wolf," Michi answered accusingly. "He is due back on An Ting soon, isn't he? That is why Colonel Arbuthnot is going there."

"Whether it is my true motive or not, my inquisitive friend, I will not say. I do intend to speak to Jaime Wolf. At least to learn how went his trip to Luthien."

"Do you think Lord Kurita will have straightened things out? Surely he has seen past the lies of Samsonov and Akuma."

"Perhaps." Minobu looked out the window at the sky. Heavy, snow-bearing clouds were moving in from the north-east. "There is a storm coming," he said. "We have no way to avoid it, and so we must prepare for it as best we can."

36

An Ting Orbital Station
Galedon Military District, Draconis Combine
2 January 3028

"DropShip *Wolf Pack One* has docked at Bay Twenty-Seven," the voice repeated for those who might not have understood the first announcement in Japanese. The words of the announcer were clipped as though it annoyed the speaker to repeat the obvious.

"See. I told you that was about the Colonel's ship." Susan Lean looked like her name, and seemed far too youthful to be wearing a Captain's star. She was pleased at the small intelligence victory over her three fellow Captains. Lean was especially pleased that she had caught something that Anton Shadd had missed. She considered the hot shots in the Seventh Kommando entirely too cocky.

"But when we boarded, they said it would be Bay Twenty-Two," Dechan Fraser complained.

"Whether they lied or just made a mistake don't matter, kid," drawled Shadd, a compact, muscular commando. His large hands, marked with an astonishing number of scars, fidgeted with an unlit cigarette. He wore a dress uniform that looked too new for someone who had served so long in the Dragoons, and his twitches and shrugs showed that he was uncomfortable in the uniform's restrictive tailoring. The announcement of Wolf's imminent arrival had awakened

Shadd from the mood of sullen preoccupation that had dominated him ever since shuttling over from the *Hephaestus*. "What matters is that we meet the Colonel when he comes aboard."

With that, the commando tossed his cigarette away and headed for the corridor. The fourth member of their group was a step ahead. William Cameron's long legs put him in the lead and kept him there as the Dragoons trotted along the curve of the wheel. Passengers awaiting transport and gray-and-tan uniformed station crew all dodged out of the way of the purposeful quartet. They passed occasional station monitors, whose pendant chestplates distinguished them from regular crew, but none questioned their haste.

Cameron turned the corner into the waiting area for Bay 27 and pulled up to a sudden halt. Dechan and Lean piled into him, almost knocking him down. Stepping to one side of the tangled Dragoons, Shadd reached for his sidearm. He stopped when he saw why Cameron had stalled.

Lounging at his ease in the reception area was *Chu-sa* Jerry Akuma. Dressed in his Ryuken duty uniform, the man was immaculate, as always. The chain that proclaimed his position as PSL officer glinted coldly on his chest. Akuma removed his polished boots from where he'd propped them on a table, and rose to his feet, adopting a nonchalant pose. He seemed not at all surprised by the Dragoons' sudden appearance.

Shadd assessed Akuma's half-smile and the look in his eyes as amusement over something that had turned out exactly as expected. It was a petty victory that would cost the Dragoons nothing, and so the commando relaxed. Akuma wasn't the kind of threat he could deal with using a laser pistol. Not yet, at least. Shadd let his contempt of Akuma's petty maneuvering show in his face.

This fellow is a small surprise, Akuma thought. *He does not wear the designation of a MechWarrior. Yet he carries himself as one, not like some half-trained support trooper or out-of-tone staffer. His reactions are quick, attuned to the world in a way that a MechWarrior is not. He is almost as sharp as Quinn, standing quietly in the corner. This Dragoon has none of the cocky air of invulnerability that is such a pitiably common flaw in 'Mech pilots. He is a man who re-*

lies on himself and what he can hold in his hands. An interesting find among the Dragoons. Is he an anomaly, Akuma wondered, *or do the Dragoons have assets not listed on their personnel rosters?*

When Akuma saw Shadd relax, lowering his guard before noticing Quinn, he decided that perhaps the man was not so dangerous after all. Even an entire battalion of Dragoons like this Captain could do little to halt the inevitable. Those who slackened their attention in the presence of potential danger were no threat.

"Come in, officers," Akuma invited. "I expect you are here to meet Colonel Wolf. The boarding locks are completing their cycle now, so you won't have long to wait."

The Dragoon officers stepped cautiously into the chamber, spreading out around the padded benches of the waiting area. Akuma noticed the sharp turn of the head when Shadd became aware of the tall, blond man in the corner. Though Akuma knew the black-clad Quinn was acutely aware of his surroundings, the man moved not a muscle in reaction to the Dragoons. Shadd pretended the Kuritan was not there, a detente that amused Akuma.

The sound of the inner airlock door cycling preempted any further interactions. Pneumatic cylinders whined as they released the locks that sealed the waiting area from the passageway to the docked DropShip. The heavy metal door slid back into the wall, revealing seven figures moving down the jointed tunnel. They were backlit shadows, unrecognizable until they reached the light spill from the waiting room. Shadows became people as Wolf and his five officers stepped onto An Ting orbital station. The seventh person was a Kurita officer who bowed stiffly to Akuma and then to Wolf before striding from the chamber without a word.

Wolf's face was grim, and it did not need a *ki* master to see that he was upset. Akuma knew that it was probably because of Kurita Space Command's refusal to allow the DropShip to proceed from the JumpShip to the *Hephaestus* station until they had placed an escort officer aboard. These were, he decided, more well-placed irritants.

Wolf took in Akuma and his man in the corner, then deliberately snubbed them by turning his back. "What's going on here?" he said to his own officers.

Cameron cleared his throat to focus Wolf's attention on himself. He threw a glance at Akuma. "Ah . . . Colonel," he began.

Wolf held up a hand to stop him, then turned with a frown toward Akuma, the hand still elevated. The Kuritan stood his ground even when Wolf jerked his head in the direction of the corridor.

Akuma pretended to take Wolf's gesture as an invitation to speak. "I do not understand the reluctance of your officers to speak. They seemed anxious to see you when they arrived." Then he feigned a look of sudden revelation. "Ah, perhaps, they have unkind things to say about the Combine. Let them be frank. I am your Professional Soldiery Liaison, after all. If there are complaints, you should be able to air them in my presence. There might be something I could do."

"Doesn't matter whether he stays or not, Colonel. I expect there isn't anyplace on this station where we won't be overheard," Major Stanford Blake said as he stepped up. His hostility was evident in his scornful tone.

Wolf nodded.

"All right, William. Let's have it."

Cameron began almost reluctantly "Well, Colonel, it's like this. There's been a lot of friction with the Draconians since you left. Our reputation among the civilians is being undermined by constant misrepresentation in the Kuritan media. And we're getting the same raw treatment on all the garrison worlds. The result has been demonstrations, protests, brawls, and strikes, but nothing we haven't been able to handle. So far. The troops are getting itchy, Colonel. I think we have trouble brewing."

"Brewing!" burst in Dechan Fraser. He had been impatient throughout Cameron's speech. "Boiled over, more like! Quit dancing around it, Cameron."

"At ease, Captain Fraser," Blake cautioned.

"What are you talking about, son?" Wolf asked quietly, his eyes showing deep concern."

"There was a fight last night. Some Dracs got themselves hurt."

"How bad?"

Dechan's eyes were on the floor. "They got themselves hurt dead."

Wolf's tone was calm, but it was now a glacial calm. "Exactly what happened?"

Dechan hesitated and Shadd stepped in. "Five members of Fraser's company, three of Lean's, and two of my . . . er . . . friends, were taking their off-duty in a bar called Munnen's. It's an O.K. hole. Ever since our people started to frequent it, the crowd has become all Dragoons or friends. The locals knew it. The bar was crowded last night, some kind of festival, I guess. Lotsa out-of-towners, some Ryuken Jocks and a few of the former regulars, but mostly strangers. Things got a bit noisy, and some of the strangers had some things to say about the Dragoons. Our people took it unkindly and answered with their fists. When the smoke cleared, we had five of ours for medevac, one critical. There were three Dracs for the bag. All wearing civvies."

"This is most disturbing, Colonel Wolf," Akuma said indignantly. "I am appalled at your Dragoons' lack of restraint."

"Those troublemakers only got what they asked for," Dechan insisted.

Shadd put a hand on Dechan's shoulder as he cut him off. The pressure calmed Dechan in a way that the commando's words couldn't. "Take it easy, kid."

The commando addressed his next words to Wolf. "The fight was fair enough. Those Dracs were playing with fire and got burned."

"There will be repercussions," Blake pointed out. "I'm sure we'll be hearing from eyewitnesses who'll say that the Dragoons provoked the confrontation."

Akuma ignored the intel officer's stare. He shifted his own eyes to Wolf's face, trying to gauge how the mercenary Colonel was taking the situation. Wolf's expression gave no hint.

"Perhaps," Akuma prodded, "that was the case. Perhaps your troopers thought that they could use the opportunity of the New Year Festival to hide their criminal actions. Perhaps they provoked innocent citizens to create violence that would soothe their own savage souls. Deliberate provocation by a trained warrior against an untrained civilian might be considered murder."

"Murder! Those malking Snakes weren't civilian or untrained! They put five good soldiers into hospital. We're being set up!"

"Fraser!" Wolf snapped. "Damp it!"

Akuma's tone was ominous. "This incident could lead to worse things."

Wolf glared indignantly at Akuma. "Such as the DCMS stepping in?"

"Military intervention would be a most drastic course, Colonel. It is certainly not one I would recommend in this matter. Your own officers report that the troops were off-duty. By the terms of contract, they fall under civilian legal jurisdiction if they leave designated military enclaves while off-duty. It would seem, therefore, to be a civil matter—one suited to the Civilian Guidance Corps and under the jurisdiction of the Ministry of Justice. If an investigation shows guilt, your soldiers will most assuredly pay for their crimes. Until that time, I expect that the troopers in question and any others involved in the case, as witnesses or peripheral participants, will remain on planet."

Several of the Dragoons grumbled at that, which pleased Akuma, though he hid it well. His face was smooth and his voice bland. "I assure you, Colonel Wolf, that there will be no military involvement in civil problems."

"You're not going to make it easy, are you?"

"Whatever do you mean, Colonel?" Akuma asked, pretending puzzlement he did not feel.

"All right. We'll play it your way for now."

Wolf turned to Cameron. "William, set up your shuttle to take Kormenski and her crew back to *Hephaestus*."

"What about us, Colonel?" Shadd spoke for the assembled captains.

"I want the four of you to go planetside with Blake and me on *Pack-One*. Let's move it." As the Dragoons moved to follow orders, Wolf turned back to Akuma as though struck by sudden thought.

"As our *liaison*, will you answer some questions concerning our interaction with your Draconis Combine?"

"Of course, Colonel. That is my job."

"Why didn't I hear anything about these problems on the way from Luthien?"

Akuma spread his hands to indicate helplessness. "I have no knowledge of this lack of information. My office forwarded regular reports to the systems on your route. They should have been waiting for you. Did you not receive them?"

A frown was Wolf's only reply.

"I am a simple soldier, Colonel Wolf, not a ComStar Adept. Perhaps you should speak with them, for it is they who handle all interstellar communications. Perhaps you should question your officers as well. If you have received no reports from them, it may be because they fear to report their own negligence and incompetence."

Wolf raised his head at the last allegation. Akuma knew it was false, but was once again gratified to have raised the Dragoon's hackles. Wolf would not believe it, but once voiced, the hint that he could not trust his own would always rankle. It would be a worm to gnaw at the mercenary's belief in his subordinates, a seed to be nurtured.

"Why have Dragoon communications been jammed insystem?" Wolf asked, ignoring Akuma's thrust.

"Do not be paranoid, Colonel. The jamming is part of a duly scheduled exercise by my Ryuken-*ichi,* whose maneuvers should be concluded in a few hours. Until then, you are not the only ones affected. You will soon be able to do all the talking you wish." In a performance calculated to further agitate Wolf, Akuma added patronizingly, "I look forward to seeing how you handle this."

Akuma started for the tunnel to the DropShip, Quinn falling in behind. Wolf was left standing. "Shall we go downstairs?" Akuma called back.

Wolf answered him with a cold stare, but then set his jaw and followed along.

37

Hoshon Mansion, Cerant, An Ting
Galedon Military District, Draconis Combine
2 January 3028

Minobu roamed through the house, having finished packing his ceramics. All that remained was to prepare his *kyudo* equipment for shipment. Except for the disruption inherent in the packing for a move, things were normal. Yet a vague unease nagged at him. Something was wrong, out of place.

The Hoshon Mansion had been his home for almost five years, and those years had been full ones. His eldest son Ito had applied to the Sun Zhang Academy and been accepted, bringing pride, and secret relief, to the father. His daughter Tomoe had grown from a rowdy gawk into a beautifully mannered young lady. Little Kiyomasa, no longer so little, had become a sturdy youth who promised to outstrip his father's own two-meter height in a few years. That boy was going to find any 'Mech cockpit a tight fit.

They had been good years, and the mansion had been lit with warmth and happiness. There had been shadows, too, for business had intruded here far too often. The darkest memory that this house held for Minobu was the near-estrangement of Tomiko after his injuries on Barlow's End. At first, she had been unable to accept it, refusing to look at him unless he was clothed. Even then, her eyes would avoid the black plastic hand that protruded from his sleeve. Yet even that had eventually passed, as do all things in this universe.

During Minobu's last leave from the regiment on Misery, Tomiko had put aside her distaste for the artificial arm and leg and returned to his bed. She had avoided touching the replacements, but that was understandable. She had not had as long as he to get used to their dry, unyielding surfaces.

From her tearful account, Minobu had learned that Marisha Dandridge was instrumental in Tomiko's turnabout. The sage counsel of Wolf's lady had helped his wife accept that Minobu had not changed, that he was still her husband, no matter what. Tomiko realized finally that the man, the essence she loved, was still there.

Despite the relief of his wife's return, Minobu was struck by the cosmic jest of it. She had come back because she believed him the same. He knew only too well that he was not.

Certainly, he still loved Tomiko. Without a thought, he could forgive her foolishness over his artificial limbs. Such a reaction was to be expected of a woman, especially one like Tomiko, so concerned with appearance. His love for her remained strong, but he was not the same man she had married sixteen years before. These last five years had changed him.

The roots of that change went back to Dromini VI, where he had committed an action that resulted in his being relieved of his command. Minobu had never understood why, but he had not questioned it. It was a samurai's duty to obey, not to question. Indeed, it was that belief in duty that kept him from despair. But the messages he had received—the dismissal from command and the promotion that accompanied it—were contradictory. And then another promotion followed, this one accompanied by a warning that it was only a sham. When assigned to the Dragoons, Minobu had been a very confused man.

He knew now that the assignment had been a turning point. His confusion began to clear as he began to realize that many of his long-held assumptions were false. Against the falsehoods, he had held to his honor, which had sustained him through those times. Honor was, after all, the foundation of a samurai's existence.

Standing on that bedrock of honor, he had met Jaime

Wolf, a man with the name of a ravening beast but the heart of a true warrior. Another contradiction, but Minobu had been curious enough to look below the surface. Beyond the exterior of the driven mercenary Colonel, Minobu had found a man who believed in honor, and that man looked at those around him, the way he dealt with others. When he had changed Minobu could not guess, but the transformation continued even now to affect his life.

Oh no, he was not the same man Tomiko had married.

Yet, he was still Minobu Tetsuhara, loyal Kurita samurai and even stronger than before he had encountered Jaime Wolf and his Dragoons. After Lord Kurita had removed him from the Second Sword of Light, Minobu had lost his inner peace and with it, his *ki.* His years of loyal service as PSL Officer and the confidence fostered by Jaime's friendship had helped him to regain his balance and to renew his inner strength. After the crippling accident on Barlow's End, he had been able to call upon his *ki* to fortify himself through the trials of recovery. This time, he had not lost *muga.* Its peace fueled his *ki* and that gave him more from his prosthetic limbs than the doctors had ever thought possible. They did not believe in *ki* and scoffed at his explanations, but that did not alter the truth.

His *ki* told him that something was not right here in the mansion today. Nothing more than a sense of unease . . . a sense of deception . . . came to him. There was no warning of immediate danger, no focus to the disturbance.

Headed down the corridor toward the garden, a servant bustled by, carrying a wrapped package. So busy was his tasks, the servant made no more than a brief bow to his master. The move, Minobu thought, is very disruptive to the patterns of everyday life.

He decided that it could be the only explanation for his feeling of unrest. This was, after all, more than a simple translocation. Tomiko and the children would not be joining him on Misery, but would go to the family estates on Awano, where they would be safe. Given the state of relations between Wolf's Dragoons and House Kurita, he could not allow them to accompany him to Misery. To protect all involved, Minobu had resolved to keep the destination secret even from Tomiko. Though his deception was based in good intentions, its disharmony with the universe would add to his feeling of disturbance.

Minobu walked down the passageway to the bed chamber. From the doorway, he could see Tomiko and Marisha busily rearranging piles of carefully folded garments. They moved the clothes from one chest to another, all the while debating the best way to pack the wardrobe. From their talk, Minobu could tell that Tomiko was assuming she would accompany him to Misery, as should any dutiful wife. He had stood there only a few moments before she looked up to see him watching. Tomiko smiled at him, but the smile faded slightly as she discerned his troubled state of mind.

"The packing is going slowly, husband. I hope we shall be finished in time," she said, wondering if his concern was about that. "When do we leave for Misery?"

"I return to the regiment tomorrow."

"Tomorrow! Then we had best get fin . . ." Tomiko stopped in mid-sentence when she realized what he had said. "You? If it is just you, why have you had me packing my things and those of the children?"

"Because you are leaving An Ting."

Tomiko glanced at Marisha. Not a word passed between them, but Marisha understood the wordless request. She excused herself to check on Tomoe's progress. With Dandridge gone, Tomiko gave Minobu a stern look. "You have an explanation, husband?"

"Only I am going to Misery. It is no world for women and children." He stilled her objections by putting a finger to her lips. "I understand your devotion, wife. But I will hear no protests. You are going to Awano with the children."

"Awano." Tomiko turned her back to him and hung her head forlornly. "There is more to this than the living conditions on Misery."

"No, it is only that."

When Minobu reached out to take her shoulders in his hands, she shrugged clear of his embrace. She had heard the lie in his voice. He lowered his hands and stared helplessly out the open panel at the archery range. At the far end of the range, he saw the servant who had passed him in the corridor disappear into the shadows of the tower. Minobu wished he could disappear as easily.

Tomiko turned toward her husband and reached up to touch his face, fingers carefully avoiding the pale scars of the reconstructive surgery. The faint pressure of her touch turned his face to hers.

"Can you look at me and say that it is only the conditions on Misery?"

Minobu's eyes searched hers. He saw that he could not tell her all that he feared. She had her own fears. Lost in his concerns, he did not speak, and his silence gave her the answer she was expecting.

"You have put me aside. That is why I have seen so little of you."

"That is not so," he said, wiping away the tear that wet her cheek.

"Do not do this, husband. I have changed. Truly, I have. I can accept it now," she said, touching his artificial arm. There was need in her voice. It warred with the revulsion that she still tried to hide.

"We can return to what we had," she added in a tiny voice.

"You have indeed changed. Now you no longer understand me. I wish no gulf between us, Miko-*chan,* but you cannot come to Misery."

"Then, at least, let me be with you now," she sobbed, throwing her arms around him.

He returned the embrace with his natural arm, then, carefully, with the artificial one. She did not flinch. Instead, she held him closer with a fierceness she had never shown before. They kissed, each responding to the other's desire. Their passion led them to the *futon,* with their clothes scattered behind them.

As they lay quietly after their lovemaking, Minobu felt the return of the day's nagging tension. It was a siren call, a message that he could neither understand nor ignore. It prodded him to action, but did not tell him what that action should be or what should be its target. He only knew he could not remain still.

Tomiko dozed against his right side, the replacement parts of his ravaged left side away from her touch. He was reluctant to disturb her, but he must rise. As gently as he could, he slipped his arm from beneath her head. Half-asleep, the motion barely disturbed her. When she rolled over, he was free to stand up and began to pull on his kimono. Just as he was reaching for his sash, Minobu caught his wife watching him with eyes wide and full of worry.

"What is the matter, husband?"

He wrapped the sash around his waist. "Something is wrong," he said.

"With me?"

Minobu shook his head. "Never. I do not know what it is, but it is not a problem between us. That, at least, is at rest."

"Then you should rest. Come back under the covers," she said, holding out her arms. The gentle light that came through the *shoji* panels made her flesh shine with an alabaster radiance.

Minobu was tempted. Very strongly tempted. "I think I would find little rest under those covers."

Her smile confirmed his suspicions.

"No, Miko-*chan,* I cannot. Much as I wish to, I cannot." It was the truth. His unease had grown and began to pull strongly at him. He could not lose himself in her arms now.

"*Shigata go nai.* Do what you must. I will understand."

"I know."

Minobu moved toward the veranda. He walked as though on another plane, Tomiko forgotten behind him. Whatever disturbed him was not in this house. With the cool breeze blowing through his light kimono, the feeling intensified. Yes, the source was somewhere out here.

The unease crystallized into a clear warning of danger, a sensation Minobu had never experienced before except on the battlefield. His head jerked up, eyes settling on the corner tower. There, crouched on the balcony of the third level, was a figure. The shadowy shape was manipulating a long object that glinted coldly in the afternoon light. A rifle.

Trusting his *ki*, Minobu acted.

A shrug and a twist of his torso freed the left side of his body from the confines of the garment. Dark skin and darker plastic drank the late afternoon sunlight. Minobu threw open the cabinet that held his archery equipment and snatched a bow. Muscles bunched and coiled as he bent it and slipped the string into place. Arrow in hand, he turned to face the tower once more.

The figure was leaning against the railing, the rifleman steadying his weapon on the rail as he sighted at some target in the city. Minobu's sense of danger peaked.

He fitted the arrow to the string and rested the shaft against the plastic of his artificial hand. In a smooth, continuous motion, he raised the bow above his head, lowered in the draw, and loosed. The arrow sped true, striking the target just as the other man squeezed off his shot.

The weapon twinkled in the light as it fell from the tower. The dark figure crumpled.

It was too late.

38

Central Square, Cerant, An Ting
Galedon Military District, Draconis Combine
2 January 3028

Akuma's staff car had slowed progressively as it moved through the city of Cerant. At the edge of the central square, the driver brought the vehicle to a halt. For the moment, its bulk, even reinforced by the Draconis Combine ensigns flying from its fenders, could gain it no headway. The square and the streets leading to it were choked with people. Angry people.

"It seems you have a reception committee, Colonel Wolf," Akuma commented, indicating the crush of bodies beyond the one-way windows of the vehicle. Wolf and Blake watched the throng but said nothing. Quinn seemed oblivious to his surroundings.

Wolf glanced through the back window to be sure that the second car was still behind them. It had stopped with its bumper nearly touching Akuma's car.

"Checking to see if your hotheads are about to get into trouble, Colonel?"

"Just making sure your driver didn't take a wrong turn."

"Hardly necessary," Akuma harrumphed. "Driver, take the car as close as you can to the Dragoon headquarters. We don't want to make our passengers walk too far."

The car crept forward. Progress was slow, but relatively

steady. Even the most vociferous and obstinate members of the crowd eventually gave way when it became clear that the vehicle was going to proceed whether they moved or not.

The mob's attention was directed toward the administrative HQ, where a cordon of Dragoon soldiers stood at the base of the steps. They wore combat armor and full helmets, their faces invisible behind the visors. Each trooper held a Ceres Arms M-22 Crowdbuster, a formidable stun rifle. The weapon's bulky appearance made it intimidating, and it was well-balanced for use as a bludgeon.

Halfway up the stairs, a pair of Dragoon officers divided their attention between the mob and a detail of Dragoons erecting barricades to link the columns of the portico into a defensible perimeter. Two sandbag emplacements flanked the main doors, each with a semi-portable laser and crew. The heavy weapons were a statement to the mob that the Dragoons were ready to answer serious violence with serious firepower.

Outside the cordon, the crowd roared as a straw effigy in a mocked-up Dragoon uniform burst into flame. It burned with the fierce heat of gasoline-fed flames, and people came forward to spit on it. Every time the breeze fanned the flames, the mob's cries peaked. The red-and-white striped uniforms of the Civilian Guidance Corps were nowhere to be seen.

The staff car came to a halt at the ruins of a festival wagon. In the press, there was no room to maneuver the vehicle. The car following had pulled close again, and that prevented the driver from backing up. They were still twenty meters from the steps to the Dragoon HQ. "We're not getting any closer, *Chu-sa-sama,*" the driver told Akuma.

Wolf reached for the door handle.

"Be careful, Colonel," Akuma warned.

"I didn't know you cared," Wolf replied dryly. Blake smirked at the sarcasm in his Colonel's voice.

"I would not care to see you the victim of random violence."

Wolf forced the door open and stood beside the car. As soon as the Colonel had elbowed out enough space amid the milling throng, Blake followed. No longer protected by the baffled interior of the vehicle, they could now hear the jeers, taunts, and recriminations the crowd hurled at the Dragoon soldiers. "Cowards" and "turncoats" were among the milder epithets that rose above the general uproar. Then a single voice stood out above the hubbub, screaming that the Dragoons were wanton murderers of innocents, and naming them *teki*.

Wolf marked the speaker as the crowd took up the chant of "Enemy! Enemy!"

"Keep your eye on that one in the red tunic, Stan," Wolf ordered as he started to force his way toward the rabble-rouser. Too short to see over most of the crowd, the mercenary relied on Blake's directions, correcting his course whenever their target moved.

A sudden shift of the crowd left Wolf facing his quarry's back. Stepping up to close the distance, he threw a back-handed slap against the man's shoulder blade.

"Hey, you!" Wolf addressed the man in his best battlefield voice, speaking Japanese for the crowd's benefit. "You've got a big mouth for somebody who needs to hide in a crowd. If you have accusations, you say them to me, to my face. I'm Jaime Wolf."

The man turned around. He stood a full thirty centimeters taller than Wolf and was built like a wrestler. Throwing out his chest and tensing his muscles, he frowned disdainfully at the short mercenary. The practiced ease with which the man went through those motions showed how used he was to intimidating people with his size alone, especially those smaller than him.

Wolf was unimpressed.

"Lost your taste for speeches now that someone is here to call you on your lies?" Wolf demanded.

The man's eyes narrowed beneath his bushy eyebrows. They darted to the left as the man glanced over Wolf's shoulder.

Trusting Blake to warn him of treachery, Wolf turned his head to follow the rabble-rouser's line of sight back toward the staff car. Akuma had gotten out and was standing on the vehicle's door frame, his tall, lanky frame visible even to Wolf. Wolf thought he saw Akuma nod, but a disturbance near the second vehicle distracted him. The Dragoons who had been traveling in it had disembarked and were working their way through the crowd. When Wolf looked back, the Draconian bully was ready to bluster.

"So you are the barbarian Wolf. You seem an insignificant package to have caused so much grief to the people of the Draconis Combine."

The mob around them had quieted.

Wolf was getting the confrontation he had asked for and now he had to deal with it. "And you seem to have gotten away from your keepers, lackwit. I didn't come here to trade insults. You've called the Dragoons murderers and I call you a liar."

"I am no liar! You are the liar if you deny what the Dragoons have done. These people here have all heard of the butchery your bandits performed against the peaceful people on the planet of Kawabe. Now you have brought your violence here to An Ting."

"We have killed no peaceful people on this or any other world."

"Hear his lies, fellow Draconians! You know me. I am Albert Nitta. You know I am an honest man. I myself saw two of his men brutally attack and kill an innocent man in a bar last night. They had no cause—the poor fellow merely got in their way." Nitta raised his arms and shouted, "Citizens, we must rid ourselves of these vermin before they decide our children are in their way!"

"You've got your facts wrong." Wolf's tone held a clear note of warning.

"Now the cowardly cur wants to call facts to his defense. His kind of facts will have little truth to them," Nitta called out. "He hopes to slip away from our justice on the grease of a facile tongue, to blind our eyes with glib lies. I can tell you the facts. The truth is that three loyal sons of the Dragon lie dead today, their blood on the hands of mercenary scum. Those are facts, villain. Can you deny them? Can you silence my voice of truth?"

A new voice broke in before Wolf could answer. It was shrill and cut through the crowd's murmur like a laser slicing paper. "Look out, the *teki* has a gun!" The words were punctuated with the report of a gunshot.

Nitta stiffened as though about to hurl himself at Wolf, then a thin trickle of blood escaped from the corner of his mouth. He toppled forward at the mercenary Colonel in a disjointed sprawl.

Wolf got one arm around Nitta before he could hit the ground. The man was heavy, dead weight. Nitta's body slipped from Wolf's grip, its mass and the slick blood covering the man's back making it impossible to hold. Wolf's right hand and arm were covered with Nitta's blood.

With a howl of rage, the mob surged forward. Bodies crashed into Wolf. Hands struck and pawed at him. He smashed out with his elbows. He kicked and bit. The tide of humanity was too strong for his efforts, and the mob overwhelming.

Blake was attacked as well, but his greater mass and lesser age let him strike back more effectively. Several Kuritans whirled away, screaming their pain, before the weight of multiple attackers caught and pinned the Major's arms. A few seconds later, Blake, too, went down under a snarling mass.

The screeching of a stunner rifle cut the air as the Dragoon guards on the steps opened fire. Draconians fell in windrows on either side of the melee around the fallen Wolf. The Dragoons dared not fire too close, however. If one of their burst caught the Colonel, Wolf would have no chance against his attackers.

Lieutenant Riker was about to order his men to form a wedge to charge through the mob when the Dragoons from the second car began to force their way toward the Colonel. They were considerably closer. The Lieutenant redirected some of his men to fire on the portion of the throng between the struggling Dragoons and the scuffle where Wolf had disappeared under a pile of Kuritan bodies. Riker's decision proved to be a wise one.

Struggling to come to the Colonel's aid, Anton Shadd didn't know why the pressure against his advance had eased, but he took advantage of it. A few well-placed punches at the Dracs in front of him opened a relatively clear path through the mob. Only sprawled bodies and a few stumbling, half-aware Kuritans were between him and the knot around the Colonel. Galvanized at seeing flashes of the Dragoons uniform, the commando bolted forward.

Behind him, his companions broke through as well. He

heard Fraser's whoop as the kid pounded after. Shadd didn't have time to look back, so he missed Cameron's tumble over a fallen Draco. Lean stopped to help her comrade, leaving only Shadd and Fraser in the first assault against the snarling mob around the Colonel.

Without thought of backup, the commando threw himself into the knot of Snakes pounding on Wolf. Bodies flew as eighty-two kilos of hardened muscle and bone struck. Shadd went down with them, but he was prepared. He struck out with hands and feet, knees and elbows. Rough and tumble was the way he liked it. Five seconds later, he was on his feet again, but those he had bowled over were not.

Fraser arrived in time to lay low a street punk who was using a brick against Blake's head, then the young Dragoon immediately engaged with two of the Draco's friends. Or so they seemed, dressed in the same gang colors as the fallen punk.

Wolf was on his hands and knees, battered, bloodied, but still alive. He was moving slowly and seemed unaware of the screaming harridan who rose up beside him with a knife. Fraser and Blake were occupied with their own problems. Cameron and Lean had just resumed their progress toward the melee. They were too far away to be any help.

It was Shadd who launched himself into a flying kick. His *kiai* shout carried above the bedlam, momentarily stilling it. The crack as the woman's neck snapped was audible over most of the square. Even before her body hit the ground, Shadd was up and had recovered the knife.

"Come on, Colonel. We've got to get you out of here."

Shadd had to help Wolf stand. The Colonel was shaky, disoriented, and covered with blood, some of it his own. Shadd could not tell how serious the injuries were. The Colonel was too old for this kind of ill-use.

Cameron and Lean arrived in time to help Fraser and Blake finish off the last of their immediate opponents. For the moment, the mob held back, unsure what to do about the new furies in their midst. Shadd did not want to give them time to recover. Hit them and vanish was the rule in Seventh Kommando. Vanishing with this crowd around them was going to be a little tricky.

"Major!" Shadd shouted. "We've got to get the Colonel inside. He's hurt."

"Right." Blood streamed down the side of Blake's face from a gash on his scalp. He looked worse than Wolf but was considerably steadier on his feet. "Everybody else functional?"

A quick chorus of ayes replied.

"Shadd, on point. Fraser, rear guard. Lean, right flank," Blake ordered. He himself took up the left side. He didn't need to give Cameron an order, for the comm officer was already supporting the Colonel. Somebody had to do it, and Cameron was the least effective fighter of the group. "Let's move it!"

The rescue of Wolf, and the speed with which the Dragoons had organized, caught their tormentors off-guard. Shadd's sudden plunge into the midst of the press had gained the fugitives a fair bit of ground, as much from surprise as from his liberal use of the knife he still held.

They had made it only a quarter of the way to the steps when Shadd went up against an armored figure. He almost struck the trooper down in a reflexive move before he recognized the Dragoon's equipment.

After making it possible for Shadd and his group to reach Wolf in time, Lieutenant Riker had organized a sally by the cordon guards. Once the beleaguered Dragoons were safely inside a ring of armored bodies, the guards opened up freely with their Crowdbusters. Only fallen bodies opposed the Dragoon retreat to the steps.

The mob, cheated of its prey, stormed up behind them in an attempt to reclaim the victims they had let slip from their grip. A volley of concentrated stunner fire took out the leaders, and the crowd recoiled. Belligerent Kuritans hurled rocks and bottles. Bits of rotten food rained down on the steps of the barricade.

Safe behind that shelter, Blake turned. In a voice loud enough to carry over the abusive shouting of the mob, he shouted, "Clear the steps! Go home!"

The crowd only jeered him.

"All right," he said more quietly. "Lieutenant, sweep the steps with the stunners. I don't want any Draco standing on our property."

"Yessir!"

Blake didn't need to see the face behind the helmet visor to know it wore a pleased smile. Riker passed the order to his men. Blake watched as they opened up, the keening wail of massed Crowdbusters drowning out the roar of the crowd. With no protection and nowhere to run, people began to fall. The mob's nerve broke. They routed.

Though the stunners were not aimed at him, Blake's head ached from more than the head wound he had taken. Without the sound baffles of a helmet, the close-range buzz from the weapons affected him. That ache would be with him for hours, but he did not care. He felt a savage satisfaction. Some of the Kuritans had taken multiple stunner hits. Such abuse heaped on a living system often had serious results. Blake hoped some would die.

In minutes, the square was empty of rioters. The bodies lay where they had fallen. A few semi-conscious Kuritans wandered about. In their dazed state, they were more a threat to themselves than to anyone else. Broken festival wagons littered the pavement. The square looked like the aftermath of a battle.

39

Dragoon Administrative HQ, Cerant, An Ting
Galedon Military District, Draconis Combine
2 January 3028

The two Kurita staff cars stood silently in the square, reefs in a sea of debris and bodies. They were scratched and dented and their surfaces were marred by smears of food, but they were otherwise unharmed.

The rear door of the first limousine opened and Akuma stepped out, ever pristine in his uniform. Picking his way toward the Dragoon HQ, he carefully avoided the fallen bodies and clutter left behind by the fighting. The hulking blond mass of his bodyguard trooped behind him.

No Dragoon made a move to stop the approaching Kuritans, but Blake could tell from the way trigger fingers twitched that several thought about it. When Akuma shifted his path to pass by Blake, the intel officer stepped into the Draconian's way.

"I believe that I should see Colonel Wolf," Akuma announced, undaunted.

"*I* believe the Colonel will want a few minutes before he talks to you."

Akuma inclined his head. "A reasonable request. Shall we wait inside?"

Malking Snake, Blake thought. *As though nothing had*

happened. I can be unreasonably reasonable, too. "If the *Chu-sa* would accompany me to the waiting area."

"Certainly," Akuma replied.

After sending a runner to inform Wolf of their presence, Blake silently escorted the Draconian. Accepting the Dragoon's silent treatment, Akuma sat and waited. After a few minutes, Lean came back with the runner.

"Colonel wants to see you now," she said. When Akuma started to rise, she said, "Not you, Colonel Snake. Wolf wants to talk to Major Blake first."

"As he wishes, Captain. I do suggest that your Colonel not delay over long."

"I think Colonel Wolf knows what he's doing," she snapped back.

"So long as the wait is his doing and not yours." Akuma knew it was petty to agitate Lean this way, but he enjoyed seeing the angry color flush her face. After all, soon there would be no Dragoons to bait.

"Five minutes," she ground out.

"I can certainly wait that long. I will see you then, Captain." He dismissed her with a wave of his hand.

Lean came back exactly on time to escort the Kuritans to the planning room. With her were two security troopers. Unlike the men stationed outside, these carried Ryonex subguns. Akuma decided that this was a warning that any trouble inside the headquarters would be met with deadly force. *How pathetically juvenile,* he thought.

The Dragoons had removed the teak conference table from the center of the planning room and replaced it with a holotank from one of their DropShips. Technicians were busy with it, calling up a map of Cerant. Even the brief glance he allowed himself showed Akuma that the city was reproduced in intricate detail. That surprised him, for his own maps were not as good. What his maps did do, however, was indicate the exact positions of all Kuritan forces as well as the carefully plotted locations of all Dragoon assets. The Dragoons had misplaced several key Ryuken units.

Knowing that it was not wise to show too much interest, he looked around for Wolf. The mercenary Colonel was in conference with Blake on the far side of the room. Though the man looked much the worse for his tumble in the square, he did, unfortunately, seem fully functional. Now, while Wolf was still rattled, would be the time to press matters. Akuma strode up and interrupted the conversation.

"That was quite a demonstration you set off, Colonel Wolf."

Wolf's eyes glittered. "I suppose you didn't know things were this bad."

"I knew that your Dragoons had disturbed the local populace. I had no inkling that they had brought things to the brink of riot."

"So we are to blame."

"How can it be otherwise? You were dissatisfied with your contract and were looking for an excuse to break it, while still preserving your highly overrated sense of honor. But this! I had no idea that you would stoop to murdering innocents to further your ends. That you would slaughter civilians merely exercising their lawful right to protest your criminal behavior. Now you will no doubt claim that the riot was deliberately incited and that you are free from the obligations of your contract. Will you produce evidence that I or my officers organized this threat to you? What is your next move, butcher?"

Wolf said nothing into the stillness that had fallen on the room.

"Have I struck too close to the truth?" Akuma swept his right arm to encompass the Dragoons in the room. "Some of your officers look surprised. Have you not shared this grand plan of yours with them? Are you, in your megalomania, seeking to drag down the good reputations of honest soldiers along with your own? Are you afraid that they would not believe your lies about Kurita treachery? Did you have to manufacture a cause to get them to follow you down your brigand's path?"

"Shut up!" Blake shouted.

"You need lackeys to speak for you?" Akuma threw a contemptuous look in Blake's direction. "Will you silence me as you silenced Nitta? What will you get from that?"

"Nothing," Wolf said at last. "I didn't do him and I won't do you. Loud-mouthed troublemakers aren't worth it. It only dignifies their lies. Silenced or not, I get trouble I don't want. All of our posts on planet are under siege by the mob."

"That is hardly unexpected. You have unleashed the many-headed beast. See what your violence has wrought. You will bring death to your own people."

"Where's the vaunted Civilian Guidance Corps? Your civilians certainly need some guidance." Wolf's voice was cool, but his hands were clenched at his sides. Akuma noticed and was pleased.

"The Corps was hardly expecting this and was probably overwhelmed by this beast you have loosed. But that was in your plan, wasn't it? Now yours is the only force-in-being in Cerant. Do you expect a commission empowering you to restore the peace? Will you then continue your bloody work and suppress the mob? I am sure your 'Mechs will be able to restore order. Kurita casualties will, no doubt, be light."

"So that you can claim we fired on civilians, that we took the law into our own hands?" Wolf shook his head in refusal. "No. You won't get that. Bring your Ryuken into the city."

"So you can claim we march on you? I will not give you an opening to start the battle you so clearly want. The Ryuken will stay clear of the city at this time. I will not provide the threats you seek. Find some other way to convince those who do not believe your lies that House Kurita wishes the Dragoons dead. Find some other way to win back the loyalty of your troops. Your actions shall be on your own head."

Wolf turned from Akuma to Cameron.

"Call all the posts, William. Everyone stays put. No provocations." Wolf looked over his shoulder at Akuma. "Satisfied?"

Akuma was most definitely not satisfied. He had hoped to provoke the Dragoons into rash action. The gambit had failed, but all was not lost. There were a few more turns left on the wheel of the rack. "Your performance has hardly been satisfactory. I assure you that Kurita troops will not strike the first blow."

"Then you had better get ready for a quiet night in the barracks with your boys."

Akuma felt the sting of Wolf's implication. Anger was not

something he could afford here in the nest of his enemies. He turned and stalked off. Quinn gave Wolf a tight smile before following.

When the Kuritans were gone, Shadd approached Wolf. "You took a lot of cop from that Snake, Colonel," he said in a low voice.

Wolf was slow to look up, for he had been lost in thought. "I wanted to get a handle on where he stood in this mess."

"Think he's behind it?"

"Hard to tell. He's certainly taking advantage of it."

"You want he should have an accident?" Shadd fingered the knife he had acquired.

"That's their style, not ours," Wolf admonished him.

Shadd shrugged. "Your call, Colonel."

"I've got something more important for you, Captain. I want to get a message out over the ComStar net, and I need somebody I can trust to get through in one piece. Things are pretty dicey outside right now. One man is less conspicuous than a squad, and you're the only member of the Seventh here."

"I understand, Colonel. Is this the word?"

"No. Not yet. I just want to warn the other garrison planets to watch for trouble. This may be the start of what we've feared. It may not. But we can't afford to take the chance."

40

Dragoon Administrative HQ, Cerant, An Ting
Galedon Military District, Draconis Combine
2 January 3028

"Any word from Shadd?"

"No, Colonel," Cameron replied. "We're still getting jamming from the Kurita ships in orbit. It's blanketing all comm frequencies."

Wolf took a seat near the holotank. He rubbed his face with both hands as though trying to massage away the weariness. It didn't work. He ran his hands up through his close-cropped hair, wincing at each bruise and cut he touched. It had been a long day.

"What about the barracks?"

"We still have hard lines through to them and to the landing field. All report quiet for the past two hours."

"Looks like you can stand down for a while. William, get somebody to take over for you. You could use some rest. Tell your relief that I want to know as soon as we hear from Shadd or get through to the *Hephaestus*."

"Yes, Colonel." Cameron beckoned to another officer to take over the console he was using to monitor the few lines of communications the Dragoons had open. After briefing the woman, he walked over to where Wolf sat. "Perhaps the Colonel should get some rest while it is quiet."

"You're a little young to be my mother, William."

"Just trying to do my job, Colonel. Communications are my responsibility. You're nearly dead on your feet, or would be if you were standing. You can't communicate effectively if you're asleep on the deck."

"How can I argue against such an expert opinion?"

A sudden shouting and commotion came from the corridor. Wolf was up from his seat in an instant, all trace of tiredness gone. He and Cameron ran to the corridor to find it filled with Dragoons. The main doors were open and through them, they could see the shapes of agitated people, silhouetted by the harsh glare of spotlights illuminating the steps.

Wolf grabbed a trooper who was forcing his way toward the planning room.

"What's going on, soldier?"

The trooper almost shrugged off the hand that held him by the shoulder. The look of annoyance vanished when he realized that the man who held him was the one he had been sent to seek. "Armed Dracs, sir. They have a body."

"A Dragoon?"

"I don't think so. Couldn't see for sure. They want to come in. Lieutenant Riker won't let them, per your orders, sir."

"I'm sure they want to see me, too."

"Yessir," the trooper said, surprised that Wolf already knew.

"Well, I'm not in the mood. If the body's not one of ours, tell them to come back tomorrow. If it is one of ours, put the Kuritans on ice and don't worry about being gentle."

Wolf dismissed the soldier and started back to the planning room when the disturbance at the entrance increased. Above the deep tones of the men, Wolf heard a feminine voice.

"Jaime! Jaime, tell them to let us through!" It was Marisha Dandridge.

Wolf was down the corridor as though it were empty. On the steps, he found Marisha standing in front of about a dozen Kuritans. Wolf brushed past the Dragoon guards and embraced her.

"I thought you were safe on the *Hephaestus*."

"Marisha was at the mansion when the riots started," a new voice stated.

Wolf pulled back from his lady to look at the tall, dark Kuritan he had passed without a second thought. He had not expected to see Minobu here. In the stark shadows, he had been just another Draconian to a man who only had eyes for his loved one.

"It was my duty to see her safely into your custody," Minobu continued. "I apologize for the delay, but I waited until I thought it was safe. As it was, we had a little trouble getting here. I hope you were not unduly worried."

"If I had known she was in your care, my friend, I would have had no worries at all," Wolf said, relaxing his grip in Marisha. Still encircled by her arms, he turned toward Minobu. "I didn't know you were on An Ting. We have a lot to talk about."

"We do, indeed. I also brought this," Minobu said, indicating the body one of his men had slung over his shoulders. "I'm afraid it is in no shape to answer any questions, though it poses several."

The Kurita trooper dumped the body at Wolf's feet. The pale skin of its face reflected the light, revealing a visage fixed in a final expression of surprise. The body wore a Kurita uniform with the insignia of the Ryuken-*ni*. It stank of blood and excrement.

"It is not one of mine, despite the clothing. The man had been working at the mansion for several weeks. He was only a servant hired in my absence when the household became shorthanded. He came with excellent references."

"Forged, no doubt," said Stanford Blake, appearing at the edge of the group around the corpse.

The glance Minobu gave the Dragoon suggested that he found him slow-witted and a bit boorish. "A man may be good at more than one thing. Does it matter whether he was a real servant?"

"No, I suppose not," Blake conceded.

Wolf suddenly became aware of all the people standing around. "Let's go inside," he said. "Riker, haul this garbage out of here."

Minobu's men were left in the waiting area, having submitted without a word to being relieved of their weapons.

After detailing a pair of Dragoons to clear away the corpse, Riker returned to his protective vigil. Minobu, Marisha, Wolf, and the Dragoon officers withdrew to the planning room.

Minobu told them of the discovery of the gunman on the tower and of the events that followed. "We were unable to recover his weapon, but we found this on the body," Minobu said as he came to the end of his narrative. "There was nothing else."

Minobu tossed an object onto the table in front of Wolf. It was a package of cigarettes.

Wolf picked it up. Its weight alone betrayed that it was not what it seemed. After poking at it a bit, Wolf triggered a catch. The bottom of the package fell back and a flat black panel with tiny, lozenge-shaped buttons slid out. A second panel popped open and an antenna extended from the package.

"What do you make of it, Blake?" Wolf asked as he handed the device to the intel officer.

Blake looked it over, licking his lips in thought as he considered the object from every angel. "It's a communicator. Short-range. Its pattern fits one used by the Lyran Commonwealth's Bondians."

"Bondians?" Marisha interjected incredulously. "What in Unity's name is a Steiner secret agent doing shooting up Kurita insurrectionists? I would think the Lyrans would be happy to see trouble on a Combine planet."

"Their people certainly like to stir it up," Blake confirmed. "Dropping that loud-mouthed rabble-rouser was a sure way to set the mob off."

"We don't know who the gunman really worked for," Wolf reminded him.

"Just as we do not know his intended target," Minobu added.

At that, Wolf looked sharply at Minobu. The Kuritan's face was impassive, unreadable. Wolf was about to question him when Cameron interrupted. The Captain was back at his comm console, having gone back to work as soon as the group had entered the room.

"Message from Captain Shadd, Colonel. The interference

is still there. This came in uncoded on a hard line from a public utility. Here's a playback."

Cameron touched a stud on his unit and Shadd's voice came from the speaker.

". . . Shadd here. Tell the Colonel that I can't get his message out. The ComStar facility is crawling with armed Robes and Snakes. Locked tight. The Snakes are all in civilian clothing, but most are toting military hardware. The Adept says the HPG is forbidden to the—get this—'outlaw' Dragoons. He says to remind the Colonel of ComStar sanctity and that he'll blow the generator if he sees any 'Mechs. Tell the Colonel I'm headed for the barracks. It's closer and my . . . friends . . . are there. Will call on arrival."

"How long ago did that come in?"

"Just a couple of minutes. He won't have reached the barracks yet."

"Keep a line open to them. Tell the commander that he's on the way and to keep an eye out. A sally is authorized, if necessary, to get him inside. I want to speak to Shadd as soon as he gets there."

"Yessir."

"Blake, I want you to have a talk with ComStar. Find out what this outlaw business is all about." The intel officer was halfway to the comm console by the time Wolf finished speaking.

"This is an unfortunate turn of events, Jaime-*san*," Minobu observed.

"Yes, and it's going to be even more unfortunate for whoever started it," Wolf pledged.

41

Dragoon Administrative HQ, Cerant, An Ting
Galedon Military District, Draconis Combine
2 January 3028

Minobu could see from the set of Wolf's jaw that the mercenary had not taken Shadd's report of the situation at the ComStar facility well at all. Wolf's attitude promised that violence would come from this latest obstacle, violence that would make the riots in the streets pale in comparison.

Minobu listened while Wolf queried his officers for their views of the situation. Some held it was only exaggerated rhetoric that made the ComStar official call the Dragoons outlaw, but the rest believed that the Adept's statement reflected ComStar's official position on the Dragoons. If ComStar branded the Dragoons as outlaws, no one would hire them. They would become targets, hunted fugitives. Even the full force of the largest mercenary group in the Inner Sphere could not stand up to the hosts that the Sphere would bring against them. Every man's hand would be raised against them and no place in the Sphere would be safe.

First to attack them would be House Kurita.

Minobu hung his head. The clouds had gathered even faster than expected, and the dark shadow of those thunderheads now fell between him and his friend. His hope that the ComStar Adept had been merely speaking for effect was slim, but had to be nurtured. Minobu resolved to have the comm officer patch him through to the facility. Despite Samsonov's warning against aiding the Dragoons should they go rogue, Minobu would do what he could for his friend.

Minobu turned to find Cameron listening intently to some communication. The Captain looked up, his face ashen. His blue eyes met Minobu's brown, and the Kuritan read the naked fear in the younger man's eyes.

"The interference has stopped, Colonel." Cameron's voice was as soft and carrying as usual, but it held a quavering note. To anyone who knew him, it was a warning that something was seriously wrong. "We're getting a broadcast from the *Hephaestus*."

Cameron switched on the speaker.

". . . Kurita patriots. We are not terrorists. In the name of the Dragon, we hold these criminals and their orbital facility to ransom. We demand that they answer for their crimes. We demand that all the forces of Wolf's Dragoons on An Ting and on any other planet they defile by their presence lay down their arms. We demand that they surrender to the justice of the Draconis Combine.

"Loyal as we are to the Dragon, we are but ordinary men. We could not hope to stand before the might of trained MechWarriors. We freely admit it so that all will understand why we have acted as we have.

"We are here to see that justice is done. It is not our wish to harm those guilty only by association with the foul curs who lead Wolf's Dragoons. We hold the people of this station hostage to force their villainous superiors to hear our pleas. We call upon whatever shreds of honor remain in the hearts of the Dragoon leadership. Surrender yourselves.

"We wish no harm to innocents. We have taken control of this station without a single death. To prove this, we shall allow the commander of the station to speak." The voice paused for a moment. "State your name and position."

"I am Major James Quo, station master of *Hephaestus*. Our command section is held by this band of . . . Kurita patriots. They have killed no one as yet. From the master console, they have control of all life-support functions. They have it in their power to kill all personnel currently aboard the *Hephaestus*. No one remaining aboard has the ability to threaten the . . . boarders. No one has been killed. I have been given this chance to speak because I promised I would advise all Dragoon officers to listen to the demands of these . . . patriots . . . and to act accordingly. I gave my promise freely. I advise all Dragoon officers who can hear my voice to stand up for themselves. If you cannot convince your officers, take matters into your own hands. Scrag the Snakes!"

Sounds of a shuffle came from the speaker.

Quo's voice came again. He spoke rapidly, a man who knew he had little time. "Aft's free, Colonel. Seventh on hull. Hold out! We can—"

A gunshot cut off the Major's words.

The first voice returned. The speaker was out of breath, as though he had been violently exercising. "Quo is a fool and a liar, like all the Dragoon commanders. This station is totally under our control. He sought to engender more of the violence he worshipped. If you follow his advice, you will meet death.

"We are resolute. Any attempts at violence or retaliation will force us to make examples of the populace aboard the station. Their blood will not be on our heads. The responsibility belongs to the Dragoon High Command. We await your reply. Honor to the Dragon!"

The frequency went dead.

"Link up all units, William." Wolf waited impatiently while Cameron began the process. "Conference on a secure line, all commanders. Nobody moves without orders."

Wolf turned to Minobu to find the Kuritan shaking his head. "What is it?"

"I have seen how the populace reviles the name of Wolf's Dragoons in the streets. I have heard how ComStar labels the Dragoons. Now there is this word. You cannot avoid what is happening. Whether you wish it or not, trouble has come."

"You can help us," Wolf said. "Together we can make them listen. Stop the fires before they get out of hand."

"Not this time. Matters have gone too far." Minobu knew he was too small an obstacle to divert the gathering forces. He felt tired. What had he done to deserve such karma? He clenched and unclenched his good hand in frustration. "The earthquake may be far offshore, but the *tsunami* rumbles in, unstoppable. At best, one has warning and can flee for the safety of the mountains."

"Are you fleeing then?" Wolf asked.

"I wish I were. I cannot. I am bound to my duty." Minobu paused. Wolf had mistaken Minobu's advice for a statement of his own intent. Minobu refused to take offense at the lack of faith in their bond that Wolf's question implied. Wolf could not think that Minobu would abandon him simply to save himself. He had to be distraught, overtaxed by his concerns for his Dragoons. Minobu tried again to make his advice clearer. "Consider your own course."

"I have my own duties," Wolf said, waving a stiffened arm to encompass the Dragoons working throughout the chamber.

"I understand." Minobu understood that there could have been no other response. Sadness filled his heart. He and his friend were locked on their respective courses. The fate that loomed was inescapable. Minobu could feel its weight descending. "It seems that each must face his own karma."

Minobu walked to where Marisha sat.

"I must leave for Misery in the morning." He did not need to say that he considered this a final goodbye. "Thank you for all you have done."

Marisha, careful not to offend the dignity of a Kuritan samurai, stood and bowed when she would rather have embraced Minobu. "Give my love to Tomiko and the children."

"I do not need to give them what they already have and hold dearly."

Wolf stepped up. In his eyes, Minobu could read understanding and regret that this was to be a parting of ways. The mercenary seemed to be searching for words.

"It has been a long time since I had a brother. May you always defeat your enemies, warrior," Wolf said at last.

Minobu was taken aback, disturbed by Wolf's words. Wolf meant well and was surely giving what he thought was a proper goodbye to a samurai. Perhaps he did not see as clearly as Minobu did what must follow soon.

"An old cautionary proverb warns one to be careful of what one wishes because the wish might be granted."

Minobu turned and left the room.

"What do you mean?" Marisha asked as he retreated. She turned to her lover. "What did he mean?"

Wolf made no reply. He simply stared at the departing figure.

"You know, don't you?" Frustrated by his silence, Marisha turned to Major Blake, who had been watching the exchange.

"I think he meant it as a warning," Blake said, when she insisted again. "House of Kurita's *Dictum Honorium* states that anyone not committed to the Draconis Combine is an enemy. I think the Iron Man is letting us know that if we face off, he won't be holding back."

"All unit commanders on line, Colonel," Cameron announced.

42

Dragoon Administrative HQ, Cerant, An Ting
Galedon Military District, Draconis Combine
3 January 3028

Dechan Fraser blinked and tried to focus on the face of the person shaking his arm. The pale skin and oval shape might have been those of Jenette Rand. Strands of hair brushed against his nose, making him want to sneeze. How could that be? Jenette's hair was cropped close and she didn't have a pony tail that hung over her shoulder to hit him in the face as she bent over him. Susan Lean did, though. She was almost as pretty as Jenette. She was . . . *Lean*!

"Yeah, Lean. I'm not your dream girl, so you can let go." Lean straightened up as he loosened his grip on her arms. "Come on, Fraser. Wake up. The Colonel wants all company commanders in conference."

Lean stood in the doorway while Dechan slipped into his duty uniform. She tapped her foot impatiently.

"What are you waiting around for?" he asked. He wasn't used to being watched while dressing At least, not by a pretty woman with a scowl on her face. They usually smiled.

"Well, it's not for the show. The Colonel sent me after you. He's in a mood, so I'm not going back there without you."

Dechan caught a note of worry in her voice, something

deeper than anxiety about a potential chewing out. "It's serious?"

"You could say that."

"If it's serious, this is no time to be coy."

"You're right. Sorry." She told him about the capture of the *Hephaestus*. "I think it's Hegira," she concluded.

"Hegira? What's that?"

She smote her forehead with her hand. "That's right . . . I forgot you're adopted!" She cocked her head and looked at him with mock severity. "What's the matter, foster? Did you fall asleep during the intro session when you made company commander?"

"No, I didn't," Dechan snapped defensively. Foster! Who did she thing she was! The slang term was used for new MechWarriors until they had been accepted as full-fledged Dragoons. No one had called him that for five years. "I never had one. I got my star just before we left for Udibi. Things have been too hot since then."

"Unity save us from too-busy Majors," Lean exclaimed. "As a foster who made company commander, you should have been briefed. Hegira is the escape plan. Ever since New Delos, the Dragoons have been ready to run with the civilians if some dim-witted Successor Lord tries the hostage trick again. When the word goes out, we move."

"That's what's going on?"

"Not yet. But I think that's why the Colonel has called the meeting. In case of a disaster, he calls together all officers on-site. Everybody from company CO on up has a say."

"And if the vote is to go?"

"Then all Dragoons not under specific orders to the contrary will assemble at a previously determined, uninhabited star system. Once assembled, we will convoy somewhere safe."

"But that would go against the contract," Dechan objected. The notion of the contract as something sacred had been drilled into him during his early indoctrination to Dragoon discipline and procedure.

"Are you still asleep?" Lean queried, shaking her head in disbelief. "If we go with Hegira, the contract will already have been vaporized—by somebody else."

The implications began to sink in. Dechan buckled on his sidearm. "Let's not keep him waiting, then."

The two Captains moved at a trot through the administration building. When Dechan tried to turn down the corridor that led to the conference room, Lean grabbed his arm and tugged him on.

"Wrong way, foster."

The Dragoon officers had convened in the communications center. Its facilities were being used to reach all Dragoon locations on An Ting. Wolf and the dozen other officers present were seated in a circle on the broadcast floor of the studio. Bright lights illuminated their worried faces. Lean and Dechan joined them.

Once seated, Dechan could barely see the banks of monitors that had been set up to face the seated officers. The rest of the Dragoon officer corps on-planet were attending via two-way video link. Each monitor carried a strip identifying the unit or location of the transmission's source. One row of screens was dark except for the white letters that read "*Hephaestus*." A last monitor came to life, revealing the face of Colonel Jeremy Ellman of the Training Command.

"Now that you're on-line, Jeremy, we can begin," Wolf said. The Colonel's voice cut through the hushed babble of conversation and drove it down into silence.

"I realize this is irregular, but we are unable at this time to contact the rest of the Dragoons. I require the advice of all command-level officers."

Wolf paused, and the whispered comments of the officers resumed. Most of them already had a good idea of what the call meant. Wolf's words were merely a confirmation.

Lean elbowed Dechan's side in an "I told you so" gesture just as Wolf began to speak again.

"Gentlemen and ladies, we are in a difficult position. You all know about the problems we've had over the last two years. Our employer has been pushing us hard, but we haven't pushed back. But now they're trying to force us into actions that could be branded outlaw. They've been very careful, too. Everything they've done can be disavowed or explained away as the actions of independent parties. And we can prove nothing.

"For those of you who have not heard, Captain Shadd reports that the ComStar facility is barred to us. The Adept in charge is already referring to us as outlaws. We don't know if this is ComStar's official position or if the man has simply become the dupe of our local enemies. It doesn't really matter. Without access to the hyperpulse communications, we must rely on courier service to contact the rest of the regiments.

"We are hamstrung there as well. An Ting System Command is refusing all our requests to change orbit or depart for the jump point. They are referring all requests to the PSL office, which has suddenly become too busy to deal with the problem. All they've had time for is a warning that any repositioning of Dragoon aerospace or deep-space assets will be construed as hostile. Obviously, they do not want us talking to the rest of the regiments.

"I think you can all guess what they're using as an excuse.

"The *Hephaestus,* or at least some part of it, has been captured by parties claiming to be Kurita patriots. Major Blake's intel operation suggests that the hostiles were introduced as part of a batch of local technical talent taken aboard the station to supplement our strained repair force. They are terrorists. I believe that they are also agents of House Kurita. Again, the truth doesn't matter. The situation does.

"It's New Delos all over again. This time, it's on a bigger scale—better-organized and more ruthless. Twelve years ago, we failed in our oaths to protect our civilians, some of whom were taken hostage and killed. We failed our oath, but swore to prevent it ever happening again." Wolf paused, giving dramatic emphasis to his next words. "Will we let it happen again?" he called out.

The outraged roar was a clear answer.

"Hegira?" Wolf shouted his question.

The room went silent, a silence louder than any voice.

Jeremy Ellman was the first to break the stillness. His face was grim and his movements slow, weighted by decades of a soldier's hard life. He stood and repeated the single word, "Hegira." One by one, each Dragoon officer stood and spoke the same word.

Dechan, as a junior officer, was among the last. He didn't

understand all that was happening, but he believed in the Dragoons. He had faith in his fellow officers. Trusting their judgment, he stammered out, "Hegira."

Finally, after all had spoken, it was Jamie Wolf's turn to stand. He spoke with a strange, almost old-fashioned accent that Dechan had never heard any other Dragoon use before. From the faces of the other commanders, both those in the room and those on the screens, he could tell they understood the Colonel perfectly. Lean had been right, he was still a foster. Only Tech Chief Scott, who, like Dechan, had joined the Dragoons in Steiner space, looked puzzled as he strained to make sense of Wolf's words.

"In conclave we have deliberated, trothkin. Sealed and bonded, I stand as Oathmaster. The rede you have spoken is my will. Thus shall it stand until we shall fall."

A chorus of voices answered, "Seyla!"

The Dragoons sat down. Dechan and Scott, taken off guard by the sudden move, awkwardly followed suit. For a full minute, there was silence.

"Then the word must go out," Wolf said. He turned to face a monitor bearing the label of Boupeig barracks and spoke to one of the officers assembled there. "Captain Shadd, execute Contingency Plan Mohammed."

"The Seventh is on its way, Colonel. The Robes will never know what hit them," Shadd said with a savage grin.

Blake nodded his approval. "That's the way it has to be, Shadd. No evidence," he cautioned. "Nothing to link the Dragoons to the raid."

"We're ghosts, Major. We won't let the people down." Shadd saluted and moved out of the camera's range.

Wolf turned to another screen. This one showed the face of a single Dragoon, Colonel Jason Carmody, head of aerospace operations. Carmody's dark face tensed as Wolf addressed him.

"Jason, barring word to the contrary from me or from the *Hephaestus,* you will begin Operation Recovery on Captain Shadd's transmission. In the meantime, we negotiate with the brigands holding our people and pretend we'll do business with them.

"We are committed, ladies and gentlemen," Wolf announced to his assembled audience. "Ready your 'Mechs."

43

ComStar Compound, Cerant, An Ting
Galedon Military District, Draconis Combine
3 January 3028

"Malkin' bugs!" the ComStar Acolyte muttered, slapping his neck at the sting. He scratched at the spot and cursed again.

"They're always bad this time of year, Seldes," his companion said. His grin at his friend's discomfort vanished when one stung him, too. "Damn! They're big this year. If they get worse, we'll need antiaircraft artillery."

"We'll need the artillery all right, but not for the bugs. The Dragoons won't take it lying down that ComStar has refused to let them send out messages. Mark me, Kent. They're gonna try something."

"What can they do? ComStar is neutral, protected by all the Successor States so it can serve them all. Even if the Dragoons weren't on Kurita's bad side, the Draconians would defend the compound. This guard duty is a waste of time. Standing out all night trying to look watchful. What a pain! We should be getting a good night's sleep. We've got nothing to worry about. Anybody who tries to get in will get caught at the wall. You've seen those Kurita volunteers, haven't you? Tough mothers. I wouldn't want to cross any of them, would you?"

The answer was a ragged snore. Kent glanced over at his

companion. Seldes had slumped against the archway, his head leaning against the lintel.

"Guess you're gonna get your sleep anyway." Kent stifled a yawn. "It's not a bad idea. Hope the Precentor don't catch . . ." The rest of the thought went unspoken as his knees buckled and he crumpled to the ground.

A man-shaped shadow detached itself from the darkness and passed between the sleeping guards. It entered the building and joined the blacker darkness within. A few seconds later, it was back in the archway, waving twice before it vanished again.

More shadows materialized from the night and crept after the first. All seemed to move with feline grace, except for one who stumbled over Kent's rifle. At the slight clatter, the other shadows dropped into defensive crouches and froze into immobility. They remained fixed a few seconds before resuming their progress. One hustled the clumsy silhouette-man through the archway. Two others took hold of the fallen Acolytes and dragged them into the building. A fourth scooped up the abandoned weapons, and brought up the rear.

The shadow men flitted through the outer building and across the inner courtyard, stopping for a short, hushed conference at an unguarded inner door. Moments later, all but two remained at the entrance, sheltered in darkness.

Those two, one slim and graceful and the other stocky and clumsy, penetrated deeper into the edifice. The two shapes moved silently on soft-soled boots through the darkened corridors. Near a cross-corridor, the taller figure stopped its gliding progress and motioned to the other to wait. The second figure shuffled to a halt and leaned against a doorway. The first slid around the corner, out of sight. No one was there to see the waiting black-clad figure tremble as he huddled against the dark wood of the door.

Without warning, the door on the opposite side of the hall opened, spilling light into the corridor. The man who opened it wore the elaborate robes of a ComStar Precentor. By the look on his face, he was almost as startled as the shadow he had surprised. His hand reached again for the knob, but the intruder's gun spoke in a series of stuttering coughs before the Precentor could take the first backward step.

Bright bursts of blood starred the man's robes, and his

body jerked as he staggered back into the room under the force of the continued impacts. He tumbled backward over a chair to land splayed on the floor. Slugs continued to tear into his body long after it had stopped moving of its own volition.

The first shadow returned. Its head-covering hood had been removed, revealing the face of Anton Shadd. The commando leader's face was set in a mask of rage. His hand snaked out to slap the pudgy, black-clad figure across its concealed face. The blow broke the paralysis that had welded the man's gloved finger to the trigger of his weapon.

"Unity, Scott!" Shadd gritted out. His voice was low to keep it from carrying too far. "What the hell do you think you're doing?"

Tech Chief Scott gasped like a gaffed pisciform. His left hand came up and dragged the hood and Blackwell night goggles from his head. His face was pale and slicked with sweat. He gobbled air. It took two tries before he could find his voice. Imitating Shadd, he spoke in a whisper.

"He came through the door. I thought he was going to give the alarm."

"So you shot him!" Shadd's voice was full of disgust. "That was the Precentor. We needed him for the transmission codes."

"He surprised me. I thought he was going to give us away."

"You panicked."

"So what if I did?" Scott shot back. "I wasn't trained for this. I'm a Tech, not a professional killer like you Sevens."

Shadd clenched his jaw, biting off a retort. Instead, he said, "I found the HPG control chamber. Let's go." Shadd closed the door on the carnage and returned the corridor to darkness. "Next time, leave any killing to the professionals."

Not a word passed between the two Dragoons on the short walk to their destination.

Smoke from the presence lamps hung in a greasy haze below the chamber's high, domed ceiling. The red-tinted glass filled the room with a ruddy glow, and incarnadine reflections glinted from shiny chrome and pale plastic hardware.

The HyperPulse Generator's bulky regulator equipment and horseshoe-shaped control board dominated the center of the room. Heavy, shielded cables emerged from the machinery and ran to the north wall, behind which was hidden the massive generator. Lesser communications devices, computer consoles, and data storage units lined the walls.

An open stairway led from the entrance to a catwalk that circled the chamber three meters above the floor. The walk extended out to a platform overlooking the controls. The velvet-draped, high-backed chair was the Precentor's throne, positioned to give him a view of the actions of his Acolytes as they performed the transmission rituals.

Shadd checked for other entrances while Scott walked to the control console and studied the layout. The commando found a small door on the south wall. From the orbital photos of the compound that he studied, he knew it opened into the private garden of the Precentor's residence. There was little likelihood of disturbance from that quarter. The only other portals to the outside were the shuttered windows along the catwalk.

A rattling sound made Shadd swivel suddenly, his subgun at the ready. Seeing that the noise was only the Tech Chief removing a panel from the front of the control board, he relaxed. Scott was poking and prying at the exposed wiring and circuit boards in a desultory fashion.

"Come on, Scott. Every minute you waste fiddling with that thing means we're more likely to get caught."

"This isn't easy, Shadd. This malking machine's a patchwork. It's been crosswired eight ways to Sunday. There are patches on top of patches in the wiring. So many that I can't be sure what circuit is what. I don't think the Robes had any idea of what they were doing."

"I don't want to hear it," Shadd growled. "You're supposed to be a communications wizard. Prove it!"

Scott grimaced but bent back to his work. His curses rose in a regular stream while Shadd busied himself checking the locks on the doors. At the back entrance, he was sliding a pair of file cabinets across the door when a subgun suddenly barked outside the chamber.

"Damn!" Shadd muttered. Somebody had slipped up, or else they'd found the Precentor's body. Either way, their penetration had been discovered.

An alarm began to sound as Shadd bolted up the stairs to

the catwalk. He halted beside the window looking out over the inner court. The firing was coming from that direction. Careful to minimize his exposure, Shadd slid open the shutters.

Searchlights were sweeping the grounds. In their stark light, Shadd could see ComStar troopers and Kuritans trying to force their way across the courtyard. His team was laying down a withering fire with their silenced weapons. The sounds of the attackers' guns and the hooting alarm completely covered any sound those weapons were making. Shadd could not tell how many of his men were holding the entrance.

Shadd called down to Scott. "You've just been put on deadline, wizard."

"It had better not be a short one," Scott replied. His voice echoed out of the cabinet where he had stuck his head.

Returning his attention to the courtyard, Shadd spotted a trio of Draconians moving along the far colonnade, well on their way to achieving a flanking position. From the angle, Shadd could tell that the Snakes were out of line-of-sight from the entrance his men guarded. He swung into the window, fired a burst at the runners, and ducked back as soon as he lifted his finger from the trigger.

When no slugs came searching for him, he knew that the flash suppressor on his Ceres Arms Ranger had done its job. None of the enemy had marked his position. He risked a look to check the results of his fire. Two of the runners had dropped, sprawling. The third was skittering back the way he had come. The defense of the entrance was secure for a while longer.

Scott's shout of triumph brought Shadd around in time to see lights flicker, then stabilize into a steady glow along the control boards of the Hyper-Pulse Generator. A whine began that climbed in a steady tone before dropping into a steady hum.

"It's ready," the Tech Chief announced with satisfaction.

"What about the codes?"

"Bypassed them."

"Then send the message. Exactly as the Colonel gave it to us. Not a word out of place."

"I'm not a novice, Shadd," Scott grumbled, turning to the keyboard.

With the lull in the fighting outside, Shadd listened to the clack of the keys that seemed to mark time like the ticking of some ancient clock. But time was in short supply. Every passing moment reduced the strike force's chance of escaping from the compound.

The crackling roar of a plasma flamer echoed across the courtyard, announcing the renewal of combat.

Shadd looked out the window to see the upper body of a BattleMech visible above the roof of the outer building. Silhouetted in the predawn light, the machine resembled a headless scarecrow. Shadd recognized the shape as that of a *Vulcan,* a fearsome antipersonnel 'Mech.

When the machine's right-arm flamer belched a second burst of plasma, the backflash lit its torso. Shadd recognized the symbol that decorated the 'Mech's left chest as the black dragon of House Kurita. So, the Snakes had raised the ante.

The *Vulcan*'s plasma burst scorched everything it did not set aflame. Screams came from the entryway. Good men were dying.

Kurita soldiers came boiling from the outer building. Nothing slowed them as they rushed across the courtyard. No gunfire. No grenades. His men at the entrance to the generator building were dead. Shadd hoped that some had been able to retreat deeper into the building and take up a new defensive position where the 'Mech couldn't reach them. If they had, the Snakes wouldn't winkle them out easily. The commandos would trade their lives for time.

The lights on the HPG console dimmed briefly with the power surge as the generator sent its interstellar pulse into space. Shadd found the Tech Chief grinning in pleasure, oblivious to his surroundings. Shadd could do nothing but shake his head.

The commando leader keyed his comm unit. "Muhammad to base."

The response was immediate. "Go ahead, Muhammad," said Jaime Wolf.

"It's a Snake nest here. 'Mechs too. Don't expect us home."

"Success?"

"The word it out, Colonel. Get the people out, too."

"You will be remembered in the halls."

Shadd cut the circuit. The men of Seventh Kommando lived and died in darkness and deception. Remembered in the halls, the Colonel had said. He couldn't ask for more. Clicking a fresh magazine into the Ranger, he walked to the door to await the assault.

44

Dragoon Administrative HQ, Cerant, An Ting
Galedon Military District, Draconis Combine
3 January 3028

Dechan chewed at his thumbnail. In the long hours since the Hegira vote, the tension of waiting had soured his stomach. Enforced idleness had never sat well with him. He longed to do something . . . anything. What he really wanted was to be in the cockpit of his *Shadow Hawk* chasing Snakes, but the Colonel's order was to stay put. Besides, his 'Mech was at Boupeig barracks halfway across Cerant, and the mob still roamed the streets.

He could see Wolf across the planning room. The Colonel's shoulders were slumped with fatigue as he took a break from the almost continuous negotiations with the terrorists. Negotiations! A strange word to use for political speeches. The criminals holding the *Hephaestus* didn't seem interested in listening at all. They wanted to talk, condemning the Dragoons and exclaiming the virtues of the Dragon. It seemed to Dechan that they would rather discuss the games on Solaris than actually work out terms.

He didn't envy Wolf. The Colonel's nerves must be stretched tighter than any Dragoon's in the headquarters. After all, he was in the decision-making slot.

Two hours ago, a Dragoon DropShip's orbit had brought it near the station. After conducting a visual scan, the crew had confirmed Major Quo's assertion that members of Seventh Kommando were on the hull of the *Hephaestus*. That is, they'd been able to confirm that spacesuited figures were working their way toward the command section. When the ship had tried to radio the figures, the terrorists had murdered one of the hostages and threatened more deaths if any more transmissions were beamed at the station. Wolf had forbidden further attempts to communicate with the men on the surface of the station.

Dragoon hopes had risen with the sighting of those figures. It meant that at least some of what Major Quo had tried to tell them was true. If the spacesuited figures really were members of the Seventh, things might not be as bad as they seemed.

Operation Recovery was put on hold when Wolf decided that the commandos—if commandos they were—had a better chance of rescuing the hostages than would a full-scale assault. If a Dragoon DropShip moved into position to attack the station, it would be in direct defiance of the Kurita Command System and might provoke a military reaction. Wolf still had hopes of limiting the incident. How could he be blamed for actions of any commandos already on the station?

Wolf's orders meant that there was little to do at the command center, except to wait, updating plans as bits of new information arrived. That was even more true for Dechan, who was only a MechJock, not a planner.

When the word had first come in from Shadd at the ComStar facility, there had been a flurry of activity. The cheers at his success died quickly, however, when he announced the Kurita assault. Everyone knew there was no way the commandos could survive it.

Shadd and his commandos were gone now. Dechan thought about the gruff man who had insisted on calling him "kid." He had not known the man very well, but no one outside the Seventh ever really got to know the Sevens. Within the tightly knit Dragoon clan, they were a separate family. Shadd had seemed to be a good man in a fight, even if a little too quick to start one. He would not have made it easy for the Snakes.

In the name of protecting ComStar, the Kuritans had done

the raiding team, and the Dragoons could do nothing about it at the moment. If they tried to seek compensation, it would mean having to claim the commandos as Dragoons, drawing down the wrath of ComStar and much of the Inner Sphere against the unit for violating ComStar neutrality. Yet that was exactly what the Dracs had done by going after the commandos.

Dechan wanted to avenge the unit's loss by smashing the Snakes the way they had wiped out the Dragoon commandos. Shadd would approve, he thought. Shadd wouldn't stay cooped up at the command center. Shadd hadn't let the mob stop him from getting to Boupeig barracks.

"Colonel Wolf!"

Dechan looked up at Cameron's shout. The man's unflappability was a byword in the 'Mech regiments. If he was excited, it meant that something was up.

"Colonel, the terrorists are broadcasting on the wide band again!"

"Put it on the main screen, William," Wolf ordered.

The wide band meant that the terrorists were cutting into the public-broadcast frequencies so that the whole planet would hear. The face that appeared on the monitor was drawn and haggard, with dark smudges under the glittering, fanatical eyes. The terrorist's head bobbed once in acknowledgement of something, then his attention centered on the camera. His face became animated as he spoke, his eyes boring into the viewer.

"In a foul blasphemy, the outlaw Dragoons have attacked the ComStar compound in An Ting. They have slaughtered hundreds of innocents and destroyed the compound. This is an unconscionable act. It is beyond the bounds of civilized behavior.

"By this outrageous deed, Wolf's Dragoons have proven that we did not lie about them. They show it now to the entire Inner Sphere. Wantonly. Without regret or denial.

"We are vindicated!

"They are the enemy!

"Such enemies of mankind must be exterminated. Ground into the dust. We must make an example of them so that no others will dare the same abominable acts. They will not be allowed to leave the sacred space of the Draconis Combine unpunished.

"We are but insignificant patriots, armed only with our dedication to the Dragon and House Kurita. There is little we can do to hurt the murderers who call themselves Wolf's Dragoons. We cannot stand against their BattleMechs. We cannot fight their spaceships. But we will do what we can. Look to the sky. See the star of dawning truth. Heed the call to justice! Glory to Warlord Samsonov!" screamed the terrorist, shaking his fist at the camera. Then the screen suddenly went dead.

"What happened to the signal?" Wolf asked anxiously. "William, get it back."

Cameron made no move toward the control board. His jaw quivered and a tear rolled down his cheek. His voice faltered.

"There's a strong electromagnetic pulse from the *Hephaestus*'s orbit. The station's gone, Colonel."

45

Government House, Cerant, An Ting
Galedon Military District, Draconis Combine
3 January 3028

Akuma laughed.

As always, *Sho-sa* Andrew Subato Chou found the sound unnerving. It made him wonder if Akuma was quite sane.

Chou flicked a glance across the richly appointed office at Quinn. The bodyguard stood by the transplex window that dominated the room. In his black uniform and backlit by the Dragoon arclights from across the square, the figure seemed more a shadow than a man. Chou would find no consolation there.

Quinn was usually paired with the shorter Panati, but Chou had not seen the squat Japanese all day. Not that his presence would have made any difference. Likely, the second of Akuma's guards would have been as cold and detached as the first. Chou detested being the only military officer with Akuma. Gazig at the swirls and arabesques in the design of the room's carpet, he fidgeted, wishing he were somewhere else.

Seeing his second-in-command fight to hide his agitation only fueled Akuma's humor.

"Look at them, Chou," he commanded, indicating the one active viewscreen among the bank on one wall. "They are confounded, demoralized."

Chou obediently turned his eyes to the screen, which showed a slightly fuzzy view of the planning room of the Dragoon administrative headquarters. In the center, Jaime Wolf stood stock still, hands clenched at his sides. Dragoons milled around him, as a young Captain in the background slipped from the room. The audio was dominated by shouting, a babble of many voices.

"The destruction of their orbital station has left them in disarray. Listen to them bawl. They scurry like ants from a mound that's been kicked," Akuma gloated.

"*Chu-sa* Akuma," Chou said, having finally heard a single word clearly through the noise. "It sounds to me as though most of the Dragoon officers are calling for revenge."

Chou knew he was contradicting his superior, but it had to be said. He was pleased that his voice remained steady.

"Does it?" Akuma ran his right index finger along his upper lip, then rolled his hand over and straightened his fingers in sequence. The gesture was nonchalant. "It does not matter. They have no target. Their anger and frustration will only ripen them for the blows to come."

While Akuma spoke, the volume of noise coming from the speakers diminished. The abrupt change drew the attention of both Kurita officers to the monitor.

What they saw was Wolf calling for order. As calm fell over the Dragoon planning room, those present began a controlled discussion. Most of them wanted immediate revenge, and many wanted to start by razing the city. Wolf adamantly opposed military action by the Dragoons until the civilians were safe. To accomplish that, he had ordered DropShips down to begin loading.

One officer violently objected to Wolf's plan and berated the Colonel as a senile old man. A heated argument followed. Vanquished but still full of emotion, the officer vented his frustration by hurling a portable comm unit at the wall.

For an instant, the device seemed headed straight for the spying camera's lens, for the image wobbled as the missile struck. When the image stabilized, it was clearer than before and showed the amazed expression of the Dragoons staring directly at the camera. Someone at the back of the crowd fired a pistol, and the viewscreen went dark.

Chou ducked when the shot was fired. He straightened, grinning foolishly, to find Akuma tapping his fingers on the marble-topped desk, an annoyed pout on his face. Chou was startled when Quinn spoke.

"We cannot place another monitor at this point."

"It does not matter." Akuma dismissed the issue with a wave of his hand. "We no longer need one. The Dragoons are demoralized, distracted by their concern over worthless civilians. Their commanders are divided. Half of them are ready to overthrow Wolf." He laughed strangely. "This will be almost too easy.

"If we dispose of the mercenaries here on An Ting, we cut off the head of Wolf's Dragoons. They may have gotten their message off, but what good will it do them? Their words will never reach the ears for which they were intended. Other hands will see to that. The rest of Wolf's Dragoons will remain ignorant of An Ting until it's too late. The remaining mercenaries will be easy prey to be hunted down at our leisure. Perhaps Ryuken-*ni* can be assigned to lead the chase." Akuma's face lit with pleasure at the thought.

Chou waited a moment before clearing his throat to remind the *Chu-sa* of his presence.

"I have not forgotten you, *Sho-sa* Chou."

Something in Akuma's voice suddenly made Chou wish that he had.

"This is your moment of glory," Akuma continued. "Send out the attack orders. You may personally lead the assault on Boupeig barracks."

46

Cerant, An Ting
Galedon Military District, Draconis Combine
11 January 3028

Sho-sa Chou brought his *Dragon*'s nose back into line with his course through the northeast quarter of Cerant. As his 'Mech pounded past apartment buildings battered by eight days of combat, bricks cascaded in a dusty roar as one wall crumbled from the vibrations created by the sixty-ton BattleMech's passage. Gray dust billowed up.

The predicted outflanking maneuver by the Dragoons had failed to materialize. Like so many reports of their movements in the last eight days, it was false. The Dragoons were phantoms, striking and disappearing. They seemed to roam the city almost at will.

It was a sorry state of affairs. An Ting was a Combine planet, and Cerant a Kurita city. Vagabond outsiders should not have so easy a time, nor should they be able to lead loyal Draconians on such a chase. Time and again, the mercenaries had drawn Ryuken 'Mechs into costly ambushes or made lightning raids against supposedly secure rear areas.

Combat in a city did not usually lend itself to such bandit tactics. It was almost as though the Dragoons could see everything that moved in Cerant, though Chou knew that was impossible. The orbital space above the city was a hotly contested no-man's-land. DropShips and fighters became instant targets, and so were unable to make surveys of the planet below. The mercenaries had to be relying on ground reconnaissance, as were the Ryuken.

If the Ryuken's reconnaissance was poor, its combat performance was worse. Chou had marshaled his 'Mechs for the assault on Boupeig barracks in textbook-perfect order, but the offensive had gone wrong from the start. Though the Kurita 'Mechs reached their jump-off points without incident, with no indication from the Dragoon commnet that they were expecting an attack, a company of BattleMechs had suddenly blasted through his lines.

The lead machine was a dark blue *Shadow Hawk* whose chest was painted with a falcon. Its pilot fought with a fierce courage, outshining his fellows. The Dragoon machines swarmed through the assembling Kurita 'Mechs, catching them totally by surprise. They surprised the Ryuken pilots even more when they continued forward without stopping.

The Dragoons had created havoc in the brief fight. Two Ryuken 'Mechs were out of commission and several more damaged before the Kurita assault even got underway. If the Dragoons had sustained more than light damage, Chou did not know of it.

Though the blow to Ryuken morale was bad, the greatest harm was that the Dragoon company had alerted the barracks compound to the presence of the Kurita 'Mechs. By the time the assault forces went at them, most of the defending BattleMechs were already powered up and ready for it.

The mercenaries managed to put up strong resistance, and the Ryuken failed to achieve many of their early objectives. When the fighting became prolonged, the timetable slipped further and further. The attack finally shuddered to a halt when two mercenary 'Mech lances hit the Ryuken flank. Chou later learned that those had been simulator 'Mechs, piloted by green trainees. At the time, it hadn't mattered, for the mere appearance of fresh forces was enough to crumble his flank.

A nearby explosion brought Chou back to the present. A black cloud mushroomed ahead of him, flames licking at it. He brought up the *Dragon*'s speed, heedless of the low traction on the paved city streets. Chou was afraid he knew what had happened.

Two minutes later, those fears were confirmed as he skidded the *Dragon* to a halt and gazed dejectedly on the scene of devastation. While he and the Ryuken had been distracted, the Dragoons had slipped in a force to hit the Ryuken field command. The command camp was a shambles, and the two little guard 'Mechs were scrap heaps. The explosion had come from an ammunition supply carrier and destroyed Chou's comm tent and Ryuken-*ichi*'s last coolant vehicle. The fire raged out of control, spreading eagerly to the nearby buildings. There was nothing Chou could do here.

Second Battalion had been holding the city south of First Battalion's position, but he'd received no word from them since noon. Third Battalion was engaged with Lean's Company on the far side of Cerant. To get there, First would have to cross Dragoon-held portions of the city. Considering the First's depleted force, that would be a fool's errand.

The high and mighty commander of Ryuken-*ichi* had been absent from the commnet all morning, attending some kind of planning session. A strategy session without the Ryuken field commander? It made no sense. Damn Akuma to all the seven hells. His machinations had inflamed the Dragoons to raw hatred and brutal savagery. How could Akuma have gotten Warlord Samsonov's approval for such wrong-headed plans? Didn't the *Tai-sho* understand what he was dealing with? Did he believe that Akuma could manipulate these people at will?

The Ryuken were now in the trap Akuma had intended for the Dragoons, but Chou was not going to allow the regiment to be destroyed. What was left must be saved to fight again in service to House Kurita. With Chou unable to contact Akuma, he was in charge. For the first time, he considered Akuma's absentee generalship as a benefit.

Before Chou could save Ryuken-*ichi*, however, he had to save First Battalion. There *had* to be a way out. Calling up a tactical map to look for a way south to join with Second Battalion, he found several paths clear of Dragoon positions. That is, they had been when the map was last updated. Chou chose to believe that it was accurate, for otherwise all hope was lost.

The *Sho-sa* summoned the remnants of First Battalion to

rally on him. Once consolidated with Second, they could fight their way to Third and retreat from the city, leaving Cerant to the mercenaries. The Dragoons were acting as though they owned it already. To contest it would be death for the regiment.

Two lances joined him almost at once. Chou sent a *Panther* ahead to scout and ordered the rest to spread out and advance along parallel streets. For fifteen tense minutes, they proceeded through empty streets. Chou was sure every man was expecting to meet a Dragoon ambush at every intersection. He certainly did. It was a fear they had all lived with for days now, a fear that killed morale. The real deaths of the soldiers would follow unless Chou could get them out.

As Chou's radar pinged out warning of incoming aircraft above the city, a red blip appeared on his screen. A second later, the IFF system flashed the bogey to green. Checking the identification panel, Chou learned that it was the Kurita DropShip *Alabaster*. He halted the *Dragon* and tried to pick up a visual. The 'Mechs nearest him stopped as well.

When he finally caught sight of the ship, Chou wished he hadn't bothered. The DropShip was flying erratically, foundering and bucking as it plowed through the atmosphere. As the craft suddenly veered sharply to port, viscous black smoke began to pour from a gap that had once been covered by a cargo bay door. The DropShip disappeared from sight behind the buildings. Though it was kilometers away when it crashed, the tremor swayed Chou's BattleMech.

The *Sho-sa* scanned the skies. He knew his eyes could not see anything that the *Dragon*'s senses would miss. Perhaps, he chided himself, he was looking for salvation. The crash of the *Alabaster* did not bode well for a Kurita victory in the orbital battle.

Had the Dragoons planned the DropShip's fall, they could not have halted the Ryuken 'Mechs in a better position for the ambush. Rockets roared out of the surrounding buildings, and hidden emplacements opened fire with the eye-searing pulses of laser and charged particle beams. A heavy Dragoon 'Mech bulled through the front of an apartment building and slammed into a Kurita *Stinger*. Both 'Mechs vanished in the dust and falling masonry.

When the air had cleared enough, Chou saw the Dragoon

Thunderbolt standing over the mangled remains of the lighter machine. The *Thunderbolt* raised both arms and slammed them down into the *Stinger*. Again and again, the fists smashed into the already destroyed Kurita 'Mech.

The MechWarrior's savagery shocked Chou to his senses. He ordered his men to leave the ambush site at top speed. No longer would they fight on the mercenaries' terms. Chou took rear guard to assure that none of his men became trapped into a prolonged duel with the Dragoons.

Reserving his laser and missile fire for the part of Dragoon BattleMechs advancing toward him, Chou raked the infantry positions with a rolling volley of autocannon fire. At the moment, he was thankful for the *Thunderbolt*'s preoccupation with the downed *Stinger*. The two 'Mechs he faced were both lights. Combined, they massed less than his *Dragon,* giving him the advantage. He was going to need it against these blood-crazed mercenaries.

After the first exchange of fire, Chou noticed that the Dragoons were allowing him to increase the range by failing to make use of their superior speed. This action was so uncharacteristic of the last few days of combat that Chou wondered if they were waiting for something.

The pinging of his radar unraveled the puzzle. He had been caught in a second phase of the trap. Dragoon 'Mechs were jetting down from the tops of nearby buildings.

A dark blue *Shadow Hawk* landed to his right. Lurching out of the steam and dust of its landing, the *Hawk* came at him at high speed. Its Armstrong autocannon was pivoted back in transport position, both arms raised above the cockpit. The 'Mech's hands clasped a monstrous steel I-beam, which it must have torn from a nearby structure. For one absurd moment, Chou imagined the BattleMech to be an ancient samurai, sword raised above his head to deliver the pear-splitting stroke that would cleave through his enemy's helmet. The instant was frozen in time for Chou as he saw the stroke coming. In a moment of perfect clarity, he knew he could do nothing to avoid it.

The I-beam came down on the *Dragon*'s cockpit.

47

Government House, Cerant, An Ting
Galedon Military District, Draconis Combine
13 January 3028

"What did I miss?" Jerry Akuma said to the air in his tower office of the Government House. The only answer was the faint susurrus of the air cooler.

He shoved his chair back from the desk, threw himself to his feet, and began to pace the room. When Akuma passed the desk for the third time, he stopped with a jerk. His hand struck out, closing on the bronze dragonhead that decorated the desk. Then he whirled, hurling it at the wall. The paperweight smashed one of the video monitors, and shards of glass scattered over the floor. Circuits sparked and a thin plume of smoke crawled from the ruin, only to be sucked away by the room's circulation system.

Frackencrack!

Two days ago, *Sho-sa* Chou had died in a Dragoon ambush, and the Ryuken had begun to fall apart. Without Chou's leadership, the unit was no match for the numerically inferior Dragoon forces.

Things had looked so good at first. The riots and the capture of the *Hephaestus* station had seriously distressed Wolf's Dragoons. Though Akuma had not been able to incite Wolf to attack the local populace, he had succeeded in deeply angering the hard-shelled mercenary. Angry men made mistakes. But if Wolf had done so, Akuma had not detected any.

When a Dragoon BattleMech company had unexpectedly reached Cerant Square before Chou could begin the attack on Boupeig barracks, Akuma thought he had gotten his overreaction. The Dragoon 'Mechs had not attacked any Kurita assets, however. Instead, they had overseen the evacuation of Wolf and the other Dragoons at the Administration HQ. Taking this as a sign that the Wolf's nerve had failed, that the Dragoons were on the run, Akuma had believed that the principal thrust of his plan was still on target.

Later, when word came that the same company of 'Mechs had disrupted the assault on Boupeig barracks and thereby warned the defenders, Akuma got his first taste of what commanders throughout history had learned—no plan survives contact with the enemy. He had not liked the flavor at all.

Indeed, he learned to hate it as it became his main course. Boupeig barracks refused to fall. Day after day, the Dragoons failed to show the morale collapse he had predicted. Fighting with efficiency and tenacity, they had forced Ryuken-*ichi* to split its battalions to protect sensitive areas of Cerant.

The Dragoon reaction did not make any sense to Akuma. Their mewling morality placed a foolishly high value on their civilians. The losses he had arranged among those civilians should have broken the MechWarriors' will to fight. Instead they had resisted, each day more fiercely than before. Even attacks against the grounded DropShips loaded with those worthless laymen seemed only to fuel the martial fervor of the Dragoons.

The Ryuken had been a disappointment. From the start, the pitiful line officers could not even handle the disorganized Dragoons. Each day brought new tales of disaster at the hands of the ravaging bands of mercenary 'Mechs and infantry. Malking infantry! In Akuma's day as a MechWarrior, no Kurita soldier would have feared infantry. But these Ryuken officers cried every time they had to go near a building, afraid that some sweat-soaked groundpig was going to jump out and gut their 'Mechs with a vibroknife. Incompetents and cowards!

There was nothing left to do on An Ting. While Chou had been in command, there had been some hope of reversing the military situation. That hope had died when the fool had gotten himself ambushed and killed two days ago. It was time to withdraw and revise the plans, to continue the destruction of the Dragoons from somewhere else.

Once Akuma had set up a new headquarters, he would order the release of all the carefully gathered evidence of Dragoon disobedience, as well as the meticulously created "evidence" of their misdeeds. Once that material was in the hands of the public media of the Successor States, the Dragoons would be universally condemned. Everyone would consider them to be outlaws, which would validate any action the Combine might take against them. Should any mercenaries survive the Dragon's onslaught, they would never again find employ, destined to die broken men with evil reputations.

Jerry Akuma considered the failure on An Ting as an annoyance, not a defeat. He would not give up. The destruction of Wolf and his Dragoons was no longer just a sideshow, a way to torture that sanctimonious bastard Tetsuhara. It was personal now. Only Wolf's death and the elimination of all that the gray-haired bastard held dear would satisfy Akuma.

The sounds of distant explosions reached him through the room's outer transplex wall. Looking up, Akuma saw the flashes of energy weapons and the gray trails of missiles arcing over the battle site. The Dragoons had begun their assault. He held no illusions about the Ryuken-*ichi*'s ability to hold them back, however. In an hour, the Dragoons would be storming Government House. It was time to leave.

The door to his office opened to admit Quinn, returning from his last errand. Akuma turned his gaze back to the distant battle. "Is my 'Mech readied for the trip to the DropShip?" he asked, without turning around.

It would be only a short run to the ship. There was some small element of danger involved in the trip up the gravity well, but the scheduled diversionary attack by Kuritan aerospace forces across the Dragoon-dominated orbits would provide sufficient distraction for Akuma's ship to clear the planet. Once away, he could continue to arrange the Dragoons' downfall. A smile crept over his lips. Despite the recent setback, he would have his revenge. He was in no hurry.

The thought of hurry made him remember that Quinn had not answered his question. When Akuma turned toward him, the words froze in his throat, for the bodyguard had him at the point of a blazer pistol.

Akuma had always considered the blazer to be a sleek and finely designed weapon. At the moment, the double-barreled laser weapon looked remarkably ugly. It might have been less ugly if Akuma was not aware how expert was Quinn in its use.

"You have exceeded your authority," Quinn said, as though pronouncing sentence. "You have been allowed to do this in the past, but this time you have failed. The ISF does not tolerate failure.

"You have manipulated Samsonov into giving you a free hand. Together, you and he have forced Lord Kurita into a corner. The Director has learned of Lord Kurita's response to Samsonov's constant prodding, and he is not pleased. He only wanted Wolf's Dragoons discredited so that they would be forced to work for the Combine when no other would employ them. He thought that you understood that. You have disturbed his plan so gravely that the Dragoons have turned on the Dragon and our Lord.

"You must pay for that now."

Cold sweat beaded Akuma's upper lip. He had seen Quinn kill too many times to mistake the way the assassin held his body. This was no test or bluff, and nothing Akuma could say would sway him. The man's dedication to Indrahar was unshakable.

There was also no way to take him out. Had Akuma been the one holding the gun, he could never have killed Quinn without taking some injury himself. The assassin was too good at his craft. What had made Quinn the best choice as an agent now rendered him the worst as an enemy.

"*Sayonara,* Jerry," Quinn's voice had taken on a hint of emotion. *Could it be regret?* Akuma wondered. "The Sons of the Dragon had hopes for you," the assassin said.

Quinn's finger was tightening on the trigger when the entire building shook. The shot went wide of its mark, but still seared off Akuma's right ear as the dual bolt sizzled across the room to vaporize a two-centimeter hole in the transplex. The bolt went little farther, though. The aligned-crystal steel armor of a BattleMech drank the energy and showed no effect.

The room shook again as the BattleMech shifted its position to improve its grip on the skyscraper. Slabs fell from the ceiling as Akuma was dashed to the floor beside his desk. The desk's bulk saved his life as a chunk of the ceiling shattered against the marble top, spattering him with fist-sized particles.

Quinn was not so lucky. A piece of masonry the size of a computer deck caught him in the back of the neck and sent him sprawling to the floor. Before more falling debris buried most of the assassin from sight, Akuma saw that Quinn's head lay at a sharp angle.

Then the shaking stopped.

Akuma looked up at his savior. The 'Mech clinging precariously to the outside of the building was a dark blue *Shadow Hawk*. The golden falcon on its chest glittered in the morning sunlight as the dust-smeared battlefist shattered the transplex and thrust into the room.

Dechan Fraser's Command Lance had paid heavily to get into Cerant Center ahead of the Dragons' main force. West's *Griffin* was sidelined, with its right leg blown away by a vibrabomb. When last Fraser had seen Ellings and Alcorn, they had also taken heavy damage while engaged with a pair of Kurita *Panther*s. His own *Shadow Hawk* had lost its head-mounted SRM launcher to a PPC hit from a *Warhammer*. That shot had cracked his cockpit armor and sent shrapnel tearing into his left arm. The pain was unimportant now, for Dechan had made it to Government House in time.

He was looking in on Jerry Akuma, the Snake who had caused all their trouble. For years, Akuma had done nothing but try to hurt the Dragoons. Though Dechan would have preferred Samsonov on his viewscreen, the Warlord was too far away. Eliminating his tool would have to do.

IR showed another man in the room. Though he was mostly buried under rubble, his still-visible hand gripped a pistol. No sane person would bother to draw a pistol against a 'Mech, but Dechan had no idea what had been going on. No matter, he was here for revenge and he would have it.

He slammed the *Hawk*'s fist through the transplex window wall. Fragments of the tough plastic rained across the debris-strewn carpet as the 'Mech's hand opened to reach for the cowering Draconian. The hand closed, fingers straining briefly against the massive desk sheltering Akuma.

That delay was all the Snake needed. He squirmed free of the juggernaut fingers and staggered through the open doorway of the room.

"Come back and die, you scum," Dechan bellowed in frustration over the 'Mech's external speakers.

Myomer pseudomuscles strained as the *Shadow Hawk* ripped its way through the building's outer wall. The 'Mech flopped on its belly, legs extended into space through the hole torn for its entry. Dechan rolled the 'Mech to one side to get an optical on the fleeing Kuritan. The heavy construction of Government House blocked his machine's sensors even more successfully than the heavy walls impeded his forward progress.

Akuma threw himself into a waiting elevator car. Before Dechan could reorient his 'Mech to bring any weapons to bear, the doors slid shut. The car cleared the level as the *Shadow Hawk*'s laser pulse slagged the outer doors and sizzled through the back wall of the shaft.

Dechan cursed. Based on the trouble he'd had bulling into the executive office, he knew he couldn't plow the *Hawk* toward the elevator shaft before Akuma had finished his ride. He carefully noted which of the shafts the fleeing officer had taken, then began to back his 'Mech out of the hole. At one point, the *Hawk* would have toppled from the building except for Dechan's quick grab at the edge. An uncontrolled fall from that height could scramble even a BattleMech.

Once steadied and oriented, he cut in his jump jets and released the 'Mech's grip on the skyscraper. The ground came up quickly, but the superheated steam cushioned the drop. Myomer pseudomuscles flexed to absorb the last of the inertia.

Dechan pivoted the *Hawk* and piloted it around the corner of the building. Ahead of him stood the dark glass cylinders of the elevator shafts. Dechan marked the one in motion. His lips drew back in a snarl as a quick count assured him that it was Akuma's. He brought his sights to bear. As soon as the crosshairs of his heads-up display kissed the sinking car's center, he cut loose with his Martell laser.

Pulse after pulse flashed into the shaft. Flames and smoke erupted through the holes each pulse burned through the shaft's walls. Sheared free from its cables, the flaming elevator car crashed ten stories into the building's basement.

Dechan cut off the laser, satisfied that nothing Human could survive that inferno.

"That's for Shadd and all the others," he said. Magnified by the *Hawk*'s external speakers, his words echoed off the surrounding buildings.

Dechan had gotten his revenge, yet he didn't feel satisfied. He just felt empty.

48

Central Square, Cerant, An Ting
Galedon Military District, Draconis Combine
14 January 3028

Dechan stood on the sloping surface of his *Shadow Hawk*'s foot and leaned back against the 'Mech's leg. By draping his arm through a climbing rung, he was able to relax a bit, to the relief of his exhausted body. What he really wanted to do was lie down and sleep for a day or three, but that was a luxury he'd have to forego a while longer. After Wolf's announcement that he would address the Dragoons about their course of action, Dechan had decided to acquire a good view of the noisy square where the speech would take place. He was not about to sleep through it.

The 'Mech's shadow covered him, protecting him from the hot sun. The other still-functional BattleMechs of his company were scattered around the south edge of the central square. Like Dechan, their pilots sheltered in the shade of the machines.

Below him, Thom Dominguez stood in the shade between the *Hawk*'s legs. Sergeant Dominguez's *Wolverine* was still in the repair shop, but the rest of his Recon Lance was present. Battered, but present.

"I don't think we'll have any trouble from the Snakes today."

Dominguez's comment dragged Dechan back from his near slumber. "Huh," he replied intelligently.

"I mean, I ain't seen a Snake all day. City's been a ghost town since the Ryuken pulled out yesterday."

"Lucky for you, since you're naked," Dechan responded, referring to Dominguez's temporary lack of a 'Mech.

"Unity! A man don't need a 'Mech to chase these worthless worms. A toddler with a simulator could rout them. Some samurai," Dominguez huffed, spitting on the pavement near the *Shadow Hawk*'s left foot. "I thought we were going to have a fight of it. The Ryuken Jocks were reasonably competent on Barlow's End."

"They still are. The guys we fought here were mostly greenies. Most of the Barlow Jocks went over to the Iron Man's regiment on Misery. Bet they couldn't stand that Akuma bastard."

"They must've really hated him to trade a bunk on a soft planet like this for a slot on that frozen hellhole." Dominguez rubbed the back of his neck and yawned. "Poor trade."

"I think I might have considered it, too, if Akuma had been my CO."

Dominguez thought about that a moment, then nodded. "Yeah, I know what you mean."

Dechan looked around the square. The once-shining wood and marble facades of the public buildings were chipped and stained. The pavement was littered with debris from the street riots, overlaid by the more plentiful debris of the recent fighting. The biggest chunks of rubble had been bulldozed into heaps to clear space for the hundreds of Dragoons who would be coming to hear Wolf's address.

Across the square stood more BattleMechs. They were from Lean's Company and were already waiting here when Dechan's troops arrived. Like Dechan's 'Mech unit, they had arrived ahead of the bulk of the Dragoons. That had been planned for safety's sake, for no one wanted the tired pilots of the giant machines to accidentally trample any of their own people.

Lean had gotten to the square even earlier and grabbed the area in front of Government House, which annoyed Dechan because he'd wanted the spot for his own company. He knew that it was the only one in the square that was going to offer enough shade for several BattleMechs by the time Wolf began his address. Already the building's tattered bulk blocked the early afternoon sunlight.

From his vantage point, Dechan could see the MechWarriors of Lean's command gathered at the feet of her *Archer*. They looked even more exhausted than his own crew. The long days of city fighting had taken their toll. No Dragoon had slept through a full night in over a week.

Dragoon foot soldiers, support personnel, and dependents had been arriving for nearly half an hour. The square was almost full, with every Dragoon present on An Ting anxious to hear Wolf's address. The only ones not attending were those charged with keeping the remnants of Ryuken-*ichi* away from Cerant or with maintaining high guard in the aerospace above the city.

A familiar sound reached Dechan's ears, carrying easily above the noise of the milling Dragoons. It was the unmistakable thunder of giant BattleMech feet striking concrete. Dechan slid his arm free of the climbing rung. Gripping it tightly, he swung his body out to get a better viewing angle.

"What is it?" Dominguez called. From his position, he couldn't see through the crowd.

A smile lit Dechan's face. "It's the kids."

As the crowd nearest the street raised a hurrah at the sight of the new arrivals, the shouting became contagious and spread across the square. The cheering took up the rhythm of the pounding feet.

A half-dozen machines entered the square. Each was a training 'Mech and carried the insignia of the Training Command. These young pilots had distinguished themselves by saving the Dragoons at Boupeig barracks from the first onslaught of the Ryuken and had continued to prove themselves as warriors in the fighting that followed. They had served as the mobile reaction force for the defense of the barracks area, freeing the more experienced warriors of Lean's and Fraser's companies for the tricky work of city-fighting. The young pilots were to be decorated today, which was the last time they would pilot the training machines. After this, they would be assigned to BattleMechs and duty among the regiments. They had earned their places.

The heroes of the Training Command piloted their 'Mechs

into the roped-off area reserved for them and powered down. The open-topped groundcar that had been following in their wake pulled through their formation and halted before the steps of the administration building. Dechan could see a white-haired officer, who had to be Colonel Ellman, exit the car. Though exhaustion slumped his shoulders, he still radiated pride in his charges. That pride was well-justified, Dechan thought. Those kids had come through in a spot that would have challenged experienced MechWarriors.

The excitement of the trainees' arrival died away, and the gathered Dragoons returned to their mutterings. From his perch, Dechan listened in on a few within earshot. The desire for revenge was on everyone's lips, and people seemed to differ only in their opinions of the best way to go about it. Most seemed to want to burn Luthien around Takashi Kurita's ears and to use Warlord Samsonov as kindling.

A flash of movement in the darkness inside the administration building caught Dechan's attention. Eyes straining, he squinted through the sun's glare before remembering that the Binox goggles, which he had brought along for a better view, had a polarized setting as well. He pulled them up from the thong around his neck and snugged them into place. Now he was able to peer into the gloomy hallway that ran from the open doors deep into the building.

Colonel Wolf was on his way up the corridor, his step steady and strong, his head held high. Dechan couldn't understand how a fifty-plus-year-old man like Wolf could bounce back so quickly. It was the young ones like himself who were supposed to be resilient. Dechan knew that Wolf had to be as exhausted as the rest of them, but the Colonel didn't show it.

The crowd quieted when they saw Wolf approaching the microphones that would carry his words to the repeaters scattered throughout the square, and even further to the Dragoons stationed in orbit.

"Dragoons," Wolf began, gazing around at the gathering. "Today we welcome new MechWarriors to the ranks of our fighting forces. I call upon all present to witness that honor." Cheers followed the former trainees as they marched up the steps to receive their badges of rank from the hand of Colonel Wolf.

Rituals completed, the young MechWarriors filed down from the steps and returned to their training machines to hand the neurohelmets over to the new trainees who would take their places. Colonel Ellman did not go with them, but took his place behind Wolf, joining Colonel Arbuthnot and the other senior Dragoon officers present on An Ting. Dechan took it as a sign of solidarity among the upper ranks.

From somewhere in the crowd, a voice shouted a question to the Colonel.

"When are we going Snake hunting, Colonel?"

Somehow Wolf spotted the speaker and fixed him with a hard look. "Your answer's coming, Rodrigues. Sit tight." Both the question and answer were transmitted through the repeater system. When the thronging Dragoons heard Wolf's words, they roared their approval, anticipating vengeance.

Through the binox, Dechan could see the Colonel close his eyes at the crowd's response. For an instant, the strength that Wolf projected faltered and his exhaustion was there for Dechan to see. Then the shields slid back into place and Wolf was the quintessential commander again. He positioned himself squarely behind the microphones.

"Blood has brought us here today," he said. "Blood shed by our comrades. Blood shed by our enemies. But most of all, blood shed by the men, women, and children of our kin. That blood calls us. It calls for vengeance."

The Dragoons roared their approval.

"We stand where we are today because of the actions of others. We have been forced to this crucial point through no choice of our own. We gave fair service, but self-seeking men have betrayed us. They have cost us dearly, and we have only begun to make them pay.

"We have choices," Wolf said over the cheers.

"We can take the torch to Luthien and burn out the cancer at the heart of the Draconis Combine. We can avenge ourselves as we did at New Delos. Is that what you want?"

Hundreds of voices screamed, "Yes!"

Dechan did not feel the same way, though. He had not been a part of the Dragoons at New Delos, yet he had felt the pain of the losses here on An Ting. He had wanted revenge, too, but what he had done to Jerry Akuma did not bring a single Dragoon back to life. It had not made anything better. It had not let him sleep easier. He looked to where Wolf stood, hoping that his commander would say something to help resolve the contradiction.

Wolf stood impassively while the crowd took up the chant of "Blood! Blood!" When he held up his hands to quiet the crowd, they gradually complied.

"We would indeed see blood on that course. Our blood as well as Kurita blood. It is a long, hard road to Luthien. It is a road that would be under constant attack by Kuritan forces. The Draconians would not take kindly to our march through the Combine, and they would send strong forces to intercept us. Stronger forces would defend Luthien. It is, after all, their capital planet, a focal point to their own sense of unity. That is something we did not face at New Delos. On Luthien, we would face a unified people, not one split by civil war. The might of the Draconis Combine cannot be dismissed.

"We are the Dragoons. No unit, House-sponsored or mercenary, can match us. But even we are not invincible. If enough pressure were brought to bear, we might crack, crumble. The road to Luthien would be our path to oblivion."

A low grumbling began in the crowd. The mob animal growled, sensing it was about to be driven from its prey.

"I cannot ask you to forgo your revenge. I, too, swore that there would never be another New Delos. What I do ask is that you think about where we are, what we want to achieve. Think about those we have to protect.

"Here on An Ting, we had to fight. We will have to fight again. Nothing we do can prevent that. The Kurita High Command knows that they have lost us and that we will leave the Combine. You have all heard what the terrorists said aboard the *Hephaestus*. Surely you can see that Kurita means to target our kin, to hold them hostage against our actions? We must protect our people."

Wolf's appeal to the real concerns of the individuals who made up the crowd struck home. Having won them again, he pressed on.

"We could simply go with them. That would lead the Dragon right to them. The Draconians are alerted now; they will follow the regiments to the rendezvous point. We cannot allow that to happen. We must distract Kurita from our people.

"To do this, we will call the Draconis Combine to the field of battle. We will present a challenge to their honor. They will not be able to refuse. Even if they call us outlaws, they will not resist the chance to crush us completely.

"When they accept, they will come to a place of our choosing, and we will fight. The troops of House Kurita pride themselves on being warriors. We will show them what being a warrior really means.

"As I speak to you, our challenge is on its way via the ComStar network from the facility here on An Ting. As insurance, couriers are en route to other planets, to use their stations. The Inner Sphere will hear our side of the story. Once that word is out, House Kurita cannot deny us what we want . . . a chance to make them pay. And I promise you that we *will* make them pay."

The roar of the crowd was pure approval.

"That is why I am now ordering all the regiments to Misery."

Excited, curious babbling interrupted. The Colonel waited patiently for a few moments, then raised his hand for silence. When he had the crowd's attention once more, he continued.

"You want to know why I have chosen Misery. There are several reasons.

"Misery is well-suited to the operations we have planned. The system is within short-term transport range of our fighting units. At this time, we can expect to land and consolidate onworld without facing significant opposition. Once we are down, the resources for fortification are plentiful. These are all valid reasons, military reasons.

"The planet's name is appropriate, too. House Kurita will learn that betraying the Dragoons has brought them Misery.

"The most important of Misery's qualifications is that it is far from the rendezvous star, and so our people will be able to assemble out of harm's way. They can safely begin the trek out of Combine space. When we have finished with the Kuritans, we will join them.

"You have all proved yourselves true Dragoons. I will be honored to have you with me on Misery. Together, we will meet whatever Lord Kurita sends against us, and we will kick the Dragon's tail out through its teeth."

49

DCMS Headquarters, Laerdal, Misery
Galedon Military District, Draconis Combine
1 February 3028

Minobu stood rigidly at attention, waiting for Warlord Samsonov to acknowledge his presence. The Warlord had ignored Minobu for the past twenty minutes, busying himself with requisition authorizations. It was nothing new. Samsonov had been ignoring him ever since he had arrived and commandeered the office two days ago. No explanation had been given. Even the Warlord's subordinates had nothing to say to Minobu's officers.

Shuffling the papers aside, Samsonov looked up, his face flinty. "You have, of course, heard the ridiculous challenge that Wolf's Dragoons has flung at the Combine."

"I have seen the text."

"And what do you make of it?"

Minobu scented a trap. The Warlord would be looking for a scapegoat after the calamity on An Ting. Any officer showing sympathy for the Dragoons might be singled out. Minobu knew he had made an enemy of Samsonov years ago when he had taken Wolf's side during the Warlord's attempt to gain control of the Dragoons. Every time he had spoken out against Samsonov's plans, the Warlord's hatred of him had deepened. Samsonov would probably be glad to find evidence implicating Minobu in the recent disastrous events. Minobu's previous service as PSL Officer to the Dragoons and his known friendship with Jaime Wolf would prejudice many staunch Kurita officers against him. As much caution as honor would permit was in order.

"As the Warlord must know, I left An Ting on the morning after the rioting started. At that time, *Chu-sa* Akuma seemed to believe that he was in control of the situation.

"Many things are claimed in the Dragoon statement. If their allegations are true, their challenge offers House Kurita more honor than it deserves." To forestall the expected outburst and to soothe Samsonov's ego, Minobu went on quickly. "But you are Warlord of Galedon and you would not allow such infamous deeds to take place in your district. Therefore, the Dragoons must be lying. Their challenge is so much bluster, sheer bravado to hide their own criminal nature. As a man of high position, you will, of course, ignore the empty braggadocio of your social inferiors."

Samsonov gave him a predatory smile, as though Minobu's words pleased him. "On the contrary, I cannot ignore the situation."

The Warlord's reaction caught Minobu off guard. *Shimatta,* he thought. *I have given Samsonov whatever it was he wanted.*

Obviously pleased to see Tetsuhara off balance, Samsonov went on. "I am a loyal samurai and know my duty. This battle that the Dragoons desire must come to pass."

"I doubt that combat is their desire," Minobu offered, angry at Samsonov's enjoyment of his discomfort.

"Do not doubt it, Tetsuhara," Samsonov said, eyes sparkling like a cat playing with its quarry. "Wiser heads have expected as much for some time. The Coordinator has known this day was coming and has prepared for it. The mercenaries' challenge fits smoothly into his plans."

Minobu was confused. He did not understand what the Warlord meant. The Coordinator had always sided in favor of the Dragoons. If Minobu had been able to speak with Wolf about his visit to Luthien, perhaps this might make sense.

Leaning back in his chair, the Warlord folded his hands over his paunch. His next words brought Minobu's attention back to the present.

"Armed forces of the Draconis Combine will meet the foolish Dragoons in battle here on Misery. You shall lead them, *General* Tetsuhara," Samsonov announced, tossing a small box onto the desk. The lid of the box popped open, revealing the *Tai-sho* rank insignia nestled within. One, with no clip to restrain it, tumbled free to lie, pin up, on the desk.

Minobu was shocked. Lead the fight against the Dragoons? He had known that the battle would come, but he had hoped to stand away from it. That hope was dashed as he listened to the order to command the fight against them.

And now he was a *Tai-sho*. Another empty promotion. No, worse than empty. This one held a sharp, sharp spike to pierce him.

"You are overcome by this honor," the Warlord said, voice dripping with false sympathy. "You may even think it coincidental. But then, you do not have the farseeing eyes of our Lord Takashi."

Samsonov rocked forward to place his elbows on the smooth surface of the desk. He interlaced his fingers, holding them to one side of his face. "Yes, indeed. Last October, I was favored with a *haiku* from Lord Kurita. As you know, he often uses such forms for his more significant orders. I believe that you will find its intent quite clear."

Samsonov produced a sheet of rice paper from the central drawer of the desk and offered it to Minobu. He settled back in his seat, a smug grin on his face as Minobu read the poem:

Dragon feels spring's chill.
Iron hunter aims the shaft.
Running wolf must fall.

Like the Dragon in the first line, Minobu felt a chill.

"You are the iron hunter, Tetsuhara," the Warlord spat out. "You are chosen by the Coordinator to execute the purge of the rebellious Dragoons. He knows of your loyalty to House Kurita and respects it. He knows that you will not fail him."

"I shall do my best."

"Ah ha. No false modesty, Tetsuhara," Samsonov said mildly. His voice shifted to diamond hardness. "You have *my* every confidence," he said. "You will succeed."

Samsonov heaved his bulk up from the chair and strode to the wall, where he pulled down a map of the district. Grease pencil lines covered the slick plastic surface, all converging at the pale yellow dot that represented the Misery system. "Already Kurita units are moving to take up the challenge."

"Then you have a strategy in place."

"Of course, *Tai-sho*. The Coordinator may wish you to lead the forces that will destroy the mercenaries, but this is still my district. You command through me. *Wakari-masu-ka?*"

"*Hai,* Warlord," Minobu responded instantly.

Samsonov's eyes were hard and glittering. "See that you remember it," he commanded.

"Look here," he said, pulling down a second map, this one showing the local sun and its five planets. "We will meet the renegade Dragoons here on Misery, as they desire. But we will have a few surprises for them.

"You will be in command of the ground forces, including all regiments of the Ryuken and elements from the Seventeenth and Twenty-First Galedon Regulars. Also under your command will be the Eighth Sword of Light. Quite an honor for a new *Tai-sho*.

"My Fifth Galedon Regulars and the Third Proserpina Hussars will remain in space, hidden here behind the fourth moon. We will allow the Dragoons to land unmolested so that we may destroy them without risking our own valuable space assets."

"But their BattleMechs will be most vulnerable in the landing phase," Minobu interrupted.

"I did not ask for a critique of my strategy," Samsonov growled. "A space battle will increase the risk that the ambush forces will be spotted. The Wolves must not be aware that they are really lambs going to the slaughter."

Minobu did not see how an orbital battle would endanger well-hidden DropShips on the far side of a moon, but he held his peace. The more detailed Samsonov's planning was, the less responsibility Minobu would have in executing the loathsome orders to fight the Dragoons.

Samsonov seemed to take Minobu's silence as confirmation of his superior intelligence. "Once battle is joined, you will entice the bandit Wolf to commit his troops fully. When he has done that, my forces will leave the moon and drop in behind him. The Dragoons will be caught in a vise and we will crush them."

"The basic strategy is sound," Minobu said, careful not to offend the Warlord again. "It will depend on the details."

"And those I am leaving to you," the Warlord replied drily.

Minobu should have known *that* was coming. His karma would not allow him to escape easily.

"I will leave a small staff while I conclude the troop transfers. See that they are aware of your arrangements. The drop forces are to be informed of landing zones and expected opposition. You will, naturally, see to it that any opposition to the landings is minimal. My 'Mechs must land intact, able to bring their full fighting strength to bear."

"I understand, Warlord."

Samsonov looked at Minobu and almost smiled. It was as though the Warlord knew some secret joke, to which Minobu's words were the punchline. A moment later, he swaggered out of the room, leaving Minobu alone with his thoughts. No matter how many times he went over it, the answer always came out the same: he was bound to duty. But what had he done to deserve this karma?

Despite his words to Samsonov, Minobu could not believe in the guilt of the Dragoons. He had worked with them, fought at their side. He knew their nature. More important, he knew Jaime Wolf's nature. Wolf must have been as forced into his actions as Minobu would be from now on.

Ninjo.

He wanted to help Wolf and his Dragoons. For years, the mercenary had been his friend. All that they had shared flooded into Minobu's mind. An honorable man was honor-bound to come to the aid of a friend in trouble. Yet Minobu was being asked to kill his friend.

Giri.

Minobu was an officer in the Draconis Combine Mustered Soldiery. His superiors had ordered him to action. It was his duty as a soldier to obey. Minobu was also a samurai of House Kurita. A samurai's principal duty was obedience to his lord. The obligations of honor demanded that nothing come between him and his duty.

He was trapped, cornered by his duty. He had always been

a good samurai, loyal, faithful . . . dutiful. It was his nature. He could not be otherwise.

Minobu walked slowly to the door and opened it. Michi sat in the outer office, awaiting his lord's attention. He leaped to his feet as the panel swung wide. His eager questions were unspoken as he registered Minobu's emotional state.

"Fetch the maps and rosters," Minobu ordered tonelessly. "We have a campaign to plan."

50

Ryuken Field Headquarters, Misery
Galedon Military District, Draconis Combine
22 April 3028

Michi threaded his way through the maze of consoles, machinery, and hanging cables obstructing passage through the bunker. The heaters had been running for over a week, since the command staff had moved into the structure, but they seemed unable to banish the frigid cold that ruled Borealis, Misery's northern continent.

Michi turned into the alcove that held the planning center. The chamber was dominated by the holotank taken from Ryuken-*ni*'s MHQ. The tank displayed a detailed version of Borealis's eastern half. Tiny red images of BattleMechs clustered around the city of Farsund, marking the location of the gathering Dragoon forces. Similar blue symbols stood in a vague line from coast to coast across the continent's two thousand kilometers. There were concentrations near the city of Boras in the north and the city of Laerdal and the magma mines in the south. In the central region of the Trolfjel Highlands, azure bands indicated the passes held by the Ryuken.

All the Ryuken *Chu-sa*, including Charles Earnst, who had been promoted to fill Minobu's place as commander of Ryuken-*ni*, conferred around the tank. Minobu stood at one end, a *Tai-sho*'s insignia shining at his collar. He was in conference with *Sho-sa* Saraguchi, now chief of staff at the command center.

Michi approached Minobu and waited for his attention before speaking.

"Report from the scouts, *Tai-sho*," Michi announced, slipping a datacard into the holotank's input slot. Miniature red DropShips appeared, joining a cluster of similar shapes near a tiny representation of a city. "They have spotted new DropShip landings outside of Farsund."

"That will be Alpha Regiment arriving from Delacruz," Minobu theorized. "DropShip types?"

"Only 'Mech carriers and cargo ships, as before. No troop ships are reported. Preliminary reports indicate only 'Mechs and their standard support vehicles being disembarked. No fighting vehicles have been seen."

"Huh," Earnst grunted, shaking his head in disbelief. "What can Wolf be thinking? An unsupported 'Mech force is not the Dragoon style at all."

"It seems that Wolf may intend this to be a combat of the lords of the battlefield," Minobu pointed out.

"Your pardon, *Tai-sho*," Michi said. "I would suggest that Colonel Wolf is only being reasonable. He's aware that there are over a hundred kilometers of difficult terrain between his chosen base at Farsund and the defensive positions occupied by our forces in the Trolfjel Highlands. There are no suitable approaches for vehicles. Wheeled or tracked machines would founder in the drift fields to the south. Of course, hovercraft could negotiate that terrain with ease, but the moraines would defeat them. Metal fan blades, frozen by the cold, would shatter as soon as a rock slipped the skirting. Even the most rugged craft would break down after four or five kilometers of that abuse, and they would have to cover at least twelve kilometers. 'Mechs are the only practical way to move through the valley."

Minobu had been studying the holotank depictions of each type of terrain as Michi was describing its difficulties. He could see that Michi was right, and knew that Wolf would have reached the same conclusions. Terrain considerations would have been part of Wolf's decision, but only part. "Sometimes, Michi-*san*, you are too practical. What you say is true, but the Dragoons rarely let terrain stop them. Though the space between our two armies is daunting, vehicular forces inserted behind our position could present a threat. It is not a threat we should fear, though. Wolf has declined to bring such forces. He has his reasons."

"I don't see why," Earnst announced. He scowled for a moment before articulating his objection. "If, as you say, there's a way to employ non-'Mech forces, why didn't the Dragoons bring them? I thought the Dragoons wanted to shed as much Kurita blood as possible."

"They do want blood, and they will get it," Minobu confirmed sadly. "This will be a hard battle. I think, however, that Wolf is looking beyond this battle. 'Mech forces are the easiest and fastest to evacuate from a planet. It would mean that they could rejoin their dependents sooner."

"You make it sound as if he's sure of victory," Earnst scoffed.

"Do you doubt it?" Minobu asked in a deceptively mild voice. His eyes swept the row of officers, who had by now all turned toward the head of the holotank. Each shook his head in turn.

"Gentlemen, Lord Kurita expects that we will win. Expectations do not win battles. Planning, leadership, courage, and weaponry win battles. Please return yourselves to the first, that we may apply the others."

The *Chu-sa* were quick to take the opportunity to escape the bright, sharp gaze of their *Tai-sho*. Michi turned and started to return to his post at the comm center, but Minobu reached out and took his arm.

"This landing brings the last of the Dragoons to Farsund. There will be no other bases. Recall the Sword of Light from Laerdal and the Regulars from Boras," Minobu said. "I want all of our forces gathered here as soon as possible. Route the Sworders through Voss Gap. It will save them at least two hours."

Michi looked at the holomap. It showed Voss Gap within twenty kilometers of Farsund, which was as he remembered it. "The Sword of Light would be strung out moving through the pass," he objected. "They will make a tempting target for an ambush."

"There will be no ambushes until the main fighting has begun," Minobu said confidently.

"How can you be sure? The Dragoons have not made an offensive move since the announcement of the challenge, but Alpha is here now. How do we know that Wolf has not already positioned some forces? How do we know he is not ready to strike?"

"*We* do not. *I* do," Minobu answered. "It is good that you think independently, Michi-*san,* but you are not yet ready to question my every decision. Pass the order."

Michi ignored the dismissal in his superior's tone. "At least let me put up a DropShip for a reconnaissance run," he protested.

"No. The Dragoons have grounded all their ships. We will observe the same courtesies."

"They have other DropShips further out. Their troops and vehicle ships are waiting in reserve out there."

"Those are guards for their JumpShips. They are no threat to us on-planet. Remember, we have our own forces in space. Samsonov's reserves are waiting out there as well. His 'Mechs will be more than a match for any number of Dragoon footsoldiers that might be dispatched as an emergency reserve."

Minobu leaned on the holotank, turning his attention to the hypothetical troop movements the *Chu-sa* were projecting. Michi still refused to leave.

"How can you be so sure Samsonov is there? We've had no word."

Minobu sighed. "Nor should we have. To achieve surprise, the fleet must remain undetected. They are there.

"We are all under the Coordinator's orders. Even Samsonov must see that this battle is too important to take chances. The lure of the glory to be won by destroying the Dragoons will guarantee his participation. He will not leave us unsupported, as he did Yorioshi on Galtor.

"Now go. Your procrastination is delaying the arrival of the Sword of Light. We will need their experienced warriors when the Dragoons attack."

Minobu watched Michi leave.

The young officer had valid concerns. Despite Minobu's words, he, too, was concerned over the lack of communication with Samsonov, but there was nothing to be done. The Draconis forces onworld had their orders. With careful strategy and a little luck, they could carry out those orders even without the Warlord's participation. Minobu rejoined the group around the holotank. Some of the officers' schemes must be critiqued.

The session lasted for hours. Minobu finally called a halt, and the other officers dispersed to their quarters. Minobu remained in the command center and ran more simulations of his own until he fell asleep at the console. He didn't know how long it was before a hand on his shoulder shook him awake.

"Reconnaissance reports BattleMechs departing the Dragoon base at Farsund." Michi looked as tired as Minobu felt. The younger officer had probably not had any sleep at all.

"They are leaving their fortifications?" Even as he asked, Minobu realized that the question was redundant. His sleep had left him groggy, slow to respond.

"Yes."

"How many?"

"Scouts report more than four hundred."

That roused Minobu to full awareness. "All five regiments, then. It seems that Wolf is making a grand gesture."

"When they've moved beyond the envelope of their anti-air, we can hit them with our fighters, cut their numbers before contact with our own 'Mechs," Michi suggested. "They'll be an easy target if the fighters can get in before today's snow. I've ordered the pilots to stand by."

"Are the Dragoons advancing under air cover?"

"No," Michi replied reluctantly.

"Then have our pilots stand down," Minobu ordered. "This will be an honorable battle. We will accept the combat under the terms."

"Is that wise?" Michi was clearly upset. "Do not our orders require victory? The Dragoons are five regiments of BattleMechs piloted by elite troops. We may outnumber them, but few of our MechWarriors can match their experience. We must do what we can to gain advantage. Think of your future, Minobu-*sama,*" Michi warned.

When Minobu shrugged, he noticed Michi's exasperation at the gesture. The young man tried to hide his emotion, but Minobu knew him too well. "The future has no meaning to a warrior. The way of the samurai is death. *Shigata ga nai.*"

Michi was silent for a moment. "Do you expect to die in this battle?"

"I expect nothing." Minobu's voice was neutral. "If it is my karma, I will die."

Again Michi went silent, apparently considering Minobu's words. "Will you let yourself be killed?"

The pleading note in Michi's voice told Minobu that his protégé feared that he had given up all hope, that he would seek death in battle to escape the problems that beset him.

"A warrior must embrace death if he is a true samurai, but that does not mean that he will throw away his life. A samurai must fight on, as long as he can advance his lord's cause. Failure to do so is dishonorable."

"Dishonorable," Michi echoed. "What if you survive the battle, but we are defeated?"

"If we are defeated, the situation will be most difficult. Until then, I will do all I can to my fulfill my duty and to maintain my own honor. If I survive, it will be because I have fought as a warrior should. As commander, I will have dealt honorably with my opponent. The *Dictum Honorium* requires that we treat our enemies as though they are as honorable as well. I have no doubts about Jaime Wolf's honor, and so I must deal honorably with him.

"Even in the hour of battle, he maintains his own honor."

Michi's brows drew together, signaling his confusion at his *sensei*'s last comment.

"Michi-*san,* did you not note at what hour the Dragoon 'Mechs began to move?"

"It was midnight," the young man said. "Wolf waited until it was finally dark before beginning his march. That's not unusual."

"The cover of darkness had nothing to do with it, Michi-*san.* At midnight, the Dragoon contract with House Kurita expired. Wolf and his Dragoons are now free agents."

51

Hamar Valley, Misery
Galedon Military District, Draconis Combine
23 April 3028

"Cut right, West!" Dechan shouted over the taccomm.

The big *Griffin* shifted at his order, vacating the spot where the Kuritans were concentrating their fire. Explosions shredded the granitic extrusion, but melted snow and ice refroze almost instantly.

The Dracs had given a good account of themselves, considering that Fraser's lance had caught them by surprise. Their biggest machine, a *Crusader,* had been crippled in the first rush. That blow had gutted the Kuritans' firepower, and the Draconians were wavering now under the Dragons' relentless hammering.

"They're fading. Keep on the pressure. Wakeman, full spread on the leader."

Dechan fired his own missiles, adding to the barrage from Wakeman's *Trebuchet.* High explosive rained down on the retreating Kurita lance. The *Crusader* and another already-damaged 'Mech went down in the raging fury of the explosions. The remaining two enemy machines vanished into the rills that eons of summer meltwater had cut into the ridges of the moraine.

"Got 'em," Wakeman crowed.

"Watch yourself and hold cover. They've still got live ones out there."

Dechan's *Shadow Hawk* followed West's *Griffin,* up to the crest of a ridge.

"What's holding you up, West? We've got Snakes to catch."

"Take a look for yourself, Captain." The massive right arm of West's 'Mech pointed with its hand-held Fusigon PPC.

Directing his attention that way, Dechan saw an assembly of Kurita BattleMechs about two kilometers away. The two survivors of the enemy lance were hightailing it straight to their buddies.

"So that's where the rest of their battalion is."

"Too many for us without support, Captain."

"We're not supposed to beat them, West. Just find them. We're on a good, old-fashioned recon mission."

"Why? Why don't we just put some of the DropShips up? Make those flyboys earn their pay."

"We're doing it this way because that's how the Colonel wants it."

"Seems bassackward to me," West groused.

"The Colonel must have a good reason."

"Well, he didn't tell me."

"He didn't tell me, either, but that don't change anything. We still got a job to do."

The two 'Mechs backed down the ridge, moving slowly to avoid attracting the enemy's attention. Once blocked from view, they picked up speed and headed for the fallen Kuritan BattleMechs, where Gatlin's *Ostscout* was standing over the *Crusader.*

"What's the salvage?" Dechan asked.

"It's better than salvage, Boss," Gatlin replied. "We've got a live one over here."

"You can fix that with a stomp of your dainty little foot," Wakeman suggested. "It'll be one less Snake to bother with."

"Ease off, Calvin. According to the markings on the cockpit, this Jock's an officer," Gatlin announced. "I don't exactly con the rank, but it's at least battalion level."

"Then we've got ourselves a prize," Dechan concluded.

"West, get over there and winkle that Draconian out. The Colonel will want to have a chat with him. Gatlin, watch your sensors. Target Wakeman on anything that gets too curious about us."

BattleMechs moved to his command, but not fast enough. The Kurita battalion could be headed their way. Unity! He should have left somebody on watch at the ridge. But then, he hadn't known that they would be spending time acquiring a prisoner. "Come on, West. I want us on the road."

"Keep your vest on, Captain. You don't want me to damage the Colonel's property, do you?"

"Just get on with it and save the smartass remarks for when we're out from under Kuritan guns."

West had no more to say as he fell to work separating the *Crusader*'s head, which held the pilot cockpit, from its body. It took the *Griffin* five minutes to wrench the head assembly free from its moorings. Each twist must have tumbled the Kurita MechJock painfully within the cockpit. With the head tucked safely under one arm, the Dragoon 'Mech joined its lancemates for the high-speed trek back to the command post.

Fraser's lance passed the sentries and clomped down into the basin where Wolf's command complex stood. The camouflaged canvas was heaped with snow, both as insulation and for disguise in the stark landscape. To the left of the entrance, Selden's *Wasp LAM* and Vordel's *Victor* stood guard. To the right, Cameron's *Cyclops* towered over the tents. Beyond it, more 'Mechs could be seen. Among them, Dechan recognized the sinister black form of Natasha Kerensky's *Warhammer*. He hadn't realized that the Widows had made it to Misery, but he should have known that nothing would keep them from this fracas.

The hatch on Cameron's *Cyclops* was open, and the cockpit heaters threw waves of distortion around him as he stood there, bundled heavily against the cold. He waved in acknowledgement to Dechan's radio call.

Dechan requested a security detachment to meet him. Cameron made the arrangements, then passed on the coordinates of a repair park so that the lance could resupply. Before the other 'Mechs turned off the track, Dechan relieved West of his burden.

The *Shadow Hawk* continued forward onto the flat space before the command center. Halting before the assembled security troopers, Dechan lowered the captured head to the ground.

"Here," he announced over the external speakers. "See if you can crack this open while I get down."

By the time he had struggled into his cold-weather gear and popped the *Hawk*'s hatch, the security team had convinced the captured pilot to open his own hatch. As Dechan scrambled down the ladder, two troopers were helping the prisoner out of his cockpit. The man was battered and bleeding from several wounds. Despite his shivering, no one offered to get him something warmer than the light uniform he wore.

Dechan led the way into the tent, followed by Major Kormenski and two troopers with the prisoner in tow. The guards had to drag the Kuritan when one leg collapsed under him.

The air temperature was noticeably higher inside the heatlock. After passing through to the greater warmth of the inner tent, Dechan still felt chilled from his short stay outside and was reluctant to remove his coat. He compromised by letting it flop open. In the short walk through the corridor to the main tent, he noticed that he could smell things again; sweaty bodies, old food.

"Colonel, we caught something that might interest you," he announced on arrival.

The Dragoons around the holotank were expecting him, and no one seemed surprised at his announcement. That professional detachment vanished when Dechan turned to the prisoner, who hung slumped in the grip of the security troopers. He pulled the man's head up by his hair.

"Singh," hissed Major Blake.

The prisoner shrugged off the hands that held him, but his barely suppressed grunt of pain told what the effort cost him. He coughed and spit out blood and tooth chips before turning his face toward the Colonel.

"Hello, Wolf."

Fadre Singh squared his shoulders, which made his rank bars of a Kurita *Tai-sa* glint in the light. He took a halting step toward the mercenary leader. The guards moved to restrain him, but Wolf waved them back. Singh continued until he was face to face with Wolf.

"Surprised to see me, O great master of the Wolf Dragoons?"

"In this condition . . . yes."

"When have you ever been concerned over my condition? I spit on your concern, fossil. You are nothing and your command is even less. The Draconians have you where they want you. Your days are numbered.

"I'm glad that I'm free of you. My eyes have been opened to what you and your cronies are doing. It was clear from the way you all treated me after Hoff. My skill and my achievements meant nothing to you. You cast me away, though you had to know I was in the right. You sided with senile and cowardly old Parella. You must be senile yourself, old man."

"Watch your mouth," Blake interjected.

"Why should I?" Singh snapped at him.

"I've got no respect for him," he said, waving his arm to encompass all the people present. "Or for any of you. You've all fallen from whatever you once were. You can't see ability when it's under your collective noses. If I could have gone back, I would have, but you cut me off there as well. You cut me adrift.

"What did you expect me to do? Roll over and beg for favor from your gray-haired tyrant? Plead to be restored to the clan? I've been making my own way."

Singh's laugh was ragged. He swung his head back to Wolf.

"I owe nothing to you and your puppet Dragoons, Wolf. I don't need any of you. I fooled you all and found somebody who can appreciate my abilities. Warlord Samsonov knew a commander when he saw one. He gave me the command I deserved." Singh paused and locked eyes with Wolf. A cruel grin split the prisoner's face. "All it cost was the name of your bolthole."

The sound of indrawn breaths was loud in the shocked silence. Jaime raised his hand to strike Singh, but the man's body spun away before he could connect, driven by the impact of several heavy slugs. Wolf pivoted, looking for the gunman.

Natasha Kerensky stood calmly, no hint of remorse on her face. Smoke rose from the barrel of her Marakov.

"Those who break faith with the unity shall go down into darkness," she quoted.

52

Opdal Glacial Fields, Misery
Galedon Military District, Draconis Combine
25 April 3028

Minobu stood in the open hatch of his *Dragon*. The cold wind whipped in eddies between the 'Mech's bulky shoulders, chilling him through the cold-weather gear he wore. He was careful to avoid contact between his exposed skin, already chafed from this brief exposure, and the cold metal of the Binox forty-powers. Through the device, he studied the serried ranks of the Dragoon BattleMechs drawn up across the principal arm of the Opdal Glacier. They stood tall among the naked fangs of dark rock jutting above the ice surface.

Motion caught his eye and he focused on it. Black 'Mechs, stark against the snow, were moving into place on the Dragoon left flank. Through the Binox, he could easily distinguish the red spider insignia, which told him that the Black Widows had arrived to join the Assault 'Mechs of Zeta Battalion. A powerful anchor for the Dragoons line.

The days of preliminary skirmishing were over. Here amid the peaks and glacial surfaces, the armies had come together, reaching an unspoken agreement on the battle site. It was not the site that either general would have chosen, but each found it acceptable. Barring static defense of an important point, Minobu knew that a commander could rarely expect to fight on terrain of his own choosing.

Minobu slid back into his 'Mech and dogged down the hatch. Out of the wind and back in the heat of the *Dragon*'s interior, he found his clothes suddenly too warm. He squirmed out of the jacket and clambered into the pilot seat.

"All commands report status. Code twenty-three," he ordered. Slipping the neurohelmet onto his shoulders and connecting his cooling system, he watched ready lights flash green on the command board his Tech had rigged over the comm board, crowding the cramped cockpit even more. Minobu bore the loss of space easily. Although the jury-rigged system offered nothing like the capabilities of a Tacticon computer, it did increase his ability to communicate with his command. That capacity more than compensated for the personal discomfort. By the time he had finished hooking up, only one light remained unilluminated. Minobu keyed open the channel to the commander of Ryuken-*go*.

"*Tai-sa* Sullivan, I have a no-show from Sword of Light. Explain."

"No explanation, *Tai-sho*." The reply came at once, but Sullivan sounded nervous. That was understandable, though. The Sword of Light Regiment was supposed to be in position on his flank. "My scouts have not sighted them. I will try to set up a relay."

While Minobu waited for word, the Dragoon BattleMechs began to move, advancing en masse.

"Steady," Minobu advised his commanders. "Hold fire till we are reasonably assured of good hits. No sniping." He listened to the order being passed, pleased by the response of his troops. Only a few pilots in Seventeenth Galedon broke discipline by firing without permission, and their officers swiftly restored order.

Just as Minobu was about to give the command for harassing fire with energy weapons, the Dragoons stopped their advance. He watched in puzzlement as a single BattleMech continued forward from the center of the Dragoon line. The lone machine registered on his identification program as a *Victor*, an eighty-ton Assault 'Mech. After half a kilometer, it too stopped. The taccomm crackled as a Dragoon voice came over the open channel.

"I am Hans Vordel, Lieutenant in Wolf's Dragoons. I am a fourth-generation MechWarrior. I have seen twenty-four-cycles and have fought on more worlds than I have years. Who among you has the courage to face me in single combat?"

His challenge was awkward and his Japanese abominable, but the intent was clear. Silence greeted it. No one in the Kurita force spoke, on either the open channel or any of the protected frequencies. The challenge was unexpected. A *teki* acting like an ancient samurai? It shocked them into immobility.

Suddenly a *Thunderbolt* broke from the Kurita ranks, pounding out to within a kilometer of the Dragoon *Victory*. The comm channel reverberated with the pilot's response to the Dragoon.

"Villain. I am Tadashi Bolivar, a mere *Chu-i* in the grand forces of the Draconis Combine. I am not so old and decrepit as you, but I am a fifth-generation samurai of House Kurita and have slain three Davion MechWarriors single-handedly. I accept your challenge. Pray to any gods you hold dear, *teki,* and prepare to die by my hand."

A ragged cheer came from his comrades of Ryuken-*san*. Some of them keyed on their external speakers, and their cheers reverberated from the surrounding peaks.

Encouraged, Bolivar drove forward at his opponent. Vordel's 'Mech fairly leaped from its standing pose and accelerated rapidly. Minobu saw the flaw in Bolivar's approach vector that was sending him directly toward a zone of broken ice. Vordel must have seen it, too, because he shifted the *Victor* to take advantage. Bolivar reacted to his opponent's shift and headed his 'Mech further into the dangerous terrain.

When the *Thunderbolt* stumbled, the Dragoon *Victor* opened fire. Its paired lasers raked the Kurita 'Mech, catching the pilot by surprise. Reacting like a novice, Bolivar decelerated to pull his 'Mech around. The moment his opponent's speed slackened, Vordel triggered a burst from the massive Pontiac 100 autocannon that was the *Victor*'s right arm. Shells cratered the armor across the *Thunderbolt*'s upper surface and smashed into the cockpit area. The Kurita 'Mech shuddered and collapsed.

Dragoon cheers rang off the mountains.

The *Victor* raised its left arm and fired twin ruby flares into the sky before heading back toward its lines. Before it had reached them, a second Dragoon 'Mech left the line and advanced toward the center of the field.

Another challenge boomed out, as awkward as the first. In response, another Kurita 'Mech went forward to meet the Dragoon. Minobu recognized it instantly as Michi Noketsuna's *Ostroc*. Shouting, "I accept!" Michi roared down on the Dragoon without stopping. This fight was longer, but when it was over, the Dragoon *Catapult* lay broken on the field.

This time it was the Kuritans cheering the victor, rocking the mountains.

Minobu wondered what Wolf was thinking, to allow such dueling. The mercenary had probably decided that it would appeal to Minobu. Perhaps he thought that this was how one conducted a battle of honor. At one time, it had been.

Today, though, it was a luxury Minobu's forces could not afford. The Kurita forces outnumbered the Dragoons, but not overwhelmingly. Man for man and 'Mech for 'Mech, the Ryuken were no match for the mercenaries. The Galedon Regulars were even worse off. A series of duels would only deplete the Draconian resources.

There was another consideration. Sullivan reported that the Sword of Light had not yet appeared. During the duels, they should have time to break through the Dragoon delaying force and reach the battlefield. Then the Kuritans could attack with a better chance of success. In the meantime, Minobu would let the single combats continue. He hoped he would not lose too many good pilots before the Sworders put in their appearance.

The battles became a blur, one after another. Dragoon as well as Kurita 'Mechs failed to return, but far more of the latter lay shattered on the field. Few of the duels were as short as the first, but all were brutal. Minobu was gratified to see that none of the other victorious Dragoons returned unscathed.

The finale of a battle between a Dragoon *Spider* and a Kurita *Panther* finally ended Minobu's waiting game. The *Spider* was on its back and the *Panther* closing in for the kill when blue lightning lanced from the Dragoon line. The beam struck the Kurita 'Mech full in the chest. Weakened armor collapsed under the hellish energies. The electric discharge from the PPC overloaded the *Panther*'s circuits and caused the autoloader to cycle a reload for the SRM launcher into the path of molten metal. The *Panther*'s upper torso vanished in a fireball.

This breach of combat etiquette was too much for the Kuritans. All across the field, their BattleMechs surged forward and howls of outrage echoed from the peaks. There would be no more duels.

Like a startled flock of birds, the Dragoons turned and fled before the onrushing horde. Despite the apparent failure of morale, their fire was well-coordinated and surprisingly effective. Firing wildly, the Draconians streamed after them across the glacier's surface. From what Minobu could see the huge barrage of missiles, shells, and beams seemed to have little effect.

Uneasiness seized Minobu as he moved his 'Mech forward. If his force was advancing, he had best advance with them if he hoped to maintain even the slightest control. He was still puzzled by the Dragoon actions, which had been uncharacteristic from the first. Offering formal duels and then violating the code made no sense. The enemy's sudden flight made even less. It had to be a trap.

Almost at the moment he reached that conclusion, Minobu noticed the Dragoon left flank slowing and turning. They had reached the rocky hummocks of lesser mountains projecting through the ice and were taking cover there.

"Hold! Hold!" he screamed as he pulled his own *Dragon* to a halt. "Hold the advance!"

His orders went unheeded. The first Kurita 'Mechs rushed on past the original position the Dragoons had held. When the medium 'Mechs and the faster of the heavy machines hit the former enemy position, the mercenaries sprang their trap.

In a sudden burst, the ice beneath the Draconian machines lit up with blue fire, glowing like some crazy New Year's decorations. Cracks appeared in the ice, spreading across the field. In places, the ice shattered as easily as a frozen puddle. Yawning pits opened and swallowed Kurita BattleMechs.

The Draconian rush turned into chaos as two dozen 'Mechs immediately plummeted from view. Others scrambled from the crumbling surface. A few gained the safety of ice that had not been undermined, but most crashed down, along with the multi-ton blocks they gripped. Several more 'Mechs were forced over the edge by eagerly advancing fellows who were unaware of the danger. Devastated by their losses, the Kurita units were in total disarray.

A kilometer away, the Dragoons halted their feigned retreat. Weapons blazing, they turned on the Draconians. Their furious charge struck with ruinous effect.

Minobu saw now that Wolf had had his own reasons to delay the battle. While the duels were taking place, his engineers had been tunneling under the glacier's surface, preparing the pits and carefully placing the explosive triggers. In one clever maneuver, the Dragoons had cancelled out most of the Ryuken's numerical advantage.

Knots of Kurita 'Mechs were scattered across the glacier, and the Dragoons set out in pursuit over stretches of intact ice. The battle spread across the Opdal Glacial Fields. Instead of a head-on, multi-regimental battle, the fighting dissolved into a series of unconnected struggles by units of company or battalion size. Swept forward with the advance, Minobu's *Dragon* was being dragged along by the ebb and flow of the Ryuken-*ni*'s retreat down Hamar Valley.

Pressed and harried, the Kuritans fought fiercely, but the Dragoons allowed them no quarter. In the smaller battles, most of the advantage went to the mercenaries, who had far more experience in such combat.

Disrupted by the surrounding mountains, Minobu's comm channels were filled with static, cutting him off from most of his command. When he finally managed to break free from his own pursuers, there was little he could do to reunify his forces. Minobu knew it was only a matter of time until the Dragoons reduced his troops to a point beyond effective opposition.

Suddenly, the pressure on the Draconians let up. Everywhere across the now extensive battlefield, Dragoons pulled back. Praying over the open channel, someone thanked Buddha for the miracle. From his own vantage point, however, Minobu was able to discern the true reason for Dragoons' unexpected withdrawal. The reprieve to his troops was not of supernatural origin.

The Eighth Sword of Light had finally arrived.

Faced with the arrival of fresh enemy troops, the Dragoons contented themselves with the havoc they had caused. Scattered as they had become in pursuit of the Ryuken and the Galedon Regulars, they were in danger of being defeated in detail. Rather than face the concentrated troops of the Sworders, the Dragoons retreated.

Their withdrawal was orderly. They knew, as did Minobu, that there would be other battles.

53

Trolfjel Highlands, Misery
Galedon Military District, Draconis Combine
20 May 3028

A pale glow on the horizon marked the coming dawn, and colors began to appear to Minobu's night-sensitive eyes. Another morning on Misery, another day of battle with Wolf's Dragoons. It was almost a month since that awful battle on the Opdal Glacier. The Kuritans had recovered somewhat from the bad beginning, but the fighting had continued week after week, with neither side gaining a clear advantage.

As the light grew, he watched men and women scurrying about the camp, stocky in their cold-weather gear. Through the speaker set into the transplex window, he could hear the faint sounds of the Techs powering up BattleMechs, getting them ready for their pilots. Reloads from the dwindling stocks of ammunition were being distributed to the machines.

He turned to the man who had stood by his side in silence for the last half-hour.

"It is time for you to rejoin your troops, Michi-*san*."

"*Hai,* Minobu-*sensei.*"

Minobu almost laughed at his protégé's renewed use of the honorific. "This is hardly the time to let your rebellious streak show."

"There may not be another time."

Minobu's amusement evaporated. "Then you feel it, too. That this will be the last battle."

"Hai, sensei."

There seemed little to say.

"Fight well," he enjoined Michi.

"I am samurai, *sensei*. It goes without saying."

Michi's words pleased Minobu. The young man's inner strength had grown. He was no longer the unformed boy whom Minobu had taken on as an aide. Minobu reached out to touch the other man's shoulder. Looking down into Michi's dark eyes, he said, "I hope that each of my sons will grow to be as honorable a samurai, Michi Noketsuna."

"Your sons should follow in your footsteps rather than mine, *sensei*. It is a path of great honor."

Minobu restrained his emotion. "Enough, my young friend," he said, dropping his hand. "There is a battle to fight and your place is out there. Go now."

Michi bowed, deeply and respectfully. Minobu returned the bow, with proper consideration to his own superior rank.

Michi bowed again before pivoting on his heel and vanishing into the heatlock.

When next Minobu saw him, Michi was an anonymous figure under the bulk of cold-weather gear and goggled breath mask. Minobu watched through the transplex as Michi braced against the wind, heading for his 'Mech.

Like all the Kurita 'Mechs, the red *Ostroc* was battered, and the hasty repairs necessary to keep it fighting showed in patches of armor coated only with dark antirust sealant. Battle and the harsh climate of Misery were taking their toll. It was small comfort to learn from the scout report that, even with their superb technical staff, the Dragoons were showing the strain as well. A month of constant skirmishes and several pitched battles had worn them all down. Neither side would be able to endure the pressure much longer.

Things might have been different if Samsonov hadn't deserted them. Twice after the disastrous first battle, Minobu had maneuvered Wolf into committing his whole force. Twice the signal for Samsonov's attack had gone out. Twice the Warlord's regiments had not arrived, and Minobu's command had barely extricated themselves before being overwhelmed.

The first time might have been an accident, a missed signal. The second left no room for doubt. The Warlord had betrayed them, abandoned them to the mercy of the Dragoons. More, Samsonov had betrayed House Kurita. The Draconis Combine could ill afford the damage the Dragoons were inflicting. Even if the Dragoons were finally put down, the cost had run too high.

Samsonov would not be allowed to escape justice this time, as he had after Galtor. There could be no pardon from the Coordinator. The crime was too blatant, Samsonov's hand in it too visible.

But that did not improve the current situation. Minobu was still bound to follow the Coordinator's orders, still committed to destroying the Dragoons. When Samsonov did not arrive with additional troops, Minobu had no choice but to make do with what he had.

Now, for the first time in weeks of struggle, there seemed to be a hope of achieving that end. Many of the 'Mechs taken out during the trap at Opdal Glacial Fields were back in the line, having been repaired with parts from other machines crippled in subsequent battles. The Kuritans were stronger than they had been since that terrible day on the glacier. Even so, this was a last gasp, their final chance at an offensive action against the Dragoons.

Wolf's main body had been maneuvered into position. Minobu's own forces were also in place, awaiting word from the Eighth Sword of Light, who should have reached their jump-off points two hours ago. Any minute now, Minobu thought, they would signal that they had begun their assault.

As if on cue, a commtech approached. He bowed deferentially and presented a message flimsy. "From *Sho-sho* Torisobo, Eighth Sword of Light, sir."

Minobu ignored the outstretched hand and its paper. "What does he have to say?"

"He reports success, sir. The Dragoons are moving down onto the plain. He reports all is proceeding according to plan."

According to plan. Such a simple phrase for something so complicated. If Torisobo's message was accurate, the Dragoons, surprised by the Sworders' assault, would be moving in front of the Ryuken and the Galedon Regulars' hidden positions. Unaware of their enemy, the Dragoons would be exposing their flank. In the usual morning snow-storm, visibility would be low. The Dragoons would move close without realizing their danger, and short-range fire would devastate their ranks. The Kuritans would be among them in the first rush. The battle would be brutal, but it would reduce the Dragoons' advantage of trained gunners, giving the Draconis forces a chance to win.

Minobu had placed all of his hopes on that slim chance.

There had been no brushes with Dragoon reconnaissance for two days. He was sure that his forces had reached their positions undetected by enemy scouts. Surely the plan would succeed. Why then, he wondered, did he feel this tremendous sense of impending disaster?

Brooding would do no good, he decided. With the Dragoons on the move, his place was in the commcenter, where he could coordinate the Draconis forces. His step was firm as he walked the corridor to the center.

The first unit he checked was his own former command, the Ryuken-*ni*. It took some time, but he got *Chu-sa* Earnst on the hard line that kept the Dragoons from intercepting Ryuken communications. The *Chu-sa*'s voice was confident.

"The morning snow has arrived as scheduled, *Tai-sho*. Visibility is less than fifty meters most of the time. No sign of . . . wait." The empty line hissed slightly. Earnst was back in a few seconds. "I see . . . yes, they are . . . BattleMechs, *Tai-sho*. The Dragoons are walking into *our* trap this time."

"Commence the attack at your discretion, *Chu-sa*. Make it count," Minobu urged.

"Understood, *Tai-sho*. We'll . . ."

Earnst's words dissolved into static.

Minobu knew that the hard line they were using would not turn to static unless it had been cut.

Something had gone wrong.

"Break radio silence," he ordered the commtechs. Communication with his officers was now vital. "I want all commanders in the net."

The commtechs looked up, surprised by the vehemence in his voice.

"Move, sluggards! Open the net right now!"

The commtechs reported heavy traffic on the net. It took

them several minutes to override and break in. "Ryuken-*ni*," one announced as a voice came up on the speaker.

"Negative! Negative! Fire forward!"

"Where is *Chu-sa* Earnst?" Minobu demanded.

"His 'Mech is down. We've lost contact with him." The voice had taken on an hysterical edge.

"Calm down! This is *Tai-sho* Tetsuhara. To whom am I speaking?"

The authority in Minobu's voice seemed to reach the man on the other end. He gobbled a couple of times before responding in a slightly steadier voice, "*Chu-i* Benedict Kerasu, sir."

"Report, *Chu-i*."

"It's the Dragoons, sir. They aren't fleeing. They're heading straight in on us, attacking. I don't know how, but they know our position. We haven't fooled them." The hysteria returned to his voice. "We're being slaughtered! We're being overrun! There are Dragoon 'Mechs everywhere!"

The transmission broke up.

"Get him back," Minobu ordered brusquely.

After several tries, the commtech reported, "Enemy jamming is blanketing Ryuken-*ni*'s position. We can't punch through."

"Keep trying."

While Minobu was trying to get sense out of the distraught *Chu-i*, his staff had been laboring feverishly to sort through the garbled reports from the front and to update the situation map in the holotank. The link to Kerasu lost, Minobu turned to inspect their labors.

"It is very bad, *Tai-sho*," Saraguchi announced. "We have break-throughs throughout the center. All Ryuken Regiments are reporting heavy Dragoon assaults. Twenty-First Galedon is completely out of touch."

"What about Seventeenth Galedon?"

"They report their sector quiet."

"Well, we can't afford to let them sit idle. Have them move to back up Ryuken-*go*. If we can stabilize that flank, it may give Sword of Light time to come to our relief again."

Minobu didn't really think that was likely. Things had gone too far.

He spent the next two hours ordering shifts in the Kurita dispositions. Each time he thought he had gotten a unit across the enemy line of advance, a Dragoon unit would show up on the flank or in the rear, rendering the new position untenable. It was as though Wolf were reading his mind. The Dragoon assault began to seem unstoppable.

Suddenly, the command post shook with the violence of a nearby explosion. Around him, men pitched to the floor. Beating a constant tattoo under the sound of missile detonations came the familiar vibrations of high-speed 'Mech movement. Explosive thunder echoed hollowly within the walls of the center.

A nearby salvo ripped a hole in the commcenter's back wall, and the blast floored everyone in the room. When he had regained his feet, Minobu rushed to the hole, hurtling over the shattered remains of the holotank. Heedless of the frigid wind, he stared out at the BattleMechs assaulting the compound. At their head was a blue and gold *Archer*.

A Kurita *Panther* appeared from nowhere to contest the passage of the Dragoon 'Mech. The *Archer* bore down on the defender, crashing its full seventy-ton mass into the lighter 'Mech. The *Panther*'s PPC flared, a puny beacon against the gathering storm clouds. The *Archer* smashed the *Panther* with its right arm, toppling the Kurita 'Mech, which crashed into a workshed and out of sight.

The *Archer* strode into the main compound as though it were master of the place. Following behind, its lancemates continued to pour destruction on the compound. The *Archer* loomed over Minobu and halted. Its next step would have taken it into the flimsy prefabricated structure that was Minobu's headquarters.

Time seemed to stop.

Man faced machine; neither moved.

Minobu, tiny against the 'Mech's mass, looked up, searching for a glimpse of the pilot behind the cockpit screen of the silent BattleMech.

The 'Mech suddenly rocked under triple explosions on its left shoulder. White-hot fragments of ceramet showered down, forcing Minobu to take cover within the hut.

The *Archer* pivoted and ripped off a volley from its undamaged right-shoulder launcher. The rockets screamed wide of their intended victim, which was too close for the Dragoon MechWarrior to target effectively in the little time he had. Laserfire scorched the air around the Dragoon 'Mech, and several pulses caught it cleanly.

Damaged, but still far from imperiled, the *Archer* backed up. The Dragoons were outnumbered by the sudden appearance of two Kurita lances of heavy and medium BattleMechs. They moved into a mutually supporting formation and withdrew from the compound.

Minobu risked a glance outside the hut to learn who were these new arrivals. The red *Ostroc* in the lead was very familiar.

54

Trolfjel Highlands, Misery
Galedon Military District, Draconis Combine
20 May 3028

The effect of Michi's rescue was short-lived. In minutes, Dragoon 'Mechs renewed the attack on the command center. The blue and gold *Archer* was not among them.

A quick look at the shambles in the hut's interior and the smoking wreck of the holotank told Minobu that there was little point in remaining. He scrambled across the field to his *Dragon*. Michi's MechWarriors provided cover while he climbed aboard and powered up. Secured and ready, he opened the taccomm.

"Form on me. We will try to punch through to join the bulk of Ryuken-*go*."

"What good'll that do?" asked an unfamiliar voice.

"Little. But we should then have enough force to fight our way to the bunker line. Once there, we should be able to hold till the Dragoons tire."

The *Dragon* began to move as Minobu spoke. It lumbered past Michi's *Ostroc,* picking up speed. Half a dozen Kurita 'Mechs fell in behind it as Michi ordered them into a loose wedge formation.

Fire from the attacking Dragoons was light at first, for only one or two of the pilots had seen the Kurita machines start out. As soon as the Dragoon commander got word of the Kuritans' movements, however, he ordered a shift in his line of attack. BattleMechs that had been pounding the facilities of the command center moved to intercept the Kurita machines. In the sharp firefight that followed, the Kuritans lost half their number. Five of the Dragoons' own 'Mechs were smoking when their commander pulled back and let his opponent go. Only desultory long-range fire followed the Kuritans as they headed away from the command center. The morning storm finally closed in, and swirling snow hid them from view of the marauding Dragoons.

As soon as it seemed safe, Minobu ordered a standard cooling halt, which would not take long in Misery's chill climate. He really wanted to take stock of the condition of his troops and to attempt contact with Sederasu at Ryuken-*go*.

Minobu's *Dragon* had seen less action than those he had joined. Though his 'Mech had come through the skirmish with relatively light damage, he had already used up a fourth of his autocannon ammunition. He knew that the others had to be even worse off.

He looked around at what had become, by default, his Command Lance.

Michi's red *Ostroc* was the heaviest of the other 'Mechs, and it had suffered more damage in the last fight. The housing for one of the Fuersturm lasers dangled from its chest, shattered. Michi reported all other weapon systems functional, but did not mention the 'Mech's left arm, which hung loose and dysfunctional. Daylight showed through much of the shoulder assembly.

The next heaviest 'Mech was a *Panther*. Steam leaked from a gash in the side of its cockpit. The shredded and warped armor plates distorted the shape of the head, changing it from a hunting cat's snarl to a leering, half-decayed skull. The pilot said that he was experiencing excessive heat buildup, but that otherwise his 'Mech was functional.

The fourth of the Kurita 'Mechs was a heavily scarred *Jenner*. Its non-humanoid shape showed fresh damage almost everywhere. The only thing that seemed intact was the pilot's armored dome, which sat on the boom projecting from the base of the body. The MechWarrior, incongruously cheerful, recited a list of mechanical failures and half-functional systems that left Minobu wondering how the machine had managed to get this far.

Survey of his tiny force complete, Minobu tried to contact Sederasu. The storm that hid them from pursuit also disrupted what little long-range communications the mountain peaks allowed. Minobu could not get through.

The commcenter was destroyed, disrupting Minobu's contact with his command. He had hoped to use the Tacticon computer and powerful communications equipment on board Sederasu's *Cyclops* as a substitute. If he could call together the scattered Draconian forces and lead them to the bunker line west of Hamar Valley, the Dragoon momentum might be broken, giving the Kuritans a chance to recover.

Minobu ordered his lance into motion. Each time they crested a rise or cleared the lee of a peak, Minobu tried to reach other friendly units, but the contacts were too brief or garbled to be of any use. Finally, the wind shifted, blowing back the covering curtain of snow. Minobu hoped that it signaled a break in their luck.

It did, but not in the way he wanted. Instead of giving the Kuritans a chance for communication, the storm's capricious shift brought them a company of Dragoons.

Without conscious thought, Minobu aimed and triggered his long-range missiles at the oncoming 'Mechs. The *Dragon* belched fire, but the enemy was already spreading out into an attack formation. His rockets roared past the leading pair, a white *Griffin* and a dark blue *Shadow Hawk,* and delivered their payloads to their target. Clouds of steam and smoke erupted around the shadowy shape of an *Ostscout,* which had been advancing cautiously in the trailing slot of the lead lance. The 'Mech staggered under the barrage and stumbled back, its upper torso savaged and one sensor arm amputated. The machine's sophisticated sensors had tracked the Kuritans, even through the blinding snow and the magnetic field distortions of the mountains. Guided by his *ki,* Minobu had canceled that advantage with his first shot. Now his troops had only to contend with the BattleMechs that outnumbered them three to one.

Surprise lost, the Dragoons opened fire. The Kuritans returned it.

Minobu concentrated his attacks on those enemies furthest

away because his *Dragon* was the best equipped to engage those targets. Any Dragoon 'Mech that he could take out before it closed to its own effective range was one less enemy to hurt the lance. He trusted Michi and the others to deal with the remainder of the leading Dragoon lance.

Minobu slipped into *mushin,* thought and action becoming one. He was the *Dragon* and the 'Mech was the mighty Dragon of Kurita, breathing forth destruction on its enemies. He moved with a fluid grace, myomer pseudomuscles shifting his armor-clad body no more and no less than necessary to dodge enemy fire while setting up his own shots. The *Dragon* was deadly. Several of the lighter Dragoon machines collapsed or withdrew from combat.

Having exhausted its long-range missiles, the *Dragon* turned to the closer-ranged fight and found that the odds had not improved. The *Jenner* lay crumpled, its cockpit dome still strangely untouched. Of the *Panther,* only scattered pieces were to be seen. Michi's red *Ostroc* remained standing, locked in a hand-to-hand struggle with the *Griffin.*

A blast from the *Ostroc*'s chest-mounted lasers sent the *Griffin* staggering back, one hand raised as though to shield the exposed inner structure from further damage. Its foot slipped and it went down heavily.

The 'Mech's fall gave its partner the opening the pilot had been awaiting. The staccato roar of the *Shadow Hawk*'s autocannon drowned out the sound of its missiles launching.

The pilot was a good shot. The *Ostroc* shuddered as armor sprayed from its surface. Under the steady pounding, it jerked and shook.

The *Dragon*'s own laser hit the *Shadow Hawk,* breaking the pilot's concentration. The Dragoon cut his fire and rolled to cover.

The relief was too late for Michi's 'Mech. Sparking and smoking, the *Ostroc* began to topple.

Through the billowing dark cloud, a glittering package rocketed. Michi had waited a second too long to trigger the ejection system, and the chair flashed out at a dangerously low angle. The chute deployed but barely managed to slow the chair's furious speed before it plowed into the ground.

Dragoon rockets burned toward the *Dragon,* but the big 'Mech moved with surprising speed and grace. The missiles exploded harmlessly behind him as Minobu moved toward Michi's crash site.

A heavy laser pulse caught the *Dragon* in the back of his left leg. Dysfunction lights flashed red in the cockpit as the actuators froze and locked the leg in a slightly bent position. The *Dragon* lurched on, slowed by his wound. More and more of the *Dragon* lasers found enough purchase on his armor to burn through.

The interior of the *Dragon*'s cockpit was suffused in the bloody glow of failure lights, while sensors flashed warning of an approaching mass. Minobu pivoted and twisted aside. He brought his battlefist down on the *Shadow Hawk* as the Dragoon 'Mech stumbled past. Tubing and framework crumpled as the fist tore across the backpack. Only the resistance provided by the Armstrong autocannon as it crumpled into uselessness saved the *Shadow Hawk*'s cockpit from being split open. The Dragoon 'Mech crashed to the ground. It twitched once and was still.

The *Dragon* returned to his course.

In the twisted wreckage of the ejection seat, he could see motion. There was movement in his three-sixty screen as well. Lost in concern over the fallen Michi, the *Dragon* was slow to react.

A 'Mech crashed into his left side, but the attacker was too light to topple the *Dragon*'s sixty tons of mass, even had it struck cleanly. Though Minobu's reaction was slow, he sidestepped enough to reduce considerably the effect of the Dragoon's charge. The light machine clung to the *Dragon*'s side, punching with its fist in an effort to destroy the domed cockpit.

The *Dragon*'s autocannon arm swung around, shoving its muzzle into the side of the enemy 'Mech. Minobu's last shell cassette emptied into the unfamiliar machine. The pounding thunder beat against his ears as the backblast of the explosions sent shrapnel ripping into the *Dragon*'s side. The damage was negligible compared to what the explosions did to the Dragoon 'Mech. It fell away from the *Dragon* and lay on its back in the snow like a crushed insect.

The desperate maneuver had ruined the *Dragon*'s Imperator-A autocannon. No matter. There was no more ammunition for it.

The Dragoons abandoned their physical attacks and returned to showering the *Dragon* with energy beams and short-range missiles. With only one 5cm laser left in its offensive armament, the wounded *Dragon* staggered forward to bring the fight to his tormentors. Close combat would be the most effective way for him to continue the fight now.

The *Griffin* announced its return to the battle with fire from its PPC. Electrostatic discharge ionized the air around the *Dragon*'s crippled leg as blue lightning tore through the weakened armor. Frayed myomer pseudomuscles ripped loose from the structural system, no longer able to bear the 'Mech's weight. The leg failed. The *Dragon* swayed on his good leg for a moment, listed to the left, then crashed down.

Minobu hung dazed in the restraining straps. Shaken loose from *mushin,* he was once again a man piloting a machine.

Sensor warnings pinged at the approach of the Dragoon 'Mechs. He focused his *ki* to block the pain that shot through his body. Detached, he watched the *Dragon*'s left arm rise. A ruby pulse lanced out to strike one of the advancing Dragoons.

The Dragoons responded with concentrated laser bombardment.

More failure lights flashed red, telling of the accelerating weakness of the *Dragon.* The weapon board beeped malfunction in the laser. One by one, the lights went out as the *Dragon* died around him. Finally, the sensors failed, isolating Minobu in the smoky murk of the cockpit lit only by the fitful flickering of electrical fires.

The *Dragon* shuddered from some outside impact, throwing Minobu violently about. His head struck the side wall of the cockpit. Even through the neurohelmet, the shock doubled his vision. Blood trickled down across the bridge of his nose and over his upper lip until he could taste its sharp tang. Through the ozone-laden air, he thought he detected the scent of cherry blossoms. Before he could puzzle out that mystery, darkness claimed him.

55

Dragoon Base, Farsund, Misery
Galedon Military District, Draconis Combine
26 May 3028

"*Seppuku?*" Wolf repeated incredulously.

Minobu looked up with weary eyes at the man who stood over his bed. "I have no other choice, I have failed my lord."

"Failed? You've crippled our fighting force. It'll be months before the Dragoons are ready for a major operation. Far too many of our best pilots—men and women who have been with me since we came to the Inner Sphere—are buried out there in the snow. If you call that failure . . ."

Minobu turned his gaze to the ceiling. In his peripheral vision, he could see Michi Noketsuna seated at the foot of the bed, looking distinctly uncomfortable. Minobu could tell that the discomfort came not from Michi's bandaged head or the arm that hung across his chest in a sling. It was not even the raw red skin, a legacy of his exposure to the harshness of Misery after his 'Mech was destroyed. Like Minobu, he was distressed at Wolf's words. Partial success was no balm to a samurai. The warrior who did not accomplish the task set for him had failed in his duty. It was nothing more or less than that.

"I'm not going to go away because you ignore me," Wolf

said when Minobu did not respond. "Your lord can't hold you responsible for failing."

"Can he not?"

"It wasn't your fault," Wolf insisted. "You played by the rules and were beaten. There's no dishonor in that."

Minobu continued to stare at the ceiling. What could he say? In Wolf's world, the attempt was enough, and partial success was often acceptable. Wolf did not understand that a samurai either succeeded or failed. There were no half-measures.

Frustrated at the lack of response, Wolf sighed, rubbing the stubble on his jaw. "Look," he said. "You didn't have a chance. You played by the rules, but we didn't. You fell for our gambit with the duels and charged right on cue when we played that *Panther* Jock dirty. Even that trick wasn't good enough to stop you.

"While you were following our apparent lead in not using aerospace forces, we were setting you up. We didn't want any interference with our recon satellites in orbit. They were our secret advantage. While you groped like a blind man, we knew where your troops were every minute. And you *still* damn near beat us."

Minobu listened to Wolf's confession without interruption, disturbed by Wolf's unrelenting presentation of Minobu's difficulties and near triumph over them. Wolf had fought according to his own rules of war and maintained his own honor. His confession of not fighting by Minobu's rules changed nothing. The fact was that Minobu had not succeeded at his lord's task. And if he had succeeded, he would have brought to ruin both his friend and that friend's cherished, and almost certainly wrongly accused, Dragoons. Such a success would have been too much for Minobu.

To make things worse, many brave MechWarriors on both sides had died uselessly, for neither side had achieved its avowed goal. The Kuritans had failed to destroy Wolf's Dragoons, and the mercenaries were still a functional entity.

The Dragoons had exacted a high price in blood and had scattered the Draconians, but had not been able to completely destroy the forces arrayed against them. It was true that the Twenty-first Galedon had been mauled and the Seventeenth Galedon Regulars had probably been shattered beyond recovery. The Eighth Sword of Light had survived well, however, and almost half the Ryuken MechWarriors would fight again. All the survivors were now hardened veterans, forged into tempered steel by those who had fought to destroy them.

The Dragoons themselves had been mauled. Though losses varied according to the intensity of combat each regiment and independent unit had seen, some casualties ran as high as 60 percent. Despite their losses, the mercenaries managed to retain cohesion and had been able to hold the battlefield. Material losses could be replaced, but trained veterans could not. Wolf's Dragoons would no longer be able to maintain their exclusive recruitment policies if they wished to field their full forces. Still, they had won their battle for survival. Several JumpShips had already left the system, taking Dragoons to join their dependents.

When Wolf lapsed into silence, Minobu heaved himself up into a sitting position, ignoring the protest of his muscles. The sudden shift narrowed his vision into a dark-edged tunnel and made him light-headed, but his voice was steady. "Why are you telling me this?"

"I'm trying to make you see that your lord should be proud of you. You've done more than any man could be expected to do."

"Yet I failed."

Wolf huffed. "Unity, you're a stubborn man!"

"Tenacious is a better word," Minobu corrected mildly. "I have lived my life trying to be a virtuous man. The Dragon admires tenacity, and the code of the samurai upholds it as well. Therefore, I have tried to cultivate it. I am loyal to the code."

Wolf started to shake his head, then stopped. A crafty look appeared on his face. "The code values loyalty above all, doesn't it?"

"You know it does."

"Don't you know your lord betrayed you before you had a chance to fail him?"

Michi's indrawn breath did not distract Minobu, who looked directly into Wolf's gray eyes. Reaching out with his *ki* for the truth in the mercenary's words, he felt the glow of conviction around the tough core of Wolf's deeper being.

"It wasn't the Dragoons who held up Torisobo and his Sworders," Wolf said, pausing to let that sink in. "They were under orders from Samsonov to hold back and let the Ryuken get mauled. After we had kicked each other to pieces, they were supposed to step in and clean up the mess. Any inconvenient survivors, of either side, would have found themselves on the business end of a PPC." Wolf shook his head sadly.

"It sounds crazy, but it's true. That old bastard is insane."

Minobu knew that Samsonov was doing foolish things, but he had never thought of the Warlord as insane.

"We overran the Sword of Light headquarters before they scampered offplanet with tails between their legs," Wolf said. "Among the captured documents were Samsonov's orders. I can show them to you."

Minobu shook his head.

"So, you see Samsonov never meant to have a force waiting to ambush us from space. He was out there in the dark all right, but not in this system. He and his troops had other business—they were chasing our families. The big, brave Warlord wanted to kill our civilians. Not exactly the actions of an honorable man, are they? Like Akuma before him, he seems to have believed that attacking our non-combatants would distract us and weaken our resolve. He's a fool as well as cowardly betrayer.

"Samsonov is the dishonored one," Wolf concluded. "Your lord betrayed you, failed you. *He* broke the bonds of loyalty."

Wolf's plea was plain in his face. He was fighting to change Minobu's mind and desperately wanted to sway him from his chosen path.

Minobu could not see how he could give Wolf what he wanted and still maintain his own honor. Nothing that any other man had done could lessen his own responsibility.

Minobu stood shakily, and Michi leaped to his feet to steady him. As soon as he felt stable, Minobu removed Michi's hand from his arm. Drawing himself up, he said, "Samsonov is not the lord whom I failed."

Wolf's disappointment was clear, but so was his determination. "He was following Takashi Kurita's orders to betray you."

Wolf's accusation was a serious one. If the ultimate lord of all Kurita samurai had ordered dishonorable behavior, if he had himself broken the bond of loyalty, the situation would be changed. Under certain circumstances a lord who ordered his samurai to improper behavior justified rebellion against himself. Minobu drew a deep breath, ribs paining him as he did so. He let half of it out before speaking.

"Do you have proof?"

"I don't need it." Wolf's response was quick, full of certainty.

"I do."

The slim hopes that Wolf had raised were dashed. Even the true belief of an honored and honorable friend was not enough on which to base rebellion. Minobu stepped to the wall and leaned against it, far more tired than his brief physical exertion could justify.

Wolf hung his head and rubbed his exhaustion-smudged eyes. "Look. You don't have to do this. Give up your allegiance to House Kurita. Join us. I'll make you a place in the Dragoons."

The offer did not surprise Minobu. Rather, it confirmed the goodness he knew dwelt in his friend's heart. Much as he wanted to accept, Minobu could not. "I understand and appreciate your offer. You must try to understand why I cannot accept it.

"From the day I saved your life on Quentin, I was responsible for you. What you did, I was accountable for. Whatever karma you earned became part of my karmic debt.

"Thus, I am responsible for all the Kurita forces your Dragoons have destroyed."

Wolf opened his mouth to object, but Minobu shook his head.

"The Dragoons were the heart of the Combine forces in the Galedon District. Now you will be taking them away. That alone would weaken our border defense," Minobu continued. "Our battles here on Misery have gutted the Regular troops that defend the Galedon border, leaving it nearly unguarded and open to our enemies. I am responsible for this terrible blow to House Kurita.

"Because of this failure of judgment and ability, I have no choice but *seppuku*. There is no other way to restore my honor. In all the time I have known you, friend Wolf, you have understood the demands of honor."

Minobu searched Wolf's face, but found bleak despair instead of comprehension. There was nothing more to be said. It was nearly sunset, a moment Minobu did not wish to miss on this day.

He leaned away from the wall, bringing his weight back onto his feet. An ache began in his flesh leg as he stepped through the door. The guards started to block his path, but Wolf waved them away. Minobu continued down the corridor unmolested.

At the end of the hallway, there was a small lounge normally used by the soldiers assigned to the barracks in their off-duty hours. It was empty of people. Minobu limped to the transplex pane that looked onto the landing fields where Dragoon 'Mechs were boarding DropShips in the last light of day. He lowered himself into the lotus position and gazed out. The brilliant refractions of light through the layers of ice crystals in the atmosphere was soothing. Reflecting on the transient beauty of nature, he dropped into a light, meditative state.

Back in the small room, Wolf turned his attention to Michi.

"And what about you? Are you going to slit your belly, too?"

"No."

Wolf seemed surprised at the answer. Michi had not intended to explain anything to the mercenary, but the compelling pressure of Wolf's scrutiny brought words to his lips.

"I will not follow my lord Tetsuhara at this time, for I have work to do. I will avenge my lord on those who trapped him into this dead end."

Wolf nodded understanding. He thought for a moment before speaking. "If we leave you here, your Kurita masters will have your head. That won't give you what you're looking for. In honor of your lord, I extend my offer to you as well.

Michi bowed. Like Minobu before him, he was tempted. Also like Minobu, he was bound to the path his honor demanded.

"It is not right that I join you while this obligation remains unfulfilled."

"Who said we'd keep you from fulfilling it? We aren't letting it stop here, you now. We are going to continue to fight Kurita. Samsonov caught some of our people before we could warn them of the change in the rendezvous star system. We want our own revenge."

"I don't know whether I am pleased to hear you say that," Michi said. He was still a Kuritan. His quarrel was not with the people of the Combine or the MechWarriors who defended them. They would be the ones facing the Dragoon guns. "Even though you fight my enemies, my place is not at your side."

Putting his words into action, Michi stepped into the corridor and gazed at the seated figure in the lounge. After a moment, Wolf came to stand beside him.

"What can we do for you then? You can't stay here."

Michi thought for a few minutes, weighing his few options. No matter which path he chose, he would be outcast. Wolf was right about one thing, though. Any attempt to remain in the Combine was tantamount to suicide. "Let me travel with you to some place where I can begin my quest."

"That's all you want?" asked Wolf incredulously.

"I cannot ask more."

"You mean, will not?"

Michi shrugged.

"You're a crazy samurai, Noketsuna, but you've got guts."

56

Dragoon Base, Farsund, Misery
Galedon Military District, Draconis Combine
27 May 3028

Michi was leaving Minobu's room when Wolf arrived in full-dress uniform, its resplendence a sharp contrast to the mercenary's haggard face. Michi was exhausted as well, but his own uniform, though clean and freshly pressed, did little to disguise the fact. The House Kurita badges had been removed, and he wore a red armband with a black wolf's head to mark his release from captivity. Even though his right arm was still in the sling, a holstered laser pistol rode on his right hip. He bowed to the mercenary Colonel.

"*Ohayo,* Colonel."

"Good morning, Michi."

"I wish to thank you for my parole, Colonel. You are generous to a former enemy."

"Former is the operative word, Michi." Wolf nodded his head at the closed door. "Is he in there?"

"Yes, Colonel. He is waiting for you."

Michi stepped aside and bowed again. Wolf opened the door and entered the room. Michi closed the door behind him.

Seated in lotus position on the bed was Minobu. From somewhere in the nearby city, Michi had acquired the shimmering white silk kimono that he now wore. It shone against his dark skin. His eyes were closed, his face calm, relaxed.

Minobu opened his eyes as Wolf stepped into the room.

"You wanted to see me," Wolf said.

"Thank you for coming."

With a wave, Minobu indicated that Wolf should sit in the chair at the bed's end. Wolf ignored the gesture and remained standing.

"Have you changed your mind?" Wolf asked.

"No."

Minobu raised his hand again to forestall Wolf's objections. "Please, do not argue. There is nothing that you can say to change my mind.

"The points at which this fate might have been averted have come and gone. The road opened when Akuma began his campaign to tie the Dragoons to the Combine. The last chance was lost on your trip to Luthien. After Samsonov received Lord Kurita's *haiku,* the path to disaster was inevitable.

"It is curious that many links in the chain of events took place in the autumn, for that is the season of changes, is it not?" Minobu paused, not really expecting an answer. Wistfully, he continued, "I had always liked the season of change."

Minobu could tell that Wolf wanted to say something, but he cut the mercenary off. "I have a favor to ask of you," Minobu said.

"Name it and it's yours."

"You agree before knowing what it is?" Minobu gave Wolf a look of mock surprise. "That is not the suspicious Jaime Wolf I have known for years."

"You would not ask anything that I could not do," Wolf said with perfect assurance.

Minobu looked up into the gray eyes of the friend who stood before him. His inner senses agreed with what his heart and eyes told him. "You truly believe that."

"I do."

"Very well." As Minobu unwound his legs to stand up, Wolf backed up to give him room in the small space. Minobu adjusted the kimono into place, and bowed deeply to Wolf. "There is a formal position in the ceremony that I wish a trusted friend to hold." Minobu paused for a moment "I ask that you serve as *kaishaku-nin* for the ceremony."

"All right."

Wolf's quick answer made Minobu wonder if he understood the request, but he did not wish to discuss it. All he said was, "Thank you," and bowed again to Wolf.

"It is time," Minobu said. "Michi will have everything ready. Let us go. Even I do not have iron resolve in all things."

Minobu opened the door for Wolf. Outside, Dechan Fraser and Hamilton Atwyl, also resplendent in Dragoon dress uniform, waited. As Wolf and Minobu started down the hall, they fell in behind. Minobu had worked with them during his time as Professional Soldiery Liaison and was mildly curious about how they had come to be the honor guards. A minor mystery, he decided, to take with him into the dark.

The small group walked down the corridor to the lounge in silence. Michi was waiting for them at the doorway. Beyond Michi, Minobu could see that the room had been arranged as well as could be expected. It was, in fact, remarkable that Michi had been able to acquire so many of the articles necessary for a proper ritual. Misery was a barren frontier world, little concerned with courtly proprieties.

Straw *futon* mats covered the room, in the center of which lay a large white cushion. To the left of the cushion was a tray bearing rice paper, a brush, and an ink block. Behind the cushion and to the right, Minobu could see a wooden bucket, with a small dipper lying across its mouth. Next to the bucket stood a lacquered sword stand. His *katana* lay sheathed on the upper hooks. The lower hooks held his empty *wakizashi* scabbard. Dragoons, quietly conversing among themselves, knelt on the floor. They formed an aisle between the door and the *futon*-covered area.

Minobu recognized all of the faces. He was impressed that the regimental commanders were all in attendance. Other important Dragoon officers were present as well, Natasha Kerensky among them. He was honored by the presence of such notable warriors.

Minobu stopped five meters from the door and let Wolf go on. The mercenary stepped up to Michi and said quietly,

"He has asked me to serve as *kaishaku-nin*. Where do I stand?"

"Next to the water bucket. You will be slightly behind him, to his left. Kneel there until it is time." Michi noted that Wolf showed none of the tension he would have expected. Suspecting that Wolf did not understand the nature of the *kaishaku-nin,* he asked, "Are you well-versed in the sword?"

"What's that got to do with it?"

"The *kaishaku-nin* strikes off the head of the principal before the pain grows so great that he shames himself."

Wolf's eyes went wide.

"You did not know?"

"NO!"

Michi lowered his head. "I understand. I shall serve then."

Wolf grabbed his arm.

"No. He asked me. I'll do it," Wolf ground out. "Is that the sword I'm supposed to use up there?"

Michi looked Wolf full in the eye, gauging his emotional state. "If you strike poorly, you will shame yourself and his memory."

"What choice do I have? I'll do my best."

"In unusual circumstances, the *kaishaku-nin* is permitted other weapons," Michi said.

"Like what?"

"A pistol."

"At least that's something I know how to use."

Wolf started into the room, but Michi stepped into his way. The Kuritan fumbled at his holster with his left hand. "Please, Colonel Wolf, use mine. Allow me to share in the honor."

Wolf took the offered laser pistol and walked to his place. The assembled Dragoons fell into silence as their Colonel entered the room.

Minobu waited until Wolf was settled. He stepped through the doorway, and bowed to the gathering. Calmly, looking neither left nor right, he walked to the cushion and knelt facing the door.

He sat quietly for a minute, composing his thoughts. Settled into a state of peace, he reached to his right, picked up the tray, and placed it before him. With great care, he mixed the ink and dipped the brush in it. For an instant, his hand poised motionless above the paper, then it began to move, creating *kanji* characters in short, precise strokes. Speaking clearly, he spoke the words he wrote:

War bares a sword's steel.
Autumn leaves reflect color,
A samurai's blood.

He laid the brush across the ink dish and returned the tray to its former position. Sinking back into his kneeling position, he waited as Michi approached up the aisle formed by the Dragoons.

Michi carried a white lacquered tray, balanced carefully in his good hand. On it were a ceramic drinking dish and a small flask of sake. Michi knelt and placed the tray before Minobu. They bowed to one another.

Minobu took the flask in his left hand and filled the dish in two pours. He returned the flask precisely to its place. Raising the dish to his lips, he took two sips. After a pause, he drained it in two more sips and returned the dish to the tray.

Michi bowed and removed the tray to the back of the room.

Minobu knelt quietly, a great calm reigning within. One minute stretched into two, then three. At last, he spoke.

"I, and I alone, am accountable for the unfortunate losses among those for whom I was responsible. For this failure, I disembowel myself. I beg all of you present here to do me the honor of witnessing the act."

Minobu bowed to the assembled Dragoons. Their faces showed reactions ranging from disgust to dignified concern to vengeful satisfaction. Through the insulation of his detachment, Minobu noted that only Kerensky remained as dispassionate as he.

As Minobu straightened from the bow, he shrugged his torso free of his upper garments. He tucked the sleeves of his kimono under his knees. Naked to the waist, he waited, hands resting lightly on his thighs. His face was expressionless.

Michi again approached, bearing another white lacquered tray. This time Minobu's *wakizashi* lay on the shining surface. The sword was closely wrapped with rice paper, which was tied at three points with a red cord. Only three centimeters of the blade's shining steel was visible at one end. At the other, the lacquered wood handle was bare, showing the Tetsuhara family *mon*.

Carefully, he knelt and placed the tray in front of Minobu. The sword lay with its edge toward Minobu, pointing to his left. Michi bowed, rose, and walked around to Minobu's right. He crossed behind his *sensei*. Stopping slightly behind Wolf, he knelt next to the Dragoon.

"*Jumonji,*" Minobu said in a low voice that did not reach beyond the two men kneeling behind him.

Michi leaned over to Wolf and whispered, "He asked you to wait until he has made the second, crosswise cut."

Wolf's nostrils went wide as he sucked in air, but he nodded slightly to confirm his understanding.

In a deliberate motion, Minobu reached out a steady hand and took the sword that lay before him. He looked down at it. In its shining surface, he saw reflections of all that had made his life worthwhile. Its shine was the sheen of his honor.

He turned the point toward his abdomen and focused his *ki*.

He stabbed the sword deeply into his flesh, on the left side below his navel. He drew it slowly across to the right. Turning the sword in the wound, he cut upward toward his heart.

He felt no pain. His *ki* liberated him from that. There was a small click behind him to the left.

Oblivion.

Wolf's nostrils stung from the sour scent of bile and singed hair. Tears blurred his vision as he knelt to free the short sword from Minobu's limp hands. He shoved the bloody blade into its scabbard and picked up Minobu's long sword as well.

"What are you doing, Colonel?" Michi asked, appalled by the lack of respect shown to the sword. "The swords must go to his family."

"Don't worry, Michi. They will. I only want to arrange for a suitable messenger."

Epilogue

ComStar First Circuit Compound
Hilton Head Island, North America, Terra
17 August 3028

"You are most welcome here, Colonel Wolf," Julian Tiepolo almost shouted.

Heads turned to stare at the black-jacketed mercenary. Wolf threw the ComStar Primus a contemptuous glance and returned to scanning the crowd in the room below him. His gaze swept the festive assembly gathered for the occasion of the marriage of Prince Hanse Davion of the Federated Suns to Melissa Steiner, heir to the Archonship of the Lyran Commonwealth. Wolf was a predator searching a flock for his prey.

The mention of the mercenary's name cut through the noise around Takashi Kurita and captured his attention. He turned to look across the room at the short man standing at the top of the stairs. Despite his size, the mercenary's presence suddenly dominated the room.

It was plain that Wolf was agitated. He hefted a meter-long bundle swathed in black and silver-brocaded fabric. The motion made his wolf's-head epaulet glitter with a hard light that matched the look in his eyes. People sidled away from that cold stare.

Wolf's gaze met Takashi's. The Coordinator knew instantly whom the mercenary was seeking.

Wolf started down the stairs in Takashi's direction, the crowd melting away from him. Even the gallant senior officers and officials who surrounded Takashi slipped out of the mercenary's path. All except Yorinaga Kurita.

Takashi read the tension between the two MechWarriors as they stood face to face. Almost imperceptibly, Wolf nodded. Yorinaga relaxed. Satisfied that Wolf was no physical danger to his cousin, Yorinaga Kurita nodded in return, but held his ground.

Takashi laid a hand on Yorinaga's shoulder, signaling his acceptance of the mercenary's presence with a squeeze. The younger Kurita bowed and stepped back to take a watchful position a few meters away.

Wolf stripped the fabric from his burden. As the paired swords came into view, Yorinaga took a half-step forward. ComStar had forbidden all weapons at the festivities, but somehow Wolf had managed to bring in these. Yorinaga halted when the weapons clattered to the floor at Takashi's feet.

Takashi looked down at the swords. The shorter one had landed atop the longer. A dark reddish stain marred the lacquer on the upper sword's hilt and covered one of the *mon* symbols. The other symbols were still clear and white against the black background. He recognized the Tetsuhara family crest.

When Takashi raised his eyes toward Wolf, the mercenary launched into fluent and rapid Japanese of a blunt and disrespectful form.

"Those are all that is left of a good man! When you return them to his family, you won't have to lie. You can tell them he stood by his honor till the end. I hope you're satisfied with what you have arranged. You were a fool to force him to this."

Takashi's face was hard. By sheer force of will, he restrained his anger. He started to speak, but Wolf forged ahead.

"You thought you could do better than Anton Marik, didn't you? Thought you had the answers he missed. You were wrong!

"You certainly spilled more blood. You even cost us more property, but that counts little against the lives you took. We

Dragoons set great store by our people. No one touches them and gets away with it. *No one!*

"It's all been for nothing, you know. You've failed. The Dragoons are clear of the Combine and ready to fight. We have survived both your puny schemes and your overrated military might. We've whipped your Warlord and left him licking his wounds. You really should get a better thug to do your dirty work."

Wolf paused, his immediate rage spent. The gold braid cord looped under his right armpit trembled with the tension in his body. When Takashi spoke, his voice was calm and even, like one trying to calm a dangerous beast. "You misunderstand, Colonel Wolf. This," he said, indicating the swords at his feet, "was never my wish. I valued Minobu Tetsuhara.

"Samsonov did not act with my approval. I warned you that others would take independent action . . ."

"Save your lies for the gullible," Wolf snapped. "You've paid a high price and you don't even know the whole of what you've bought. If I thought you were an honorable man, I'd make it personal.

"From this day, the Dragoons are at war with you and your House, Takashi Kurita! If you think you can take us, go ahead and try. We'll see you in ruins. Watch your border!" Wolf stopped, slightly out of breath.

Takashi could see that Wolf might have run out of words, but that his store of rage was far from emptied. Nothing Takashi could say could change the man's heart. The Coordinator bowed slightly to acknowledge his understanding.

Wolf's nostrils flared and his jaw clenched. He turned his back on the Coordinator and stalked off across the hall, black boots striking hard against the polished surface of inlaid marble.

With a peremptory gesture of his hand, Takashi summoned one of his officials. His face was a mask, only the eyes alive. They never left the retreating back of the mercenary Colonel as he spoke, "I want to know how Wolf got here before I was given word of the result of the fighting on Misery. Find out who is responsible and have him shot."

The nervous official started to leave, but Takashi stayed him with a lifted finger.

"Also arrange for the delivery of Grieg Samsonov's head. His bungling has cost too much this time."

The official scurried off.

Takashi frowned as he watched Wolf fall into conversation with Morgan Kell. While he pondered the possible subject of the mercenaries' conversation, Yorinaga returned to his side. "Wolf is strong-willed," he said. "A dangerous man."

"Yes," Takashi agreed. He smiled at his cousin. "But then, so am I."

Across the room, Wolf suddenly looked up to meet Takashi's gaze. In Wolf's steely eyes, Takashi read hatred and defiance, masking a well of pain. No compromise with this man would be possible. The Wolf would not be satisfied until his jaws had closed on the throat of the Dragon.

Glossary

Throughout this book, the Kurita officers are referred to by their ancient Japanese rank names. The equivalent ranks in English are:

Warlord	General of the Army
Tai-sho	General
Sho-sho	Brigadier
Tai-sa	Colonel
Chu-sa	Lieutenant Colonel
Sho-sa	Major
Tai-i	Captain
Chu-i	Lieutenant

List of Abbreviations

CLG

Combat Loss Grouping. A measure of mean time to failure of the combat systems in a BattleMech unit.

DCMS

Draconis Combine Mustered Soldiery.

ETA

Estimated Time of Arrival.

HPG

HyperPulse Generator. An interstellar communications device controlled by ComStar.

IFF

Identification: Friend or Foe.

IR

Infrared.

ISF

Internal Security Force. The Kurita Secret Service, a combination CIA, FBI, and KGB.

LAM

Land-Air 'Mech. A BattleMech that may be modified into an AreoSpace Fighter. The LAM has some of the advantages of each and the disadvantages of both forms.

LOS

Line-of-Sight.

LRM

Long-Range Missiles, indirect-fire missiles with high-explosive warheads.

MAD

Magnetic Anomaly Detector is a system used to detect hidden or camouflaged BattleMechs.

MHQ

Mobile Headquarters. A command vehicle stocked with communications and tactical planning computers.

PPC

The Particle Projector Cannon, a magnetic accelerator firing high-energy proton or ion bolts, is the most effective weapon available to a BattleMech.

PSL

Professional Soldiery Liaison. The branch of the Kurita military responsible for coordinating mercenary units with the regular military.

SRM

Short-Range Missiles, direct-trajectory missiles with high explosive or armor-piercing explosive warheads.

VTOL

Vertical Take-Off/Landing vehicles, including helicopters and other rotary-wing aircraft.

YOUR OPINION CAN MAKE A DIFFERENCE!

LET US KNOW WHAT *YOU* THINK.

Send this completed survey to us and enter a weekly drawing to win a special prize!

1.) Do you play any of the following role-playing games?
Shadowrun _____ Earthdawn _____ BattleTech _____

2.) Did you play any of the games before you read the novels?
Yes _________ No _________

3.) How many novels have you read in each of the following series?
Shadowrun _____ Earthdawn _____ BattleTech _____

4.) What other game novel lines do you read?
TSR _____ White Wolf _____ Other (Specify) _____

5.) Who is your favorite FASA author?

____

6.) Which book did you take this survey from?

____

7.) Where did you buy this book?
Bookstore _____ Game Store _____ Comic Store _____
FASA Mail Order _______ Other (Specify) _____

8.) Your opinion of the book (please print)

____

____

____

Name _______________ Age _____ Gender _____
Address ____________________________________
City __________ State ___ Country ______ Zip _____

Send this page or a photocopy of it to:
FASA Corporation
Editorial/Novels
1100 W. Cermak Suite B-305
Chicago, IL 60608